PRAISE FOR

THE MAINE CONSECRATION

"Decisions made by generations before him make it impossible for Daniel to control the direction of his own life as he becomes a feather in its dangerous slipstream. Determined to survive and committed to protecting those he loves, he must adapt quickly to a constantly changing array of environments. Readers will root for his success, but like Daniel, they won't know whom to trust from among the repertoire of colorful characters.

"Author Currence offers an exciting tale of intrigue and adventure laced with historical and philosophical insight. Those familiar with the geography and communities along the Eastern Seaboard of the United States will delight at the descriptions of favorite sites and businesses. Contemporary coverage of the methods and atrocities of modern-day terrorism in our world will make aspects of the story chillingly familiar to most readers.

"A highly recommended, topical, and entertaining novel!"

—E. A. Coe, Author of *Pedaling West*

"A fast-paced ride through terrorist terrain in the midst of financial conspiracies and paramilitary action. But the historical and religious reflections along the way clearly separate this novel from its action-packed field and are often the most captivating."

—Gerard Healy, Author of *Originally from Dorchester*

"Brandon Currence's first two books already show his range as an author. *Looking for the Seams* reminds me of a descriptive novel like *The Painted House*. It has rich development of characters, principally a young man leaving the innocence of youth and entering a dangerous new reality. *The Maine Consecration* is more like *The Firm*, a page-turner which kept me on the edge of my seat, ready for the next turn of events. I am already hooked on the *Turtle on a Fence Post* series, and I am eager for more!"

—John Suddarth, Reader, Richmond, VA

"*The Maine Consecration* abounds with action, plot twists, and heartfelt emotion, pulling you further into the life of main character Daniel and his boss, Victor. Take an entertaining road trip with these two; whether by car, plane, or boat, you'll feel like you're riding shotgun. But brace yoxurself for the end of their journey."

—Helen Anspach, Reader, Yorktown, VA

"Brandon Currence is my new favorite author. *The Maine Consecration* keeps you engaged on so many different levels—a great story interspersed with love and life lessons for Daniel and for the reader. Can't wait for the next in the *Turtle on a Fence Post* series."

—Becky Dove, Reader, Hampton, VA

The Maine Consecration

by Brandon Currence

ISBN 978-1-64663-988-5

Published by

 köehlerbooks ™

3705 Shore Drive
Virginia Beach, VA 23455
800-435-4811
www.koehlerbooks.com

THE MAINE CONSECRATION

Turtle on a Fence Post
BOOK TWO

BRANDON CURRENCE

VIRGINIA BEACH
CAPE CHARLES

To our daughter, Catherine Audet Conner,
who gave me encouragement and insightful critiques as I wrote this,
and who has given me and Nancy four delightful grandchildren.

Table of Contents

Chapter 1: The Phone Call 7

Chapter 2: The Revelation 26

Chapter 3: A Swim in the Gulf 30

Chapter 4: Daniel's Dilemma 34

Chapter 5: The General 39

Chapter 6: Swimming Home 43

Chapter 7: Daniel's Respite 51

Chapter 8: A Murderous Story 54

Chapter 9: Daniel's Decision 66

Chapter 10: The Flight 71

Chapter 11: The Citadel 83

Chapter 12: Iowa 97

Chapter 13: Saint Simon's Island 113

Chapter 14: Jekyll Island 123

Chapter 15: The Chinese Connection 141

Chapter 16: The Ranch 151

Chapter 17: Leaving Jekyll Island 160

Chapter 18: Brad's Story 168

Chapter 19: Breakfast at Sunset Beach 183

Chapter 20: Driving 191

Chapter 21: The Blue Sedan 199

Chapter 22: Emerald Isle 206

Chapter 23: Carova 219

Chapter 24: Richmond 230

Chapter 25: Paul's Epitaph 243

Chapter 26: Linden Row 256

Chapter 27: Favors 272

Chapter 28: The Road to Quantico 287

Chapter 29: The Race to Maine 297

Chapter 30: The Consecration 315

Acknowledgments 329

If you are new to the *Turtle on a Fence Post* series, and have not read *Looking for the Seams*, please note that chapter 1 of *The Maine Consecration* is a recap of that book, so *The Maine Consecration* can be read as a stand-alone novel.

If you have read *Looking for the Seams*, then you will recognize some of the story at the beginning of the book. Hopefully this synopsis will refresh your memory as you continue with the series.

Enjoy!

"Think as I think," said a man,
"Or you are abominably wicked;
You are a toad."
And after I had thought of it,
I said, "I will, then, be a toad."

—Stephen Crane, as a young man.

CHAPTER 1

The Phone Call

Daniel Furman sat on the edge of his bed at his beach cottage in Galveston, Texas, hands trembling as he entered the phone number on his telephone. Once again he read the want ad for a thirty-eight-inch avocado oven and made sure each number was correct. His breathing was very shallow, almost small gasps of air. He had been looking for this bogus ad for two years, waiting fearfully for the time to come when he would make this call. And now he could not bring himself to press the send button, terrified of what the other end of the line would reveal.

He stared again at it. His mind kept prodding him that something about it looked vaguely familiar, but he could not quite get it. Perhaps he had looked at so many want ads searching for this one that now they all had a vague familiarity. But he could not let go of this feeling as he stared again at the number and then opened Mishael's final note and compared them. Nothing in her words and the ad had any semblance of commonality. The paper her note was written on was well-worn and tearstained from Daniel obsessively handling it these past two years. Again he read it and again he had trouble focusing through his tears.

My dearest,

If you are reading this and have honored our vow not to open this note unless I have left unexpectedly, then Father has discovered us and I am on my way home to an arranged marriage. I am helpless in preventing this, but please know that you are the love of my life and without you I cannot endure. Should I find a way to freedom, I will contact you with an ad for a 38-inch avocado oven in the Sunday edition of the Palo Alto paper. Call that number. If a man answers, hang up—I am gone and you are in grave danger. You must go on with your life, my love. I beg you not to wait for me.

Please be careful, as Father is a vengeful man and could have you followed for a long time. Please do not try to find me; it will be useless as well as dangerous. We were born into cultures which will keep us apart in this life, but I believe in my heart, we will be together forever as one.

Know that I will die before I marry another. Pray that I have courage for that.

I love you for eternity.

No names, no references. Mishael left no trace of their identities in case the note was found. Daniel folded the note and put it back in the small envelope, then picked up the phone to dial the number.

Instead of a customary "Hello," the clearly male voice on the other end quietly and deliberately asked, "Who is calling please?"

Daniel's voice failed him.

Again the male voice said, "Please confirm your identity, and your reason for calling."

Daniel hit the end button on his phone and fell backward across his bed, panic welling up inside of him.

What did I think would happen? He was afraid to admit he had hoped and dreamed for Mishael's voice to miraculously say, "Hi, Trip," but now his dreams were dashed, truncated by a bland, anonymous male voice that gave no hint about his beloved Pakistani princess.

Her last note clearly warned him that a male voice meant she was gone and he was in grave danger. What did that mean? He would not dare take her warnings as lightly as he had as a student at Stanford, naively ignoring their cultural and familial differences that had driven their worlds eternally apart.

He touched each digit of the number again, almost as a religious rite, willing Mishael back from the other side of the world.

As he touched the ninth digit, it hit him—it was the phone number itself that was familiar. He could picture himself looking at it while reading something. It was so vague a memory he could not construct the time or place, but he could now visualize the pattern of the numbers. His memory raced through images of reports and letters, contracts and pages, letterhead and business cards, but he could not settle on any that matched the image in his mind.

It must be somewhere in Dad's papers, he surmised, and went to the storage closet where he had packed them. He lifted the heavy, paper-filled boxes two at a time and carried them to the living room. He began methodically going through them, unpacking each one and repacking in chronological order as he examined each folder and each page.

Nearly three hours later he resealed the last box and pushed it against the wall. Nothing. Absolutely nothing matched his memory. He went back to the storage closet to look for any other boxes from his father, but they were just the files he had brought home from VCM, a property management company in downtown Houston. He had joined VCM after college but had left the lucrative position a year ago to pursue his passion of teaching baseball and coaching top tennis players at Galveston Racquet Club. He had grown up playing both sports, concentrating on baseball in high school where he was recruited by a professional team, but switched to tennis in college, which he found he enjoyed more.

He decided to start going through them too and opened the

first box. He set aside the large envelope that contained the deed and other information about the property in Maine that Victor, VCM's owner and CEO, had given him. Victor and Daniel's father, Joseph, had been lifelong friends, and after Joseph's untimely death, Victor had given Daniel the property. He started sorting through the various files and folders that Jennifer, his administrative assistant at VCM, had so carefully organized and packed for him when he left. He glanced at his watch, the Patek Philippe Victor had given his father for his last birthday, not realizing it would be their last time together. Daniel wore the watch in remembrance of his father who had died during his last semester at Stanford, shortly after Mishael's father had whisked her away from school after learning that she and Daniel had been seeing each other.

The second hand swept smoothly past the minute hand as it neared the XII, then toward the hour hand that split II. *Two a.m.,* Daniel thought, *and still no clue about that number.*

He put a kettle of water on the stove and turned on the gas flame. He filled his tea strainer with black tea and placed it in his mug along with a spoonful of brown sugar. As the kettle whistled and he poured the hot water, his mind turned from thoughts about Mishael and that final note she had left in their special meeting place on the eleventh floor of the Stanford library, to scenarios of meetings and reading sessions, searching for a clue to where he had seen that phone number before.

He returned to the first box and finished looking through it. Finding nothing, he carefully repacked it, resealed it, and pushed it toward the living room wall. He did the same with all the others, and as he resealed the final box, pushing it toward the wall with the others, he glanced at his watch again.

Four-fifteen. Still no clue. He decided to take a short nap and resume the search after sun-up. It was now Saturday. His first tennis clinic was scheduled at ten o'clock followed by a baseball session with Jonathan and his teammates. Normally he looked forward to seeing

Sarah, Jonathan's mother and Victor's personal assistant, whom he had met at VCM. But today all he could think about was Mishael and finding her. He would cancel today's activities and concentrate on finding where the telephone number had originated from.

As he began brewing a fresh cup of tea, he thought about his first night with Sarah and the events that led to it. He still marveled at Sarah's patient understanding that had brought them together the night after the Westmoreland Country Club tennis tournament. Sarah was nearly a decade older, but the age difference never seemed to bother either of them as their friendship grew.

It had been nearly two years since the tennis tournament where Daniel had humiliated his narcissistic co-worker, Eric, who had a nasty habit of building his own ego by berating others, including their shared assistant, Jennifer.

During the week leading up to the tournament, Eric had bragged incessantly about how he would be the Westmoreland tennis champion again that year. Westmoreland's club tournament was unique in that it was a charity tournament and the entry fee was an agreement by the participant to give to their favorite charity as they exited the tournament. Since the charity and monetary value were publicly announced, hubris among the participants was the real prize, with bragging rights as to who gave the most and to what charity. An engraved plaque in the club's entrance hall recorded a history of the winners, while all the names, charities, and amounts were published in the monthly newsletter. Eric never missed an opportunity to show that his name was on the plaque for the past three years, and his charity amounts were enormous.

What Eric kept secret was that his chosen charity was always an organization that he coaxed into leasing a property he managed or could claim a fee for, and the charity amount neatly equaled his fee for a year's lease payments.

Unknown to Eric, Victor had caught on to his scheme when a large piece of property leased to the ASPCA was owned by one of Victor's LLCs, and Eric was named as the listing agent with a fee of ten thousand dollars—exactly the amount of his tournament charity to the ASPCA. Suspecting deviousness, Victor researched the previous years and easily found the pattern. He decided to keep his knowledge secret and let the tournament proceed. He did, however, encourage Daniel to study narcissism after his and Eric's confrontation in Victor's office. Daniel did his homework.

In the finals against Daniel, Eric had a seemingly insurmountable lead, having to win only one more game to take the championship, while Daniel had won no games. At this point, Daniel played to all of Eric's narcissistic pressure points, cajoling Eric into agreeing to pay Daniel's enormous charity contribution if Daniel won, and Daniel would pay Eric's if he lost. So confident was Eric that he could not lose, that he agreed to the deal. What Eric didn't know was that Daniel had been the top college tennis player in the country. Back then he had been known by his nickname, Trip, and had led Stanford to the NCAA finals two years in a row.

With the bet secured, Daniel began playing to his true level, and Eric could not win a point against his overpowering game. Discovering he had no chance against Daniel, Eric had quit, humiliated. He was suddenly deeply in debt with no resources to pay Daniel's charity. Daniel had given Eric a massive dose of his own medicine and the Westmoreland crowd was ecstatic watching Eric get his just reward. Eric never returned to his office at VCM, since he knew his failure to pay constituted a breach of contract and the consequence was immediate dismissal from VCM.

Instead of celebrating the victory and enjoying the satisfaction of belittling Eric as Eric had done to others in his sphere of influence, Daniel had gone to the locker room to brood, discovering he did not relish revenge.

Sarah found Daniel in the locker room, sulking, and began listening to his story as well as his feelings of disappointment with himself for stooping to Eric's level of behavior.

Daniel told Sarah how he had met Mishael in the library tower and been immediately drawn to her, but when he asked to see her again, she refused. She told him when he could meet her at a local restaurant, but to his dismay she was surrounded by her friends and he could not sit with her. He remembered their first conversation in the restaurant.

• • •

"Can we go somewhere else so we can talk?" he asked from his seat across the table.

Mishael leaned back in her seat and shook her head.

"I'd love to fix dinner for you. My apartment is close, and I'm not a bad cook, especially if you like seafood. I can't entice you away from here?"

Again, she shook her head, then responded, "I hear you play tennis."

Trip was encouraged as this meant she had inquired about him, so there was some interest.

"Yes," he said. "I play a little."

"A little?" she replied with a smirk. "You're the number one player for Stanford, ranked second in the country in college tennis, and it looks like you'll lead our team to the NCAA finals next month. Understating is an admirable quality, Trip, but I believe you've taken it to new lows."

"So, will you go out with me?" Trip pushed.

"No."

"Why? You don't like tennis?"

"Tennis is okay, and as much as I'd like you to cook for me, I cannot go out with you."

"Why?"

"I'm a music major. We spend more time practicing than athletes do. This is my one night away from the conservatory, so meet me here next week, same time."

"Can we go out after that?"

"No."

"I don't get it. Why not?"

"You'll never understand, Trip, but hopefully I'll see you here next week. And please don't ask me again to go out. The answer will always be no." She got up and left.

Before Trip could maneuver his way out of the jumble of tables and catch up to her, she had slipped out the door and was gone.

She was an enigma, and he couldn't get her out of his head.

• • •

Daniel told Sarah about the tennis finals his first year at Stanford and the shot that changed his life. Mishael was in the stands with her friends watching and cheering for him, and his father was in his box seat with his coach, Frank Hornbrook. It was a very close match and his opponent, Heath Whitman, hit a shot that looked like it was going long, but Daniel watched as it nipped the back of the baseline. The line judge had called it out which would have given the match and championship to Daniel. Daniel confessed to Sarah that he couldn't have lived with himself if he hadn't questioned the call. To the dismay of the Stanford crowd, he had immediately gone to the chair umpire to overrule the call. After that, close calls did not go his way, and Daniel lost the match.

"And how did that change your life?" Sarah asked.

"After the match I went to meet Mishael at the restaurant, thinking it would be another date in a crowd of her friends, but instead her friends told me she was at the library," Daniel explained. "I knew that meant the eleventh floor where we had met. So I ran there hoping to finally get some alone time with her."

"And was she alone?"

"She was, and waiting for me in a private area in the book stacks. I can still remember how she immediately put her arms around me and kissed me. Her passion melted my knees and we eased to the floor in an embrace. I thought she was impressed by my tennis, and I remember our conversation as if it just occurred. What I didn't realize is that the missed shot was the reason she was there and not at the restaurant as planned."

"She wanted to talk to you about overruling a call?" Sarah asked, not understanding the connection.

"Sort of, but not exactly," Daniel said. "Sarah, when you fell in love with Jonathan's father, do you remember the moment?"

Sarah looked at him rather quizzically, then answered. "I remember him coming off the football field in the eighth grade and hugging all the cheerleaders after scoring the winning touchdown in our first game. I remember the sweat and his smell, and thinking he was the most handsome guy in the world. After that, we just never were apart. I thought it was love, but maybe it wasn't. I'm still not sure. It was convenient to date the most popular guy in the school, and I just considered it was the way life was meant to be."

Daniel was quiet as he let Sarah have his complete attention, then he confessed. "Mishael asked me a similar question."

"Oh?" Sarah said. "And?"

"Well, the conversation was rather surreal at first, but she knew exactly what she wanted to say to me, and I was so rapt, I just followed her lead."

• • •

After the kiss, Daniel held her on top of him. "So, I take it you liked my tennis game?" he murmured.

"It was okay," she whispered.

"Okay?" Daniel said, surprised. "With a reception like this, I figured you must have really enjoyed it even though I lost."

"This has nothing to do with tennis, my dear Trip. This has to do with you."

"I don't get it. What are you talking about?" he said, amazed by her passion, but puzzled that it had nothing to do with his tennis game.

"You didn't hesitate to question the bad call, even though it cost you the match," she said.

As Daniel tried to pull her close for more, Mishael pushed herself away and flung her long black hair behind her head. Then she looked down into his eyes.

"Why did you question the call?" she asked. "You know your teammates are mad as hell that you cost them the championship. They think you're an idiot."

"Do you?" he asked.

"Does it appear to you that I think you're an idiot?" she responded.

"I guess not," he said, trying to pull her closer.

She stiffened her arms against his chest, preventing him from reaching her, but driving him crazy with desire.

"Trip, have you ever been in love?"

Daniel looked up at her, trying to think of an answer. "No. Well, yes. Lots of times. I mean like I've loved a lot of girls, but I don't know. What do you mean in love? Like in love enough to spend my life with someone? Like deeply in love? I don't think so, if that's what you mean."

Daniel knew everything he was saying was wrong, but he couldn't stop talking. It was like when his dad asked him a question, and he knew the answer would be wrong, but he couldn't help saying it anyway.

Mishael smiled at Daniel's fumbling, watching as he tried to squirm his way out of an answer. She bent down and kissed him to stop his talking, then sat up again and threw her hair back.

Daniel marveled at her beauty. She was small, barely five feet tall, and slightly built. Her emerald green eyes and heavy dark eyelashes exuded an intensity that couldn't be ignored or forgotten, and were framed by her long, jet black hair and generous lips, so common among the people of the Mediterranean. The olive tone of her skin accentuated the only word he could think of to describe her—exotic. He was mesmerized by her and felt as if he were drowning in a quagmire of desire.

She whispered, "If you fell in love, do you think you'd know the exact moment you did?"

He looked up at her and didn't answer. He wanted to scream, "Yes!" And he knew that the moment was right then, and right there. Suddenly he felt like he never wanted to be without Mishael. What was it about her? He didn't know, but suddenly he knew he was in love like he had never dreamed love could be.

Finally, Daniel answered quietly. "I'm sure I would know the exact moment I fell in love."

"Me, too," she said. "I fell in love with you when you walked to the umpire's chair and did what was in your heart. You knew what was right and you did not hesitate. After that, I knew I could never love anyone but you. This is not about tennis. This is about you. I love you."

Daniel started to respond, but she quickly covered his lips with her delicate fingers.

"I don't want you to say anything right now, Trip," she said. "I don't want you to love me or say you love me because I said it. It's okay if you don't love me. I understand and expect nothing from you. But I have never seen anyone do what you did today. Everyone hesitates and weighs the consequences of doing the right thing—as if the cost of the action is more important than the action. I saw you today. I saw the man I thought I would never see. I will never see another like you, but I know that I fell in love at that moment, and the rest of the tennis match was irrelevant to me. I watched you after that—not tennis. Your passion overflowed in me, and I'll never be fulfilled by another man. I know you can't understand this because you don't know my family or my culture. But know this—if you stay or if you leave, I will not judge you any way but as the one love of my life. Do you understand?"

"No," he told her. "I don't understand how you can see so clearly.

I see you, and I see this moment. And I see that the moment I fell in love is right here and right now. I know that I never want to be without you. That is what I understand."

"I'm sorry," she said, "but you'll have to understand much more than that or we cannot see each other."

He tried to argue with her, but to no avail. "Of course we can. If we love each other we can be together forever. No one can come between us!"

"No," she said. "Listen to me carefully. You have no idea who I am or where I'm from."

"I don't care! I'll learn," he protested.

"Don't interrupt me," she said. "Hear me. We cannot be seen alone together. My family will not allow it."

Daniel started to speak again, but Mishael put her fingers firmly over his mouth. "Listen," she said. "When we are in public, we must be in a crowd. Do not touch me or pay too much attention to me. We will be watched. Believe me. You may not call me, ever. I will leave notes for you here in a special book on the shelf. You can do the same and we can stay in touch that way. I'm going to leave a sealed envelope for you to open only if I've had to leave suddenly. I want you to do the same and leave me a final note, too. My final note is already there and sealed with my lips. Promise me you'll not open it."

"I promise," he told her, confused by her motivation.

That was their vow to each other.

She continued, "Also, I practice in the conservatory at night. I must be out by midnight, or the consequences will be dire. When I leave, it will be by taxi which my parents send for me. There's a study hall in the conservatory near my piano. Start studying there, and when everyone leaves, we can be together. Wait for me to be gone a long time before you leave the conservatory. Do you understand?"

"I hear you," he said, "but I don't understand you."

"Then we cannot see each other again, ever. Do you understand that?"

"I can't bear that," he told her. "I'll do what you say. One day things will change. I'll figure out a way for us to be together forever. I'll do whatever it takes."

"I know you will, my love," she said. "But it will be fruitless. I'm sorry. I have to go now. Come to the conservatory tomorrow evening around nine. Don't be early. Now you must stay here for a time so we are not seen leaving together. I love you."

She leaned down and kissed him, then quickly got up and left.

Daniel laid on the library floor for a long time, both heartsick and overjoyed. His emotions were tearing him apart, and at the same time he had never been happier. *This is how far the East is from the West,* he kept thinking. It was like life was right in front of him, but an eternity away. He fell asleep dreaming of Mishael.

The next evening he went to the conservatory and that became their private world. Every morning he would go to the library to find a note from her, and would leave her a note in return. They called it their "mailbox."

• • •

Sarah had, in turn, shared with him her story of Jonathan's dad and the several unsuccessful relationships she'd had since. She had started seeing Jonathan's dad after the eighth-grade football game. They dated throughout high school and when she was accepted to the University of Texas he decided to move to Austin with her and attend Austin Community College. Following the pattern begun in high school, she did most of the schoolwork for him and tutored him so he passed, while he spent most of his time playing. He did have a knack for photography and ended up with a degree in photographic technology. Then he started photographing the sports venues at the university, making enough money to stay in Austin while Sarah finished school. Unfortunately for Sarah, after Jonathan was born she discovered he wanted to be taken care of and did not want her to take care of anyone else. So when Sarah's attention turned increasingly towards Jonathan out of necessity, he left. She bought herself a wedding ring and wore it out of convenience and for Jonathan's sake, but they were never married.

After finishing her story, Sarah asked about what happened with Mishael. Daniel held back tears as he told her of their last night together.

• • •

One Saturday night as they lay together under her piano, she fell asleep in his arms and he watched as she breathed peacefully. He was so content to be with her. He marveled at her beauty as well as her playing, which was unlike any music he had ever heard. Sometimes, she confessed, she played her soul for him—and only him. This night, he too fell asleep and did not awaken her in time for the taxi.

A door slamming woke them up.

Mishael sat up and looked around, getting her bearings, then panicked. "Oh, my God, Trip! What have you done?" she screamed. Before he could react, she was out of his arms and gathering her music books.

"What's wrong?" Daniel asked her.

That's when he saw the two men in black suits standing at the end of the piano, glaring at them. One of them grabbed Mishael's arm to pull her away.

"Don't you dare touch me," she seethed. "I'm Ameerah and when Father hears you touched me he will have your head!"

The man stepped back, fear evident in his eyes. The other man spoke. "You missed your taxi. Your father is outside waiting. You must come with us." He cocked his head toward Daniel and said. "Your father will deal with this infidel, I'm sure."

"Mishael, what's happening?" he screamed.

She didn't answer, but started for the door. Daniel tried to catch her, but one of the men blocked his way, forcing him backward.

"Mishael! Wait!" he screamed.

She turned to him, tears streaming and said, "Oh, Trip! What have you done! What have you done! My God! I'm afraid I'll never see you again! I have to go! Can't you see? You must let me go! Why didn't you wake me? I have to go!"

He tried to jump around the man to get to her, but was expertly blocked. "Mishael!" he pleaded, "You don't have to go. I'll protect you! I'll do whatever it takes! Don't go. Please don't go! I just don't understand. Why do you have to go like this?" He followed her to the door as the man stood between them.

She ran, not looking back, and got into a black Mercedes.

Daniel stood paralyzed, watching, not knowing what to do. He could see Mishael holding her head in her hands, sobbing, as the car sped away.

After walking around the campus in a daze, he decided to go to the library and wait until her first class the next day. He thought that they would be able to talk then and straighten everything out. But impatience and fear overcame him, and he broke into a run to the library. He flung the doors open, waking the night guard, and ran to the elevators. When the elevator was too slow to open, he went to the stairs, running up them as panic consumed him. He nearly passed out at the eleventh floor and literally crawled to the mailbox, unable to get a breath. The books had been moved. His final letter to her in the sealed envelope was gone as well as his last note, but there was no reply note from her—just her sealed envelope. He ripped it open. Her handwriting was beautiful, but what she wrote was devastating.

About a month later his dad came to see him to help get his life back together, but Daniel was in no mood to talk. His dad had a heart attack that night and Daniel never saw him again.

Victor came to his funeral and he and Daniel had dinner together, then talked all night about Daniel's dad. Daniel decided not to go on the professional tennis circuit and went to Houston for a sabbatical.

He figured getting rid of his nickname and going by Daniel would help him deal with his losses. Working for VCM gave him something to do while he waited for Mishael.

If that tennis ball hadn't clipped the back of the line, he probably would've never gotten close to Mishael, and would probably be a pro tennis player now. But losing both Mishael and his dad within a month was more than he could handle. Now he doubted he would ever get his game back in shape enough to get on the pro circuit.

• • •

This was the beginning of his deep friendship with Sarah, and instead of joining the gala on the country club's lawn, they left for the beaches of Galveston. There they spent the night talking and getting to know each other on a more personal level.

For Daniel, it was a welcome catharsis after months of grieving the loss of his father and his beloved Mishael. He found Sarah easy to be with as she quelled the restlessness of his youthful spirit—not endeavoring to solve his issues, but letting him work through them as a lighthouse guides wayward mariners.

After that night in Galveston, their relationship grew cautiously beyond the friendship stage and they began spending occasional weekends together, but were very careful of her son, Jonathan, and her position at VCM. The VCM issue resolved itself when Daniel left the company a year after the tennis tournament to take a job at a racquet club in Galveston teaching tennis. Sarah's weekend visits to his cottage became more frequent, and as Jonathan found friends on the beach to hang out with, Daniel and Sarah were able to enjoy time alone with each other.

In preparation for leaving VCM, Daniel set up management strategies for his projects and handed them off to other associates. He sold his dad's condo in Houston, where he had been living while working at VCM, and moved to a small cottage on the beach in

Galveston, close enough to the racquet club where he held his clinics so biking there was feasible. He kept his dad's pristine Porsche 912, which he had inherited along with the condo, covered and garaged to protect it from the salt air. He used his BMW for daily transportation, and saved the Porsche for weekend trips with Sarah when she could find a friend of Jonathan's willing to keep him overnight.

Their time together was fun; he appreciated her edgy sarcasm and maturity, and she enjoyed Daniel's playfulness while privately gawking at his terrific physique. At five feet eight inches, Sarah was a tall woman and usually looked almost directly into the eyes of men she dated, but Daniel was six inches taller, and she savored looking up into his pale blue eyes. She worked hard to keep up with his active lifestyle and discovered that hiking, biking, swimming, and skiing had brought back some of her youthful figure and vitality. She had even begun buying new clothes to fit her smaller size, but was very surprised when her weight did not go down very much. Her masseuse at Westmoreland informed her since muscles were heavier than fat, maintaining the weight was a good sign. And she was looking toned and terrific.

As Sarah and Daniel's friendship grew, Sarah knew she would never supplant Mishael. She knew if he did come to love her, it would be a very different kind of love than the passion that burns with a first love. She accepted this without rancor and as they spent time together, they discovered they enjoyed each other's company immensely. They genuinely liked each other and so could go days without seeing one another, then pick back up immediately upon contact, just like old friends do after long periods of absence.

Daniel found that being with Sarah was never stressful. She harbored no jealous expectations, which he attributed to her maturity. He felt completely at ease with her. He found he could talk with her without reservation about anything and she'd respond without judgmental emotions clouding the issues. Her self-assurance while listening to him was like the rock of Gibraltar, and then she would raise one eyebrow with a hint of a smile and his serious conversation would disintegrate into the silliness of adolescent intellectualism. His only escape would be to carry her to the nearest bedroom, letting her excitement allay all of his boyish meanderings. Later, spent, she would inevitably fall asleep in his arms, and he would, for a brief spell, be at peace from the futility that haunted him. He marveled at how she could fall asleep so easily anywhere, and sleep so soundly. She attributed it to the rigors of being a single mom with an executive position in a major corporation, but he considered it was because she knew how to let the world go and enjoy what peace there may be in nothingness.

Still Daniel's heart burned for Mishael, but he found himself falling in love with Sarah—a different kind of love, but it was indeed love. He tried to keep the feeling at bay, honoring his love for Mishael, but the endeavor was fruitless. Sarah never broached the subject, and for that he was grateful.

He did find she had a temper and it would surface quickly at an injustice. But he also found it was a healthy temper, much like the anger Jesus displayed at the moneychangers in the temple. It was born of intelligence and she had a penchant for caring for others, so it was not an anger based on self-interest. Her singular angry moment with him had been a result of their diverse sleeping habits—he would sleep for a few hours at most, and she was able to sleep up to ten hours if given the opportunity. This discrepancy gave him a lot of time by himself when they were spending weekends together, and he would spend his alone time nocturnally wandering. The first time she woke up to find him gone had been on a weekend trip to Caddo Lake in the bayou country of Louisiana. His cell phone was left on the table and there was no note or hint as to where he was or when he would return. When he came back he found her furious that he had been so inconsiderate of her. She did not mind him leaving, but she found it intolerable that he left her in the dark when they were together. Keeping her informed was just common courtesy from her perspective. He apologized, having never considered the situation from her position, and being so accustomed to just leaving and wandering at any time of night. He promised to leave her a note and remember his cell phone. If he was swimming, which he loved to do at night, he would message her when he went in the water and send another as soon as he came out. She reminded him of the dangers of swimming alone at night, but on this he would not concede. He accused her of sounding like his mother, which indeed she did since his mother had also found his nighttime swims recklessly dangerous and told him so often. At this, she grabbed him behind both ears, pulling his face close to hers, and, looking into those soft blue eyes, told him he better not end up as shark bait, then kissed him passionately. He lifted her up and carried her to the bedroom as she wrapped her legs around his waist. No more was ever said about it, but he did try to always be considerate of her when he left.

CHAPTER 2

The Revelation

D aniel woke up suddenly, having fallen asleep on the floor by the boxes, and immediately checked the time. Six-fifteen. He made a mental note to call the tennis center by seven to cancel the first appointment. Before going on his coveted morning swim and grabbing breakfast at the fishing pier, he decided to put the boxes back into the storage closet. He really didn't have an appetite, so as he loaded the boxes, he decided to skip breakfast and instead start researching the phone number. Maybe, he thought, when he called Sarah to cancel the baseball clinic, he could get her advice about what to do. Maybe she would help.

This thought allayed some of his anxiety, and Daniel began considering again the ad and the number, and the fact it was answered by a guarded male voice. What could it mean? Possibly Mishael was back in America and wanted to get in touch? Maybe she was married and saw the ad as a way to communicate with Daniel without her husband knowing. It would be a way to get Daniel to call without raising any suspicion, since she would not be initiating a call. If so, maybe she would retrieve the number and call him when it was safe to do so. He would ensure he kept his phone nearby and answered all the calls, even the obnoxious sales calls that he normally wouldn't take. He would also look up the area code as soon as he finished his swim. It seemed like a good place to start.

As he picked up the first box, he noticed the large envelope from Victor. *Crap,* he thought, *I've already sealed the box this goes in.* He reached for the knife to cut the tape and it hit him. The envelope— that's where he had seen the number! The series of numbers had a unique pattern that his brain had keyed on as he was pressing the keypad. Now, looking at the envelope, the pattern emerged again in his mind's eye. Several weeks after Victor had given him the envelope, Daniel finally had time to study the deed and property information in depth, and the unique pattern of the ten numbers had been etched in his psyche. He turned the envelope over, emptied the contents on the table, and started reading through the deed and instructions about the Maine property. He found the phone number as part of the contact information for the group that paid to rent the property several weeks a year. He compared the numbers and they matched. He looked for a name to go with the number, but couldn't find one. It had not occurred to him before, but now it seemed outrageously odd that this number would be here with no hint of who it belonged to. But whoever it was, they were obviously known to Victor, and they knew something of Mishael.

Now Daniel began to question everything he knew about Victor. If Victor was a lifelong friend of his father as he professed to be, why had he not met him before? He had heard his father mention a man named Victor, but had never seen him before his father's funeral, nor was he ever given any detail about him, only that Victor was someone he had known since childhood. But that wouldn't explain why Victor would have had a connection to Mishael.

He remembered Victor showing up at his father's funeral and befriending him. He was such an easy person to talk to about his grief and his father and seemed genuinely concerned for Daniel's welfare.

Had it been an elaborate ruse? But why? Daniel was a nobody, and his father was just an athletic scout who expertly guided Daniel's education and athletic career. And what could Victor possibly have to do with Mishael?

Daniel felt like he was going down a rabbit hole. He hated conspiracy theories and conspiracy theorists, feeling like they were just paranoid idiots, but now he felt like he was engaging in one of his own. There had to be a simple explanation.

He decided to contact his best friend in Houston, Jeffrey, who had been one of his studio-mates at VCM and had helped him deal with Eric's horrible demeanor. The property management division of VCM was set up as a studio with a reception area where Jennifer, the studio administrator, coordinated the activities of four property managers, Jeffrey, Eric, Marlene, and Daniel. Each manager had a private office and they shared a conference room. Eric's narcissistic behavior cast a horrible pallor over the studio, but Jeffrey and Jennifer had taken the youthful Daniel under their wing and shielded him from Eric's venomous outbursts. Marlene just ignored him.

Daniel and Jeffrey often traveled together on one of VCM's private jets. This gave them a lot of bonding time and Jeffrey, although older, was easy to get along with and became more than a studio-mate— he had become a good friend. Perhaps he could shed some light on Victor since he had been at VCM for a long time.

Funny though that Jeffrey and everyone he had come in contact with in Houston had a connection to Victor and VCM. Maybe Jeffrey wasn't someone he should ask about Victor. Who else could he trust? He hated the feeling that he was somehow being manipulated. He hated that he was thinking like a conspiracy theorist and putting distrust and an evil motive behind every situation in his life. It was just a telephone number, and possibly just a coincidence.

No—he knew it wasn't a coincidence. He was missing something and now had no one to turn to for advice. Even Sarah was part of VCM. Was her relationship with him also a setup?

Maybe he should go straight to the source and confront Victor.

Although it was nearly impossible to get an audience with him due to his busy schedule, he would have to try. He had to have an explanation for the number, the want ad, and the male voice that Mishael had warned him about. If he was going to find Mishael, Victor was now his only clue. He had to know something. It couldn't be a coincidence that the phone number for the group who occasionally rented the mountain property in Maine was the same phone number listed in the want ad.

That was another enigma. Why give him a million-dollar property with the only explanation being it was his father's wishes? Did Victor and his father really own the mountain together, as he claimed, and will it to Daniel? What did Victor expect Daniel to do with the property? Victor could've sold it, pocketed the money, and Daniel would never have known about it. It was paid for in full and had enough income from rentals to cover all its expenses. But would he tell Daniel anything? And could Daniel even believe him? Suddenly Daniel was overwhelmed with anxiety and impatient for Monday so he could contact Victor.

Daniel sat at the table for a long time staring at the number, his brain trying to resolve the question of the phone number and this apparent connection between Victor and Mishael. Those periods of his life had been totally separate and half a country apart. After his father's death, Victor had become like a surrogate father to Daniel, mentoring and advising him as he navigated his mid-twenties alone. With his father gone and his mother busy with her second husband and their children, Daniel essentially had no family. And since he required nothing from Victor, Victor had graciously taken him under his wing, treating him as the son he never had.

Now, this bizarre connection changed everything. Daniel knew he was missing a critical piece to a puzzle and feared his naivety had once again thrust him into a futile and hopeless quagmire that would slowly swallow his soul.

CHAPTER 3

A Swim in the Gulf

Daniel's kettle began to whistle, and as he poured his morning cup of tea, his doorbell rang. *Who would be at my door this early in the morning?* he thought, suspicious. He peered at the visitor through the door's peephole before opening it. A Middle Eastern man of medium build with close-cropped dark curly hair stood waiting. It looked like he was carrying a package to deliver, but his casual, expensive attire screamed he was no ordinary delivery person.

The words of Mishael's note rang in Daniel's mind.

If a man answers, hang up—I am gone and you are in grave danger.

Please be careful as Father is a vengeful man and could have you followed for a long time.

Was he in danger? And if so, what kind of danger? It had been two years since Mishael left. Would anyone even remember him?

But a man had answered the call, and now there was a stranger at his door. Daniel's nerves began to fray. He cautiously opened the door and looked down into the dark brown eyes. The man was at least eight inches shorter than Daniel, but obviously in excellent physical shape, appearing very strong for his stature. His erect stance and demeanor belied his military background.

"I have a package for Joseph Daniel Furman, the third," he

announced crisply.

"That's me," replied Daniel.

"Do you have identification?"

"Why?" asked Daniel, feeling uneasy about this entire bizarre situation.

"Mr. Furman must sign for the package, and I must compare the signature with an official picture ID before I can hand it over," he responded.

Daniel began to back up cautiously to get his wallet which was on the entry hall table. He saw the man move slightly toward the door, so he stopped, not liking how close the man positioned himself to the open door. Daniel's eyes never left the man's torso, and Daniel noticed the man's dark, intense brown eyes never wavered from Daniel's midsection. Both men obviously knew that although a person can feint many body movements, the torso is the key to where the body is actually going to move. Daniel had received his training in athletics and he had correctly surmised his visitor's training was military.

"You can either step back while I get my ID or leave," Daniel said, his heart racing. The man did not move. "Step back or I call the police, swine!" Daniel saw the vein in the man's neck expand and pulsate and he knew he had struck a dangerous chord, confirming his suspicion this guy was not American born, and may even be Pakistani, like Mishael. Daniel finally began remembering the several times since Mishael's departure that he seemed to be followed—his first trip to VCM when he was almost rear-ended by a black Mercedes that had been behind him; the strange visitor in Jeremy's restaurant that Jeremy asked him about; and again at the Galveston Racquet Club when he thought maybe a potential sponsor was stalking him, hoping to be the first to sign him to an endorsement deal. *Why had he never connected the dots and realized that Mishael's warning was serious? Was he so blinded by grief that he could not see the obvious?*

Daniel's hand remained on the door, muscles flexed, ready to slam it on the intruder if he did anything except retreat. Slowly the man stepped backward and Daniel quickly grabbed his wallet and phone from the table, but his eyes never wavered. Daniel removed his driver's license and showed it. The man reached for it and Daniel quickly snatched it back from his grasp. He obviously surprised the man with his quick reactions and the man hesitated.

"I must examine the signature," he said.

"Bullshit," Daniel said, "you saw it. Now either let me sign and give me the package, or get the hell out of here." Daniel turned on his phone and started pressing numbers.

"No need to get upset," the man volunteered quickly, "I have my orders."

"Orders?" Daniel exclaimed.

The man immediately recognized his mistake and retracted. "I mean instructions."

"Right. Where do I sign?"

The man handed Daniel a clipboard with a delivery record sheet on it, but no other signatures were on the lines. Daniel knew it was a fake, but really didn't care. He was anxious to see what type of package warranted this level of scrutiny. His hand was shaking as he tried to sign. He paused, took a deep breath, and signed as quickly as he could while maintaining awareness of the man's position.

The man took the clipboard, handed Daniel a five by seven-inch padded envelope with no name or address on it, and stepped backwards off the porch before turning around and heading back toward his van. Daniel noted it was a new black Mercedes van, very expensive for a delivery service. He photographed it with his phone and as it moved away he got another photo of the rear, hoping it was clear enough to get the license number. He didn't know why he was compelled to be so cautious, except that the whole night had been surreal and his nerves were on edge, so it seemed to make sense to photograph the van. He considered maybe he just wanted to irritate the delivery man who creeped him out anyway.

He watched the van until it turned a corner and was out of sight, then he went back inside and locked the doors. His tea was cold now, so he turned the stove back on to make another cup, opened the envelope, and peered inside. It contained a small flash drive. He turned his computer on and then thought, to be safe, he would use his dad's old laptop to view it. It took a few minutes to turn on since the battery was dead.

Finally the screen came to life, and, standing by his kitchen table, he inserted the flash drive. It contained a single document in an MPEG format, obviously a video, the name indicating it was a clip from Al Jazeera. He double-clicked on the icon and as the clip began, the subtitles noted it was a street in a commercial section of London known for its restaurants that catered to government officials.

The street was empty except for a lone female figure emerging from a restaurant's double doors, her burqa flowing elegantly as she walked. She positioned herself in the middle of the street and slowly looked around until the small mesh screen through which she was peering was facing the news camera. As the camera zoomed in, the girl released the burqa and it fell to the ground.

He was looking into the eyes of his beloved Mishael. She was clad in Western clothing—the same as she had been wearing the last time he saw her, except around her midsection was a knapsack. As she raised her arms Daniel gasped at the sight of her gauze-wrapped, fingerless hands. He saw a string around her wrist connected to the knapsack. She raised her arms until the string was taut, and, looking deep into the camera lens she shouted, "I love you, Trip!" then jerked the string upward and the screen flashed white as the explosion devastated its surroundings.

Daniel yelled a blood-curdling scream as he fell to his knees and then sideways onto the floor, writhing and wailing in anguish. Gasping for air, Daniel's demons of futility overwhelmed his will to exist, and he scrambled off the floor, bolting for the door. His basic instinct to run overtook all else and he darted for the Gulf, shedding clothes, and sobbing and shaking as he ran into the waves.

CHAPTER 4

Daniel's Dilemma

"Hello?" Victor said rather groggily. Saturday mornings were his respite time, away from the pressures of incessant phone calls, appointments, board meetings, and all the trappings that came with riding the tiger that is the life of a conglomerate's chief. The only allowed interruption would be an emergency phone call on this private number; a number very few people had. Sarah had never used it before this morning.

"Victor, something's happened to Daniel," Sarah said hurriedly, her voice quivering with fear.

Victor was immediately alert. "How do you know? What's going on?" he asked, his impatience surging.

"He didn't show up for his clinic this morning nor for Jonathan's practice. He's never even been late before, so I came to his house to check on him."

"And?" Victor wanted to know everything in two seconds, so one could never tell him anything fast enough. Sarah knew this, and her mind was racing to try to make sense of the situation, but her fear was paralyzing her.

"I'm here now. His front door was locked as usual, but his patio door is wide open, and his shirt, pants, and shoes look like he tore them off on his way to the beach." There was a pause as Sarah walked into the kitchen. "There's a full cup of tea beside an old laptop that has a video running . . . oh my God, Victor, it's a suicide bombing . . . a young girl . . . my God, my God, Victor what's this mean?"

"Sarah! Sarah! Slow down, get your wits about you! You've got to pull yourself together. Daniel's in extreme danger and I need your eyes and ears right now."

As Victor was trying desperately to rein in Sarah's panic, he was calling out on another phone. The answer was immediate.

"Yes, Victor?"

"Billy, how fast can you get to Daniel's house?"

"I'm headed toward Dallas now; probably forty-five minutes."

"You've got to make it there faster. I'll call the state police to let you go through. Book it, now! Who's the closest agent who can get there immediately?"

Victor paused and changed phones. Sarah was obviously weeping now. "Sarah, hold a moment, I've got help on the way."

"All right," Sarah responded through her sobbing, but Victor was already talking on the other line.

"Dave Barber lives in Galveston, I'll call him," Billy said.

"Tell him to go in quietly, raise no alarm and protect the area until you get there. Tell him to look for any suspicious people or vehicles in the area but not to give himself away," Victor replied.

"Dave knows what to do."

"I know he does. Just make sure. Time is not on our side right now." Victor heard the squeal of the tires and Billy's customized Mustang exhaust roar as he reversed course and accelerated into triple digits toward Galveston. Billy Saunders was one of a close circle of Victor's associates with exceptional training in private investigations. A former SEAL and CIA agent, he was well aware of the gravity of the situation and wasted no time setting up surveillance of the area while he headed toward Galveston. Dave Barber was part of his covert team.

Billy reached into a concealed compartment in his door panel and thumbed through a series of IDs and badges, selected a set labeling him as Texas SBI, then pressed a button under his dash, resealing the compartment. He knew Victor would clear his route with the state police, but when he left the interstate, a local sheriff's deputy might decide to slow him down, and he didn't want to be stopped long. The badge and ID would avert any prolonged questions. He came over a rise and saw a highway patrol car running radar. He flicked his lights and as he passed he saw in his mirror the trooper flash his blue lights momentarily, but not move. He was always impressed with the speed Victor could put wheels in motion. Even the governor could not have worked so fast.

Victor made another quick phone call and then got back to Sarah. "Sarah," Victor's voice was calm, but very deliberate now, "don't touch anything. Look around carefully. Is his bike there?"

"Yes, in the living room where he keeps it."

"Phone? Wallet?"

"They are on the table in the entry hall."

"Can you see the street?"

"Yes."

"Anyone suspicious?"

"A black van down the street I've never seen before, but otherwise quiet and normal."

"Sarah, take his phone and wallet and head to your car. Stay out of sight of the van for as long as possible and get to your car quickly. Lock the doors and get out of there as fast as possible. If anyone approaches or gets out of the van, run to your car. Do you still carry the spray?"

"Yes, but it's in the car."

"Look in Daniel's cleaning supplies for something with ammonia in it and pour a glass full. Don't hesitate to use it."

"What's going on, Victor?" Sarah's panic was turning to deep concern.

"I'll tell you when you get here. Stay on the phone with me until you're in your car and then come to my office. Come in on the Robin Street garage entrance, door C. Someone will meet you. If you're followed, don't worry, they won't get past Gillette Street. Where's Jonathan?"

"He's at Steven's. He's not in any danger is he, Victor?"

"No, but I'll have an officer nearby him until we resolve this. Are you ready to head to the car?"

"I want to go get him, Victor."

"No, Sarah. It's best to follow my instructions until we are sure all is okay. Don't worry, the officer I send will be able to handle anything. Ready?"

"Yes, I'm walking around the house now. The van is still there and it's running. I can see its exhaust."

"Can you make it to your car?"

"I'm not sure . . . "

"Hide the phone and wallet outside and make sure no one is watching. Then walk calmly to the car as if nothing is wrong. If the van moves, run, and throw the ammonia in anyone's face that comes close. Sarah—these people are not nice. Keep your eyes open and be careful."

"Don't worry about that, Victor. I'm so on edge right now . . . Okay, I'm coming around the house . . . in view of the van now . . . it's moving, Victor!"

"Run, Sarah!"

Sarah didn't need to be told to run as she was already at a full gallop, but she saw she would not be able to get into her car safely before the van blocked her path. A white sedan appeared from the other direction coming toward the van and veered into its path, giving Sarah enough time to get to her car as horns blared. The van jumped the curb barely avoiding an accident.

She opened her door and fumbled to get the key in the ignition. Her nostrils burned from the jar of ammonia she had dropped as she opened her door while holding the phone and not losing contact with Victor. She threw the phone on the seat, started the car, and jerked the gear lever into reverse, then quickly into drive as she got out of the driveway. The van had now moved around the sedan and was back on the street, following her as she sped through the neighborhood. As she neared an intersection, she saw the white sedan again approaching from the right. She crossed the intersection with the van close behind. The sedan collided with the rear of the van, sending it careening into a spin, and into a hedgerow. Through her rearview mirror, she saw a man jump from the sedan and run in the direction of Daniel's house. The van door opened with a cloud of smoke from the airbags, and Sarah saw a dark-skinned man with close-cropped black hair jump out. She turned at the next street and headed toward Houston, her heart racing and tears streaming as the events of the morning overwhelmed her emotions. "Oh, God, let Daniel be okay," she prayed as she merged onto the interstate. She felt like Houston was an eternity away.

CHAPTER 5

The General

"Brad, this is Victor."

"Hello Victor, what's up?"

"Our old friend Abu has set his scheme in motion against our boy. Abu's henchman, Babel, delivered the video of Mishael to him this morning."

"Is Daniel okay?"

"Don't know yet. Apparently, after viewing the video, he went for a long swim in the Gulf and we haven't found him yet. Billy and Dave got to his house, but not as quietly as I had hoped. Dave had a little run-in with Babel when he tried to get Sarah."

"What was Sarah doing there?"

"Looking for Daniel after he didn't show at the tennis courts this morning. Billy determined from the scene at the house that he's probably been in the water at least five hours."

"You know he has the endurance of a marathon runner, so he could be miles out by now, if he's even still alive!"

"Yes, and with the tide running south, he could be drifting toward Corpus. But the tide's been slack an hour now and it's turning so our pilot is headed to that area."

"Who'd you send?"

"Jack, with four SEALs."

"Four, huh? That's good. Did you warn them our boy might be tough to handle if he doesn't want to be rescued?"

"Oh, yeah. Jack protested a little and thought it was overkill. One SEAL could handle him in the water and one in the chopper, but of course Jack followed orders. He'll put three in the water."

General Bradley Brigham was officially an active-duty marine, one of the oldest active officers in the service, and special advisor to the president on homeland security. As such, he quietly oversaw the actions of that department, secretly briefing and advising the president on terrorist activities inside and outside the country's borders. What his security clearance didn't give him access to (which was very little), his network of friends and acquaintances provided him when necessary. Unofficially, and known to only a dozen men and women in the world, he was one of Victor's associates on the Panel of Twelve, or P12 as they called themselves. P12 headed an organization called MALTA, where membership was a lifetime commitment.

"Did Jack take Nathan?" General Brigham asked.

"Of course. I wanted to make sure we had the best team out there," Victor responded.

"Well if he can be found, they will find him. What about the Coast Guard?"

"I'll call them in two hours whether Jack finds him or not. Hopefully Jack will find him and the Coast Guard will declare him lost when they finish their search and rescue mission."

"So I guess the video sent him over the edge. You still think he's our choice?"

"Absolutely," Victor responded. "We haven't had a recruit with his potential while I've been with MALTA."

"That's a long time, Victor," the general commented. "What do you think your chances are of success with him?"

"I'm sure after I tell him the whole story, he'll come aboard. His training IDs are all in place, so he's a go as soon as he says yes."

"Well, nobody's a better judge of character than you, Victor. So I'm sure you'll be successful. Did he make the phone call?"

"Yes."

"What did he say?"

"Nothing, he just hung up."

"You think he recognized the number?"

"Very slim chance of that," Victor conceded, "but if perchance he did, then he's even better than I expected. He's tenacious and smart, but I don't know for sure he even read the deed information, which is the only place he would've seen the number. That was nearly two years ago. In any case, he'll find out if they bring him in."

"What do you think Abu will do when he doesn't get the call?"

"Oh, he got the call. We set up a cloned phone with Daniel's number and called the number in the newspaper before Daniel called us. We wanted to know how they would answer and what they would say. Only Daniel's copy of the newspaper had our number in it."

"What happened?"

"Just a bland male voice asking Daniel to confirm who was calling and why. It went to the mosque in Phoenix where Abu runs his cell. We're sure they were just confirming Daniel was the intended recipient since they started their execution plan this morning."

"And you're positive they don't already have Daniel?"

"According to Billy, they don't. He's sure Daniel ran into the water after viewing the video, and it was set to keep repeating, so unfortunately Sarah saw it. Billy sent the flash drive to our lab for testing. He should be able to tell us something about it this evening. Besides, why would Babel be there if they had Daniel? Billy thinks he was waiting for him."

"Well he's the best, so I hope he's right on this one. Are you sure you don't want me to come down and sit in with you?"

"No, thanks. This is one I want to handle alone. I'll call you afterward."

"Okay. Since you don't need me, I'm headed to Phoenix. We'll take care of Abu's network. Let me know how our boy is, if and when Jack finds him."

"Will do." Victor hung up the phone and said another prayer for Daniel. He really wasn't as confident as he sounded on the phone with Brad.

CHAPTER 6

Swimming Home

The sun was still low in the cloudless eastern sky as Daniel ran headlong into the small waves of the Gulf of Mexico. He crawled along the sandy bottom until he was out of breath, then surfaced, and swam toward the sun. *Florida,* he thought, *I'll swim home to Florida and my childhood, then this nightmare will end. Florida, where Dad will embrace me and I'll be safe again; far away from the vile evilness of men—jealous men who know only destruction of all things beautiful.*

"God!" he screamed, "how can anyone be filled with so much hatred!" *What would compel Mishael to such an end? Oh, God, I don't want to be in this world anymore. Please take me home . . .*

Daniel swam hard for an hour before exhaustion started setting in. He knew he didn't have the self-will to take his own life, but he thought if he could swim eastward far enough then he would drown before he could change his mind and make it back to land. Suddenly he saw a small triangular fin break the water's surface nearby and immediately noticed the second one a couple of feet away. *Just a ray,* he thought, but that meant fish and possibly a shark were nearby.

The thought of a shark made him think of Sarah and her warnings about him becoming shark bait. Thoughts of Sarah flooded his mind. Beautiful Sarah. So different than Mishael, but so beautiful. Maybe not so different in many ways. He had wanted to wrap himself around Mishael, smothering her with protection and keeping her safe from the world while she created their melodies. But it was the opposite with Sarah. She wrapped herself around him, taking him out of the reality of losing Mishael. Her mere presence was strong enough to envelop him with serenity and allay his desperate feelings of futility. But both women were strong, confident, and self-assured, immensely talented and intelligent, and not bent to think and act as the world of men demanded. Now only Sarah remained. He paused for a moment considering her; was she who she appeared to be? He regained his resolve and began swimming again.

The ray curtailed his aura as it breached the surface just yards away and splashed back into the water with an explosive slap. He had seen a ray do this one other time while surfing on an outer sandbar at Wrightsville Beach, North Carolina. It had so surprised him that he caught the next wave and rode it to shore, staying prone on the board for the entire ride. He had gone straight into the pier's restaurant and ordered a beer. An old salt was also enjoying a morning beer at the bar, so he sat down nearby and told him about the ray.

"You's a'lucky bo' on two o'counts," the old man had said with the heavy sound-side brogue common among the watermen of Eastern North Carolina. Daniel had trouble understanding him, but was fascinated by the accent.

"Not o'lot o' people e'er see a ray do that. Mos'n don't ev'n know it's a'pos'ble. I's a'seen 'em do it, but I's been on the wardda more'n on land, and I's a'seen the shark ne'rby too. I's alla-ways a'figur'd that the ray was a-breachin' to stay o'tta the jaws o' the shark. Great Whites cruise that bar but no'bordy knows 'cept a few o' us'n and you's a'lucky 'e didn't up 'n 'ave you for 'is brea'fast."

The sailor dragged down another gulp of beer and kept talking. Daniel tried to decipher his message through the truncated words, added syllables, and deep guttural twang. He figured that the man was trying to tell him that the rays are showing off to get a mate just like men do in a bar. But who knows when so many tales are told by men surrounded by water for weeks on end. The waterman kept the dialogue going until Daniel finished his beer and slipped away to the toilet. He didn't go back to the bar.

Now Daniel wondered if the guy was right about the shark. That would take his death out of his own hands and put it squarely onto Mother Nature. *Good*, he thought, *now hurry up*. He continued swimming as the sun climbed higher. His sobs had stopped with the drying of the tears. *Probably from dehydration setting in*, he thought. *Well if I'm not shark food then at least I'll die of thirst.*

The diversion of the ray gave him a temporary respite from his grief, but then the image of Mishael screaming her love for him came flooding back and he redoubled his effort to reach the horizon.

It was more of a mental exercise than a reality, with very little physical manifestation since his muscles were already at their limit of endurance. Time had ceased to exist for Daniel as he retreated further into his inner soul and let the waves and wind wash over his outer being. A fin broke the surface close by and brought him back from his core. The large gray fin surfaced in an arc-like motion as Daniel heard a hiss of air before it disappeared beneath the surface. Another fin came up on his left, and looking around he saw a pod of dolphins joining him. His first thought was how large they were— surprisingly large when so close. Then he realized the shark danger would be averted as long as the dolphins were nearby. This theory may have been old sailors' lore, but he had always believed it, and always felt safer when a pod of dolphins was visible as he surfed.

He checked the position of the sun again and noticed it was harder to figure out which way was east as it climbed. For the first time he turned to look back toward Galveston but couldn't see any recognizable buildings. The thin line of the rooftops gave him a sense of direction as he headed away from them. The current was obviously carrying him south, away from the city, and his forward motion was meager now as his muscles began to protest in earnest, craving rest and water. He felt the sharp pain in his calf as a cramp gripped him. He immediately took a deep breath, curled into a tight ball, and began massaging and stretching his leg muscles. He laughed inwardly at the futility of the action, but he had imagined his death would come peacefully as sleep due to total exhaustion, or suddenly and violently from a shark attack. He did not want to be gulping water in a painful fit of cramps as he sank into the depths. The air in his lungs kept a small part of his upper back on the surface as he continued to push the wastes from his muscles and ease the cramp. With his head below the surface, he did not hear the helicopter pass overhead. The helicopter quickly distanced itself from the tight ball that was Daniel. After some time Daniel expelled the air from his lungs and continued on his journey.

In the helicopter, Nathan watched his screens closely as the infrared sensors created the blips that he recognized as dolphins. He had done his calculations carefully and explained his assumptions about Daniel's swimming to Jack and the SEAL team. He coupled his theory with the known current and then created a box within which Daniel should be if he was alive. He explained the best Daniel could do was three miles per hour due east, but most swimmers zigzag as they are constantly correcting their course and looking around for their bearings. Also, Daniel's pace may be only a mile an hour after this long in the water. With this information he established points and drew a line on the chart, then directed Jack to fly that path and subsequent parallel courses until the box he created had been scouted. The first time through was quiet as the SEALs scoured the water with powerful, image-stabilizing binoculars. Nathan constantly monitored his multiple screens tied to the array of sensors, most of which were classified equipment known only to a few in the intelligence community.

Jack suggested they widen the search area and possibly fly a bit higher, but Nathan shot back testily that he didn't do wild-ass guesses because they're wrong most of the time, and their altitude was perfect for the sensors and the binoculars.

"If he's still swimming out here, we'll find him," Nathan continued. "If we don't then he's either dead or swimming back to shore twenty miles south of Galveston, so shut up and fly."

"Never mind," returned Jack. He knew how seriously Nathan took his craft, which he had elevated to an art form.

"Jack, let's go back to that pod of dolphins and fly widening circles from there," Nathan said. He had seen dolphins gravitate to swimmers before and he noticed this pod was near the center of his box, so it was a good tactical change. It also gave his SEALs a slightly different look at the same areas.

"Crap," Jack shot back, "why do you always have to make it so difficult?"

"Oh, I'm sorry Jack, I thought I had a real pilot up there. Next time I'll request one who knows how to fly straight lines and circles. Maybe someone with more than one solo flight under his belt." The friendly banter between these old friends belied the depth of their respect for each other and also served to break the ever-present tension of searching when a life was on the line. Jack responded to the request immediately and keyed in the coordinates to the center of the pod. Then he began a slow outward spiral with each lap equidistant from the previous position. No pilot flew with more precision than Jack.

"Hold!" Nathan shouted. Jack immediately went into a hover and held steady. "Eleven o'clock, one hundred fifty yards." In the midst of the pod of dolphins, Nathan had the patterned blip of the swimmer he had been searching for. He was dismayed with himself that he had missed it before, so he made a mental note to go over the recorded data and see if he could determine why. Immediately one of the SEALs called "Got him, let's go!" and pointed Jack toward Daniel. As Jack maneuvered into position, three SEALs prepared to exit the aircraft, while the fourth started preparations for bringing a rescued swimmer aboard. They had been warned that Daniel may not want to cooperate, so the preparations included a securing method. As the three SEALs exited the chopper, Jack maneuvered so each one dropped into the water about twenty yards from Daniel, equidistant around him.

Daniel heard the helicopter approaching in the distance and looked up to see it start a circular pattern, but didn't think much about it until it started to move directly toward him. *Crap*, he thought, *who the hell is this?* Daniel noticed it was a totally black aircraft with no military or life-saving insignias, so he figured it to be a corporate bird that happened to spot him and assume he needed help. Kicking to tread water, he tried to wave them off, but instead of leaving, the helicopter paused, and with a deafening roar began hovering over him. Through the thick ocean mist being churned by the downdraft, Daniel watched as they opened the door and dropped a very thick rope. Immediately, three men in snorkel gear fast-roped down, dropping into the water at precise intervals, and spreading out around him. As the helicopter moved off quickly, an eerie calm enveloped the four men.

The swimmers began closing in and Daniel spun to watch them, then yelled, "Who the hell are you?"

"Are you Daniel Furman?" came the reply.

"Who wants to know?"

"I'll take that as a yes. We're here to take you in."

"And what if I don't want to go?"

"That's not an option, Mr. Furman." As the SEAL was talking to Daniel, keeping his attention focused, the other two SEALs were closing in from behind. Daniel was watching them in his periphery and as they converged behind so he could no longer see them, he took a deep breath, straightened his legs, and with a powerful stroke of both hands descended feetfirst into the depths. He quickly reached twenty feet and as he felt the intense pressure in his ears, he began letting out air while using his hands and arms in a reverse kicking motion to propel himself downward. Suddenly he felt a vice-like grip around his legs and thighs and as he struggled to free himself, another set of arms embraced him in a stranglehold as he felt his feet being lashed together. Then his arms were quickly pinioned and a zip-tie was expertly placed around his wrists. Meanwhile, he felt the powerful thrusts of swim fins propelling him upward. As he broke the surface and gasped for a gulp of air, an arm wrapped around his neck, constricting blood flow to his brain.

His father was sitting on the edge of his bed calling his name, "Daniel, Daniel." *How strange,* he thought, *Dad never called me Daniel. And how young he looks. It's so wonderful to see you, Dad, but the roar of the alarm is deafening. Someone stop it! I'm trying to wake up, Dad. Where are you going? Wait!* Daniel woke up, disoriented, and found himself looking into the face of one of the SEALs who was calling his name and patting his legs, bringing him out of the blackout. Two other men sat on either side of him in the tight quarters of the helicopter. The alarm he was dreaming about was the roar of the machine nearly drowning out the yelling of the SEAL. Daniel immediately jerked and kicked but nothing moved; his arms and legs were bound to the seat and he was helpless. His helplessness morphed to panic and he screamed, but the placid face in front of his just looked at him, waiting. Spent from the hours in the water and the struggle with the SEALs, he finally collapsed and hung his head. One of the SEALs fit a set of earphones on him and adjusted the microphone. Daniel didn't resist. He was too tired to care and he just wanted to die—to go home and see his dad once again.

The earphone came to life and he heard the voice in front of him. "How are you feeling, Daniel?"

"Who the hell are you?" Daniel shook his head trying to focus, but dizziness overwhelmed him. "What are you doing to me?"

"I'm Danny, he's Al, that's Cabell, and behind you is Doc. He's a corpsman. We're Navy SEALs. Your pilot is Dave, and Nathan is your navigator. We're taking you to Houston."

"Up yours, asshole, I don't want to go to Houston! Now get this shit off me and let me go!"

"No can do, Daniel. Our orders are to bring you back to Houston."

"Orders!" Daniel shouted, "What the crap is this with 'orders' lately?" Daniel paused, trying to regain some strength. "Who gives you the right to *order* me? Now let me go!"

"Calm down, Daniel, everything is all right. Someone wants to talk to you before the sharks have you for lunch."

"And if I don't want to talk to anyone?"

"That's not up to us, Daniel. We're just the delivery squad. But things will go much easier if you relax."

"I don't want to relax, shithead! I want out . . ." Daniel's voice trailed off as the dryness in his throat affected his speech. He tried again to protest, but couldn't form any words.

Daniel noticed the shoreline coming at them very quickly and then realized how low they were flying, making the sensation of speed immediate. This meant they were flying under the radar and his sense of dread began to crescendo. He began to panic.

He saw Doc reach around with a syringe, place it against his rigidly held forearm and inject him. Danny's voice was asking him to breathe normally as the skyscrapers of Houston came into view and the blackness of drug-induced sleep engulfed him.

CHAPTER 7

Daniel's Respite

Daniel heard the soft voice nearby before he opened his eyes. He knew he was exhausted and for a moment he just wanted to lie quietly and get his bearings. He could not imagine where he was, so he decided to pretend to sleep a little longer until he could gather enough information to formulate a plan of action. The voice was very familiar, but he could not make out the words being spoken. As the fogginess receded, his memory of the day began to flood his consciousness and he jerked himself awake.

"Easy kiddo," he heard Victor say as he rose from his bedside seat.

Daniel struggled for a moment, then realized he was tugging vainly against his restraints.

"Sorry to strap you in, Daniel, my boy, but apparently you gave the SEAL team quite a go."

"Victor!" Daniel gasped, "What's going on? Why am I tied up? Who?"

"Slow down, Daniel. One thing at a time." Victor held up his hand to try to slow down Daniel's questioning.

Daniel started taking notes of where he was as his mind focused. At that moment he felt a soft hand clutching his and he turned his head toward the other side of the bed. "Sarah," he cried, as he saw the tears streaming down her cheeks.

"Oh, Daniel," she whispered through her tears, "I was so afraid I'd never see you again." Her voice failed her as her grip tightened and she slumped back into the chair.

Daniel turned back to Victor. "Please tell me what's going on Victor. Where am I and how did I get here? This is all so crazy!" At that moment he remembered Mishael. "Victor, Mishael's dead—she blew herself up! Oh God, Victor, why would she do that?" Daniel's body released into convulsive sobs as he struggled against the restraints to wipe his eyes. Sarah took a tissue from the bedside box and wiped his tears.

"Oh Daniel, I'm so sorry," he heard Sarah saying as she ministered to his grief. "I'm just so sorry." She stroked his curly blond hair he had let grow out since leaving VCM and took a cool rag and laid it on his forehead, soothing the burning effects of the sun and water.

"Daniel," Victor said, "you need some rest. Then we'll talk."

"I don't want to rest! I want to die!" Daniel screamed back.

"I know you're hurting Daniel, and I know how bad you're hurting—"

"How can you possibly know how bad I'm hurting?" Daniel interjected. His grief-induced venom shot through but did not disturb Victor.

"Daniel, believe me, I know. We'll talk after you rest. Now relax, the doctor is going to give you something to help."

Daniel began to protest, then he noticed the IV tube in his arm, and watched as the doctor added a drug.

He turned towards Sarah, "Help me, Sarah, please help me . . . Sarah . . ."

Sarah squeezed his hand and then felt it go limp as the drug took effect. "I'm here Daniel. I'll always be here, my dear Daniel."

• • •

Daniel felt the intensity of the déjà vu as he began stirring from coma-like sleep. Like before, he could not fathom where he was, but he could hear the same voice softly wafting towards him. It sounded like a prayer. He managed to open one eye and look down the bed sheets at the top of a head. Victor had his head on Daniel's bed, arms crossed above, and hands clasped together in a position of prayer. And he was praying; praying for Daniel.

"Victor?" Daniel called hoarsely. "Is that you?"

Victor raised his head and looked into Daniel's soft blue eyes and responded quietly, "Yes. I'm here."

"I didn't know you were a religious man, Victor."

"That's funny," Victor responded. "I chastised your father for being a religious man one time when I woke up to him praying over my badly damaged body."

"Really?"

"I think I should give you exactly the same response he gave me."

"What was that?"

"He said, 'I'm not a religious man, Vic, I'm a Christ-centered man.' He always called me 'Vic' when he spoke to me like he was older instead of younger."

"What's the difference?"

"Well, that's also exactly what I asked him. Do you want his answer to that, too?"

"I guess so," Daniel said, trying desperately to keep his eyes open.

"He said, 'My dear Vic, the answer to that will take a lifetime.' And it did. So you get some sleep now, Daniel, and we'll talk again when you wake up."

"Where is Sarah?" Daniel asked as he finally relented to the heaviness of his eyelids.

Victor did not respond as he watched Daniel's eyelids close and listened as his breathing eased into tranquility.

CHAPTER 8

A Murderous Story

Daniel awoke suddenly as his dreams became increasingly real, his thirst and full bladder creating scenarios of simultaneously gulping water while searching frantically for a dark corner to use as a toilet. Victor sensed his restlessness so when he finally opened his eyes, he was ready with a cup of electrolyte solution the doctor had concocted. Daniel's restraints had been removed, but the outer doors to the suite were secured as a precaution. Victor was alone with him now and handed him the cup before saying anything. Daniel looked at him quizzically, took the cup, drank it, and asked for the toilet. Victor pointed to a doorway behind him as Daniel flung the sheets off and tried to get out of bed. Victor caught him before he fell, helped him stabilize, then headed with him to the bathroom. Daniel used the sink as a support as Victor let go of him and closed the door.

Victor was ready with more to drink when Daniel emerged from the toilet and made his way to a lounge chair.

"Jesus, I feel like crap!" he finally said when his cotton-like throat allowed him to talk.

"You don't look so good either, my boy," Victor replied.

"Where am I?"

"My office suite," Victor replied. "I had my bedroom refitted with a hospital bed and some equipment to help you recover."

"How long have I been here?"

"Two days."

"Christ! I should be dead!"

"More than you realize, Daniel. More than you realize."

"Mishael's dead!"

"I know, son. I'm very sorry."

"Why Victor? Why did she do that? Was it my fault? Do you know what happened?"

As Daniel was shooting questions at Victor, the realizations of the past Saturday began to flood back into his awareness, and the tears returned. He fell back into the chair, unable to speak anymore.

Victor gave him a few moments to grieve, and then quietly answered him. "I know what happened, Daniel, and when you're ready we can talk about it."

Something in what Victor said, or the way he said it, triggered a memory in Daniel, and he suddenly was flush with anger. "You knew about Mishael, didn't you Victor? You've always known where she was!" Daniel's anger escalated.

"Hold on Daniel! What are you talking about?"

"The phone number, Victor! The number in the want ad was yours—or at least one of your acquaintances. Who was it? Who knew?"

Victor was rarely surprised by anything, but this sudden outburst coupled with the knowledge that Daniel knew about the phone number caught him totally off guard. He tried desperately to regroup as he attempted to fend off Daniel's questions. "Daniel, let me explain . . . you don't understand . . . calm down for a moment . . . give me a chance to tell you what happened."

Daniel was on his feet now, shaking from a combination of rage and grief, and demanding an explanation. "Don't tell me to calm down, Victor! Tell me about Mishael! Tell me now!"

"Please, Daniel, sit down. Let me tell you the whole story. There's so much," Victor paused, trying to reel in his own anxiety. "Just give me a chance."

"What do you mean, there's so much. Just tell me—did you know where Mishael was?"

"No."

"Then why was your number on the want ad?"

"To save your life, Daniel," Victor said somberly.

"Bullshit! Bullshit! Bullshit! Tell me the truth or I swear I'll tear this place apart!"

"That is the truth," Victor said quietly and sat back in his chair waiting for Daniel to explode on him. But Daniel's anger finally abated as he succumbed to his grief and slumped back into his chair. Then he asked, "What is the truth, Victor? Please tell me the truth."

"The truth is a very long story. And one you need to hear all of, in detail."

"What is so long about telling me what you know of Mishael?"

"Plenty. And the rest of your life will be totally altered from this day."

"What in the world are you talking about? I just lost the love of my life, my soulmate, and my reason for living. How can my life not be forever altered—if I even have a life when I leave here? None of this makes a bit of sense, especially your attitude right now. I'm even trying to figure out why you went to such extremes to fish me out of the Gulf. And I'm not in the mood to thank you for that right now—unless you can shed some light on this whole debacle. After that, I may just go for another swim."

"Daniel, I promise you if you allow me time to tell you everything you need to know, then afterward, if you still want to take your own life, I will not get in your way."

Daniel looked at Victor for a long moment. Victor would not make a statement like that lightly, so he began to consider that Victor really may know something that would either bring him back from the brink of suicide, or push him over the edge with his blessing. And right now Daniel could not fathom which way Victor was directing the game. Daniel's outbursts had sapped his limited energy and his fatigue was beginning to affect his ability to think clearly and ascertain the nuances of Victor's offer. It was an offer from a man whom he had trusted and admired, but now found himself questioning to the very core of their relationship. Finally Daniel sat back and closed his eyes. "Please, just tell me the truth. I beg you."

"All right, but you will have to trust that I have your best interest at heart and I love you as a son."

"What?" Daniel paused, surprised by Victor's words, then asked, "Why? For all I know you were involved in Mishael's death. How can I trust you and why would you say you love me as a son? You've helped me tremendously over the past couple of years, and been a wonderful mentor, but all of that is worthless without Mishael."

"I understand how you feel, Daniel, believe me."

Daniel viciously cut Victor's sentence short, "No you *don't* understand. You *can't* understand how I feel, and stop trying to tell me you do! You just can't!"

"Yes I can, Daniel! I've been there. I've lost the love of my life and my grief sent me over a hill outside of San Diego hoping for death! I woke up in a hospital with your father praying over me. And that was only part of my loss. The real tragedy was why I lost my wife. If not for Joseph, I would have died long ago. Believe me, living after that was much harder than dying. But your father gave me something to live for, and my grief helped me to be with him when he lost his first family in the plane crash on their way to see him. He grieved for years before meeting your mother, falling in love again, and starting a second family. I think you were the final salvation that brought him out of his despair. We were there for each other, and now if you'll allow me, and trust me, I'll tell you about Mishael."

Daniel hung his head as he nodded. "Okay. I'll listen. And I'm sorry I got angry with you. I didn't know. I just didn't know. I'm so lost right now. I don't know what I'm going to do. But I promise I'll listen and trust what you tell me."

"I'll tell you more about my wife later," Victor said as he reached for a folder on a nearby table. "First, I'm going to have to tell you some facts about the danger you're in."

"I'm in danger? Why? And where's Sarah? Is she okay?" It suddenly occurred to Daniel that Sarah had been here when he awoke the first time, and she had been very upset, but now she was missing.

"Sarah's fine. She and Jonathan are on a little sabbatical. She waited until she knew you were okay, then left while you were sleeping. She knew I needed time with you alone before you saw her again. But don't worry, she's fine. She told me to tell you she loves you and will see you as soon as you are ready."

"Ready? Ready for what? What's the danger?"

"Slow down. Have you ever seen this man?" Victor removed a photograph of a Middle-Eastern looking man from the folder and handed it to Daniel.

Daniel immediately recognized the man as the one who had delivered the video of Mishael's suicide bombing. His rage was immediate as he spat out a profanity and threw the photo back at Victor. "Does he work for you?"

"Not hardly. I think you have a few things backward. Did he deliver the flash drive?"

"Yes."

"We thought so, but I wanted to make sure you knew him. Why did you photograph his van?"

"I don't know. He creeped me out and it had been a weird night. I found out you, or someone you knew, had placed the want ad I've been looking for since Mishael left, and I knew he wasn't a real delivery guy. I was sure he was foreign and military, so I decided to take his picture just to check on him later. How did you know I took his picture?"

"Sarah got your phone and wallet when she went to check on you. She probably saved your life and it almost cost her hers."

"What do you mean?"

"Your deliveryman is no ordinary deliveryman."

"Yeah, I figured that," Daniel quipped.

"Do you recognize this photo?" Victor handed Daniel another picture; a grainy image obviously taken from a surveillance camera. It was of a hotel lobby and Daniel immediately recognized it as the location of his last meeting with his father. He could make out the back of his father's head as he was being served a drink.

"Did Joseph have his usual drink that night?" Victor asked.

"As far as I know. It looked like an Arnold Palmer, but at that time of the evening it may have turned into a John Daly. Why? What does this have to do with anything?"

"Do you recognize the server?"

Daniel looked closely at the waiter, then horror struck him as he saw the same stern face that had been at his door. "Who is this guy?"

"No one you want to mess with, believe me. But he was the beginning of a very destructive trail we, and the government, have been tracking."

"But what does he have to do with me and Dad? We're not anybody."

"You're almost right. Let me back up for a minute. Joseph, as you know, was in excellent health and kept himself very fit, even though he was older when he married your mother and they had you, so it struck me as extremely odd he died so suddenly. I talked to the EMTs that worked on him that evening. They said his heart attack was so massive his heart did not respond at all to any shocks. Nothing at all. His heart was so dead they just figured it was a massive heart attack, but I wanted to know more. So I sent Joseph's body to San Diego for an autopsy, secretly. That wasn't actually him that we buried at his funeral."

"What?" Daniel's surprise registered as a flash of anger causing Victor to raise his hands defensively.

"Hold on, Daniel. Just listen for a moment before you get mad at me."

"Sorry. I'm not mad, just a little shocked, I guess. So, the autopsy?"

"Not a classic heart attack. In fact, they couldn't find any blockage that would cause one, but his heart just suddenly seized. When I heard that, I got extremely suspicious so I had the police get the surveillance tapes from the hotel and we investigated each person Joseph had contact with that night. Only we couldn't figure out who the waiter was. No one at the hotel knew him and he wasn't an employee. We ran his face through Homeland Security and got a hit, though. Meanwhile, I asked the lab in San Diego to do another autopsy, this time looking for a particular drug. Not one that would show up unless you knew to look for it. And bingo, they got a positive result."

"So you're telling me Dad was poisoned?"

"Not poisoned in the classic sense. This drug stops the heart muscle, leaving very little trace. It's used by a few terrorist organizations, and we don't know how often since most of the time the victim is buried with the cause of death listed as a heart attack and no one's the wiser. Why anyone would want Joseph dead was the bigger mystery, but at least we knew who did it."

"So Dad was murdered by a terrorist? But why? That makes no sense. Dad was not politically active at all and rarely went out of the country."

"Well, at first I was afraid it had to be connected to me somehow."

"Why?"

"I'll get to that later, Daniel. It turned out this terrorist, who we now call Babel, is the top assassin in a terrorist cell which at the time was based in a mosque in Silicon Valley. You remember the day Mishael's father picked her up and you went to her house looking for her?"

"Yeah. The police showed up with a restraining order against me."

"I remembered you had told me that so I had it checked out. There was no record anywhere of a call to the police or any such order being issued. It was totally bogus, even the police officer."

"So what are you saying? That Mishael's father is connected to a terrorist organization or something?"

"No. Not connected. He is the terrorist organization. He is Abu, a rogue Pakistani terrorist bent on destroying America, and Babel is his right-hand man. These are very dangerous and deadly people with ISIS roots. Those are code names we use for them. 'A' for Abu means the top guy and 'B' for Babel is the second in command. He has a small army operating here and nearly limitless funds.

"But why did he want Dad dead?"

"Revenge, Daniel. Pure, simple, revenge. When he found out about you and Mishael, he exacted revenge by killing someone you love—your father. You would have found out about it sooner or later, when they wanted you to. I think they planned for him to die in front of you, but you left the meeting quickly and he didn't finish his drink until you left."

"So I'm the reason they killed Dad. God, Victor, how could I have been so stupid!"

"Daniel, you're not responsible. Abu is."

"So Mishael is dead because of me too!"

"No. Listen to me. What happened to her is not your fault!"

"How can it not be? Of course it's my fault! I killed her!"

"Please just listen for a moment! You don't understand these people. You can't blame yourself for their hatred. They are butchers. They know nothing but hatred and revenge. It's what they live for and hopefully what they will die for. The sooner the better."

"If I had just woken her up that night, she would still be alive and Dad would be too. So I'm responsible for both their deaths."

"Daniel, they both loved you beyond measure. And that love is what Abu hated and sought to destroy."

"How do you know about how Mishael felt?"

"I know she loved you so much that when her father sent her back to Pakistan for an arranged marriage, she told him she would rather die than marry anyone but you."

"How do you know that?"

"You'll have to trust me for a while, but hopefully soon I'll be able to tell you exactly how we know what we do."

"I want to know now, Victor!"

"No. Let me finish. I will tell you everything, but the context is too important. You need to first understand so much more."

"Then hurry up and finish so I can find this jerk, Babel, and rip his head off!" Daniel paused waiting for Victor to continue, then impatiently asked, "Can you at least tell me what happened to her hands?"

"Yes. Yes, I can. But I can't tell you how I know this yet."

"Just tell me something—I don't care how you know all this—just tell me before I explode."

"When Mishael got back to Pakistan and learned her fate, she swore to her father she would never marry. Of course, in her family and her religion, women are little more than chattel, and God-sanctioned slaves. They exist to serve men and have children. Mishael's words were blasphemy and her father considered her possessed by the devil. And the devil was you, Daniel. He set out to punish and destroy you. Slowly and deliberately. And in his mind, God was on his side. Mishael learned about your father and knew you would be next, so in retaliation she bound her fingers with rubber bands, essentially killing them and destroying her ability to play the piano. A side effect was that without fingers her arranged marriage was no longer viable. A man in her culture does not want a cripple for a wife. She told her father if she could not play for you, she would play for no one. Her only chance for atonement then was a suicide in which she took as many infidel lives as possible. She agreed to this if he swore to spare you. So her father arranged a suicide bombing at a London restaurant filled with government officials."

"When was that?" Daniel interjected.

"A month after Joseph's death."

"So you've known Mishael was dead for a long time!"

"Yes, but it wasn't something I could tell you until we could assure your safety and neutralize Abu. He closed his cell in California and we couldn't find him again. He's very good at hiding and travels the world with impunity. Also, we cannot let on we know anything about him— to his organization or our own government for that matter. That is our greatest advantage over him. Mishael had the last revenge, though. When she shed her burqa and proclaimed her love for you, then killed only herself, it was an extreme slap in the face to her father."

"So why didn't he just kill me then?"

"That would not punish you, Daniel. Abu seeks revenge by destroying love. I think he was waiting for you to have a wife and family, then he would destroy them. That's his style. Killing you is last on the agenda. You need to suffer first."

"So that's why Sarah and Jonathan are in danger?"

"Yes, and also why your swim in the Gulf may have saved your life and theirs. Babel was waiting for you to view the video, then I think he planned to kidnap you, Sarah, and possibly Jonathan, and start the punishment. He almost got Sarah at your house, but fortunately we were able to thwart his plans."

"So what about the want ad? Why did you run it?"

"We didn't."

"But the phone number . . . "

"We knew you were still getting the Palo Alto paper every week at the office, so we looked through it before Jennifer forwarded it to you. She told me what you were looking for. When we found the ad, we had our art department switch numbers so you would call us. We called the real number. That led us to Abu in Phoenix, and also set in motion the events of Saturday morning. Abu must have found out about the want ad plan somehow and tested it by running the ad in the paper. We made a grave mistake that nearly cost you your life in that we didn't realize how quickly he would act. We were setting up surveillance in Phoenix while Babel was at your doorstep. Thank God you went for a swim when you did and didn't return."

"So Sarah came looking for me and stepped into a death trap!"

"Yes, but one of our agents got in the way and she escaped. She and Jonathan are at a safe house now for a while."

"And Babel?"

"He thinks you're dead, and we want to leave it that way. But of course that's up to you."

"Does Mom know?"

"She knows you're missing, but since you haven't been declared dead yet, she's still hoping. I flew her to Houston and she's staying at one of my suites nearby."

"Can I see her?"

"That would be extremely dangerous, Daniel. Abu is already looking for Sarah and until your body shows up, I don't think he will give up. So far he has left your mom alone. I think he thinks you and her don't get along, so he didn't care to do anything with her. Right now everyone is safer if you're dead."

"I can't just leave her hanging like that, Victor."

"For everyone's safety you may have to, but like I said that must be your decision."

"Jesus, Victor, I've made such a mess of everything. What am I going to do? How can I ever end this mess?"

"You are a victim here, not a perpetrator. You need to remember that. You were a college student who fell in love, that's all. We're all guilty of that, but fortunately we all are not punished for it. You just happened to step on the wrong side of a vengeful religious zealot and by the grace of God you're still alive. And you're also in a position to do something about it, if you so choose."

"What do you mean? What could I possibly do to these people? My only option is to run for the rest of my life and hope they never catch me, or Sarah and Jonathan. That's not much of a life, Victor. It looks like Abu has destroyed me."

Victor sat quietly letting Daniel draw his conclusions, knowing that once Daniel was finished, his frame of mind would allow him to offer other options. But Victor knew he had to be patient. He was at a critical juncture with Daniel and he needed for Daniel to decide his next move. Victor could not push him there, but he could set the scenario so the decision would be obvious for Daniel.

"I'm very tired. Do you mind if I take a nap now, then we can continue? I have so many questions, but I can't organize them. I need some sleep."

"No problem. We have a lot to talk about, and right now there's no hurry. I'll order breakfast for later. You get some rest."

"Breakfast? Jeez, I have no idea what day it is or the time."

"It doesn't matter right now, Daniel. Get some rest. I'll be in the other room if you need anything."

"Thanks, Victor. Victor?"

"Yes?" Victor had stood up to leave, but paused at the door and turned when Daniel called.

"Thank you. And I'm sorry. I'm so sorry to have caused so much trouble."

"There's no need for apologies, Daniel. I'm just glad you're still with us. Hopefully you'll decide to stay with us for a while." Victor watched as Daniel's eyelids closed and knew he was asleep before the sentence was complete. "Sleep tight, my boy," Victor said to himself as he watched Daniel's breaths become slow and rhythmic. "We have a lot to do when you wake up." He turned out the light and left.

Daniel's Decision

Victor quietly opened the door to check on Daniel and found him sitting in the chair. The room was dark.

"Feeling better, kid?" Victor asked.

"A little hungry and a whole lot curious," Daniel responded.

"The hunger we can take care of immediately. The curiosity may take a little longer."

Daniel knew Victor was trying to lighten the atmosphere, but couldn't bring himself to make any jovial remark. His heart was too heavy and his thoughts too jumbled. He needed answers, and Victor was his only source at the moment. He was hoping Victor could stay with him long enough to settle his burning soul. Victor's patience with him had been incredible; something he still did not quite understand, and Victor showed no signs of wanting him to leave. He marveled at the consideration shown him, even to the point of bringing his mom to Houston and looking out for her. Daniel couldn't help but wonder what was behind the immeasurable kindness. Had he underestimated the depth of the friendship Victor and his father shared? Certainly they had been lifelong friends, but did that warrant this level of commitment by Victor? It occurred to Daniel that Victor could easily have turned the situation over to the police or FBI, taken Daniel to the hospital, and gotten back to his own business. Business for Victor was a twenty-four-seven ordeal, and interruptions were unfathomable. Daniel was lost.

"Food is on the way," Victor announced as he flipped a switch near the door and Daniel marveled as the black out shades began to lift and the bright Houston sunshine flooded the room. "You're looking better. Your face took quite a beating from the sun, but doesn't seem to be much worse for the wear. Are you drinking plenty?"

"Yes, sir," Daniel answered politely, trying not to transmit his agitation at Victor's talkativeness.

"Good. Dehydration is tricky business. I've got bacon and eggs on the way, and a plate of sandwiches, if you prefer. I'll serve them myself, though. I gave Robert the week off and sent him to Mexico on vacation so he wouldn't be tempted to pop in on me unexpectedly." Robert was Victor's French valet and pronounced his name "Ro-Bear," rolling the R and accentuating the last syllable.

"Why's that?" Daniel perked up as his curiosity was further aroused.

"The fewer people who know you're alive, the better."

Daniel was quiet for a moment, considering this, then asked, "What if I don't want to be dead?"

"Well," Victor began in a resigned tone, "we'd have to have you come ashore in Mexico on a fishing boat as if they had rescued you and made it difficult to get you back to the US. That would answer the timeline questions, but the police investigation at your cottage might be a little trickier."

"What police investigation?"

"Foul play is suspected in your disappearance."

"Why?"

"Neighbors are telling police about the suspicious car chase, and a black van that was in an accident in your neighborhood. It tore up some bushes and took out a light pole. The driver disappeared and it turns out the van had a bogus registration. A lot of curious paraphernalia was in the van. Guns, shackles, military grade explosives—things that shouldn't be in a quiet Galveston neighborhood. When the police showed up at your house, they found a broken glass in the driveway with an ammonia residue around it."

"What was that? Where'd it come from?"

"Sarah had it as a defense in case Babel got to her before she got to her car. She must have dropped it getting into the car. It was a close call."

"Jesus, I had no idea."

"It's okay now. But the police have tape around your house and are investigating it as a homicide, which suits us just fine. Babel will lay low for a while, and Abu is probably seething. He doesn't like failure, and he really hates attention. He likes to work quietly and be nowhere around when the results of his actions hit the media."

"But if I show up, then there's no more investigation. And I don't know anything about the van, so that shouldn't affect me either. I can go home and get back to killing myself."

"Is that what you want?"

"No, of course not. I couldn't do it in the Gulf, so I know I can't do it now, or ever. To tell you the truth, every time I wanted to give up out there, I thought of Sarah and Jonathan, and couldn't bring myself to finish the job."

"Jack says you went for the bottom when the SEALs came for you."

"Yeah, that was just a reaction. I was nearly delirious by then anyway. I don't know if I could have made it back to shore, but I do know my last thoughts would have been of Sarah if I hadn't made it."

"You'll have to tell her one day. Right now she's torn between grief and anger, and I downplayed the real extent of the danger she and Jonathan are in."

"I guess she does have a huge reason to be mad at me. I never considered how selfish it was until I was here thinking about it. I just blindly ran, wanting to stop the pain. But I do know she saved my life out there, and though I'm torn up over Mishael's suicide, I really consider Sarah and Jonathan my family here in Houston, since I really have no other family now that Mom is remarried and has other children. I should have had more regard for Sarah and Jonathan."

"Hopefully you can explain all that to them and they'll understand. The video was very shocking. Even Sarah has had trouble lately after viewing it."

"Really? Is she okay?"

"The doctor has been giving her something to help her sleep, but between that and worrying about you, she's in need of some recovery of her own. And she doesn't realize how close she came to dire consequences with Babel, so let's keep that low key for a while."

"Sure. Where is she? Can I see her?"

"I sent her to a very private place. She thinks just for a sabbatical, but mostly it's for her safety until we can take care of Abu."

"We take care of Abu? What d'you mean? How can we ever get close enough to him to do anything? I think it will be all I can do to stay out of his way. You think if I move away from Sarah and Jonathan, he'll leave them alone?"

"No. Not if he knows you're alive. He'll kill them for spite, now. It's in his DNA. So what's your decision?"

"What decision?"

"Do you want to be put ashore in Mexico or remain dead?"

"How can I remain dead? What am I going to do?"

"I can help, but you have to decide."

"Will that keep Sarah and Jonathan safe?"

"I'm pretty sure Abu will not waste any time on them if you're dead. He has much bigger wars to fight."

"Well then the decision is a no-brainer. I've either got to be dead for real or play dead very convincingly. That's not something I know how to do."

"Like I said, I can help, but we'll talk about that later. Right now we need to catch a helicopter to Hobby Field. The jet is waiting."

"Waiting for what?"

"What do you say we take a trip to Maine? We can talk on the plane and I could use some rest and some time to satisfy that curiosity of yours. Joseph and I used trips to your mountain to rejuvenate. Maybe you and I could do the same and get to know each other better. Maybe even catch a few trout? Joseph used to say that fly fishing was spiritual."

"You've already done so much, though. Why? I don't get it. You and Dad must have been better friends than I imagined for you to commit so much to me. I mean, I really appreciate it, but I don't quite understand it. I doubt you'd rescue other former employees, nurse them back to health, and fly them to Maine for a little R&R!" Daniel grinned, trying to make light of the dire situation and understand Victor's motives. "Is there any way I can see Mom before we leave?"

Victor put his hand on Daniel's shoulder, trying to calm his restlessness and obvious confusion over the bizarre twist that had disrupted his tranquil life. "She's in Sarah's office, waiting. I've explained everything to her, so when she leaves here it will be as though you are dead and she will make all the arrangements. As next of kin, she'll take care of your property. Frederick in legal will be assisting her. Let's go say goodbye."

Daniel was incredulous, and as Victor headed for the door Daniel blurted, "Wait, Victor!"

Victor turned to face Daniel and just raised his eyebrows.

"You knew what my decision would be and had already arranged all this?"

"You're a smart kid, Daniel. I knew you'd make the right decision."

"Shit! One day I'm going to get tired of being played by you," Daniel said laughingly.

"I hope not, kid. Life might get a little dull without you to look after." Victor pressed the buttons to let the shades down, turned out the lights, and locked the door to his private quarters. He paused for a moment in his office and looked around as if saying goodbye. Daniel assumed he was just ensuring he didn't miss anything and opened the heavy wooden door to Sarah's office and into his mother's arms.

CHAPTER 10

The Flight

Daniel kissed his mom's cheek as she hugged him through the tears and said her final goodbye for an undetermined period of time. Victor handed Daniel a bag of clothes suited for the Maine climate then opened the door to his office and motioned for Daniel to go in.

"But I thought we were headed to the helipad now?" Daniel protested.

"We are. Come on," Victor responded.

As the office door closed behind Daniel, a wall panel nearby slid open revealing Victor's private elevator connecting his basement garage, his office, and the helipad. Victor inserted a key and entered a code, bringing the elevator to life. He pushed the upper of three buttons and immediately the doors closed and they were on their way up. "Impressive," Daniel said. "There are stairs beside the shaft that connect these areas also aren't there?"

"How'd you know?"

"I was never able to complete the plan of the building in my head when I worked here. I just assumed the lost space was for mechanical equipment, but could never find an access. I didn't want to be nosy, so I just let it be an enigma."

"Thoughtful of you," Victor smiled. "And perceptive."

"Well, it is very well concealed, which I assume is the whole idea."

"Yep," Victor said as the doors opened to reveal the helicopter, blades already in motion.

"I didn't realize it had gotten dark," Daniel said. "But thanks for letting me visit with Mom for so long."

"No problem," Victor said with a kind smile. "It may be a long time before you're able to see her again, so it's the least I could do."

"Least? That's a funny word to use after all you've done."

Victor didn't respond, just handed Daniel a set of headphones and instructed his pilot to take off. A few minutes later the helicopter was circling Hobby Airport with the copilot scanning the area with high-powered night-vision binoculars.

"What's he doing?" Daniel asked Victor, pointing to the copilot.

"Just making sure no one is watching as we land. I want you to stay back against the seat and be very still until we get into the hangar. Don't be tempted to look out. We've seen several of Abu's men watching the activities of VCM. We figure he's just fishing, hoping we'll tip our hand in case we know anything about you. Everything we do from now on will be handled as a covert operation. You'll get used to it, but it's not pleasant, I warn you."

The helicopter landed close to a hangar door that opened as soon as they touched down. In seconds they were connected to a powered cart and whisked inside, the doors closing immediately behind them. The jet was waiting with its door open and Victor ushered Daniel aboard with his bag slung over his shoulder. Victor carried only a briefcase.

"No baggage, Victor? I thought you were taking a week off," Daniel puzzled.

"I have clothes all over the place, and a wardrobe on the jet in case I go somewhere unexpected. Robert keeps up with it and he's very meticulous about everything pertaining to my food and clothes. It's actually one of the most enjoyable perks of wealth; and one of the very few."

"I would imagine there are plenty."

"For every perk there's a freedom lost, so pretty soon you're a slave to the wealth and just have to appreciate the bennies."

"Oh," Daniel conceded. "I never considered it that way."

"It's a choice you make early and don't have the luxury of reversing."

"Dad thought it was a personality trait more than a choice."

"He was probably right. He was right about a lot of things, I've discovered."

"Really? Like what?"

"Make yourself comfortable, Daniel, while we take off. We'll eat and then talk."

Daniel began to notice how much Victor was putting off conversations with him. It seemed like *later* was always a more convenient time to talk. Daniel puzzled over this as he buckled his seat belt and watched Victor head toward the cockpit and engage in a lengthy conversation with the pilots. Finally he came back, handed Daniel a cold beer, and took a seat across the table. He buckled his belt as the jet began its acceleration down the runway.

"Everything okay up there?" Daniel asked motioning toward the cockpit.

"Nothing we can't handle. We found a couple of low-lifes hanging around outside the hangar. They were pretending to be TSA agents, but their IDs were bogus so we turned them over to real TSA agents."

"How did you know they weren't real?"

"We know every agent here, so we knew they were imposters. Their costumes were good, but ours are better. They tried to pull rank and escape, but since they didn't know we had no authority over them, we had the advantage. They'll be on ice for a while and then get deported. I doubt they're Americans."

"Jesus, is this all because of me? Does it happen much?"

"I'm not positive it had anything to do with you, but it pays to be careful. We'll find out who they were working for soon enough. Another beer?"

"Thanks." Daniel looked around and noticed there was no flight attendant. It seemed strange Victor would not have someone here to attend to what he wanted.

Victor was watching him, amused at his puzzlement, and then as if to let him off the hook said, "The beer and our food trays are in the kitchen through that door. How about fetching them for us? We'll be serving ourselves on this flight, my boy. It's just you, me, and the pilots. And we'll be zigzagging around before we head to Maine. It's safer that way. We never head directly to Maine, and then we just land as if it's a fuel stop only. It will look like I'm headed to London for the week."

"That seems like a lot to go through just to get to Maine."

"One of the not-so-fun perks," Victor said facetiously.

"Right," Daniel said with a smile as he headed toward the kitchen. Daniel got Victor's food first and then went back to the kitchen for his own.

They ate quietly for a time as Victor perused some paperwork. Then Daniel picked up the trays and asked, "Another beer?"

"No thanks. But a Perrier would be nice."

"Mind if I have another one?"

"Hell no, kid. Help yourself. And don't feel like you have to ask."

"Thanks."

After Daniel had cleared the trays and returned with the drinks, he sat down and looked intently at Victor who finally noticed the look and set his report aside.

"Something on your mind, Daniel?"

"Plenty."

"Like what?"

"Like, why are you doing all this for me? Why did you think Dad's murder was connected to you? And what about your wife? How did you lose her? And why was she only part of your loss? All these questions keep running through my head whenever I start thinking about what you've told me so far. Nothing seems to square. I just can't seem to make sense of it. And why did you think it was so special when Dad called you Vic, 'like he was older' I think is the way you put it. Seems like just a friendly way to say Victor. So I just don't get it, and I don't know what to ask first. One question seems to lead to ten others and time after time you just said we'll get to that later. Well, is it later yet?"

"I suppose it is," Victor said quietly. "Can you get me another Perrier and I'll tell you a story that might tie up some of the loose ends."

"Are you putting me off again, Victor?" Daniel said, half grinning.

"No. I just need a moment to collect my thoughts. Better get yourself another beer while you're up."

When Daniel sat back down, Victor had his hands crossed in front of him and his head down as if he were praying. Daniel slid the Perrier across the table. Victor looked up at him and nodded a thank you.

Victor lifted the bottle to his lips, sipped, took a deep breath, and began. "When your father called me Vic, it was special because at that time 'Vic' was not short for Victor. That's not my name. Victor is actually an alias Joseph suggested for me."

"An alias? What's your real name then? Or can you not tell me?"

"Well, I have a born name; I have an adopted name; and I have an alias I go by."

"Why an alias?"

"Like you, Daniel, I'm better off dead. I killed a man, so if I'm dead, nobody cares."

"You killed a man?" Daniel exclaimed. "When? Or who?"

"My father."

"Christ! You killed your father?"

"Yes."

"Why?"

"My born name is Ivan Yurkovic. My father was Goya Yurkovic, an immigrant from Yugoslavia—when there was a Yugoslavia. He was Croatian, and a real lady-killer. He liked young girls, and he was very good at impressing them. This I learned later from my adopted father."

"You were adopted?"

"It's part of the story. I'll get to that. Anyway, my mother thought he was the most handsome man in the world, and, at age sixteen, when a man like that gives you the right attention, well, it works. And she ended up pregnant. That's when his true nature started to surface. He was very abusive and it didn't help that her family disowned her. They told her she was a disgrace and if she didn't marry him they would send her to a home for *wayward* girls, as they described it. The sheriff had different ideas though and told my father to marry her or go to jail for statutory rape. He married her and moved away."

"Where'd they go?"

"They moved from Atlanta to Greenville, South Carolina, where I was born. He worked odd jobs there but his temper usually ended up costing him the job. He mostly worked as a forklift operator, making enough money to support his drinking, yet barely enough to keep Mom in an apartment with food to put on the table. Mom cleaned houses and was able to keep me with her as she worked. One of the houses she cleaned belonged to Doc Heidi, an emergency room doctor at Greenville General. He got the nickname 'Heidi' while he was in the Navy, apparently because he sounded like he was yodeling when he was barking orders during surgery. Emergency room surgery, like field surgery, is often very tense, and seconds matter. He was very fast, and very good, and didn't take kindly to any degree of slackness in his theatre. After the military, he became a lifelong emergency room doctor. It was his passion. And everyone just called him 'Doc Heidi.'"

"Did you know his real name?"

"Davidson was his real last name. That's all I know of his original name."

"Original name?"

"Yeah. When I was about two years old, my father's abuse turned toward me, and after a particularly bad night, my mom had to take me to the emergency room. Apparently my testicles were the size of lemons. Doc Heidi was on duty, and after treating me, insisted on examining Mom. Then he called the police. By then, my father had arrived looking for me and Mom. Doc Heidi confronted him and had the police take him out of the hospital, but not before he had threatened everybody involved. Mom was petrified and knew there would be a beating awaiting her when she got home. Of course, spousal abuse in that day was not taken as seriously as it is now by most authorities, but Doc Heidi knew we were in grave danger. The courts and justice system really weren't much help and Mom had no choice but to return home and face the music. It seemed Doc Heidi's warnings fell on deaf ears, and keeping a family 'together' seemed far more important than keeping a child safe. But Doc Heidi wasn't to be dismissed so easily, and when the abuse resumed, Mom called him as he had asked her to do and he provided a safe haven for us. Long story short is after a lengthy court battle over the separation and divorce, Doc Heidi married my mom and adopted me. But it didn't end there. My dad tried several times to get us back by force, even trying to kidnap me from school. I'm sure it wasn't because he loved us, but more because his ego wouldn't allow him to lose something. He ended up in jail for a time and Doc Heidi moved away and changed our names in the process. He knew that as soon as Dad got out of jail he would come looking for vengeance. By then Mom was pregnant again and Doc Heidi knew our only protection was to never be found."

"So where did you move?"

"Florida. Doc Heidi had no trouble getting into another hospital, and with some legal help he got us new identities, buried our old ones, and continued emergency room work the rest of his life. Dad never found us, but Doc Heidi kept close tabs on him."

"So that's why your last name is no longer Yurkovic, but why Victor?"

"Victor is a name your father gave me after my 'death'. He used to call me Vic privately, as a throwback to when that was my last name, and he thought it was necessary to keep the history alive. So he suggested it, and I agreed, but I never liked it."

"So Dad knew about your previous life?"

"Oh yes. He knew the whole story."

"So you don't have Doc Heidi's new name now, but can you tell me what it is? Or was? Or is that a secret buried in an archive in Washington somewhere? I take it he's no longer alive."

"I may tell you eventually, but it's a closely guarded secret only one other person knows. If it were to become public, I could still be tried for murder."

"Can you tell me about killing your father? And what did you mean by your 'death?'"

"I was getting to that. Like you, I met the love of my life in college. I went to The Citadel so marriage wasn't an option until I graduated. We married immediately and she wanted to start a family right away, which I was all for. But after a year of trying with no success, we decided to seek help."

"Fertility testing?"

"Yes. I was at Camp Pendleton in California by then, and after the testing the doctor wanted to see me privately. He asked if I had ever had any trauma to my testicles. I told him what I knew of the first visit to Doc Heidi, so while I waited he placed a call to Florida to find out more. An hour later he gave me the bad news that my sperm was DOA. My father's abuse had done irreparable damage and I was sterile."

"God, I'm sorry." Daniel paused a moment as Victor sipped his Perrier, then cautiously asked the burning question. "How did your wife take the news?"

"Divorce."

"No! No way! So having a family was that much more important to her than you!"

"Apparently. She told me she was going to visit her parents, but instead went to see a lawyer. When I got the letter, I crumbled. I was lost between grief, heartbreak, humiliation, and anger. That's when I went for my own 'swim.' I found my dad working as a valet in LA and caught him as he was parking a Mercedes SL. The look on his face when he saw me told me he knew I was out for blood. I'm not sure he recognized me at first, but it didn't take long. Then he got that shit-eating narcissistic smirk on his face as if he was going to sweet-talk his way out of hell. I hit him so fast in the nose, it sounded like a cantaloupe bursting. His grin turned to shock, then pain, then abject terror. He tried to back up and cover his face, which was pouring blood, as I acquainted him with the news he had murdered all of my future children and destroyed my marriage. He tried to mumble some bullshit apology which I countered with my next blow—my heel to his throat, crushing his larynx. He slumped to the ground, and I'm pretty sure he died of suffocation from that blow. I grabbed the keys and took off for the hills east of Pendleton. By the time I went through the guardrail I had a convoy of state troopers trying to keep up with me. It's funny what I thought about when the wheel went light and I felt the weightlessness of falling."

"What?" Daniel instinctively asked in a hurried manner.

"The moment felt like an eternity although it was only a fraction of a second. All of a sudden I didn't want to die. I really regretted doing what I had done, but it was too late. I was over the edge."

"I got that feeling, too, when I was in the Gulf," Daniel interjected, "only I had time to remember Mishael's face as she lifted her arms, and I just couldn't stand it, so I continued. But always there was something pulling me back to life—like I regretted what I was doing. I didn't put that word with it until now, but regret is exactly what I felt. So what happened?"

Victor was looking at Daniel differently now, and Daniel was almost uncomfortable with it. It was the look soldiers sometimes exchange after an intense battle where they should have died, but miraculously lived. They've stared death down. There's no word for it, and nothing is spoken, but it's an unmistakable tie that binds souls forever.

"What happened?" Victor said, breaking the experiential aura. "I picked the wrong car to drive off the side of a mountain. Out of habit, and like an idiot, I had buckled the seat belt. When I hit the guardrail I heard the explosion of the belt's safety system and it pinned me against the seat. I tumbled end over end down the mountain, but at the bottom I was still alive. Broken to pieces and unconscious, but alive. That car saved my life. They had to cut me out, strap me to a board, and airlift me to Pendleton. The car was unrecognizable. I woke up from a drug induced coma in the hospital a month later with Joseph praying over me. I've got to tell you it was a little weird. Growing up, he was always in touch with God. I wasn't. I told him I didn't believe in God just to aggravate him, but it never worked. One time he turned and looked me in the eye and said, 'Of course you believe in God, Vic. You can't hate something you don't believe in.'"

"So is that when you became religious?"

"Oh, hell no. I still hated God. Even more so after the accident. How could a benevolent God take everything from me like that?"

"What did Dad say to that?"

"Nothing. Joseph never sowed seeds in the dead of winter. He was always patient and first waited for the right season to prepare the ground. And then he waited. You know from his coaching how important timing was to him."

"Yeah, I can hear him now, 'timing is everything.' What was he waiting for?"

"God. Unlike religious zealots, Joseph never tried to do God's work for Him. He knew how to *let go and let God*, an axiom he lived by. Each day he did the work set before him and left tomorrow up to God. As he put it one time, 'the Lord's prayer asks God to give us our daily bread—not our weekly bread, or our yearly bread. That's what's set before us each day.' I really didn't give a crap one way or the other. It was all a scam in my opinion. Just a way to squeeze money out of gullible idiots. Joseph never dwelled on religion with me, though, so it never became a big issue between us. And he never preached religion; he lived it."

"So you woke up to Dad praying; what then?" Daniel didn't mind the sidetracks, as he was learning things about his father he had never taken the time to find out while Joseph was alive. He knew his dad had been an intense person, but always in a benevolent way; a way Daniel never quite understood. But now, as he was getting past the self-centeredness of youth, he was finding he was more and more curious about Joseph.

From Daniel's perspective, conversations with his dad had always centered around sports and preparing for a career there. He was beginning to realize that from Joseph's perspective the conversations were about life and preparing Daniel for the world no matter what the career turned out to be. Sports was just the familiar ground Joseph used in his teachings that allowed an etched memory in Daniel's psyche, planting the seed deep into fertile ground. Surely Joseph had planned more for Daniel, but his life had been cut very short; so Daniel was coveting any nuance Victor could share with him about his father. He was now relishing this trip to Maine, hoping to finally get to know the real Joseph, even if it had to be secondhand.

Victor continued, "I woke up in a similar situation to yours; a lot had gone on while I was comatose. And, being broken both physically and emotionally, I was in no mood to have things explained to me. I just wanted my life back. Of course that wasn't possible, just as with you. I had to get used to the fact that the love of my life was gone, I was never going to have children, and to make matters worse, I was a murderer. When Joseph tried to talk to me, I got belligerent and just wanted to die. It finally dawned on me I hadn't been arrested and no police were around. So curiosity settled me down enough for Joseph to explain what had gone down."

Victor was interrupted by the pilot's voice, "We're coming into Omaha, sir. Please fasten your seat belts and prepare for landing."

Daniel saw Victor push a button on his armrest, then a small light above turned green and Victor answered. "Thank you, Steven. We're prepared. Hangar fourteen?"

"Yes, sir."

"Great. I'll be gone about two hours."

"Roger that, sir."

Victor switched off the intercom and turned to Daniel. "I've got to run an errand while we're here. Best if you stay out of sight. You're welcome to use the bed in the back if you want to stay on the plane, or you can go to the private lounge in the hangar. I'll have Steven keep an eye out for any curious visitors."

Daniel didn't hide his frustration at being put off at such a critical juncture of the story. "I think I'll just hang out on the plane, if that's okay."

Victor noted Daniel's displeasure, but let it slide without comment. "Sure. Probably a little safer. I'm sure you'll get stir crazy before we get to Maine, but you can stretch at the other stops along the way."

"Thanks," Daniel responded as he felt the light jolt of the touchdown. He was amazed at how quickly the small jet traversed the tarmac and got to the hangar as the large doors were opening. A powered cart was waiting to take them in as the engines shut down. Victor was at the door with his briefcase as soon as the jet came to a stop. He quickly exited and got into a waiting car. Daniel marveled at the speed and efficiency of Victor's world, and he remembered his first day at VCM and Sarah telling him not to be late or early for meetings with Victor. Obviously she had been very serious with that statement, and Daniel now surmised that with thousands of dollars riding on seconds of time, punctuality was not to be taken lightly. But that world was now a lifetime away, and for the foreseeable future he had nothing but time on his hands. He decided to start writing down some of his questions for Victor, but suddenly his eyelids were too heavy for him to get up and look for paper and pencil. The interior of the jet being so quiet and peaceful now, he closed his eyes for just a moment to let the intensity of his new world abate.

CHAPTER 11

The Citadel

D aniel was jarred awake as Victor came bounding up the jet's steps followed by the pilots. The preflight checklist was quickly completed as the engines roared to life. The cart pulled them out of the hangar and they began their run across the tarmac to the runway. As the ground receded beneath them, Victor put two briefcases on the table, opened them and turned them toward Daniel.

"Ever seen ten million dollars, kid?"

"You're shitting me!" Daniel exclaimed.

"Nope. Euros, hundreds, Yuan, and one gold bar."

"I take it you're buying something and the seller wants cash?" Daniel said jokingly.

"Nope. Selling, and I want cash. If the other stops go this smoothly, we'll land in Maine with fifty-four million bucks in untraceable currency, gold, and diamonds."

"Holy crap! What are you up to?"

"All in good time, my boy. All in good time. But let's just say I learned how to get off the tiger."

"What does that mean? I've heard it before, but don't get it," Daniel said.

"Sometimes business is like getting on a tiger. Once on, you can't get off without being eaten, so you just have to hang on for the ride."

"Oh. How long have you been planning this?" Daniel asked, his voice not masking his concern.

"About a year and a half. But I kicked it into overdrive after your little swim, and have been putting the final touches on it all week. I've been very busy while you were sleeping. Did they bring food while I was gone? I'm starving. Making money always makes me hungry." Victor laughed.

"Don't know. I passed out before your car was out of the hangar and didn't hear anything," Daniel said as he was getting up to check the kitchen. "Yep! Two trays."

Daniel set the trays out as Victor put away the briefcases, then went back to the kitchen for beer and Perrier. When Daniel returned, Victor had opened a bottle of Pappy Van Winkle's bourbon and was pouring shots into a glass.

"Can you bring me a couple of ice cubes?" Victor asked as Daniel set the drinks on the table.

"Sure. What mixer do you want?" Daniel noticed it was a bottle of Family Reserve 23 Year. Victor always did go for the best.

"I never screw up good bourbon with a mixer. Just ice, please."

"Aye, aye, sir," Daniel retorted as he retrieved the ice bucket and set it by Victor.

At the "Aye, aye", Victor recalled Daniel's frustration at the interruption in his story, so decided to return to the subject. "Thanks. Now where were we in my life's story you are so curious about?"

"What? Just like that? You nonchalantly make a pit stop in Nebraska in the middle of the night, come back with more money than I've ever imagined, and then just sit down and want to continue our dinner conversation?" Daniel was lifting the lid on his tray and looking in amazement at the gourmet meal before him. Some of his frustration was quelled by his enormous appetite.

"Ah, Daniel! You'll have to get used to relishing the quiet moments and occasionally leaving the world behind. Besides, if you had stayed with tennis you would have made a lot more than ten million in your career, so you must have imagined that much. Be honest."

"I guess you're right, but I didn't stick with it, nor VCM, so I'll never see that kind of money. And come to think of it, now that I'm dead, I don't know that I'll ever see any kind of money again. What the hell am I going to do?"

Victor sensed Daniel's downward emotional spiral and quickly curtailed it before it spun out of control. He had to prepare Daniel for a new life, and had just this plane ride and a few days in Maine to accomplish the mission. He had to keep Daniel's curiosity piqued and focus his attention on the story unfolding.

"Well, Daniel, have you ever tried to spend fifty million dollars of untraceable cash? It's not as easy as you may think. So maybe you can help me—if you're up to it. But first let's get it, then we can worry about spending it without raising any eyebrows."

"Huh? You've already raised my eyebrows and we haven't spent a dime!"

Victor laughed as he sipped his bourbon and felt his tension ease. Daniel noticed Victor was gauging his mood and felt Victor was feigning some of the easy bravado of the moment. Daniel had a talent for detecting the slight physical vagaries of an opponent choking on the verge of a win and had used that talent on the court to usurp an opponent's victory. Coaches called it *choking*, but Daniel and his father knew it was a far more subtle physical change that manifested the choke. Daniel now sensed that in Victor and added another question to his long list. What was he really up to? Fifty million was pocket change in Victor's world, where he regularly dealt in billion-dollar-deals on the world arena. For now, Daniel decided to play along with Victor's game and relax as Victor wished, but he would quietly stay focused on Victor's underlying tension.

"Well maybe a shot of bourbon will loosen up my throat so I can enjoy this steak. Chateaubriand?" Daniel quizzed as he found a glass and poured himself a shot.

"Kobe," Victor responded. "Wagyu cattle raised near here according to the strictest rules of Kobe, and very fresh. It will melt in your mouth. And the chef's timing was perfect, as always. Glad he was quiet and didn't wake you. He was probably on his way out as I was on my way in. Obviously I wasn't so careful boarding."

"Well, I've never woken up to ten million dollars and Kobe steak," Daniel laughed as he began eating. "Talking about waking up—you were starting to tell me what had gone on while you were comatose and woke up to Dad's prayers."

"Oh yeah. And why I wasn't under arrest. This is probably a good time to introduce you to the Brighams. You recognize the name?"

"I ran across it once or twice at VCM. A partner of yours I assume?"

"Damn, you have a good memory, kid," Victor said, remembering Daniel's recollection of the phone number. "Is it photographic?"

"No. Just pretty good, I guess." Daniel laughed, "I only remember what I remember. I can't remember what I forget."

"That makes sense," Victor smiled back at him, then continued. "Brad was a bit more than just a partner, and the family is very well known in Texas and Washington but they try very hard to keep a low, silent profile, especially in the business world. They see themselves as primarily a military family with tremendous influence as advisers to many generations of politicians. Probably the name you saw was Brad's. I call him the black sheep of the family, but he's probably the smartest of the clan."

"Why a black sheep?"

"He's a rebel, a real nonconformist, but due to serendipity, he got his stars in spite of himself."

"So he was a general?"

"Is a general. Oldest in the service. And Marine; not Army like every other male member of his family. They've been in every American war, starting with the revolution. Brad's great-

great-grandfather was with Sam Houston when Texas won their independence and stayed there afterward, creating a huge ranch south of Houston. Brad appreciates business, so his name will occasionally crop up on some of VCM's subsidiary ventures, but never with VCM directly. He's always well insulated from me."

"Why is that?"

"Multiple reasons."

"More evasive answers?"

"Not really, but sometimes the answers aren't so simple. Be patient; I'll get to everything."

"So what's the deal with you and the Brighams?"

"Mostly with Brad. We met as freshmen at The Citadel. Of course, all of his ancestors were West Point grads, so going to South Carolina was heresy. I hated him immediately and he didn't feel much differently about me."

"What was the issue?"

"He was everything I loathed. To me, he was born with a silver spoon in his mouth; his ancestry went back to the Mayflower, his military career was guaranteed since he had family at every level right up to the Joint Chiefs, and he could've gone to any college in the country. And I assumed he was a pompous ass. I figured he pegged me as a cracker with no pedigree and marginal grades who scraped his way into The Citadel and was going to do nothing worthwhile with the training. Mostly, it boiled down to cultural stereotyping, which eighteen-year-olds naturally take as the gospel truth. But one great thing about going away from home for college—you learn very quickly that your own cultural perspective is not 'normal,' no matter what it is. There is so much diversity in the world, normal just doesn't exist. But try to explain that to two young punks at a very competitive Southern school. Both of us would defend to the death our view of normal and right."

"I wish I'd learned that before I met Mishael. She might still be alive."

"Probably not, Daniel, I'm sorry to say. Her real fight was with her father and the culture that enslaves women. Sooner or later the chasm would have become untenable for both of you, and her only option was the course she chose. I hate to say it but you were just the convenient catalyst for her own private revolution."

"I don't believe that! I can't believe that!"

"Don't get me wrong; that in no way diminishes her love for you. But consider it this way: a soldier leaves his family and gives his life for his belief in his set of values. That doesn't diminish his love for his family; in fact it enhances it. But without that commitment, the soldier would not feel true love. That knowledge does not help the grieving family, or you in this instance, but it is a trait of humanity— sort of our fatal flaw."

"You're right. That doesn't help."

"For Mishael, you were a benevolent mirror that magnified the putrid culture of her father."

"I hope that's not meant to make me feel better."

"No, I guess not. I don't know what comfort there is for those of us left behind."

"Yeah. So what about this Bradley kid? What happened?"

"Well, we picked at each other until well into our second semester, and then one day at mess it came to a head. I don't remember what was actually said, but I probably started it, and he jumped on me. We both got some pretty good licks in before some upperclassmen could break us up and haul our asses to the commandant. Of course, I didn't give a shit, I just wanted to hit somebody. And I don't know that it was Brad; it was what he represented to me, and the anger issues over my father."

"Anger issues?"

"Well, Doc Heidi was a great father, and never treated me any differently than my brother, even though I was adopted. But I looked at myself as something less than his son. I had Croatian features— thick dark hair, olive complexion, and a medium build. So whenever I looked in a mirror I saw a loser, which was my father. I had no idea of the proud, rich heritage of the Croats. I just knew my real father and associated all things evil with him. My brother had Doc Heidi's features, the ruddy complexion so common among the Scotch Irish of the Carolinas, and he was taller than me. I tried to hate him, but he worshipped me, and time after time I had to be his protector. So I just gave up hating him and loved him like a puppy. Brad taught me how blessed I was to have a father like Doc Heidi who loved me and treated me as a person instead of just another star on his lapel."

"So what was your punishment?"

"The commandant gave our cadet company commander that responsibility with two choices. He could either put us in a boxing circle or put us in a locked room together until reveille. The boxing circle is a ritual where our fellow plebes form a circle, and we are thrown into it wearing boxing gloves and shorts. We fight until one of us can't or won't get up. If you get too close to the edge, the plebes push you back toward the middle."

"And why a locked room?"

"The theory is if you're stuck with someone for that long, you will work out your differences."

"So which did you get?"

"Our cadet company commander was a kid named Smythe, a real prick from Massachusetts. His vocabulary had no 'R' in it and he hated the South and Southerners, especially ones from Texas or Florida, so he was relishing this opportunity. He knew I had boxed in high school and was in the boxing club at The Citadel and also on the wrestling team. Brad was a great athlete, and played football and baseball, so the circle gave me a huge advantage. But in the confines of a room, Brad's size evened the playing field. Usually in situations like this, the circle is always chosen since it builds camaraderie and respect among all the cadets. That prick Smythe chose the room and smiled all the way there. Smythe told the commandant he was going to use the baseball equipment shed, which he had the key to since he was the baseball team manager. And what he said was true, he was going to put us in the shed, but what he didn't say was he had discovered the hole and that was what he really had in mind. Apparently a half-truth was justifiable in his eyes."

"What's the hole?"

"That's a secret very few know about, and nobody from inside the school will admit to, but basically it's a stone cellar under the shed. It was built before the Civil War, probably beneath a kitchen as food storage, but now there's just the equipment shed over it. It floods with the tides so even at low tide the floor is wet and at high tide there's as much as a foot of water in it. There's a heavy trapdoor in the floor of the shed and a rope ladder down into it. Once they pull up the rope, you're stuck in a cold, wet, stinky, slimy cellar, with a single light bulb which never goes off. You can't sit or rest so it's pretty miserable, as you can imagine.

"We were stripped and lowered in. When the trap door slammed shut, I jumped at Brad, but he was big and strong so he just grabbed me in a bear hug and held on until I wore myself out. Then he pushed me away and just said 'what the fuck is your problem with me anyway?' I looked at him, wet, naked, covered in mud and silt, and I honestly had no answer. He looked so ridiculous and I'm sure I did too, so I started laughing. Don't know why, but the catharsis just exploded into laughter. He looked at me and called me a 'fucking cracker' and I called him a 'shit-headed redneck,' and we both laughed till we cried. Then we talked.

"We found out we were a whole lot alike. He was a pretty cool guy. Hated his father as much as I hated my real father. He described his home life as being in his father's own private army. He was the youngest of four boys and, like I said before, came from two hundred and fifty years of soldiers, with ancestors in every US war including the Texas War of Independence, relatives at the Joint Chiefs' echelon, all Army and all West Pointers. In his home everything was perfectly organized and perfectly scheduled, and Brad was perfectly dressed, perfectly fed, perfectly educated, perfectly presented, and perfectly unloved. His revenge was to go to The Citadel and join the Marines. His father absolutely refused to support him unless he went to West Point as ordered. Fortunately, his grandmother stepped in; she always had a soft spot for Brad and loved his independent nature, especially when it stuck in the craw of her son. She didn't really approve of her son's manner with his boys and thought he needed to loosen up. He just got tougher on Brad trying to break him which had the opposite effect. His grandmother got him into The Citadel and supported him.

"I don't think he and his father had much to do with each other after that and I know his father and grandmother didn't speak to each other again. He made my situation look like Camelot. Anyway, we were standing around watching the tide come in and freezing our balls off when Brad screamed 'moccasin!' and started trying to climb the wall. From across the room I saw the head come out of the water and I watched it for a moment, then quietly edged over behind it and grabbed it, gently swinging it so its head could not turn back on me, but soft enough so as not to harm it. Brad was screaming at me, calling me a fucking crazy man, and an idiot, and anything else he could get out through his panic. Finally I told him to stop being a pussy and shut up; it was a harmless water snake. He called me a stupid liar and screamed at me to kill it. I tried to explain to him it wasn't a moccasin; moccasins swim with their whole body on top of the water and a water snake just pokes its head up like a turtle. And, their heads look totally different even though their bodies look alike. He asked me how I could be so sure, so I told him Texas may have a few rattlers but Florida has diamondbacks, copperheads, coral snakes, and a shitload of moccasins, along with plenty of harmless snakes like this one. My brother and I used to play with them until Doc Heidi found out and was furious with me. The good thing was my punishment entailed learning enough about snakes to be a herpetologist, and after I could correctly identify and report on every snake in the state, he left me and my brother alone to hunt them. I know other fathers would have whipped me for playing with seemingly dangerous snakes around a little brother, but that's where Doc Heidi was so good. He turned it into a positive for us. He often said lack of knowledge is what causes most of the problems in the world, like racism in the South. The more Blacks and Whites know each other, the more they find out they really should love one another and not hate so much.

"Brad looked at me curiously and said, 'Sorta like you and me?' It almost brought me to tears, but he was exactly right. I threw the snake into the water across the room, apologized to him, and offered him my hand. He took it and slapped my back and then yelled, 'Look!' I turned just as the snake was slithering through a crack in the stones. I went over to the crack and noticed the stone was slightly different than the ones around it and the ebbing tide was flowing through the crack. 'This must connect to the river somehow', I told him as we closely examined the stone. We could feel finger holes along its edges, so we started working it and felt it loosen. It took us an hour, but we managed to remove it and discovered it opened into a tunnel to the river. We figured it must have been a slave escape route or a smuggler's tunnel, and we cautiously crawled in. Brad was still afraid of the snake and said if the water snake was there then moccasins must be also. I explained how snakes are territorial and where water snakes are you won't find moccasins."

"Is that true?" Daniel interjected, fascinated with Victor's knowledge of snakes.

"Don't know for sure, but Doc Heidi believed it and would get really pissed if anyone bothered the water snakes around where we lived. He claimed they kept the moccasins away. He might have been right 'cause we would have to go to another neighborhood to find moccasins."

"So y'all escaped?" Daniel asked.

"Not really, but we were free; at least for the night. And what we figured out was we were really free! As long as we weren't caught red-handed, we could pretty much do whatever we wanted. But first we had to find some clothes and shoes. The first thing we did was check the shed. The cadets guarding us were asleep and we didn't want to wake them, so we couldn't get our clothes. But the security locker room was open and we found enough there to wear. Then we started our rampage. Smythe and his cronies were our main targets. We found some locks, handcuffs, flashlights, and other goodies in the security office, so then it was just a matter of not getting caught."

"Did y'all talk about what you'd do if you did get caught?"

"Oh, yeah. We knew we'd get kicked out, so we decided we'd transfer to Auburn and finish school there. Alabama seemed like a good halfway point between our homes, and we had heard that Alabama girls are pretty sweet. Great reason to select a school, huh?"

"Sounds reasonable to me," Daniel quipped.

"Fortunately, when cadets finally get to their bunk, they sleep like logs. The first thing we did was lock the shed from the outside. Then we snuck into the dorm and swiped Smythe's boots and underwear and cuffed him to his bunk. Brad crapped in his boots and I ran them up the flagpole. Then we shoved his underwear down the reveille cannon. We thought of anyone we had a grievance with and figured out some way to even the score. As the tide was coming back in strong we headed back to the tunnel, hid the clothes and shoes, and reset the stone.

"At sunup it didn't take long for all hell to break loose above us. By the time someone got to the trap door to let us out, there was a full-scale investigation going on, and every cadet had to give a detailed account of his whereabouts during the night. We had an ironclad alibi, and Smythe had to back us up or face expulsion for putting us in the hole.

"One of the greatest things about a military school like The Citadel or VMI is the code of honor. There is no lying, cheating, or stealing. And any collaboration or nonreporting is treated equally as the infraction would be. It's so strong, a cadet can leave his wallet filled with money on the lavatory and come back a month later and it will still be there perfectly intact. So everyone told the truth. Smythe, of course, didn't lie, but also didn't tell everything. Brad and I now had a code that was stronger than the cadet code of honor; and that was to each other. No matter what, we had each other's back for life. So it didn't matter what we were asked, we both said we were in the shed and nothing else.

"Of course Smythe swore we were behind it, but couldn't figure out how since he had the only key to the trap door. When they got him cut free from his bunk and he discovered his underwear were all over the parade ground and the flag patrol had brought him his boots in a sealed bag, he was a laughingstock. And since he was our alibi, he couldn't blame us. But that didn't stop him from trying to even the score. And it didn't help when other cadets would mention something about a stench in the air and everyone around would say in unison 'Smythe's boots.' God, he was mad."

"Did he ever get revenge?" Daniel asked.

"He tried. One evening he and five of his buddies cornered Brad and me. They were going to 'teach us a lesson.' I called him a fucking coward since it took six of them against two of us, but they figured to split us up, hold us, and beat the shit out of us. Brad and I stuck together like glue and put up one hell of a fight until security finally broke it up."

"So everyone got in trouble?"

"No. We all swore it was all in fun—just a friendly brawl, and no one would point a finger at anyone else. But word got out it was six against two and we held our own. That pegged Smythe and his buddies as cowards and made heroes of me and Brad. Nobody ever screwed with us after that."

"And what happened to Smythe?"

"Not sure. He didn't graduate from The Citadel. I heard he made it through law school up North and it wouldn't surprise me if he went into politics. But Brad and I never really cared; he gave us the best night of our lives and cemented our reputation at The Citadel.

We probably should have sent the rotten bastard a thank you note."

"So you did pretty good there?"

"With Brad's help. He was smart as shit. He loved math and I loved science so we helped each other all the way through. It was almost like a competition, except we both wanted to beat everyone else first, then each other. We tag-teamed being company commanders our senior year and graduated first and second in our class. He was first, and I was happy to be anywhere close to him, but he always helped keep my grades high. We can probably thank his father for that; he did provide Brad with a perfect education—everything it took to be tops at West Point, only he was tops at The Citadel."

"Then what?"

"We both decided on the Marines and ended up at Camp Pendleton together. He met a girl in South Carolina after a football game. She was pretty enough and smart enough and just what Brad was looking for. And she had a sister. Apparently she got the brains and her sister got the looks, drop-dead gorgeous looks. Ava Gardner-type beauty. I was in love as soon as Brad introduced us. So we ended up marrying sisters, only he got the good one and I got Miss Vanity."

"And what does all this have to do with what happened while you were comatose?" Daniel paused, hearing the harsh nature of his question, then apologized. "Sorry. I know that sounds rough, but I'm still trying to make sense of it all."

"It's okay," Victor said, smoothing out the tension. "I know I'm throwing a lot at you right now."

"Sir, we're getting close to Des Moines," the pilot's voice came in over the intercom.

Victor pushed a button and thanked the pilot, then turned back to Daniel, "Hold that question right there, Daniel. I've got an errand in Des Moines to prepare for. We'll continue when I get back. Come to the kitchen for a minute, I need to show you something."

Daniel got up and followed Victor. He had never paid much attention to Victor's looks, but now, following him, he noticed the few thick, dark strands left in a mostly white, rich, full head of hair. And he watched the assured walk of a man who could handle himself even after more than seventy years. He had never considered Victor's age before; he just seemed timeless. But obviously Victor was feeling his own mortality and was anxious to let go of the pressures of his business. He wondered if Joseph's death had prompted this. The timing was right, but would a friend's death make that much of a difference in his life? That was another question Daniel tucked away for later.

CHAPTER 12

Iowa

The kitchen was located in the rear section of the jet. Victor paused near the sink and opened a lower cabinet door.

"Ever seen one of these?" he asked Daniel.

"A water heater?" Daniel responded sarcastically.

Victor grinned, then reached into the cabinet and turned two thumb screws near the top rim of the small appliance. He then grasped the top and turned it. What appeared to be a welded seam came apart and Victor lifted the top off the water heater, exposing a compartment filled with money and an envelope. Daniel also noticed some small wires threaded into the lower tank. Victor turned back to Daniel saying, "Fancy water heater, huh?"

"Wow!" Daniel exclaimed, gawking.

Victor's tone became serious. "My next few stops could get dicey if all doesn't go as planned, so I want you to have an exit strategy. There's access to enough money here to last you a lifetime and instructions are in the envelope."

"Instructions for what?"

"Mostly how to access money, contact someone covertly, or be contacted. Also, how to get a new identity and the best places to hang out anonymously."

"Why?"

"If I'm not back here within fifteen minutes of my schedule, you take the money, turn this timer on—it's set for fifteen minutes—and get the hell out of here."

"Are you in that much danger?" Daniel's worry escalated profoundly. All of his life had been peaceful and relatively quiet and normal. Now he was racked with perilous visions of danger upon danger, all tracing back to the Saturday morning visitor and Mishael's video. Daniel's concern turned to panic. The real ramifications of his changed life overwhelmed him and he was consumed by the urge to run. But with nowhere to run, and nothing to run to, a feeling of helplessness engulfed him. He slumped into the seat behind him and buried his head in his hands.

Victor watched Daniel carefully, wondering what emotional upheaval was playing out inside his young protege. For the first time since he had coerced Daniel from California, he doubted his own judgment and wondered if he had made the correct decision to bring Daniel into the fold. He would have to be patient now and let Daniel either work through his demons and emerge with the strength of character essential to the mission ahead, or drown in his emotions.

Daniel had no idea why Victor was watching him so intently, but he sensed Victor's edginess and again got the feeling that he was choking just as he had victory in his grasp. *What is Victor after from me?* he thought.

Finally Daniel took a deep breath and stood up. In the quiet of the jet, with only the muffled drone of the engines as white noise, Daniel overcame the emotional eddy sucking him into oblivion and steeled himself for whatever Victor was initiating him into. The epiphany left him with a renewed strength and for the first time Daniel considered he was now in a war; a word he had never imagined would apply to himself. Daniel looked over at Victor and asked, "What danger are you facing, Vic, and what can I do to help?"

Victor was taken aback by the question. It wasn't the words that struck him, but the voice behind them. Daniel sounded so much like Joseph, and using the name Vic as naturally as Joseph would have, startled him. Perhaps his soldier did have the mettle necessary for an appointment in MALTA. Victor breathed a heavy sigh of relief as he sat and motioned for Daniel to sit beside him for an explanation of what lay ahead.

"Daniel," Victor began, "I am not doing anything outside the law, I assure you, so the danger I'm putting myself in does not come from any law enforcement agency."

"Hopefully that means no organized crime, either?"

"No. Not organized crime. Not that docile."

"What?"

"Even organized crime answers to somebody, otherwise the money stops flowing. And when the tap gets turned off, even mobsters can have their heads handed to themselves on a platter. Usually a golden platter."

"By whom?"

"The Bank," Victor said this as calmly and nonchalantly as if he had said, the *tooth fairy*.

Daniel thought he was joking now; just putting him off in preparation for the real answer, which he expected to be a major terrorist organization or similar conscienceless fanatical group. He looked at Victor, waiting for a crack in the stone face. Finally Daniel commented, "You're serious? The bank?"

"Deadly serious. And I'll give you a hint as to how serious since I don't have time now to go into any depth. What do the four assassinated American presidents have in common?"

"Besides the fact they were all elected in years that end in zero?"

"Yes."

"Don't know."

"They sought to end The Bank's control of the US economy."

Daniel thought for a moment, trying to recall the assassinated presidents and their platforms. "Okay, I get Lincoln, obviously, since he had an on-going battle with the eastern banks. Garfield wasn't around long enough to consider, Kennedy would've had to excommunicate himself from his father to go against the banking institutions, and McKinley, I thought, was one of the first presidents who infused the industrialists into politics in the name of progress. He was pro-union so all Americans would have a piece of the pie, but that doesn't make him anti-bank. In fact, it seems he would be pro-bank."

"You might have gotten an A in high school American history, but study the men around the presidents and look at what happened when they sought to end The Bank's control. Here's what you won't read in a high school history book. Mrs. Lincoln's words when she was being taken back to the White House after her husband's assassination were, *that dreadful House . . . that dreadful House. This awful place.* People thought she meant the Ford theater, since she was looking at it from across the street, but she was actually talking about The Bank's agent, a man by the name of Thomas House who had been watching Lincoln and his war with The Bank, and planned the assassination when Lincoln's power in the White House assured him a victory over the unregulated eastern banks. Jack and Robert Kennedy were at odds with their father over The Bank, but Johnson and Nixon were deeply entrenched. Convenient they were the next two presidents. Kennedy loathed both of them and the feeling was mutual.

"And McKinley?" Daniel was very dubious of Victor's account of history and was beginning to suspect Victor was engaging in conspiracy theory crap. The type of stuff he read about and dismissed as easily as aliens in Area 51. But the bomb on the jet was no theory, and Victor's edginess was real, so Daniel played along.

"Study Hanna, the industrialist, and the money behind his campaigns. Hanna's schoolmate was Rockefeller, and Hanna had all the trappings of a Bank agent. After McKinley was elected for his second term and began actively trying to end The Bank's control of the US economy, a 'deranged anarchist' (a la Oswald) shot him. And who became president?"

"Teddy Roosevelt," Daniel said blandly.

"The Roosevelts and the Rockefellers are The Bank's royalty in America."

Daniel was doubly concerned now. Had Victor gone off the deep end and was he dragging Daniel with him? And would he really detonate a bomb over an age-old conspiracy he suspected was directed at him? Daniel let none of this show, but let his game-face hide his concern. "So what you are saying," Daniel placated, "is an organization that can and will wantonly assassinate the president, will not think twice about eliminating you if they don't like what you're up to; legal or illegal? And obviously you're up to something the banks will not approve of."

"Bank, not banks. And yes. Moving around half a billion dollars like a pea in a shell game raises red flags very quickly in London and Bern. In forty years of business I've been an exemplary manager of tremendous debt without a hint of anything surreptitious. Even so, one call to The Bank from anywhere I make a transaction tonight and my goose will be cooked. Omaha was easy, but each stop will be progressively more dangerous. I've planned carefully, Daniel, and covered my steps as well as anyone could. If questions arise it will look like I'm loading up to purchase an entire city's industrial base in Ukraine, with stops in London and Moscow to complete the financial arrangements."

"So, if you have a history of this activity, what kind of questions would arise that would spark an investigation?" Daniel asked, trying to figure out the risk to Victor.

"Since I'm using different currencies, including rubles for plausibility in eastern Ukraine, and then changing currency again, it could look like I'm laundering money to get cash and forgoing the purchase, so The Bank will be left with some worthless contracts, and I'll have untraceable dollars."

Daniel shrugged, "I still don't get it, but I'm not a money guru. It sounds to me like you are laundering money, which is illegal, and the banks would catch on quickly and report you."

"The mechanics of the transactions are complex, but the concept is really simple. I depend on greed, and it rarely fails me."

"Greed? Whose greed?"

"Russian oligarchs."

"Oh, shit! You're playing with devils, Victor!"

"Not really, as long as I stay away from Putin and his cronies. Privately, many of the oligarchs don't support Putin, and are using foreign investments for their protection. Of course, Putin requires that most of their wealth stays inside the Russian banking system, but that doesn't do anyone much good, and even Putin's inner circle knows that. So they jump at the chance to diversify without raising Putin's ire. And since Russia stole Crimea and is looking to push into eastern Ukraine, using an industrial base such as steel factories in Mariupol gives a perfect cover."

"So where is the big risk?"

"There's only one place Russian oligarchs can bank outside of Russia and not raise Putin's blood pressure, and that's The Bank. Through The Bank, the oligarchs can have some of their money accessible in banks all over the world, including American banks. That's how they protect themselves from Putin, who is unpredictable—some call him a loose cannon—and they have contingency plans to leave Russia on a moment's notice. They know Putin has issued execution orders, even in foreign countries, on Russians he suspects of not supporting him, so they are paranoid. He's just another Stalin in that respect. So the ties between these oligarchs and The Bank are not only close, but very closely guarded, so even a casual check at the wrong time will bring a squad of auditors to my door."

"So if The Bank learns of the plan, they will certainly be waiting for your arrival in London to ensure their investment is legitimate?"

Victor nodded his head in agreement.

"And if they have questions before London, I'll never see you again."

Victor nodded again.

"So I take the money, flip the switch, and run?"

"Don't wait a second longer. If I'm not here on time, start loading the money and other items, and be careful with the sealed envelope. There's a satchel in the overhead bin. Go by foot as far as you can and stay away from cameras."

The pilot's voice came in over the intercom. "Five minutes, Victor."

Victor pressed a button on the seat and responded, then turned to Daniel and handed him a cell phone. "Use the clock on this phone for the time. Don't use the phone though, and don't turn it on until ten minutes before I'm due back. Brad will follow it, so he'll know something is up. I take it Joseph's Patek Phillippe is still working okay?"

"Oh yeah," Daniel said. "It's a beautiful watch and I guess the only thing of Dad's left for me."

"Did Joseph tell you it's a fake?"

"He left a note with it in the box telling me about it. He said he was pretty pissed at you for giving it to him. He hated to waste money on a trinket. Do you still have the original box and paperwork for it?"

"What do you mean, 'original?'"

"Dad had it checked out. He knew it was real; you just put it in a knock-off box to make him think it was a fake."

"Shit! You're kidding me!"

"No. He knew it meant a lot to you for him to have the genuine article and he appreciated that you thought enough of him to make him think you didn't spend much money on it, so he enjoyed it even more."

"Just like Joseph, dammit!" Victor laughed. "God, I miss him. I can see him laughing about it now. Yes, he would enjoy something like that and put me at ease to boot! And he was right, I wouldn't have been able to bear him walking around with a cheap knock-off."

"Yeah. Looks like now it's the only thing of his I have left, so personally I'm glad it's the real McCoy. And it keeps perfect time so I'll use it to let me know when to turn on the cell phone. Sounds like the landing gear is going down. Can we buckle up back here?"

"Sure." Victor reached into his coat pocket and took out an index card and handed it to Daniel. "This is my itinerary with the time schedule."

"Thanks. I guess," Daniel said haltingly. "I hope it all goes well for you, Victor."

"I'm pretty sure all will go smoothly. I've done similar things over the past couple of years and been thoroughly checked out by The Bank afterward. So I hope they will see this as just another routine and very profitable venture. But I always like a backup plan."

As the jet was pulled into the hangar, Victor reset the water heater, pulled a briefcase from a drawer, and headed to the door with barely a nod to Daniel as a goodbye.

Daniel stayed seated, his mind reeling from the new knowledge about Victor and this excursion. Then his thoughts turned to Sarah and he wondered when and if he would ever see her again. If Victor didn't return, then he would truly be alone in the world. He hoped the envelope contained instructions on how to contact her. Yet another question for Victor. It seemed like the questions were piling up faster than Victor was answering them.

Daniel picked up the index card and studied it; Des Moines, to Aspen, to Pittsburgh, to Toronto. Then maybe to Maine. Daniel found a map in a drawer and opened it across the small table. Hopefully, Toronto to Maine would be the final leg. He wondered why Canada, then back to the US. Studying Maine, he deduced Bangor would be their destination. It was a small airport, but an international one and seemed to be the closest to the mountain mentioned on the deed to the land. Which brought up another question in Daniel's mind. Whose mountain was it now? He assumed it was probably his mom's along with the Porsche and the beach cottage.

Thinking about Galveston conjured up memories of what he had lost, gained, and lost again over the past two years. A wave of depression engulfed him, nearly taking his breath away, but his thought process eventually led him to back to Victor. Victor needed him for something, and was trusting him beyond belief. He compartmentalized his depression and focused on Victor. He knew he would have to keep that compartment tightly closed until his mission with Victor was complete. He put on his game face and focused his concentration on this new task as if it was a final match in a major tournament. He needed Victor as much as Victor apparently needed him. Victor was his only ticket home, and oh, how he wanted to go home.

Daniel began considering his options. He now had a real enemy; a deadly enemy with deadly consequences. Daniel blamed Mishael's father for her death, and Abu was directly responsible for Joseph's death. If there was any truth to what Victor had told him, and Abu blamed Daniel for Mishael's rebellion, Sarah and Jonathan would be his next victims and then Abu would torture and kill Daniel. If Abu knew Daniel was alive, dispensing such a plan would be as easy for him as it had been for Daniel to destroy Eric on the tennis court. Abu was a master terrorist with an army and an intelligence network at his disposal, and Daniel wasn't even a weekend warrior. But Daniel had one major advantage: as far as the rest of the world was concerned, he was dead. And, unlike Eric, he would do his homework before engaging his enemy.

Daniel found a pencil and a note pad and began jotting down questions as he remembered them. Each question seemed to lead to ten others on different tangents, so he tried to organize them along the paths of conversations he and Victor had been having. Paramount at the moment was keeping Victor focused on his story.

Daniel was interested in the story of Bradley, but obviously didn't get the tie-in to what was going on while Victor was comatose. Daniel had been out for only a couple of days, and his whole life was turned upside down, so he understood what can happen when others take control of your life. But covering up murder, car theft, and attempted suicide took a lot of power from somewhere, especially from across the country. And then going from the depths of despair to building a billion-dollar corporation also took something extraordinary somewhere along the line. Daniel knew he was missing important pieces to the puzzle of who Victor really is.

None of this gave Daniel any clue to Victor's behavior toward him. Again his thoughts turned to Sarah. He missed her. He missed her face, her smile, her demeanor, her presence. She seemed to be able to quell his emotional storms just by being nearby. He thought about pressing Victor on Sarah's whereabouts, but decided to relinquish control of the conversation to Victor and try to keep him on track with his agenda. Daniel felt the sooner Victor's agenda was complete, the sooner he could start rebuilding his own life, hopefully with Sarah.

He glanced down at his notes and saw the fruitlessness of his endeavor. His thoughts went in circles, ending up nowhere closer to a resolution. And his impatience was building. He needed a marathon run, or a set of stairs in a skyscraper to climb, or a long nighttime swim. He knew he solved his most complex problems while his body was fully engaged in a mindless activity. Sitting quietly in the plane was counterproductive for him.

He recalled one of his early morning runs while working with VCM on a project for Trans Gulf Petroleum, TGP in office lingo. It was his second large account, after a successful commission on the Hudson Building.

Daniel's education had been in civil engineering and while getting his masters at Stanford, he was also able to get an MBA, so he was uniquely qualified to handle an account like TGP. Eric's prelaw degree from UVA did not give him the expertise TGP was looking for in a property manager.

Daniel had enjoyed computer programming courses in college and used that talent in his masters program at Stanford to write a construction management program as a semester project. He visualized programming like a recipe using *if*, *then*, and *else* statements to create the algorithms. He loved the challenge of figuring out how to make the computer perform tasks with these root words and usually visualized and solved his most complex problems while running, climbing, swimming, or cycling. On this particular morning's run, he focused on an issue of how to create graphically intertwined sets of data tables of cost-benefit expenditures that indicated by intersections of critical paths optimum times to purchase, replace, or overhaul equipment and facilities on oil rig platforms.

Suddenly, the key to the solution materialized as an image in his mind and he visualized the lines of code necessary for the procedure. With this vision in his head, he sprinted back to the condo and jumped into the Porsche for a fast trip to VCM's building, took the elevator to his floor, and ran into his office. As the computer fired up, he began jotting down notes, and within four hours, when most of VCM was just getting started with their day's work, he had the framework for an elegant industrial system management program he knew would seal the deal with TGP.

Within a week he had the program in a presentable format to unveil to the VCM and TGP boards, so he sent an email to Sarah requesting an audience. As soon as Victor saw the note, he called Daniel for a preview showing before the unveiling to the boards. After an hour of presentation and in-depth questioning by Victor, Daniel was asked to wait in Sarah's office while she went into a conference with Victor. As was Victor's main talent, he quickly grasped the financial ramifications of Daniel's program and immediately began the process of patenting Daniel's algorithm in preparation for developing and marketing the programs that would use it as a foundation. As Daniel watched quietly from the anteroom, a team of lawyers arrived and were escorted into Victor's office. An hour later Sarah emerged with an itinerary for Daniel which began with a trip to Seattle to present the program to a software development company owned by VCM.

After patenting the program, Victor set in motion the process of transforming Daniel's work into a world-class set of industrial management programs that were implemented first in all of VCM's industrial companies, and then marketed worldwide. Daniel watched as his acorn of an idea, developed while on a morning run, grew into a mainstay of industrial management under the auspices of Victor. VCM owned the patent and the rights, but Victor ensured Daniel a percentage of the sales that would pay dividends for many years. He surmised that now his mother would receive the benefits of his work, and for that, he was glad.

Daniel knew, in the close quietness of the plane, he needed to run to sort through the quagmire Victor had ushered him into. The curvature of the fuselage felt like it was closing in on his psyche. Suddenly he felt a tightness in his chest constrict his breathing to the point he thought he was going to pass out. He jumped out of his seat and exiting the jet he almost ran over the pilot who was ascending the stairs to begin the preflight check.

"What's going on, Daniel?" the pilot stammered as he grabbed the handrail to avoid a collision.

"Sorry, sir," Daniel quickly replied. "I just need a break from the plane. I need some exercise."

"There's a workout area in the lounge, but make it quick. Victor's on his way and we'll take off as soon as he gets here."

"Thanks. I'll just run around the hangar till he gets here. I need to expend some energy."

"Suit yourself," the pilot responded almost absentmindedly as he ducked into the jet.

As Daniel began running around the hangar, he heard the large overhead door open and saw Victor's car speeding toward the jet. It skidded to a halt near the steps and Victor jumped out, hollering at Daniel.

"Daniel! Grab a bag and let's go! Hurry up!"

Daniel sprinted to the car and grabbed the remaining satchels and bounded up the stairs behind Victor who was struggling under the weight of his packages. Daniel grabbed the end of one of them and helped Victor into the plane as the copilot was raising the steps.

"Let's hit it!" Victor ordered as he collapsed into his seat.

The pilot did not wait for a tow as he revved the engines and headed toward the runway.

"What's going on?" Daniel asked as he pushed his satchels aside and fell into a seat, aided by the jet's sudden acceleration.

Victor had his nose to the window looking toward the long, straight road connecting the interstate to the airport. He glanced over at Daniel and then pointed to the road where two black Mercedes were speeding toward the airport.

"Slight change of plans, Daniel, my boy. Our goose is cooked."

"What happened?"

"Robert happened," Victor said as he pronounced the name Robear, but with a decided hardness on the second syllable. "I always suspected him as he seemed way too intelligent for his station with me and too military with his organizational skills. I've been careful with him, and never indicated any suspicion. I knew his true colors would emerge when necessary. He knew my security system and camera locations, so I installed a second set. I caught him with those cameras. He never went to Mexico, but waited for us to leave and went into the office with a team to find out what I've been up to."

"What did he find?"

"Only evidence of you, but nothing else."

"So he works for Mishael's father?"

"I'm not sure yet, but I doubt it. My hunch is he's a Bank agent."

"So if there's no evidence, why is that a problem?"

"Well, lack of evidence can be as big a red flag as evidence."

"So couldn't you have left some false evidence?"

"I considered it, but these people are the best in the world. They would've ferreted out the false evidence and known for sure I was up to something. Then they wouldn't bother to call first. With no evidence, they will be curious enough to want me checked out carefully before they do anything. I'm pretty sure that's who's in the

Mercedes. They'll want to talk to me before takeoff, and failing that, there will be a team waiting for me when I land."

"So they know where we're going?"

"They're tapped into the FAA computer. They'll have my flight plan."

Once airborne, Victor signaled his pilot.

"Yes, sir?" the pilot immediately responded.

"Course change. St. Simons Island. Can we do that with as little fanfare as possible?"

"How little fanfare? I can chart a course to Jacksonville, feign a bit of trouble before we get there, and land at St. Simons instead."

"Great. Do it."

"Are we going to be leaving in this jet?"

Victor glanced over at Daniel for a long moment, obviously puzzled by the question and considering his answer very carefully. After an uncomfortable pause from Daniel's point of view, Victor responded.

"Yes. We won't be there long. I'll be meeting General Brigham to pick up a couple packages before we continue. Thanks."

Victor turned off the intercom and pressed another button. Daniel immediately heard the hiss of white noise in the background. Then Victor motioned for Daniel to move closer and leaned over toward Daniel's ear. Obviously he no longer trusted that what he was going to say wasn't being overheard.

Quietly Victor began talking into Daniel's ear. "Steven has been my personal pilot for twenty-five years and has been absolutely trustworthy, but he has never asked a question like that before. And his timing is too coincidental for comfort."

"So suddenly you just don't trust him?"

"I'm having a bad feeling about him. *Suddenly* as you say. His question was just too convenient."

"But you trust me?"

"Of course."

"Why?"

"Later."

"Always later. Later. Later. When is later going to be now?"

"Soon enough, Daniel. Don't get frustrated with me right now, please. I have to figure out what to do with Steven."

Daniel watched as Victor opened another cabinet housing a small safe. He took out a satellite phone and a small black device which Daniel didn't recognize. Victor then got a map and sat down at the small table. After a few minutes he turned on the satellite phone and dialed. Daniel heard the phone buzz as the call went through. Daniel felt like he was intruding in Victor's private business and motioned to Victor he was going to the main cabin. Victor shook his head and motioned for Daniel to sit.

"Brad, where are you?"

Daniel could not make out the response, but watched as Victor pointed to Fort Lauderdale on the map.

"Yeah, that's no good. I need Steven to chart a course to Fort Belvoir and you to watch where he goes. Would you call him and ask him to pick you up there?" There was a pause as Victor listened then responded, "Yes. Jacksonville, but we're going to make an unscheduled stop at St. Simons." Another pause. "Make sure Steven thinks you're filling the jet with passengers to bring back to St. Simons. I'll unload everything on St. Simons." Daniel watched Victor as he listened and responded. "Yeah. Okay. I'll call on four-twenty-one when Steven takes off. Thanks."

Victor clicked off the satellite phone and looked over at Daniel. "I need you to load the satchel with the water heater stuff and put it with your bag. When we get to St. Simons, we'll take our bags and the money off the plane to make room for Brad and his entourage, and then Steven will take off for Fort Belvoir. He'll drop us on the tarmac and we'll make our own way over to the hangar."

"Isn't that a little risky?" Daniel asked.

"It's a small risk we'll have to take. I don't want him on the ground long. Can you carry your stuff and three satchels?"

"No problem. You can load me up."

The intercom buzzed and Victor turned off the white noise generator and pushed the intercom button.

"Yes, Steven?" Victor responded.

"General Brigham is at Fort Belvoir and wants me to pick up him and his group and bring them back to St. Simons."

"Crap," Victor spat, feigning frustration. "What happened? He's supposed to already be at St. Simons."

"He said his plane is grounded up there."

"Okay," Victor said in a resigned voice. "Just drop Daniel and me on the tarmac and keep going. We'll make our way to the hangar while you pick up the general."

"Sir, he'll need all the seats and weight may be an issue."

"Okay. We'll unload our stuff and make do. You just get there ASAP. Thanks, Steven."

Daniel saw Victor turn the intercom off, so he started to say something, but Victor put a finger to his lips to keep quiet, so Daniel just nodded and finished packing the satchel.

"All right, Daniel," Victor announced. "Let's get our stuff and set it by the door."

Daniel staged the baggage by the door and sat down close by, buckling his seatbelt. Victor was quiet for the rest of the flight, obviously very troubled.

CHAPTER 13

Saint Simon's Island

"Coming into St. Simons, sir," they heard Steven's announcement over the intercom.

"We're ready," Victor responded.

"Roger," Steven automatically replied.

Daniel puzzled as he watched Victor clasp his hands together, look down at his feet, and shake his head. *Wonder what's bothering him now*, Daniel pondered. Then he noticed Victor's left thumb was uppermost in his clasped hands. The image reminded him of his father teaching him a lesson about right, wrong, and merely different. One day during practice, Joseph abruptly stopped the session and asked Daniel to clasp his hands together. Daniel was puzzled, but obeyed.

"This is about muscle memory, Trip," Joseph explained. "Look at which thumb is on top."

Daniel noticed his right thumb was uppermost.

"Now, clasp your hands again and put your left thumb on top."

Daniel had to think for a moment to accomplish the task.

Joseph explained. "Without thinking, your muscles automatically have your right thumb on top, and to change that takes thought. But if you practice putting your left thumb on top a thousand times, then that will feel comfortable and putting your right thumb on top will feel weird. Athletic mechanics are the same. We practice enough so that your body does the proper movement without you thinking about it. That leaves your brain free to concentrate on what you do need to think about, which is watching the ball.

"Now the real lesson, Trip, is about what's right, wrong, or merely different. There is no right way or wrong way to clasp your hands, so it doesn't really matter. But athletic mechanics do have right and wrong ways. Learn what's right, and never practice what's wrong. Then your body will automatically do what's right."

In seeing Victor clasp his hands, Daniel realized that, as was so typical with his father, the lesson was about life, not sports. Now that Daniel sensed a change was in the air, he realized he would have to learn that his new life may be right, wrong, or merely different, but he was going to be forced to feel uncomfortable in order to adapt and grow. He clasped his hands together, forcing his left thumb to the top, and silently thanked his father.

The jet touched down smoothly on the small runway and taxied to a point where Victor and Daniel could deplane and Steven could turn back onto the runway for a quick departure. Daniel quickly unloaded the bags as Victor was talking to Steven, then joined him on the tarmac. The stairs went up and Daniel heard the latch click as the engines accelerated the small jet toward takeoff. Victor immediately turned on the satellite phone and took out the black box. As the phone was connecting to Brad, he sat down on the baggage and opened the hinged cover of the box.

"What d'we have, Brad?" Victor said as the phone came to life. Victor pressed the speaker button and put the phone down in front of him. Daniel sat down on another satchel to take in the proceedings.

"He's changing his flight plan now. Ummm. Okay. Not Fort Belvoir. Hold on. All right, destination is Freeport."

"Any others going to Freeport?" Victor inquired.

"We're checking. Hold on." After a short pause Brad came back on the line. "There's already a private jet inbound from London to Pittsburgh. I assume Pittsburgh was a stop on your agenda? It hasn't changed its plans yet so Steven may wait to contact them after he changes his plans. If so, they would arrive in Freeport about the same time. My guess is whoever is on that plane wants to have a little talk with you. We better time this perfectly before Steven can contact anyone and give away that you're not with him. I can jam his communications for a short time. Are you prepping?"

Victor had started pressing buttons on the black box's keypad as soon as he heard Steven was going to Freeport. Daniel saw amber lights began to blink, then turn green. When three green lights were solid, Victor answered Brad.

"Ready here. Where are they?"

"Fifteen seconds to deep water. Phone and radio still jammed. Here's your window. Three, two, one, go."

Victor pressed two red buttons simultaneously on the box and held them for three seconds, then pushed another one on the side, stood up, and threw the box into the marsh grass near the tarmac. Daniel heard the muffled explosion of the box, then saw a bright white glow in the grass as the phosphorus burned for about ten seconds.

"We're done," Victor said. "See you in Maine."

"Ten-four."

The satellite phone went dead as Daniel heard General Brigham's sign-off. He looked over at Victor who was taking a deep breath as he put his head in his hands for a moment then slumped back on to the baggage.

"Was that what I think it was?" Daniel asked quietly.

"I'm afraid it was."

"You detonated the bomb just like that, and killed two men on a hunch?"

"My hunch just saved our lives."

"You don't know that for sure!"

"Here's what I do know for sure, kiddo. The Bank uses Freeport as a steppingstone into the US, always changing planes. The only reason Steven would go there instead of Fort Belvoir as directed would be to pick up a team of agents and bring them to me. Probably the ones headed to Pittsburgh."

"So what? Does that give you the right to kill him? And his copilot? Was he also an agent, as you call them, or was he just collateral damage?" Daniel exploded as his shock at the situation turned to anger.

"He was also under suspicion since Steven recommended him and hired him as his copilot. But what made me know he was an agent was when he told us we were coming in to St. Simons Island. You know how careful I am with the intercom system, right? Well I responded without pushing a button and he automatically responded back which means he had been listening without our knowledge, and responded out of habit. That was when I knew I had to get rid of him quickly. I have the plane swept for bugs often, and he is the only one besides me who knows when. Which means he could remove his bugs and then put them back after the sweep. If I was a normal businessman, you and I would be waiting here for an execution squad to arrive on our own plane, and you would be the collateral damage. But I'm not a normal businessman: never have been, never will be."

So that's why he looked so distraught when Steven answered him, Daniel thought. Now, without masking his skepticism, Daniel asked, "What are you, Victor?"

"Obviously you think I'm a cold-blooded murderer, but I hate what I just did. I hate that I had to do it."

"What about your copilot? Did you even know his name? Do you even care who he was?"

"Yes. Douglas Waters. He grew up in Raleigh, and graduated from UNC, went into the Air Force, two tours in Iraq, retired, and has been flying for me for a year. He wasn't just a face in a uniform to me, Daniel. He was a person with a family. And I just killed him to save our lives.

I'm sorry I had to do it, but that's the nature of the war we're in."

"But how could Steven work for you for twenty-five years and suddenly turn on you like that?"

"It helps to know how The Bank works. You interested?"

"Make it fast. My patience is wearing thin right now."

"Okay. As soon as I started large-scale development and managing large debt, The Bank assigned someone to keep tabs on me. As business grew and became international, their agents became covert as well as visible. Their favorite tactic though is to find someone close to you whom you trust, compromise them, then blackmail them to keep tabs on you. Even the agents who choose to work for The Bank are usually compromised at some point so The Bank can exercise complete control over them. They are ruthless and unforgiving and do not tolerate mistakes or failure."

"You know I hate to be skeptical, Victor, but whenever I hear stories about *them*, I tend to give it very little credence. Either *they* have an identity, or it's just a load of crap to me."

"I understand your skepticism, and I know I've asked you to take a lot on faith, and your questioning is sound. 'They' are family members who are the direct descendants of the original man who established The Bank in the 1600s in Europe. Through his sons, who he sent to major cities in Europe to start branches, the largest banking institution in the Western World was formed. His descendants now number in the hundreds, but they are still a close-knit and tightly run family with a patriarchal hierarchy of absolute power that is the envy of even the most powerful dictatorships and criminal organizations."

"Where are they from?"

"You mean what country?"

"Yeah."

"That's not really a question that applies to them in the sense you're asking."

"Well they have to be from somewhere and live somewhere."

"I know what you mean to be asking, but the question just

doesn't apply like it does to you and me. We're Americans, because we're citizens of the United States, so we are governed and protected by what we perceive to be an institution we call *our* government. We pledge fealty to this institution, pay taxes to it, love it, and will even defend it with our life.

"This family doesn't belong to a country. Countries belong to this family. They don't pay taxes, taxes are paid to them. They don't defend with arms, they pit people against people, arm both sides, and profit off what we call *war*. They have no loyalties except to wealth. They literally control most of the world and its wealth and consider it their fiefdom and do so by using the concept of country to their ultimate advantage. They are not captains, kings, or presidents. They are power. They don't just control heads of state, they create them and place them in power to ensure the wealth flows to their coffers. The terms democracy, monarchy, communism, socialism, and any other form of government have no meaning to them except as a management method for the populace.

"All forms of government have one objective—to tax the populace; and that, Daniel, is the one guiding principle of The Bank. Their founder realized early in his banking career the safest and most profitable investment was to a government with the capability to tax the people in order to pay interest on the debt. And every government borrows money to exist, and borrows the most money to wage wars. War, roads, infrastructure, education, welfare—everything a government needs for its people—needs money. And The Bank is the ultimate source of that money. And taxes pay the interest on the debt."

"Why? Why do they borrow? Why not just balance the budget and tell the banks to shove it?"

"Have you ever known the US to maintain a balanced budget?"

"No."

"Of course not. And you never will. Lawmakers who seek to do that are quickly voted down by lawmakers controlled by The Bank. And the debt just keeps growing—into the trillions."

"So, in your eyes, they control every country this way?"

"In the Western World. Except Cuba."

"Cuba?"

"Yeah," Victor chuckled. "Castro was their only failure, but not from lack of trying. Castro seems to have lived a charmed, but bankrupt life. He had more failed attempts on his life than any leader, and sanctions that would choke a horse, but he survived and practiced his idea of social democracy. And although he was stuck in a 1950s economy, his people still have free healthcare, free education, and quite a bit of personal freedoms. Even Russia couldn't control him, though they tried. And the US propaganda machine didn't seem to faze him. But The Bank will ultimately regain control. Probably very soon now that he's dead."

"Interesting," Daniel mused, doing little to mask his skepticism. "So what about the Eastern world?" Daniel asked.

Victor laughed. "They are the biggest enigma wrapped in a puzzle the world has ever known. The Bank considers themselves special because they've been around for a few hundred years and measure their wealth in the trillions of dollars. Banks in the East trace their business back thousands of years and intricately through families with tentacles everywhere and their wealth is immeasurable. No one really knows who controls it or how, but they make The Bank look like a monopoly game. And where The Bank uses taxes, the East uses gambling as their core. It's really fascinating. But if someone needed a billion dollars in gold bullion tomorrow and was willing to pay for it, it would mysteriously appear. And the price would be exorbitant for generations, and would include more than money."

"What d'you *mean more than money*?" Daniel quizzed.

"They deal in futures, in favors, in trades, placements of family members, and all the nontangibles the western cultures dismiss so easily. But that's how they've grown and controlled their wealth for hundreds of generations. And why it is immeasurable. And favors linger forever with them. Even Switzerland is indebted to them for more than money."

"That's a nice story, Victor, but the fact remains you just killed two people and now I'm an accomplice to murder unless I go to the police."

"Is that what you want to do, Daniel?"

"I'm thinking it's a Catch-22. According to you, if I go, then people will know I'm alive, and Abu's terrorists will kill me, and Sarah, and Jonathan. If I don't go, and you're not who you claim to be, then you, or your black organization, which may even be The Bank, will have compromised me, so you own me. And I'm sure you would kill me before I got to the police. Am I missing anything?"

"Well, from your perspective, I can see how you would come to that conclusion. So what are you going to do?"

Daniel reached behind his back and pulled a pistol from his belt, clicked the safety off and cocked it.

"The water heater pistol," Victor stated. "Are you going to shoot me?"

"Thinking about it," Daniel said rather nonchalantly. "I could shoot you, walk away with a few million and start a new life somewhere. After all, I'm dead and the world thinks you were on a plane that just disappeared into the Atlantic."

"Yep," Victor said, not seeming to be overly concerned by Daniel's threat.

"But then I'd never see Sarah or Jonathan again, and they mean more to me than a few million measly bucks."

"Seventy-four million to be more accurate, but not very much of it is untraceable now."

"Big deal. It's still worthless to me." Daniel kept the gun pointed at Victor while he reached into his bag where the rest of the water heater stash was. He groped around until he found the passport and ID he was looking for. He opened it. In the dim light of the full moon it was difficult to see detail, but he could make out his own face on the documents and his new name, Paul Williams, from Wake Forest, North Carolina. Clipped to it was a letter which he assumed was his fabricated life history. He looked at his birthday.

"I'm nineteen years old, Victor? Seriously?"

"Yep. More convenient that way. You can pass for an older looking nineteen-year-old. The photos were Photoshopped to help."

In the full moon's light it was hard to see this, but Daniel knew it would be true.

"So what's it going to be, my boy?" Victor asked as he stretched his feet out and leaned back on his elbows.

Daniel uncocked the gun and ensured the safety was on, then turned it and held the barrel, offering it to Victor handle first. "I'd rather you kill me than me kill you. I won't live a compromised life, and I can't promise I won't go to the police."

"You truly are Joseph's son, Daniel," Victor said as he took the gun, turned it, and handed it back. "Put this back in the bag. We may need it someday. And it may come as a surprise to you, but I'd use it on myself before I'd use it on you."

Daniel looked perplexed. "Why?"

"Because of who your grandfather was."

"Grandpa JD?" Daniel had heard his mother refer to Joseph's father this way but he had died long before Daniel was born, and he never learned very much about him. "What does he have to do with this?"

"When Doc Heidi moved to Florida, he wanted a new name that would reflect his heritage for his children's sake. His mother's family started Furman University in Greenville, and his favorite Bible characters were Joseph and Daniel. Make sense now?"

"Joseph Daniel Furman. JD."

Daniel watched a cloud pass before the full moon as his thoughts churned, coalescing as a revelation. His thoughts became verbal as he stated, "Grandpa JD was Doc Heidi. Dad was your younger brother. So you're my uncle." Daniel paused again in thought. "That does explain a lot."

Victor nodded and waited for this revelation to sink in.

"Why was I never told?" Daniel asked.

"Safety. Brad's the only other person who knows. I protected Joseph from The Bank, who I'm sure would have used him to control me somehow, and also would have traced me back to my father's murder. But in the end, I couldn't protect Joseph from ISIS."

"That's my fault," Daniel stammered.

"Nope. That's Abu's fault. And he will pay for that, I promise you."

"More vengeance, huh? Does it ever end?"

"When we're all dead, kiddo, when we're all dead." Victor looked up at the nearly full moon getting close to the horizon and motioned to Daniel. "We've got to get moving. Sun will be up soon and I want to be on Jekyll Island by daylight." Victor was patient, though, waiting for Daniel to move first.

Daniel was staring at Victor now, quietly letting the pieces of the puzzle fall into place as his emotions ran the gamut from shock to acceptance. Finally he responded, "Okay, Uncle Victor. How do we do that?"

CHAPTER 14

Jekyll Island

Victor loaded Daniel down with the baggage and they made their way to the shoreline south of the runway and near the golf course. It was tricky avoiding the early-morning groundskeepers, and Victor staged Daniel in the grass near the shore while he looked for a boat. As the sun was peeking up on the horizon, Victor came up to the shore in a small skiff and motioned for Daniel to load up quickly. After a short crossing of St. Simons Sound, they skidded onto the sand of Jekyll Island behind a nondescript ranch-style beach house. Daniel noticed the beach along this part of the Island was lined with boulders to protect it from erosion. While Daniel struggled to get the bags over the rocks and into the yard, Victor took the boat down the beach and tied it to the remains of an old public pier. Waiting for Victor's return, Daniel sat down on the rocks and marveled at the fiery red sky burgeoning as the sun rose over the Atlantic. He remembered his father talking to him about how the sky along the east coast displays a red brilliance as the rays of the low sun penetrate the wind-born dust from the Sahara Desert lifted to the upper atmosphere as it drifts across the ocean, borne on the same trade winds that brought the early explorers to the New

World. He realized how much he had missed this ocean, with its waters warmed by the Gulf Stream making its way northward from the tropics to Newfoundland before crossing the North Atlantic to warm the British Isles.

Daniel's trance was interrupted as Victor came up behind him. "Red sky at morning, sailors take warning," Victor announced. "Looks like we could have some rain today."

Daniel turned his head toward Victor to complete the mariners' saying, "Red sky at night, sailor's delight. Last night was a world away, though, and I doubt the sky was red due to weather." Victor grunted, unamused by the dig. Daniel stood up and followed Victor to the house. Obviously the chit-chat was over and Victor was getting down to business.

Victor carefully checked the house from the outside, then went to the satellite TV dish and opened the control box revealing a keypad. He punched some numbers and Daniel saw a few lights flicker on inside the house. Victor then went to the back door which was fitted with an electronic lock, input a code, and opened the door.

"Welcome home, kiddo," Victor said turning to Daniel. "Bring in the bags while I start breakfast. Nothing fresh, but we do have plenty in the freezer."

Daniel stood outside the door for a moment just looking around.

"Well, come on!" Victor prodded.

"What is this place?" Daniel finally asked as he finished his pondering and shoved a bag through the door.

"Sort of a safe house. We've owned property here since 1888 when one of our members clandestinely purchased shares in the Jekyll Island Club, which the original plantation owners here had sold the island to. We built this house in the fifties. Lots of advantages here. Jekyll is a State Park now and many of the major money families still have property on the Georgia Islands. Did you know this is where the meetings were held to establish the Federal Reserve? We kept tabs on that meeting from the old hunting lodge that was here when we bought it."

"Who's *we?*" Daniel asked skeptically.

"Just a small group of people who try to protect our freedom. We failed miserably with the Federal Reserve, though."

"Right," Daniel said, half under his breath. "That doesn't tell me squat. So I guess I'll have to wait till later for the real answer."

"We'll lay low here for a week or so until Brad thinks we're safe, then drive up to Maine. The good thing about Jekyll is all the cars coming and going to the island are scanned, and we have access to the computer, so we'll know if any suspicious vehicle pays a visit."

"Wonderful," Daniel said sarcastically. "Is that why we came by boat?"

"Yep. There's no record of us or a vehicle that can be traced to us coming here. And we can watch a lot of activity from here."

"How do we leave?"

"Same way we came. Brad will have a car at the airport so we just slip back across the sound and drive away."

"That simple, huh?"

"That simple. Like a turtle on a fence post."

"What?" Daniel quizzed.

"You've never heard that expression?"

"Not hardly."

"I use it jokingly with Brad to describe how I got to be a billionaire. It started when I was working on his family's ranch."

"I didn't know you were a ranch hand."

"Oh yeah, I guess I haven't gotten to that part of the story yet. I went there after Pendleton. I'll tell you more later. Let's eat now."

"What about the turtle on the fence post? At least tell me about it while we eat."

"All right. Well, one day I was driving around the ranch checking fences and I saw something strange on top of a post, so I got out of my truck to investigate. It was a turtle. So I'm thinking, how the hell does a turtle get on a fence post? Anyway, I took it down and put it under a bush to cool. That evening I told Brad's uncle about the turtle. He laughed and said that would be Pedro's doings. One thing about a turtle on a fence post is you can be sure he didn't get there by himself. When Pedro would find a turtle on the road, he would save it by putting it on a fence post and let the next traveler take it down. 'There's a message for you in that scenario,' Brad's uncle had said. So for the rest of my time as a ranch hand I would occasionally find a turtle on a fencepost and would rescue it. It would remind me I didn't get here by myself; someone put me here. So I'm always reminded I didn't get to VCM by myself; someone put me there. And now, I'm reminded I can't get down by myself. Someone has to do that, also. Jekyll is like a fence post and we're turtles. Safely out of the road, thanks to Brad, and now we wait for Brad to give us a safe way off."

"I got it. Cute. So we just sit and wait?"

"Yep."

"Well I'm tired, confused, and a little frustrated. Mind if I take a run on the beach?"

"Go ahead. I'm going to shower and get some sleep. It's been a long night. Use the first room on the right. I'll be at the end of the hall. Wake me up for lunch, will you?"

"Sure." Daniel took his shoes off and headed for the door.

"And no long swims," Victor said as he headed down the hall.

"Aye aye, sir!" Daniel quipped back. He was anxious to get to the beach for a nice long run. As he was opening the door, he paused. "Victor?" he called loudly.

"What?" Victor called back from down the hall.

"What was your name when you drove off that mountain?"

Victor walked back toward Daniel, and when he could see him, he answered. "Patrick. Patrick McCluney Furman."

"Nice name. Were you called Pat?"

"No. Patrick. Dad didn't use nick names, so I was Patrick and Joseph was, well, Joseph."

Daniel noticed this was the first time Victor referred to Doc Heidi as Dad. It sounded odd coming from him. "Okay. Thanks. See you later."

Daniel closed the door and headed toward the rocks. There was something about this granite barrier Daniel immediately despised. They were so alien to this coastline, and to Daniel they screamed of the vanity of money and man's attempt to alter nature. He had taken a geology course at the University of Florida dealing with coastlines, and he believed that the beauty of the Atlantic Seaboard with its islands, banks, and shoals, lay in its fluidity. These sand features, formed by wind and water, were constantly on the move, reshaping themselves as well as the sounds and waterways they created and protected. Hurricanes and Nor'easters continually opened and closed inlets and jetties as easily as children building moats around their sandcastles and watching as the tide takes away the entire structure.

As Daniel crested the rocks he saw the small beach was now gone and, with the tide high, the waves were breaking against the boulders. Looking up and down the artificially straight line of rip rap, he could see pools of water forming behind the barrier. Already the sea was reclaiming its sand and men would now be forced to refill the yards of the wealthy in an annual effort to protect their investments. *Vanity*, he thought. *Such vanity. To haul huge boulders from the mountains and dump them here in an artificially perfect and straight line.* Suddenly the ridiculousness of his inane judgmentalism racked him and he laughed aloud, causing an early morning artist perched on the rocks to look up from her sketch pad. He was the proverbial pot calling the kettle black. After all, had he not just spent an entire night flitting around the country in a private jet, enjoying Kobe beef and expensive bourbon while retrieving millions of dollars, and ultimately watching as the jet with its crew was poofed out of existence with the push of a button? What vanity. His senses screamed at the insanity of his situation.

Running along the beach was nearly impossible now, so he headed into the water to wash away his demons, waving to the artist as he waded into the surf.

Daniel noticed the water got deep quickly as he felt his way into the unfamiliar surf. It then got shallow and stayed just below his waist for a long time, and began to get deep again as the wide sandbar gave way to the ocean depths. He watched the waves breaking just off the sandbar and roll toward shore before dissipating in the short trench near the rocks. They then broke again onto the boulders. He saw the woman get up suddenly as a crashing wave sprayed her with a light shower of ocean mist. Looking up and down the shoreline, he saw very few people; such a contrast from the densely populated public beaches he normally had to settle for. He was anxious to see this beach at low tide as he surmised it would be a beautiful, wide beach with great waves to surf further out. These waves had a nice but short break, then a long, unrideable roll across the sandbar, ending with another short break. *Not good for surfing now*, he thought, *but possibly great when the tide goes out and the promised storm nears.* The Atlantic seemed to always be rife with storms somewhere, generating surfable waves most of the time. His favorite surfing experience though, had been on a short winter trip to Barbados when the North Atlantic was churning and sending big beautiful waves southward to the Bahamas and West Indies. Barbados, being east of the dominate arc of islands, was not mountainous like the rest of the chain, but low and flat, transitioning into a gentle beach ideal for producing wave after wave of glorious rides.

Daniel felt the gentle tug of the changing tide and waited to see which way it would run. He decided to swim with it down the beach and then run back when the changing tide exposed the sand. After an hour of swimming, he decided to go ashore at the public park and find a drink of water.

For the first time he realized he had absolutely no money. No credit card, debit card, or cash. Nothing with which to buy a snack, a drink, or lunch. The irony of it caught him again and he laughed as he came out of the surf. Seventy million dollars he had carried ashore and now, money, money everywhere, and not a dime to spend! He found a water fountain and drank the tepid liquid as he mused about the money. He caught a glimpse of a small thatched structure nearby where a man was opening the walls to reveal an open-air seaside bar. He ambled up the sidewalk to it and sat on a stool to read the menu.

As the barman was setting up for the day, he asked with an unmistakable New York accent, "Can I get you something?"

"I wish," Daniel responded, "but I don't have any cash on me."

"You got a driver's license?"

"Not with me. Why?"

"I'd run a tab for you and you can pay later, but I need your license."

"Oh. That's convenient. You're not concerned about getting stiffed?"

"This is a state park, so we turn stiffers over to the state police. If you're out of state they turn it over to the US Marshals. You don't want to mess with them. We really don't have that problem here, though."

"I guess the demographics are pretty good?" Daniel said more as a statement than as a question.

"The best," the barman replied. "Where're you from?"

Daniel had to pause for a moment before answering. "North Carolina," he finally said remembering he was now Paul Williams.

"Well, if you're going to be here for awhile, check in with me and I'll run a tab for you. You can pay online later if you want. Makes it convenient for swimmers who don't carry much with them."

"You have oysters here?"

"Raw, fried, and steamed. I can get most anything you want if you can wait fifteen minutes. We get it by golf cart from the hotel over there," he pointed up the beach, "and I prepare it here. Very fresh. If you don't see what you want on the menu, let me know. I can cook just about anything."

"Really? You're a chef and a bartender?"

"Sure am. Retired here from New York. Had a restaurant up there, but got tired of the cold. Love it here, though. Easy life, great people, and warm weather. Look at that view," he said pointing toward the horizon. "Beats a dirty street in Queens."

"I guess it does," Daniel agreed. "When do you open?"

"When I wake up. Usually between seven and twelve, depending on the night before."

Daniel watched as the bartender poured some lager into a large glass, then cracked an egg into it.

"Prairie Oyster," Daniel said, watching the guy swallow everything in one gulp. "Must have been a good night."

"Great night," he said, wiping his cheeks with a towel. "Private party," he continued with a grin.

"Put a couple of raw oysters in that, some salt, pepper, and Tabasco, and you'll have yourself an Ocracoke."

"A what?" the barman said quizzically.

"Well, the Scotsman I learned that from used to have it for breakfast at a bar on Ocracoke Island on the Outer Banks. But I think if he had been on Nantucket, he would have called it a Nantucket. Try it sometime. It's different. I was starving one morning and didn't have enough money for breakfast, so he offered me one on a dare. I'm sure he was thinking I'd just puke it up and he'd get a big laugh at the hungry kid. If I hadn't been so hungry, I might've, but I kept it down. It wasn't half bad once you got used to the texture. It's amazing what tastes good when you're really hungry. I've liked oysters ever since; raw, fried, or steamed. Favorite way is in an omelet."

"I do a pretty good oyster omelet. Stop by one morning and I'll fix you one."

"Sounds good. I might just do that."

The barman eased away to wait on a couple who had shown up for breakfast, so Daniel headed back to the beach for the run back to the house. When he neared the house, he noticed the boat was no longer at the pier, and he had to look carefully to get the right house from the returning perspective with the tide out. Finally he found where he had crossed the rocks earlier and climbed over them to the house. He found Victor at the large dining table with stacks of money on every available horizontal surface.

"Thought you'd be sleeping," Daniel said looking around at the neat piles of cash.

"I wish I could've gone to sleep, but I couldn't relax with so many loose ends to tie up. This traceable cash is a real problem so I thought I'd start organizing it for safekeeping while I figure out what to do."

"Got any ideas?" Daniel asked as he carefully walked around reading notes, quantities, and directions on papers atop each pile.

"Working on one. Time is the best way. In ten years it won't matter too much, but using it during that time is tricky. And I doubt I'll have much more than a decade to do what I want to with it."

"And what is that? And why is it whenever I ask a question, it just seems to lead to more questions and fewer answers?"

Victor laughed. "Which one do you want me to answer first?"

"All of 'em," Daniel smirked.

"Okay," Victor conceded. "I'll talk while you start loading this cash in those bags." Victor pointed to a stack of black, rubber looking items piled in the living room.

"Nice bags," Daniel said as he picked one up and carefully examined it. It appeared that once sealed it would be airtight and waterproof, and the neoprene material seemed heavily reinforced to make it resistant to puncturing. "Where did these come from?"

"A friend of Brad's brought them and picked up the boat. Hopefully no one will notice it was ever gone."

"Nice to have friends in strange places," Daniel said matter-of-factly.

"Yep. It can be very convenient. How was your run?"

Daniel told Victor about his morning venture at the bar.

Victor listened intently, then asked, "Did he have a heavy New York accent?"

"Yeah. You know the bartender?"

"I assume he asked where you were from and finagled a way to see your ID?"

"Yes, he did, but he didn't have to finagle too hard since I had no money on me. He said he'd run a tab for me if I had a driver's license."

"Where'd you tell him you are from?"

"North Carolina. Why?"

"Did he get your name?"

"No, I left before he asked. Why the twenty questions?"

"His name is Joe. He's DEA. The cartels used to run a lot of coke through here, so he was sent to keep tabs on people. Any time he encounters a new young face, he starts a file on that person as a matter of course. Almost all of the time they come to naught, but he's had enough success in getting information bartenders seem to be privy to that they keep him here even though the drug trade isn't what it once was. It's good you didn't have any ID on you."

"Why? Is there a problem with my new ID?"

"No. It's clean. But we want to keep it under the radar for as long as possible. Just to be careful." Victor reached behind him, picked up an envelope, and tossed it to Daniel. "There's a thousand dollars. Nine hundreds and five twenties. Break the hundreds every chance you get, but never two in the same place. That should hold you till you get to Maine."

"Thanks. Now what do we do with the rest of the money?"

"We'll be driving back roads to Maine and stopping at various safe properties along the way where we'll put parcels of money. After it's all safely stowed, I'm thinking about asking the Chinese to help with the money."

"You mean a Chinese bank? Will we have to go to Washington for that? I don't think I've ever seen one."

Victor smiled. "Part of the enigma of the Chinese banks is that they are hidden in plain sight, and you see them all the time, you just don't know it."

Daniel paused, prodding Victor to continue, "And?"

"We walk into a Chinese restaurant and ask for a loan."

"You're shitting me!"

"Nope. It's the largest bank in the world if you know how to be a customer. And they are immune from The Bank's influence, and from government regulators. They are shielded within veils and layers of legitimate businesses. And you cannot imagine how hard The Bank has been trying to penetrate them for two hundred years."

"How so?"

"You may have noticed, but Asians are master copiers of good ideas and prey very successfully on the West. They let us invent it, test it, market it, and then if it's successful, they take it for pennies on the dollar for their own use and profit. This is not a new concept for them but goes back to the first interactions the Western traders had with the East. One of those ideas was our corporate structure. Once they figured out how companies work, it revolutionized their whole system. The West knew nothing of the transition, but the shift enabled them to increase their wealth tenfold and infiltrate every large corporation in the West—to their own benefit, of course. They quietly gained covert control of the tea trade with England and started draining the British of their silver bullion. Once the British figured this out and sought to stop the bleeding, the Chinese banks were very willing to oblige and loaned them back the silver, which they used to establish a permanent port, Hong Kong. Now, permanent to the British may mean ninety-nine years, but ninety-nine years is the flitting of a moth's wing to the Chinese, who grow wealth for generations, not for one century. So the British built Hong Kong, even beyond the wildest dreams of the Chinese, then gave it all back to them with interest less than a century later. But that's just a minor example." Victor paused and perused a checklist where he was keeping track of the bags and money. Satisfied, he nodded to Daniel and continued his lecture.

Daniel was interested in what Victor was saying, but was taking everything with a grain of salt. He wished Victor could just answer the questions instead of giving Daniel a "history of the world according to Victor," but he held in his frustration and listened. At least packing the bags gave him something to do.

"Now the Chinese have always had trouble with their neighbors who covet their wealth and their massive resources. The Mongols, the Russians, the Japanese—all have tried in vain to control them, hence The Great Wall. And if that's not enough, their own internal politics have sometimes dealt them a massive blow. I'm talking here about Mao Tse-Tung. The world wars were also setbacks, but not fatal. They just adjusted and kept doing business, moving the central control offshore to Taiwan, Macao, and Hong Kong. What they really needed was a worldwide network to gather, distribute, and grow their wealth covertly. After all, money under a mattress just deteriorates. It needs to be worked. So after World War II they tried with a network of Chinese tailors, but misjudged the way Westerners buy clothing; we prefer mass-produced items found in department stores. Meanwhile, they watched the success of fast-food chain restaurants and came up with a solution to their problem by helping local Chinese families open restaurants. The restaurants, along with the wholesale food suppliers and distributors, are perfect for manipulating vast sums of untraceable cash. And an added benefit is getting the Chinese into the US and other Western countries. Did you know small Chinese restaurants in America out-number all other fast-food chains combined?"

"Never really thought about it," Daniel replied. "I always thought Mickey D's was the largest." Daniel was still feigning interest but becoming impatient with the long-winded answer. He noticed, though, how animated Victor was as he told the story. Business was obviously his game and he loved it, so Daniel politely showed interest in the whole subject.

"Well, McDonald's," Victor continued, "as one corporation, may be the largest fast-food company, but look at how many Chinese restaurants there are between two McDonald's restaurants. It might surprise you. And look at the investment required to open up a stand-alone burger joint compared to a Chinese restaurant. Many times when you see a stand-alone Chinese restaurant it's because a burger joint has failed and they pick up the building for a fraction of its original cost. Their favorite location is a twenty-five-foot-wide space in a strip shopping center—low investment, low overhead, and maximum cash flow. Notice they all have variations of a very few names but the same menu and the same formula. They all copy and duplicate to the max. Also, it's impossible to trace the true owners of the business, or trace where the money flows."

"How do they get away with it?"

"They don't 'get away' with anything. They're perfectly legal, obey every law to the nth degree, are fastidious about getting every license and permit, and pay all taxes on time. The government's penalty for any violation is minuscule compared to the Chinese ramifications. And the reason is simple: the cost of running the restaurant business is puny compared to the real wealth of the location. Their magic is everything is done exactly the same way in every location so nobody reinvents any wheel. Every action is time-tested and proven, and there's no room for innovation nor mistakes. It's like cars; if you want to see what innovations will be in Japanese and Korean cars in three years, look at a new BMW, Mercedes, or Jaguar today. If it works and sells, it will be copied, but never invented. If anything has been an innovation in the East, it's how efficiently they steal and copy Western ideas and technologies. And they can produce a copy better than the original. It's uncanny."

"Yeah, yeah. I get it," Daniel said trying to spur Victor on. "Restaurants are like branch banks on every corner in the world. So how do they operate?"

"I can tell you how they operate from a customer's perspective, but I don't think anyone can actually tell you how they truly operate. They are like a black widow spider's web. Filaments all over with no apparent rhyme nor reason, but deadly efficient at capturing prey. And they stay very hidden."

"I guess that's in contrast to a yellow garden spider that spins beautifully organized webs in highly visible locations?"

"That's the analogy," Victor said, smiling. "The black widow is often right under you and you never know it. But it catches more prey with less effort than any orb-weave spider. And nobody wants to cross a black widow."

Daniel laughed at Victor's sly grin as he offered this last bit of information. "Obviously, as overtly dangerous as The Bank wants to appear, they pale in comparison to the Chinese," Daniel concluded. So, Victor was committing himself to a very dangerous and risky course of action. Daniel knew becoming a billionaire doesn't happen by shying away from risk. And, knowing Victor, he would not venture into a den of danger without being fully prepared.

"So you just walk into the first Chinese restaurant you see and ask for a loan?" Daniel asked in a facetious tone of voice.

"Not quite that simple but essentially that's a start. The first thing you do is read the menu, in Chinese, not English. Hidden within the characters are the code words indicating the nature of their business. If you can't find them, you move to the next restaurant."

"Not all of them are banks?"

"Oh, no. There are still some genuine Chinese restaurants that are only restaurants. Usually they have the best food, as it's unique to their family, or their village, or their area of China. The menu will quickly let you know. And some are at various stages of the echelon, so may be used only for collecting and passing money to other branches. It's impossible to tell from the shop itself, as they all want to look and be exactly alike. That's how they hide in plain sight. But the menu will give away the opening to conduct business."

"Then what?"

"Once you know what to order, it then becomes a matter of how you order it. I will order politely in Mandarin Chinese and will be politely told 'so sorry, but that dish is not available today.' This is when you need to be very good at Chinese profanity. It's the key to unlocking the system."

"Profanity?"

"Yeah. It's great. An ancient art form, as I see it. Not at all like Western profanity. When and how you use it, and the inflections are more important than the words themselves."

"What if you screw up?"

"With seventy million on the line, I better not. I practice a lot when I'm alone, and started learning a long time ago. Brad's uncle put me with a Chinese mentor as soon as I got to the ranch. Bert foresaw the Chinese economy buying the US once Chairman Mao was gone, so he wanted us to be prepared."

"Brad's uncle was a pretty smart guy," Daniel commented.

"Brilliant, actually. And he liked Brad as much as he disapproved of his brother. Bert and his mom were pretty close, too, so they watched over Brad. My mentor wasn't lacking brain power either—the two of them were quite a team."

"What was with Brad's dad?"

"He was all right in a by-the-book kind of way. He just couldn't get past the Army. The Army was everything to him, the end-all, be-all of existence. He was intelligent enough, just not very smart. To him, the Army was the solution to all things. Brad's uncle and his mom knew it was a tool; nothing more. A very powerful tool, and one to be used very skillfully, but it's not the reason for living."

"Oh. Okay. So you're going to curse the Chinese waiter?"

"Yeah, back to the banking. The counter person will be young, usually in their twenties and dressed like any neighborhood kid—probably jeans and T-shirt. If male, I'll scowl at him for the dish not being available and tell him something like his penis is so small it won't fit in a dog's ass, and if a girl, I will call her a mongrel dog with a jade gate the size of an elephant, or something like that. It gets lost in translation, but the colorful point is taken."

"What then?"

"They act nonplussed, as if I'm just a typical stupid, rude, uncivilized foreign person, and they offer a nonapology."

"A nonapology?"

"It's how they say sorry in such a way it means *fuck-off*. It's a face-saving gesture for both of us. Similar to when a Southerner says 'bless his heart.' It sounds so sweet, but it means 'what an idiot.'"

"Yeah, I've heard that. Whereas, a Northerner will just call you a fucking idiot. No feigned finesse there." Daniel laughed. He was enjoying this episode. "And then?"

Victor just shook his head in agreement. "I insult their mother, father, family—anything up the lineage tree. Finally they will tell me they might have that dish in two days. I'll rail against their ineptitude and tell them I will be back in one hour and they better have the dish ready. They will tell me it's impossible, but maybe tomorrow. I'll continue to curse and say maybe I can wait two hours, but the dish better be perfect. They will say, 'So sorry. My uncle may have that dish available,' and give me a name. They will know the magnitude of my business by the level of profanity and how adamant I am with the bartering. That will direct their course of action."

"What's next? Do we go see their uncle then?"

"The next day, or next hour—time is not really relevant—I go to where they directed and go through the process again, only the person I will be engaged with this time will be about ten years older and dressed better; probably a collared shirt and nice slacks. Maybe a tie, but in this day and age, probably not. The dialogue will be more polite, but I will get nowhere except for another appointment. This will happen several times with each person getting slightly more knowledge of what I offer, all in a coded fashion, and each one will be another ten years older and dressed in a more expensive suit. The last one will be someone my age. That will be the signal I'm in. He'll be wearing a magnificent hand-tailored silk suit and will invite me to a small office. But he will only be the front man. Somewhere near will be the final authority. I will exchange pleasantries with him for maybe half an hour, but will conduct no business. This will let him know I am going to wait until the real power is there before I proceed. It will also indicate we are talking about tens of millions of dollars. If all goes perfectly I will be given tea. Wonderful tea, I might add, not the crap they serve in the restaurant. Shortly thereafter I will meet the real banker."

"Where will I be while this is going on?"

"By my side. Well actually slightly behind me to my left. If you were my son, you'd be on my right, but everyone else, including a nephew, is on my left. Never speak, never touch anything, and never let any part of your body, like hand or foot, get past the plane of my body. Each person we meet will be evaluating everything we do and say, and we won't proceed if we fail anywhere."

"What happens if we, or I, screw up? And how will you know?"

"We'll know because they'll send us to a false location. We'll be given another chance in a new restaurant, after we've learned how to behave. They'll check us out thoroughly during that time, and decide about business. They are very careful, but they are not in the business of letting money slip through their hands. All of these preliminaries give them a complete and absolute deniability. But don't worry, you'll do fine. Just try not to look too bored. The more they perceive boredom, the longer everything will take. You will have to feign interest but not too much interest. You're a student, nothing more. If someone asks you a question, even a mundane one like 'Hi, how are you?' you say nothing. I will respond. Everything is a test and our success depends upon our behavior. We'll get you a suit that doesn't fit quite as nicely as mine, and of cheaper material. Oh, and don't make eye contact with any female, no matter how much she flirts with you. Remember, you do not exist to the bankers, so there'll be no eye contact with you from them. They'll see the women don't exist to you. Therefore, you have self-control and they'll allow you the privilege of being in their world for a short visit. Got it?"

"I think I can do that. Except the boredom part. That will be a challenge."

"I'm sure you'll figure out something. Let's finish packing and stage these by the door. We need to leave soon."

"Today? I thought we were here for a week?"

"Brad's a little nervous and thinks we should get moving. The search for the plane is all over the news along with my face, and we need to get this money to some other safe places."

"This place isn't safe? I noticed you haven't shaved in a couple of days. You growing a disguise?"

"Yeah, I need to change my look. And this place is safe enough for part of the money, but you know what they say about all the eggs being in one basket. Why don't you get cleaned up and get some sleep. It might be another long night."

"I'd like to get something to eat first. Reading the menu at that bar while starving was not such a good idea. I'm famished."

"Tell you what—I'll fix a snack while you shower."

"Deal." Daniel ambled down the hall to his door, found some towels and got in the shower. He didn't realize how exhausted he was and felt he could sleep in the shower with the hot water pouring over him.

CHAPTER 15

The Chinese Connection

When Daniel didn't show up to eat, Victor decided to check on him and found him asleep across the large bed, clad only in a towel. Victor found a blanket to cover him and let him sleep. He put the snack in the refrigerator for later, and sat down to plan his foray into the alien world of the Chinese banking system. With the help of the internet, he studied various restaurants along the East Coast and selected several likely locations.

He had always been fascinated by the Chinese culture. Much of it was difficult for him to comprehend since he had not grown up immersed in the collective paradigms of this ancient society where the complex becomes simple and the simplest actions are fraught with complexities beyond imagining. A nuance can be more powerful than a sledgehammer, while a sledgehammer can be reduced to a whiff of smoke in the twinkling of an eye. His Western sensibility was not at all attuned to these subtleties.

On the ranch in Texas, Paul Chang had been Victor's introduction to the Chinese and within his story lay a crucible of the Chinese mentality, beginning with his name. Although he spoke perfect English and was known to everyone on the ranch as Paul Chang, he refused to speak to Victor in any language except Mandarin Chinese. And he insisted Victor refer to him as Jianhong Chen, or just Jianhong. At first Victor thought this was due to Brad's uncle but later found out it was wholly Paul's doing—a way of immersing Victor in the Chinese culture Paul had left behind so many years ago. Simultaneously, he was breathing new life into his own heritage. He took Victor under his wing to not only rehabilitate his physically broken body, but to mend his spirit as well. Paul was a remarkable rancher and, with his Zen conditioning, was equally content doing mundane chores such as mending fences as he was with breeding the cattle and preparing them for market. He expertly valued the livestock and was a master negotiator. When neighboring ranchers sought his advice on their livestock value, he always refused. He was steadfastly loyal to Brad's uncle and never swayed.

After a year on the ranch being mentored by Paul, Victor finally understood his language well enough to learn the story of how he came to Texas. And, as is so typically Chinese, it began with his name. His parents pored over his name for weeks after he was born, consulting several soothsayers in the process before finally giving in to what the soothsayers saw. From birth, Paul had a distant look about him marking him as different–a trait not valued by his culture. So his parents settled on Jianhong, which was the combination of two words; *Jian* meaning "build" or "establish," and *Hong* meaning "wide, spacious, or vast." Their dream was that he would build a palatial estate and amass a vast fortune. Unfortunately, his personality never lent itself to the Chinese ideals, so he was disciplined unmercifully to bring him into accordance with the village norms.

His Zen master tried to make him understand he was like a brick in the Great Wall and his strength lay in being part of the wall. Apart from the wall he was nothing but a weak lump of hard clay. So he needed to conform. His restlessness caused him to lose attention during his lessons and he would get caught up within his own world where he was the center of the universe. To him, whether or not he was in the wall had nothing to do with his value as a person. He acutely felt his individuality, and much to the chagrin of his family, this revelation caused him to crave attention, whether positive or negative. He pondered his fate constantly, but felt helpless to change. He just could not fit the mold into which he was born.

Then one day he heard a voice. The voice was rather a revelation, and to the horror of his family, unequivocally changed his life. The words resonated through his psyche as clearly as if they had been spoken by someone standing directly in front of him, and they stopped him in his tracks. "Be still and know that I am God." He stood for several moments and looked around. He was alone, a rarity in his crowded village. Then he replied into the thin air, "Which god?" But there was no answer. The words etched themselves on his memory and reverberated within his mind until they nearly drove him crazy. He had to find which god had spoken to him and what the words meant. His family tried to hide his quest and were ashamed of what they considered delirium, but he would not abate. Finally his parents were forced to send him to a monastery where he would spend his life as a reclusive monk. They gave him his inheritance and sent him away.

But he had no intention of going to the monastery. He considered his name meant something far different than what it meant to his family, and that his fate lay far away, across a vast expanse, where he would build his dreams. So he headed toward the sea to find work on a merchant ship and find the meaning of the words and the god who had spoken them.

What his parents called his inheritance was just enough money to get him to the monastery and pay his way in. After that, he would have to earn his own way by serving the monks in the fields while he learned The Way. He headed west out of his village as his parents watched, then, once out of sight, he turned and circled around the village to head southeast toward the sea. As the road got close to the first town, it became crowded with travelers, so he mingled in to disappear as part of the crowd.

His mother had packed food that would last for the first day of his three-day journey, but he decided to skip lunch and save it for dinner since he did not know where he would find food or a place to sleep.

As Jianhong walked, he noticed a fellow traveler who was much taller than most of the throng, and dressed in dark, heavy clothing. His curly hair hung out from beneath an odd shaped hat with a wide brim turned upward at the sides, giving it an ungainly look. Out of curiosity Jianhong maneuvered close to the man and began walking near him. Other travelers were keeping a healthy distance from him and Jianhong discovered quickly it was due to the man's odor. Jianhong had never been around anyone who wore such heavy clothing and sweated so profusely, creating a putrid body odor.

After walking near each other for a couple of miles, the man noticed Jianhong's curiosity and turned to greet him. At first Jianhong shied away as the man's behavior was extremely unorthodox, but looking around he saw the other travelers ignoring this exchange, so curiosity overcame good judgment and Jianhong responded. The man's greeting was odd, but not nearly as strange as his accent. The words were obviously Mandarin Chinese but barely understandable. He asked Jianhong where he was from and where he was going and asked about his plans. Jianhong was aghast the stranger would ask such personal questions of someone unknown to him, but because his demeanor was so different than his looks, Jianhong was drawn in and began to answer. Jianhong had trouble with the answers, though, since he was so awed by the man's size and massive red facial hair; and he could barely breathe due to the stench. Jianhong surmised he was one of the dreaded foreigners with horribly uncivilized behavior, so he decided it would be best to learn about him since he would probably be meeting more of these creatures as he journeyed farther from his village.

This aspect of his journey never occurred to him, but then very few aspects of his journey had. He just left his village to go across an ocean and did not think farther than the next step. Realizing this, he felt an overwhelming panic well up inside of him, and he would have stopped right there and returned home, but the stranger beckoned him to continue the conversation. Not knowing exactly how to behave in this giant's presence, he decided to follow the stranger's lead and ask the same questions of him. To his surprise, the stranger was very open and delighted to answer any question Jianhong posed. For Jianhong, this was like finding a key to a forbidden box and opening it without fear of reprisal. He maintained a watchful eye on his fellow travelers, but no one seemed to notice the strange ritual going on between them. As the afternoon passed, Jianhong became engrossed in this foreigner's story, although most of it was beyond belief. At first Jianhong could not imagine such a life as this person led. It seemed pointless, lost, and without foundation or purpose; but the more they talked, the more Jianhong realized it was for a different purpose than Jianhong knew existed. The stranger's life fit none of the traditional molds of Jianhong's world.

Another puzzle Jianhong could not fathom was his name, Chris. It meant nothing and was really just an almost unpronounceable jumble of a sound. Jianhong pressed him several times for its meaning, but Chris just smiled and maintained it meant nothing. It was just a name. *Maybe*, Jianhong thought, *that was his parents' intention in giving such a name. His pointless name foretold his pointless life.*

Just as Jianhong thought he had heard the most incredibly ridiculous story, Chris surprised him once again. He announced he was here to convert the Chinese. Jianhong was speechless. Convert the civilized people to be stinking heathens? It then occurred to Jianhong maybe Chris was mentally deranged. He had heard of this among foreigners who acted so strangely it could not be explained, but never thought he would witness it for himself. By now, Jianhong was so enthralled with Chris, he pressed him for more information instead of distancing himself as a rational person would certainly do. He was anxious to find out how Chris expected to convert human beings into grotesque monsters. Jianhong tried to phrase his question carefully for fear Chris would misunderstand it since his use of the language was so hampered by his strange accent. Chris was not at all disturbed by the directness of the question though. He actually seemed to relish it.

"I introduce the Chinese to God," Chris answered.

Jianhong stifled a laugh as the answer was simply ridiculous. "Which god?" Jianhong pressed, expecting another insane answer.

"The one true God, my friend," Chris answered with a serious tone Jianhong mistook as a sign of his delusional state of mind.

"Ah," Jianhong said, "you are a Muslim. We have a Muslim family in our village, descendants of the great admiral, Zheng He. They also believe in only one god, but I do not know what they do with all the other gods. Maybe you can tell me?" Jianhong said jokingly.

"No," Chris stated. "I am not a Muslim. I am a Christian missionary."

"Oh! I've heard of your sect from our Muslim friends. But you do not believe in one God, you believe in three gods. Right?"

"No, no, no, Jianhong." Chris pronounced the name as if Jianhong was a castrated rabbit, not a dream builder in a distant land. Jianhong winced every time Chris said it.

But Jianhong was not to be dissuaded in his assessment of Christians. "Yes, my Muslim friends have told me about you. They say they have been at war with you for a thousand years. They call you the *infidels*. Is that true?"

"Are you Buddhist?"

"No. Hindu. But we also have Buddhists in our village and I am instructed in Zen Buddhism. Why?"

"Buddhist; Hindu; it doesn't matter. To the Muslims, you are infidels too."

"But we are not at war with our Muslim friends, and they told me you worship three gods, not the one true God."

Chris was quiet at this point, so Jianhong took the opportunity to teach him more of what he knew about Christians. "My friends say you worship a father god, who lives in heaven, and he has a son god, who lives at his right hand, also in this heaven, but they never told me which heaven, only it is somewhere up in the sky. And then there is a spirit god who you believe lives in the people. Only that would mean there are lots of spirit gods if they live in people, so I think they meant he lives among the people, but I don't know if this spirit god has a home like our Hindu gods. We make nice homes for our gods, so why don't you make a home for your spirit god?"

Jianhong looked over at Chris to see if he was listening, but couldn't understand the expression on his face. It was almost like sadness. Jianhong tried not to stare, but the thick, curly red hair on his face and head, which Jianhong considered pubic-like, was so bizarre he fixated on it, unable to see through it to Chris's true demeanor. Finally Jianhong asked if Chris had heard him.

"Oh, yes," Chris responded. "I'm thinking carefully about what you have said and it explains a lot about the tensions we have with the people of Islam. I also want to answer your questions carefully. To dispel such a myth without further propagating it is very tricky. I will have to rely on the Holy Spirit to lead me."

Jianhong looked around curiously, hoping to glimpse this spirit god Chris was trying to follow, but he could not see or feel anything different along the road.

"I'm afraid I'm a dismal failure as a missionary, which is why they are sending me home. Missionary school teaches us how to share our faith in Jesus Christ, but forbids us any contact with Muslims, so we don't have a true idea of what they believe about us. We just know they don't believe in Jesus Christ, so they will not go to Heaven."

"Is this Jesus Christ person another god you worship?" Jianhong asked, now thoroughly confused by Chris's statement.

Chris saw the folly in his statement and it seemed that as much as he was trying to dispel the multitheistic version of Christianity

Jianhong had been taught, he was instead reinforcing it. How could he ever explain God in Three Persons to someone who has grown up believing three persons are just that—three persons, not one. Here, his Chinese failed him and he began praying in English as the tears wet his heavy beard. "Oh Lord," he cried, "help me to explain You to this heathen."

At that moment his knees weakened and he fell to the ground. Jianhong tried to catch him, but he was no match for Chris's great bulk, and he fell to the road beside him.

"What's wrong, Chris? Are you okay?"

"I think God just spoke to me, Jianhong. I've got to find my Bible."

"What is a Bible?" Jianhong asked as Chris started rummaging through his duffle bag. "And which god spoke to you?"

Exasperated and shaking, Chris retorted, "There is only one God, and the Bible is His written word!"

"Yes, I understand," replied Jianhong, not detecting the frustration in Chris's voice. We have The Tao, the book that teaches us The Way. Is it like that?"

"No! Not at all," Chris said, frustrated his Bible was not easily accessible. "The Tao was written by man; the Bible is the holy Word of God."

"Which one of your gods wrote it?"

Chris felt like he was sinking into a pit of quicksand, and every time he opened his mouth, he sank deeper. He felt worthless, and to make matters worse, he felt rebuked by God. He had to find his Bible.

"I heard a god speak one time," Jianhong confessed, wanting to assimilate with Chris. "That's why I'm here. What did your God say to you?"

Chris stopped searching and looked at Jianhong. For the first time in his life he saw the soft brown Asian eyes of a child of God, not the heathen eyes he had been conditioned to see, judge, and convert. Quietly Chris said to Jianhong, "God rebuked me. He said you are not a heathen. You are His child and He loves you. I am so sorry, Jianhong."

Jianhong was incredulous. "How in the world could a heathen like you consider me, a civilized person of a thousand generations, a heathen? You must be mad!"

"You are so right, my brother. I am a heathen. The worst kind of heathen. I ask your forgiveness. I am so sorry to have thought of you like that. Oh, please forgive me. Forgive me."

Jianhong was embarrassed beyond belief for this poor, wretched creature with his tears streaming down his dust-covered face, streaking it until his skin looked like a river delta. Jianhong looked around to find an opening in the throng of travelers so he could run, unnoticed, and continue his travels. But the crowd had left a wide berth around these luckless sojourners and were politely ignoring them. Jianhong could not bring himself to cross the gulf and rejoin the crowd, so he hid his face in shame as he crouched beside Chris.

After a few moments, Chris resumed his search and felt his Bible wrapped up in his spare pair of underclothes. He unwound it and opened it, then turned to Jianhong and asked him, "What did the voice you thought was a god say to you?"

"The god spoke to me when I was all alone and said, 'Be still and know that I am God.' But he wouldn't tell me which god he was. My parents sent me away because I was searching for which god spoke to me. But I decided to go across the Great Sea instead of going to the monastery." Jianhong paused as he saw Chris staring at him.

"Have you ever seen this book before?" Chris asked, pointing to the New Testament Chinese Bible.

"No, of course not."

"And no one has ever spoken these words to you?"

"No! A god spoke to me and you can't convince me otherwise! My whole village has tried that, but I know what I heard!"

"Jianhong, I'm not trying to convince you otherwise. I know God must have spoken to you. And He has written those same words in His book. Look." Chris took the Chinese Bible and began thumbing through the book of Psalms, scanning the English pages. Finally he found Psalm 46:10 and showed Jianhong the verse.

Jianhong could not believe he was reading the same words that had been spoken to him. "So it is one of your gods who spoke to me. But which one?"

"There is only one God, and He exists in three-persons, but let me explain that later, please. Just trust me that God who spoke to you created heaven and earth and all things."

"Which heaven?"

"All of Heaven and all of Earth. Can you walk with me for a while longer, and we can talk more about it?"

Jianhong did not want to stay with this man any longer, but Chris knew the god who had spoken to him, so he had to stay. He needed to learn the meaning of the words. After all, the god told him to be still, but instead, fate put him on a long journey, so Jianhong needed to stay with Chris until the puzzling words made sense to him.

CHAPTER 16

The Ranch

Jianhong learned that Chris was returning home to America, to a place he called Texas. He was trying to get to a seaport where a freighter was docked, and he was being allowed to work his way back to America aboard this ship.

Jianhong decided to walk with Chris toward the coast so he could learn more about America and foreigners. When they reached the port, Jianhong asked if he could join him on the freighter and work his way to America like Chris. So Chris arranged it with the captain. Jianhong did not know the freighter was not going directly to America, but was traveling to many ports picking up and delivering cargo. A year later, they cruised into Galveston Bay, and Chris and Jianhong took their earnings in American dollars and left the maritime business for Chris's home south of Houston.

By this time, Chris had taught Jianhong English while Jianhong had taught Chris about the Chinese culture, beginning with personal hygiene and proper clothing. Chris was ecstatic to finally be rid of the constant under-arm boils caused by wearing heavy western clothing in the extreme heat of southern China. He changed much of his diet to fish and rice, but still loved the red meat, potatoes, and corn he had grown up on.

As they drew closer to the port city, Chris told Jianhong he needed an American name if he wanted to be successful there. Jianhong still thought it was curious that American names had no meaning. But he had grown to trust what Chris told him, and if all Americans pronounced Jianhong as Chris did, he wanted to change his name. He did not want to go through life being called a castrated rabbit.

"Will you pick a name for me?" Jianhong asked as they watched the city of Houston come into view from the ship's bow.

"I will!" Chris said, delighted at the prospect. "I think you should be called 'Paul' because you appeared to me along the road to Zhanjiang much like Jesus came to the apostle Paul on the road to Damascus. And you opened my eyes and have taught me more than all of my missionary teachers ever could. I can now go back to China and be a real missionary to the Chinese. Jianhong, you are now Paul. Paul Chang. Chang is very easy for Americans to pronounce and they will know you are Chinese. So I suggest that. And to consecrate your new name, I want to give you my Chinese-English Bible."

"Paul Chiang," Paul repeated, marveling at his new name.

"No. Chang, not Chiang," Chris repeated.

Paul kept repeating the name until Chris was satisfied, then Chris wrote it down in the Bible so Paul would not forget. Then, holding the Bible with both hands and bowing, he presented it to Paul.

Chris helped Paul through customs and immigration, sponsoring him as a guest, and together they headed south. Chris was anxious to see his family after three long years.

Along the way to Chris's home, Paul announced he would only visit for a short time. He had been studying a map of the United States and decided he wanted to see Florida. Chris understood and, in fact, told Paul he was going to head back to China in a month or so. Chris explained how they could keep in touch by way of his parents' address. So Paul would head east while Chris went west, their intersected lives diverging. Each man left an indelible mark on the other, and this year together set the course of both their lives.

Paul visited with Chris's family for a month, learning what Christianity was all about and witnessing how they lived. He realized his Muslim friends were as confused about Christians as Chris was about Islam. He enjoyed going to their church with them, and was welcomed. It was so different than anything he had experienced growing up, and he had to watch Chris closely to follow along with the strange rituals, but then, so much about America was so different that he just enjoyed it as another learning experience. And, they called the building where they met God's house, so he was pleased they did build a home for their God. He was sure this was the god who had spoken to him, but still did not understand the meaning of the words. Chris told him to keep reading and one day he would know God, and then it would make sense. Paul could not seem to be still, though, and one day he packed his duffle bag, said goodbye to Chris and his family, and headed east. Paul planned to hitchhike along the Gulf Coast to Fort Myers, then traverse Florida to Miami and catch the recently constructed Overseas Railroad to Key West.

As Paul walked along the dusty road, he marveled at the vast unpopulated Texas range bounded by a wire fence studded with sharp spikes. Chris had shown him the long-horned cattle famous in Texas, but looking from horizon to horizon Paul did not see any of these large animals with horns stretching as wide as he was tall. His eyes studied the twin rows of fence posts lining the path of the wagon rutted road. The posts seemed endless as their spacings coalesced into one brown streak extending to the far horizon. In the distance he could detect a bump on one of them, the only unique feature in the repetitive rhythm of the poles. He decided to stop and eat lunch when he reached that denizen on the fence. As he neared it, he saw a work wagon appear from over the next hill.

Paul reached the post while the wagon was still a short distance away, and marveled at what he saw. It was a turtle. Who would put a turtle on a fence post? And why? He took it down, placed it under a clump of sage brush, and sat down to watch it as he ate his lunch. *Perhaps the driver of the wagon will know about the turtle,* he thought. So he finished eating and waited.

It took a long time for the wagon to reach him as it kept stopping. The driver would get down and walk along the fence for a short way, then get back in the wagon and continue. Apparently the horse was very accustomed to this action, since it would stop when the cowboy stopped, and start pulling the wagon again as the cowboy proceeded. Finally the wagon pulled up close to Paul and stopped. The cowboy got down and tipped his hat to Paul as a hello and Paul stood up and greeted him with a bow, then a handshake. The cowboy introduced himself as Bertram Brigham and inquired as to where Paul was going.

"People just call me Bert," Bertram said as he explained that his family owned all the land for as far as one could see. "I'm supposed to be mending fences, but it isn't easy alone. My laborer ran off on me yesterday. You interested in helping for a while?"

"But you're headed west, and I need to go east," Paul explained.

"I'm only headed west for the rest of today, then I'll turn north for a day and then head east for several days. By the time I finish, we'll be back at the main house, and I can pay you, feed you a great meal, and give you a nice bed for the night. You can be on your way to Florida the next day."

Paul thought about it for minute and then agreed. "I'll stay with you for a little while, then go to Florida."

"That'll be great," Bert said. "I see you found a turtle on the fence post." Bert was watching as the turtle revived somewhat from his ordeal and made his way out from under the sage.

"Yeah," Paul said, also watching it. "How do you figure it got there?"

"Not by itself, I can assure you," Bert laughed. "Not by itself. Put your stuff in the wagon and I'll explain what to do as we go."

Paul decided to stay with Bert for a little while.

Almost forty years later Bert brought Victor to Paul and asked Paul to look after him while he healed.

During the year Victor was on the ranch, the Brighams invested much of their wealth trying to find oil on their land, but they were obviously on the southwest fringe of the vast East Texas oil field and came up dry. Although the drilling company tried to get them to angle drill into their neighbors' land and tap their oil, they did not succumb to the temptation. They knew millions had been made by this method before the government stepped in and began prosecuting the offenders. The Brighams would have nothing to do with it.

Victor watched and listened as the Brighams began to talk about selling their land. He was also privy to the conversations around the dinner table when congressmen and senators visited for hunts on the huge ranch. There was also a bevy of generals, colonels, and their staff attending, and Victor learned quite a lot about what was coming down the pike in Washington just by being nearby. He began studying the maps in the oil drillers' offices and figured out quickly that the drillers knew they were out of the oil field. They also knew the Brighams paid well for the drilling services, so they never shared that knowledge. Victor was extremely interested when a contingent from NACA, the precursor to NASA, showed up at the ranch to talk to Bert. Victor listened carefully from a short distance away and begin to formulate an idea about the ranch. He bounced his ideas off Paul during one of their week-long working tours of the ranch. Paul was quiet about it and did not respond, but he also did not discourage Victor. He suggested Victor formalize the plan and present it to Bert.

Victor noticed early in his stay at the ranch that Paul followed a very regimented schedule. Once a month after payday, he would spend one night in town. He would first spend several hours with this tailor, where he'd pick up letters from his family and deliver letters that would be sent to them. Then he'd visit the library for a while, spend the evening with a family, attend church the next morning, and then head back to the ranch. Victor didn't know how the mail system with the tailor worked, but apparently it had been working for a long time since Paul had a footlocker full of letters from home. He told Victor that for twenty years he had gotten two letters a month, one from his mother and one from his father. Then one month he only received one from his mother. Ten years later, a letter came from his younger brother informing him his mother had passed and asking if he could send Paul's nephew to America. Paul agreed to help.

Shortly thereafter Paul's tailor closed his business, and with Paul's help converted his shop into a restaurant, making Paul's nephew the cook and manager. His tailor maintained a small shop in the rear of the restaurant. Paul never worked there, but checked in on it every month and read the letters from home, which were now delivered along with the unique Chinese condiments and special spices.

Victor took Paul's advice and created a detailed plan for the Brigham's land. He foresaw its development into towns, villages, and communities, all growing as the space age brought in new businesses and families. Bert was impressed, but saddened. He knew ranching was a dying business and had hoped oil would allow him to save his land, but now the family was nearly broke and faced selling the land just to survive. Victor explained that with his plan, the Brighams would maintain their homestead with a huge tract of land surrounding it and could turn it into a rural estate specializing in breeding longhorns. Victor explained how necessary this was in order to continue entertaining the brass and politicians who would give them the inside track on Washington's future plans.

Again, Bert was impressed, but sadly there was just no money in the coffers to begin such a venture. At this point, Paul, who had been quietly sitting in on all of the presentations, spoke up.

"Bert," he said, "I think Victor is onto something here. There's a new land investment company that just opened in the building next to my nephew's restaurant. Perhaps I can ask them for help."

"Paul, we're talking about millions of dollars of risky investment here. I don't think a small land investment company can help. Sorry."

"You may be right, but let me ask before you say no."

"Suit yourself," Bert acquiesced. "Let me know what they say. I have a realtor coming out on Friday, so we have until then."

"I'll go into town tonight," Paul said and left.

Bert turned to Victor. "Victor, this is great work and a great dream, and I appreciate what you've done. I'm afraid it's just not a possibility for us. But thank you."

Victor thanked Bert for listening, gathered his presentation, and decided to head to town. He needed a drink or two to drown his disappointment.

The next day a young man with curly red hair showed up at the ranch looking for Bert. Since he had no appointment, he was not given an audience, but asked to leave his name and told that Bert would get back to him. He told Bert's secretary that Paul had sent him and gave her a note. She contacted Bert using the ranch's radio, and he agreed to meet. She then found Victor, hungover and asleep, and got him to the meeting.

The young man introduced himself as Christopher Chermak, from Rochester, New York. He said his grandparents grew up in this part of Texas, and he had just moved here to look after them and open his investment company. He was looking to help with developments like the one Victor had laid out, and asked Victor to show him the entire plan. Then he showed Bert how his company, TOAFP Investments, Inc., could help.

Bert was dubious and asked where the money came from. Christopher explained that he specialized in small accounts. Accounts from average citizens who couldn't afford to put together large sums to command high returns, but with enough small investors, he could put together enough money to return thirty percent on the investments. And he always advised his investors to only invest what they can afford to lose, since the investments were risky. But his parent company had a very long history of success, and had averaged a very good return for many years.

Christopher presented a program whereby Bert would put up the land, TOAFP would invest their money, and Victor would manage the project. According to his pro forma, there would be a large initial investment for planning, rezoning, legal fees, and infrastructure, but ultimately a million dollars of land could be turned into fifty million dollars of value. Christopher required that TOAFP get one third of the profits, Victor get a one-tenth share, and the Brighams get the balance. With that, the Brighams would be getting twenty times what the real estate agent was going to market their ranch for.

"And what if it goes bust?" Bert asked, always voicing the conservative rancher's point of view.

"You keep your land to sell, we lose our money, and Victor is out a couple of years of income. But it looks like he has a roof over his head and three meals a day here, so I think he can make do."

"Let me think about it," Bert said. He thanked Christopher and went back to his chores. A week later he called Christopher and agreed to the deal.

Part of the deal was Victor had to set up his own management company. Paul gave him the name of a lawyer in town to go see, and then sent him to an accountant. Victor took his savings and opened up his company with an account at the local bank. When the lawyer asked for his company name, the letters VCM popped into his head so he set that as his name and he was in business. The letters meant nothing. Victor just liked the way they sounded.

Meanwhile, Christopher was looking at other ranches in East Texas in the same predicament as the Brighams. They were outside the oil field, ranching was not returning a profit, and the new generations of children wanted off the ranch and into Houston. Christopher and Bert arranged to buy the land, and Victor added it to his portfolio of land development deals. His first development netted VCM five hundred thousand dollars, and he was on his way. He began securing loans through his local bank and found that managing debt was more profitable than managing income, so he maintained maximum borrowing limits, always making enough money to pay the interest.

One day Bert asked him about this philosophy, since it went against everything Bert had grown up believing about making money.

"So, Uncle Bert," Victor said, referring to him as uncle out of respect, not because he was family. "What is the first obligation when you get a loan?"

"To pay it back, of course," Bert said.

"I don't see it that way," Victor politely responded. "To me, the priority is to make money on the loan, otherwise what's the point of the loan. And I can use my small amount of money to get ten times that amount, so I can make a lot more money. Paying it back is a moot point as long as you're making money. And getting a loan is pointless unless you're going to make money."

"Well, young man, I'm glad it's you and not me. I couldn't sleep at night with that debt hanging over me. But I guess I'm just old-school."

A week after he set up VCM, Victor found a note Paul had left in his room and took it to Bert.

Paul had stayed with Bert for a little while as the Chinese measure time. After over four decades he left the note on his bed thanking Bert for letting him stay for a while, and quietly left. He had found the meaning of being still, and now knew God.

Bert smiled, folded it into his shirt pocket, and got into his truck. "Tell Maggie I'm going to mend some fences. I'll be back in a few days." Victor saw the moisture in Uncle Bert's eyes as he started the engine and rolled up the window. Victor knew he was witnessing the end of an era.

Bert figured Paul had finally gone to Florida, and neither Bert nor Victor heard from him again.

CHAPTER 17

Leaving Jekyll Island

Victor sat at the large dining table on Jekyll Island pondering. It had been nearly forty years since he had used the Chinese language in any meaningful way. After Paul left, Victor struck up a friendship with Christopher as they began their first large development, which they called Westmoreland. Christopher spoke fluent Chinese with an accent and inflections very similar to Paul. When together, they conversed in Chinese as a way to maintain fluency. Victor learned Christopher had been born and raised in China and his parents had been American missionaries. Both had been killed during one of Mao Tse-Tung's educational cleansings of the cultural revolution, and Christopher and his sister were smuggled out of the country and made it to the American Embassy in Taiwan. From there they were placed with their aunt in New York where Christopher went to college, majoring in business. He then went to work as an investment banker until moving to Texas to care for his aging grandparents and start his investment company.

After several very successful years, Uncle Bert wanted a rest and Christopher wanted to go back to China to resume his father's work. Victor moved VCM into Houston and continued to grow, expanding his business by acquiring all the resources necessary to take raw land and create finished developments. He learned while acquiring other struggling ranches that second, third, and fourth generation businesses were subject to a downward spiral due to apathy and lack of vision; qualities not inherent in the generation that started and built the businesses. Victor had a knack for detecting these coasting businesses and also for finding small entrepreneurs on the upswing. He would show the entrepreneur how to leap-frog their business by partnering with him to buy and revamp the staid operations. In this way, he became part owner of many corporations, each with vivacious management and the skill and determination to grow successfully. With these companies and a plethora of land development deals to feed the mill, VCM blossomed.

Meanwhile, The Bank watched closely and gave Victor as much backing as he needed. As long as the deals were highly profitable, Victor was given free reign. Victor detected early he was being watched, but did not know the depth and peril of The Bank's involvement until Brad covertly met with him one day and told him a chilling story.

Due to the circumstances with which Victor was taken out of the hospital at Camp Pendleton and his fabricated identity, he could not be seen openly with Brad nor Joseph. His past identity was a closely guarded secret from all, especially The Bank. He and Joseph had their private vacations in Maine together, but otherwise could not meet. And Brad, now moving up the ranks of the military intelligence community, arranged occasional covert meetings to see him, but otherwise kept his distance. Victor knew that whenever he was out of sight for any length of time, The Bank's agents assigned to him became very edgy. His alibis had to be carefully planned and ironclad. He had unwittingly become a slave to their system, albeit a very wealthy vassal.

Now, sitting at the table, he pondered whether or not his venture back into the Chinese realm would relieve him of The Bank's yoke while allowing him his wealth to use for what he considered his higher calling.

He decided it was time to awaken Daniel, but heard Daniel stirring and waited quietly as Daniel got dressed and came out to join him.

"Feeling better, kiddo?" Victor said as he got up and went to the refrigerator.

"Much better," Daniel said. "How long did I sleep? What time is it, anyway?"

"You slept long enough and it's time to get on the road. I want to make it to the Cedar Island ferry so we can get to Ocracoke tonight. Last ferry leaves at nine o'clock and it's about a six-hour drive, so we might make it if we push. Let's get the boat loaded. Here, I packed your food. You can eat it while we cross the sound."

"Ocracoke, huh? Great place to spend some time."

"We'll only be there for the day. Then we'll go to Emerald Isle for the night, and head up to Carova the next day. From there, the plan is to use the Knotts Island ferry to get back across the sound and head to Richmond. There's a restaurant on Broad Street I want to visit. After we finish our business with the restaurants, we can head to Maine."

"Sounds like a plan," Daniel said as he took a quick bite of the food and picked up a couple of bags. "See you at the boat. Thanks for the snack."

Daniel headed out the door toward the rocks, picking his way over them carefully to the boat, which was double anchored in the shallow surf, riding the small waves of an incoming tide. Daniel dropped the bags in the boat, then turned to retrieve the rest. Victor was already struggling with them over the rocks and Daniel arrived just in time to catch him as he slipped under the heavy load.

"I'll get these, Victor," Daniel said as he stabilized him. "You get the boat going. I take it the house is already secured?"

"Thanks. There's one more bag over the rocks, and we're ready to go. I'm just anxious to get out of here. I thought I could handle them, but the rocks are slicker than I remembered."

"No problem," Daniel said as he hoisted the bags and headed to the boat behind Victor.

The ride across the sound was rough as an east wind was blowing the ocean waves in and creating an unsettled chop in the shallow sound. As they slid up on the beach of St. Simons hidden from the view of the golf course, Daniel slipped overboard and stabilized the small boat so Victor could hand him the bags. Daniel staged them in the marsh grass and anchored the boat as Victor went to find the car Brad had left for them at the airport. It took Victor more than an hour to return with the car and get close enough to where Daniel was hidden that they could transport the money to the vehicle.

"I thought you'd gotten lost or something. What took so long?" Daniel queried.

"Nothing really. It's just a longer walk than I remembered. And I'm not quite as quick on my feet as I used to be."

Daniel smiled. "Nice SUV. And four-wheel drive, too. Will we need that?"

"Yep. The only way to get to Carova is along the beach, so we'll be using it there for a few miles."

"I've heard of Corolla, but you said Carova?"

"Yeah. You go through Nags Head to Corolla, keep heading north till the road ends, get on the beach and drive nine more miles almost to the Virginia border. Great, secluded beach community. Sandy roads, canals out to Back Bay, wild horses roaming around, and not very many people to bother you. It was difficult to build a safe house there, but now that it's done, it makes a great place to hide out."

Daniel was curious about Carova, so he looked through the glove compartment and found a map. After studying it for a while he asked, "Victor, why are you going to Ocracoke before Emerald Isle? That doesn't make sense. And there's no way we can make the nine o'clock ferry tonight, even if we take the interstate."

"Let me see that," Victor said, a little agitated as he took the map from Daniel.

"And look at Corova," Daniel said. "I don't see how we get to the Knott's Island ferry."

Victor pulled into a gas station and started studying the map. Daniel decided to go into the convenience store and get some snacks for the trip. As he got out of the car, Victor handed him a hat.

"Here. Put this on and keep the brim low. And don't look at any cameras. The missing jet and my face are all over the news, but I don't think yours is. Still, it's best to play it safe."

Daniel nodded, adjusted the hat, and put it on. When he returned, Victor was in the passenger seat obviously wanting Daniel to do the driving.

"You're right, kid. I had my geography a little mixed up. It's been a long time since I've been to North Carolina. It sucks getting old and forgetting things. But at least I've got you to keep me straight, huh?"

Daniel smiled. "You're still sharper than a two-edged sword, Uncle Vic. And you don't really need me, except to get bags over rocks, of course." Daniel's smirk was enough to put Victor at ease.

"Smart-ass," Victor said, returning the smirk. "Joseph always said you had a smart-ass way about you. I think he enjoyed it."

"I don't know if he enjoyed it or not, but I do know he used to tell me the same joke over and over again."

"Oh, yeah? Which one?"

"He'd say, 'Hey Trip, why don't they send donkeys to college?' I'd always reply, 'I know, Dad, you've told me before, nobody likes a smart-ass!' And then he'd nod as if I was supposed to have learned something from that. I guess I never did."

"That sure sounds like Joseph. But I'll let you in on a little secret. I need you for more than getting bags over rocks. You make all this shit worthwhile. I've watched you grow up from a distance, and it hasn't been easy. I was at your tennis final and it was all I could stand to sit in a cheap, anonymous seat with people I didn't know and see your grief get the best of you. Your tennis was a beautiful thing to behold, and I know you'd be a top player today if you had stuck with it, but I'm sort of glad you didn't. Now I can enjoy the only family I'll ever know without hiding and sneaking around."

"Really? What d'you call what we're doing now?"

Victor laughed. "I guess you're right, but at least you and I can get to know each other now. And if I survive this last ordeal, maybe we can find some normalcy again."

"I hope so." Daniel paused, then asked, "Is there normalcy after killing someone, Victor?"

"You talking about my pilots?"

"No. I'm talking about Abu and Babel. I want to take both their heads off and stuff them in a pig's carcass."

"Whoa, kid. What brought that on?"

"I don't know. But I do know that as long as they're alive, I'll never be able to have a normal life. And I wonder if I did find them and kill them, could I ever have a normal life anyway? I just don't know. It's like damned if I do and damned if I don't."

"Well, sometimes we make choices, and sometimes choices are forced upon us. Either way, life goes on and changes. Nothing seems to turn out like we imagine."

"I guess so. You never told me how you got out of Pendleton. Looks like we have some time now. How 'bout it?"

"Okay. Get on Route 17 up ahead and let's take that to Jacksonville, then we'll get on Highway 24 to Swansboro and Emerald Isle. Maybe we can stop at Camp Lejuene and meet up with Brad."

"I'd like to meet him. Think we can make it there tonight?"

"Going 17 and staying off the interstate's slow going, so I doubt it. But it's a pretty drive through the country. We can make it to Wilmington easily and stay there for the night."

"Sounds good. Now, tell me about Pendleton."

Victor was quiet for a moment, obviously gathering thoughts about where to start this part of his story. Finally he asked a question. "Do you know what kills more young marines than anything?"

"Does that question have something to do with you getting out of the hospital?"

"It does."

"I take it war is not the answer."

"Nope."

"I guess the next culprit would be training accidents."

"Good guess, but not even close."

"What then?"

"Motorcycles. Marines, when they graduate from Parris Island, tend to believe they are invincible. And many have a little cash for the first time in their lives, so they buy a motorcycle and test it at a hundred and fifty miles per hour. It's such a prevalent issue that at graduation, the colonel warns the attending parents and family about this and pleads with them to make sure their first official leave is not spent near a motorcycle. The government spends a lot of money turning a green teenager into a formidable fighting machine, and it really torques them to see their investment being scraped up off the highway."

"I guess it does. What does that have to do with you? Besides the fact they were equally torqued you would try to fly a car?"

Victor looked sideways at Daniel, obviously a little put out by the comment. Daniel caught the look.

"Oh, sorry. My bad. I know, donkeys and colleges and all that bullshit."

"Yeah." Victor strung out the syllable for emphasis.

"Go on. I'll listen quietly. The motorcycles?"

"When they rolled me into the hospital, Brad was waiting for me and he knew the police were close behind. Shortly before I came in they brought in a motorcycle victim, and Brad watched as he died and they covered him with a sheet. As they wheeled me in, Brad got my dogtags and, acting like he knew the kid, went over to him as if to say his last goodbye, and swapped dogtags. By the time the orderlies got to my gurney to haul me to intensive care, I was another person."

"That was quick thinking on Brad's part."

"A lot of luck involved there, good and bad, and I was treated as a young private, not a lieutenant, but the care was the same. And I was unrecognizable, as was the motorcycle victim, so it worked out. The police came looking for me, found a corpse, and closed the case."

"What about the private's family?"

"He really didn't have much of a family, which is why he joined the Marines in the first place, and his next of kin were back East and not about to make a trip to San Diego, so I was lucky in that respect too."

"So, did you take his name permanently?"

"No. As soon as it was safe to get me out of the hospital, Brad had a new set of IDs for me and shipped me off to his ranch in Texas, which is how I ended up there. He took the dog tags and put them on a dead drunk in Tiajuana. I don't know how the government ever sorted out that one, but they never caught wind of me again, I do know that."

"How'd he get IDs for you?"

"Well that's another part of the story and I'll have to finish telling you about Brad to have it make sense."

"I think we have the time, so shoot." Daniel was enjoying the leisurely drive along Route 17 through South Carolina, its small Southern towns with main streets still seemingly stuck in the sixties. Without the intensity of the interstate highway, driving was quite relaxing. And Victor's story helped the miles tick by.

CHAPTER 18

Brad's Story

Victor finally took a deep breath and started telling Daniel about Brad.

"When Brad and I went from The Citadel to the Marine Corps we tried to stay together, but his uncles pulled some strings so he could get an assignment in Washington as a precursor to the intelligence community. So he ended up with a desk job in the White House as an officer on the president's detail. This happened to be during the time when the US was trying to oust Castro and the CIA was having pretty much a free reign in Latin America setting up puppet governments friendly to American business interests. Batista had been very friendly and the CIA was anxious to get him back in."

"You're going back a long way," Daniel chimed in. "I guess this will tie together somehow?"

"Patience, my boy. It ties together and will also tell you what kind of person Brad is. If we're able to meet up with him at Lejeune, it will be good for you to know something about him."

"All right. But we need gas and lunch, so where should I stop?"

"Try to find a small country store without cameras if you can. They may have a food bar."

"Okay. That shouldn't be hard along this stretch of road."

Daniel found a country store and when he went in to pay for the gas and get some food he could feel the grease in the air frizz the hair on his arms. He looked over the fried food bar and noticed the fried bologna sandwich. The slab of bologna they used was about half an inch thick and he guessed they used lard to fry it in. He grinned at the thought that he certainly wasn't in California anymore. Then to top it off, he saw the huge vats of boiled peanuts: plain, spicy, and blow-your-head-off hot. He decided he could easily forego the fried bologna, but the boiled peanuts were too much to resist. He ordered two fried chicken dinners with mashed potatoes and macaroni and cheese, made with Velveeta as the old, faded sign advertised, and apple cobbler for dessert. He got two large foam cups of sweet tea, grabbed a handful of napkins, and headed back to the car. Victor was coming out of the outside toilet and met him, taking one of the bags off his hands.

"Have you ever had a fried bologna sandwich?" Daniel quizzed as he opened the door.

"Don't tell me they have those in that store! I haven't had one since The Citadel. Did they have pickled pig's feet?"

"Yep."

"Pickled boiled eggs?"

"Nice pink ones."

"My kind of country store. They don't make 'em like that anymore. It's a wonder people around here live past the ripe old age of fifty, huh?" Victor snorted.

"From what I can see, they live just as long as the people in Cali who think the only permissible fat intake comes from eating avocados. Enjoy your cholesterol dinner." Daniel grinned as he took a giant swig of the syrupy-sweet iced tea. "I don't think we're going to make it to Wilmington tonight. Can we stop in Myrtle Beach?"

"Too many people and cameras there. I think we can make it to Sunset Beach, just over the border into North Carolina. There's a little privately owned motel there called the Continental with no security cameras and no questions. They have a one-bedroom apartment we can stay in."

"You think they'll have a vacancy this time of year?" Daniel asked.

"They'll make room for us."

"Figures. Amazing. Is there any place you don't know somebody?"

"Well, after forty years of dodging The Bank, I do have a few friends in odd places. If you would prefer, we can always go to Bald Head Island and rub elbows with some stars."

"I'm good with the Continental, thanks. Is it close to the beach?"

"Across the street from the pier."

"Perfect. A late-night swim and food at a fishing pier. Life is good!"

"Whatever." Victor finished his dinner and checked the map. "If you see a pay phone, let's stop."

"Are you joking? A pay phone?"

"You never know. There are a few still around in these small towns."

"Whatever," Daniel responded in the same tone as Victor had responded to him.

"Smart-ass."

"I think we'd be better off to ask to borrow a cell phone from a stranger."

"Either way. Wake me up when you find one. I'll call the motel and get us a room."

"What about Brad?"

"Give me some time to let this grease settle, then I'll tell you." Victor put a hat over his eyes and reclined the seat to nap.

Daniel started looking for an opportunity to borrow a cell phone since he had no confidence he would find a working pay phone. Bracing the steering wheel with his knee, he lifted the lid off the foam cup of boiled peanuts in coffee colored liquid and began the messy job of shelling the soggy legumes. The route along the old highway was beautiful and relaxing, but they were only averaging about thirty-five miles an hour, so the trip was taking longer than expected. Daniel could feel his edgy impatience growing. He longed for Sarah's company and wanted to find her; to hold her; to feel the calming aura of her presence and the peace he felt when wrapped in her arms. He was getting frustrated with Victor's procrastinations, but knew he had to play along with Victor's game. This was his court and his rules, and Daniel would be lost without his guidance. He took a deep breath and once again put on his game face. Maybe a long swim at Sunset Beach would allay his consternation.

Daniel saw a sign indicating Alternate Route 17 and decided it might be easier to find a pay phone along that road, so he turned off the main highway onto it. This stretch of old, two-lane, Route 17 was called Saint's Delight Road and was lined with farmhouses and small businesses. It then joined Highway 521 and became a very nice four-lane divided highway into Georgetown. Close to town the highway lost its grassy median and became a busy small-town main street called Highmarket Street. As Daniel was coming to the stoplight at the intersection of Fraser Street where Alternate 17 rejoins the main highway, he noticed a homeless man holding a sign asking for food or money. The man, in his mid-twenties with a full, scraggly beard was working the cars as they stopped for the light. Daniel turned into the corner parking lot and stopped.

"What're you doing?" Victor asked as he removed the hat's brim from his eyes.

"I'm going to see if I can borrow that beggar's phone."

"What makes you think he has a phone? He's panhandling."

"He's smoking a cigarette. In California you'd lose your corner for that. If you can afford cigarettes, you obviously don't need money. I guess they're not so discerning here in Georgetown."

Daniel got out of the car and went over to the young man as the traffic began to move and he came back to his spot under the road sign. "Hey man, you wouldn't happen to have a cell phone I can borrow, would you? I lost mine somewhere back up the road."

"Naw, man. I ain't got no cell phone."

"How about for fifty bucks?"

"Must be a mighty important phone call. Might have one for a hundred."

"Not that important. I'm sure you've got a buddy up at the next light. Maybe he'll want an easy fifty."

"Maybe I'll call him and warn him."

"Maybe you'll both lose out. Light's red. Customers're waiting. What'll it be?

"Fifty'll do. Wait for the light to turn and I'll get it."

"I'm in the blue SUV over there."

"Where's my fifty?"

"I'll be at the car. Here's a down payment." Daniel handed him a twenty and walked back to the car.

He watched as the panhandler walked along the row of stopped cars until the light turned green, then went to a low brick monument sign to retrieve his knap sack and fumbled through it for his phone. He looked around and saw Daniel standing beside his car and walked over to hand him the phone. Daniel took the phone and handed it to Victor through his window. It took a few minutes for Victor to look up the phone number to the Continental and make the call while Daniel was waiting outside the car. When he finished, Daniel took the phone back, put a fifty with it, and handed it back to the panhandler. "Thank you. Have a blessed day," the panhandler said, his standard line when receiving alms.

"We're in," Victor said when Daniel got back in the car. "Smart way to get a phone."

"Those guys make a pretty decent living that way. It's easy cash in Cali, but there are more bleeding hearts out there."

"Seventy bucks for a phone call seems like a pretty bleeding heart to me," Victor laughed.

"I guess I'm not so good at being wealthy," Daniel quipped back. "How far away are we?"

"About an hour and a half."

"Get your nap out of the way?"

Victor stifled a yawn. "I guess so."

"So, you were telling me about Brad during the Cuban crisis. He was working in the White House?"

"Yeah. Well, one day the president was meeting with his cabinet and some top brass. They were going over some operations called Mongoose and Northwoods. Basically these were plans proposed by the CIA to fake a terrorist attack by Cuba on innocent Americans and give the US a reason to declare war on Cuba and get rid of Castro."

"Sounds like weapons of mass destruction in Iraq."

"Except innocent Americans were going to pay with their lives so the CIA could go to war. WMD is a little easier to swallow."

"I guess so," Daniel said. "So the president was behind this idea?"

"No. Not at all. But he was in a very precarious situation. He was fighting to maintain authority over the military who didn't trust him and the CIA who loathed him. He was actually dangerously close to a coup. Khrushchev knew this and was scared as hell. That's one reason he was sending missiles to Cuba. So the president was being pressured into approving the plan, or face dire consequences."

"And Brad?"

"Patience, my boy. I'm getting to him. Anyway, the president needed time to think, so he called in the Marine lieutenant stationed at his door, who happened to be Brad. This was extremely unorthodox, but the president was in a dangerous predicament and figured he could throw a marine under the bus to buy some time to think."

"So Brad goes into the Oval Office as a sacrificial lamb to buy time for his commander-in-chief?"

"Pretty much. The president asked him his clearance and introduced him to the people in the meeting. Brad knew who all of them were, but he answered properly, saluted properly, stood at attention properly, and stood at ease when the president asked him to. Then he waited and listened. The cabinet and the brass were very edgy since Brad had no business hearing what the president was telling him."

"And what was that?"

"Basically, he told him the secretary of Defense wanted to use a couple of captured MIGs, painted to look like Cuban fighter jets, to down an American airliner they would claim, by a faked radio transmission, was in Cuban airspace."

"You're shitting me."

"Nope. He wanted to know what Brad thought about the plan. Brad knew he had just been put in an impossible situation and somebody of great importance was going to be very upset with his answer. He was a pawn in an international chess game, and he was being sacrificed to allow the king to move into a stalemate. Also, he knew if given the order to carry out such a mission, he would follow orders, as horrible as they appeared. But that's what a US Marine does."

"So what did he say?"

"Brad stood at attention, looked straight ahead, and said, 'Mr. President, I would support that operation with one caveat.' The president asked, 'And what is that, Lieutenant?' Brad replied, 'I would insist the secretary be required to place his family on that plane, sir.'"

"Damn. He actually said that?"

"Yes."

"And?"

"Brad said he could see blood boiling, but nobody said a word. The president broke the silence by dismissing him and warning him this meeting was top secret and that he was ordered to silence."

"What'd Brad do?"

"Saluted, did an about face, and left. He walked by his desk and out of the White House. He said he was so angry, he ran the entire eight miles back to his quarters. By the time he got there he had defused his anger enough that he could sit down and write a letter resigning his commission. He knew he had been sacrificed for politics and his career was over, so he accepted his fate and decided to move on. The bad thing was that since the president had ordered his silence, he couldn't tell anyone why he was resigning. He knew he was going to have a fight with his family over it. It was just bad karma."

"So what happened?"

"As he was finishing the letter, his CO came to the door. Brad answered the door with the letter in hand and told the CO he was just about to come see him. He apologized and handed him the envelope explaining what the letter was. The CO took it and just asked Brad to come with him. 'Someone wants to have a talk with you,' the CO said. By now Brad was fed up with the situation and got pissy with the CO. He told him he wasn't going to sit around for an ass-chewing after losing his career. The CO just reminded him he was still a marine and he would follow. When Brad got to the car, the CO opened the back door for him and he got in. Immediately, he recognized the Marine Corps general in the back seat as one who had been in the meeting. His CO got into the driver's seat, handed the general the letter, raised the glass separating the front compartment from the rear, put the car in gear, and drove off. The general put the letter in his pocket, smiled at Brad and told him to be completely at ease. He wanted to have a candid conversation."

"What did the general have to say?"

"Pushy aren't you, kiddo? I'm getting there. The general congratulated Brad, told him how proud he was of him, and said he might have saved a lot of lives today. He did admit the president probably would have found another way out of the dilemma, but after Brad left, the secretary closed the file and Mongoose was never mentioned again."

"What'd Brad say?"

"He asked where they were going. He didn't mention the meeting or respond, being careful to follow the president's order of silence. The general pointed toward the White House and told him his commander-in-chief wanted a word with him. Afterward, the general wanted to have a casual dinner with him. So Brad had a second meeting with the president, who thanked him for his candor and his service. He told Brad he would be calling on him from time to time for candid discussions. He needed someone with Brad's integrity and from outside the beltway politics. From that point on, Brad's career was set in stone. Something was placed in his file paving his way in gold."

"Nice. And how did the dinner go?"

"That dinner changed his life. And mine."

"Wow. I thought the meetings with the president had already done that."

"Those meetings were just a blip on the chart. The general's meeting, however, was a real game changer. But I'll let Brad tell you about that."

"That's not fair!"

"Too bad. But you know enough about Brad to know his intelligence career was set, so he knew where, when, and how to get me a clean, new identity. With that, I made it to Texas for a year of healing and learning."

Victor sat quietly for a while enjoying the ride past North Myrtle Beach, then turned to Daniel and instructed him to take Highway 179 into Calabash. "You'll turn right on Business 179 to Sunset Beach. The sun is getting low, so our timing may be perfect."

"Perfect for what? You have an appointment or something?"

"Yeah. A celestial appointment. Let me know when we're passing the golf course." Victor let his seat back and pulled his hat over his eyes.

Daniel went through the small town of Calabash, turned off the main road and crossed the Calabash River, then nudged Victor.

"I think that was the golf course you were talking about," Daniel said, pointing behind him.

"Sure is," Victor said as he readjusted his seat. "And it looks like we'll be right on time."

Daniel turned left and followed the intracoastal waterway for a short distance and then saw the bridge crossing it into Sunset Beach.

"Looks like the cars aren't moving on the bridge. Must be an accident or something on the other side."

"Hurry up and get on the bridge, kid," Victor prodded.

Daniel turned onto Sunset Boulevard and joined the line of stopped cars on the bridge. As soon as he stopped the car, Victor jumped out and went to the railing. Daniel followed as Victor pointed toward the western sky.

"This is one of the most beautiful sunsets you'll ever see," Victor said as he and Daniel looked across the marsh toward the West just as the sun was kissing the horizon. The sun was fading quickly from a bright yellow orb of fuzz into a well-defined orange ball painting the western sky with shades of crimson as its glow reddened and it descended into the tidal marshland.

"This is one of the few beaches on the East Coast facing close enough to south that you can watch the sun set while looking at the ocean. Listen for the hiss," Victor whispered as the last vestige of the sun disappeared into the marsh. Victor smiled at Daniel as the show ended and the crowd began returning to their cars.

As they turned around, they saw a young boy chasing a ball rolling along the bridge. He ducked under their car, smiled as he retrieved the ball, and nodded to Daniel as Daniel held up his open palm for a quick high five as the boy passed him.

"Are you a soccer player? Daniel asked, turning with him as he passed by.

The boy turned, and walking backwards, replied, "Yes, sir. A goalie." He then turned and continued to his admonishing parents who were obviously embarrassed by their son's antics.

"Let's check in and eat something," Victor said.

"That was beautiful. Do they stop here every evening?"

"Weather and clouds permitting. It's a tradition. Speaks volumes about the values of the people here. They know how to stop and enjoy some of the beauty the world offers up."

When they got to the hotel, Victor got out and checked in. He brought Daniel a key and instructed him to go to the rear of the building. Victor pointed to a small building across the parking lot, and Daniel pulled up to it.

"You want to eat first or swim first?" Victor asked as they took their luggage to the door.

"I'd like to swim first. I'm still feeling the grease from lunch, but if you're hungry now I can eat."

"You go ahead and take your swim. I'll be at the bar. We'll eat later."

"Great. See you in an hour or so."

Daniel put on swimming shorts, left the small apartment, and headed across the street to the beach. The water was perfect, with small swells breaking onto the grayish sand. He felt the strong pull of the tide running up the beach and decided to swim against it for a while, then just relax and let it take him back to the pier. He swam out well beyond the pier and let the darkness encompass him as his thoughts turned toward Sarah. He could see the king mackerel fishermen at the end of the pier with their double lines out; one as an anchor line, the other attached to it with a clothes pin and a bait fish hooked and swimming below. Many times he had witnessed the violent attack of a king mackerel as it struck the baitfish, ripped the line from the clothes pin, and began running toward the open ocean. The fisherman would jump to the rod, set the hook, and begin the ferocious fight to bring the mackerel in, free from extraneous weights or tackle. His buddies would quickly reel their lines in to give the lucky angler free reign of the pier for the protracted fight. Fishing was obviously slow tonight, and the men were content sitting on their coolers, sipping beer, talking quietly, and watching their lines disappear into the water.

Daniel decided it was time to prod Victor about Sarah's whereabouts, then ask to get in touch with her. He was missing her desperately, and the swim was doing nothing to relieve his angst. He turned toward the shore and body-surfed a nice breaker into shallow water, then went back to the hotel. He decided to take a quick shower before heading to the restaurant's bar.

After his shower, he dressed and left the room to find Victor.

Victor greeted him at the door to the restaurant and ushered him to a table in the back where a couple about Victor's age were already seated. The gentleman stood up as Daniel approached and Victor introduced him.

"Trip, this is General Bradley Brigham. Brad, Trip Furman." Brad stretched his hand out to Daniel who immediately noticed the firm, confident handshake.

"Great to finally shake your hand, Trip. Or should I call you Daniel? Or maybe Paul, now?" Brad said with an ease that made Daniel immediately feel like he had known this man his entire life.

"I've sort of gotten used to Daniel, sir, but—" Daniel didn't finish his sentence as Brad's wife stood to greet him. Daniel's knees felt weak and he grasped the back of a chair to steady himself as he looked into her emerald green eyes, brushed with a perfect hint of makeup, and framed by elegant salt and pepper hair, obviously natural, a delicate nose, and generous lips glossed with a subdued red shade of lipstick. He felt like he was looking into Sarah's eyes, only a few decades older. As she smiled and introduced herself, Daniel caught his breath again. She had Sarah's voice with a trace of an original low-country South Carolina drawl. Daniel was speechless as she adeptly took his hand from Brad's and clasped it in both of hers.

"Why, Daniel," she exclaimed, "your hands are freezing, and you look like you've just seen a ghost. Have a seat and let's get you a drink."

"I'm ... uhh, I—I mean ... umm, sorry ... I'm just a little surprised, that's all. You ... uhh, you remind me so much of someone."

"Sit down, sit down," she prodded.

Victor and Brad stood by watching quietly, amused by Daniel's shock, and let Lydia Brigham handle Daniel with the assured aplomb of a truly genteel Southern lady. Victor steadied a chair as Daniel fell into it and then he and Brad waited as Lydia took her seat across from Daniel before they sat down.

"Now, Trip, my dear young man, sip some water and tell me about this apparition of whom I seem to remind you." Lydia handed

Daniel a glass of water and nodded for him to drink with such an implacable gesture he found it impossible to refuse.

Daniel gulped the water and felt like a child in public for the first time as the ice cubes broke from the bottom of the glass, tumbling toward his face, and the water spilled down his chin. The speed of his embarrassment was precisely matched by Lydia's napkin as she handed it to him nonchalantly as if absolutely nothing untoward had happened. He wiped his chin as her gaze willed him to speak.

"Sarah," was all Daniel could manage to say.

"So this angel, or possibly devil, has a name. Interesting."

"Yes," Daniel stumbled. "She's a girl I've been seeing."

"A girl? Really?"

"Well . . . umm, a woman, I—I mean." Daniel felt purely adolescent as he tried desperately to regain a sense of composure. But every word Lydia spoke threw him more off-kilter. He wanted to run and hide, but he was glued to his chair by her green eyes piercing his soul.

"I see," Lydia said slowly, not taking her eyes away from his. "Very interesting. A woman named Sarah; spelled with an 'h', I presume, like our daughter." It was spoken as a statement, not a question.

"Yes, ma'am, with an 'h'. Like your daughter?" Daniel felt like he had been hit with a lightning bolt. "Is Sarah your daughter? Of course she's your daughter. You're every bit as beautiful as she is. You have to be. I mean she has to be your daughter."

Victor and Brad could hardly contain themselves as they watched Lydia toy with Daniel unmercifully, while luring him as adroitly as an ancient siren.

"Why, Mr. Furman, that's quite a compliment coming from such a handsome young man. Best be careful though. You *are* in the presence of my husband, *and* this woman's father."

"Oh, umm. Sorry. I didn't mean to be disrespectful ma'am, but Sarah is so beautiful and you look just like her. Sorry."

Victor finally burst into laughter and Brad reached over and patted Lydia's hand. "Give the poor boy a break, Lydia," Brad said, stifling a laugh.

"Oh, Bradley, we're just having a nice little conversation. Aren't we, Trip?" Lydia had answered Brad without looking away from Daniel, and her slow, Southern accent mesmerized him. As she used his nickname he realized she had known him for a long time; but he hadn't known her.

"Umm, yes, ma'am," Daniel said hurriedly. "Yes ma'am." Daniel felt as if he was drowning and could hardly breathe.

"Now what was that you were saying? Sarah is a woman you're seeing?"

"Well, more than seeing, ma'am."

"Really?"

"Yes ma'am."

"What do you mean, *more than seeing*?"

"Well, I'd like to spend the rest of my life with her, ma'am," Daniel said haltingly.

These were thoughts Daniel had never put into words, and to tell a stranger before talking to Sarah felt like a betrayal. But Lydia's coercion and her intense gaze so disrupted Daniel's psyche he couldn't resist telling her these innermost thoughts.

"You mean marry her?" Lydia placated.

"I guess so, ma'am. I mean, no, yes, I don't guess so, I really know I do." Daniel was fighting for air now, but Lydia was keeping the pressure at a boiling point as she calmly drew Daniel along.

"Have you mentioned this to Sarah?"

"No, ma'am. But when I see her again I plan to."

"And when do you plan to see her again?"

"Umm. I don't know. Well, I mean, I was going to talk to Victor about that tonight, but I haven't had the chance yet." Daniel wanted to look toward Victor for some sign of reassurance, but Lydia held his stare as if in a vice grip.

"So, Mr. Furman, let me get this straight. You want to ask my daughter to marry you, but you don't know where she is, and you're depending on Victor for this information, but you haven't asked him yet?" Lydia did not wait for a response from Daniel, but seamlessly continued her questioning while looking slightly over Daniel's head. "What do you think of that, Sarah?"

"Oh, Mom! You're awful!" said a familiar voice behind him.

Daniel's chair fell backward, almost hitting Sarah as he jumped up and turned toward her.

"SARAH!" Daniel exclaimed. "My God!"

Daniel grabbed her, crushing her into him like a castaway grabbing a lifeline, then kissed her passionately and unabashedly as the restaurant's small crowd erupted into applause. Apparently they had been watching the entire escapade as a captivated audience and now were demanding an encore with their ovation.

Sarah finally extricated herself from Daniel's clutch and took half a step backward, keeping her hands on his shoulders. "Well, my young squire, I hear you want to talk to me."

Her smile melted Daniel as he put his hands on her waist. "Marry me, Sarah. Marry me. Will you?"

"Of course, silly." She brought his face close to hers and kissed him to the delight of the cheering audience.

Lydia signaled the maître d'. "Geoffrey! Champagne!"

Brad looked over at Lydia and grinned. "You're incorrigible, my dear."

"Yes, I am, aren't I?" She smiled and put her arm around him. "Yes, I believe I am."

CHAPTER 19

Breakfast at
Sunset Beach

fter the champagne toast and a line of congratulatory patrons filing by Daniel and Sarah, the food began to arrive. Although nothing was ordered, the table was filled with seafood dishes and fresh vegetables in an unending stream. They took their seats and Daniel sampled everything, following the succulent ocean harvest with a locally brewed dark beer. Sarah sat close, eating sparingly while always in physical contact with Daniel, as if he were a dream she would awaken from if she dared let go for an instant. She and Lydia shared a bottle of Pinot Grigio from Chile while Victor sipped his port-barrel-aged bourbon and talked quietly with Brad. Daniel noticed Brad drank only ginger ale and was constantly aware of the small crowd. Several times he excused himself and checked with the men, one near each doorway. Daniel surmised they were security agents and Brad was closely guarding Victor as well as his packages.

The party went late into the night and Victor finally brought it to a close by announcing his retirement for the evening. He told Daniel to take the apartment, as he had taken his baggage to another room. So Daniel and Sarah anxiously headed to their suite, both feeling as if they had been reborn into a new life and a new beginning together.

For the first time in as long as he could remember, Daniel slept soundly for nearly eight hours. His catharsis complete, he nestled into Sarah's arms, letting her nurturing warmth become a womb of protection from his demons of despair. He finally felt like he wasn't pretending to be a new man, he *was* a new man, complete as he and Sarah joined as one new person.

Sarah slept fitfully, watching Daniel's slow, even breathing. Her anxiety over nearly losing him forever plagued her emotions, their rawness amplified by Mishael's suicide scene. She could not close her eyes without her mind filling with the image of Mishael releasing her burqa. She could not fathom the forces that could drive someone to destroy such beauty in an instant of hatred-fed terror.

Sarah knew her father had been engaged in this war for many years, and although he rarely mentioned it, he described it as a war on hate. He once told her how difficult it was to fight that war without being consumed by the hatred. He commented it was a war that could never be won, but needed to be continually waged, lest the entire country drown in hatred as so often happens in the villages of countries where extremist zealots establish roots. Then they grow their brand of fanaticism in the name of their god, preying on young, uneducated minds, fertile with bloodlust and eager to please at any cost. Sarah watched her father harden over the years as he tried desperately to maintain his own balance as well as his faith in the worthiness of mankind. Keeping the cynicism at bay was as much of a challenge as waging the war.

She found him late one night, cradled in his favorite chair, deeply distressed over a recent mission gone awry. Trying to comfort him, she began asking about his life's work and how he kept his perspective after so many years. He told her that although the battles here on Earth were unwinnable, it was his purpose to fight them and not question them. Suddenly the irony of his endeavors enraged her and comforting turned to an admonishment. She ranted to him how ludicrous she found that statement and how insane it appeared for him to continue. He accepted the rebuke gracefully, then smiled and told her that although Satan wins the battles here on Earth, the war was won long ago on Calvary, and for that reason, and that reason alone, he found all the strength necessary to continue. She marveled at his faith, asking him how he could be so sure. "I've read the final chapter," he told her, "and Satan loses while all those who know Jesus Christ dwell in victory in His house forever."

"Then why are you so distressed?" she asked.

"Man has a disconnection between his heart and his head," he explained. "What I know to be true in my head sometimes can't travel the twelve inches to my heart; so my heart is black with rage over our Earthly debacles. Sometimes I have to sit here in prayer and fasting until I find the strength to continue. When I look at you, that strength floods my soul, as love purges hate. You are such a wonderful blessing to your mom and me. We thought we would never have a daughter, and when she got pregnant so late in life after having four boys, we knew you were a gift from God. You make all things new again." Sarah couldn't speak and sat crying in her father's lap.

Now, as she held Daniel in her arms watching him sleep, she struggled to find her father's strength to persevere. An overwhelming sense of gloom embraced her as, for the first time in her life, and at the moment when she should find her greatest joy, she felt the foreboding terror of depression engulfing her.

Daniel awoke in a giddy mood. He was so happy to be reunited with Sarah he could not stop talking to her. He wanted to tell her so much of nothing. He rambled seamlessly from one inane subject to another, not realizing that although she was attentive, she was not engaged.

Victor, Brad, and Lydia met Sarah and Daniel for brunch at the restaurant and made travel plans for the day. They decided to meet for dinner at 'Possum Trot, a small beach cottage on the sound in Emerald Isle. Sarah had been staying there with Jonathan since leaving Houston, Jonathan thinking it was just a summer vacation. They had a cook and a groundskeeper with them, both MALTA agents.

While Daniel enjoyed his brunch, complete with a coveted oyster omelet, Sarah sipped her coffee quietly, unable to shake her foreboding demeanor. Lydia watched Sarah, immediately sensing something was amiss. Finally she asked Daniel if she could borrow Sarah. "We need to powder our noses," Lydia said and reached for Sarah's hand. Daniel, still oblivious to the undertones, just shrugged and helped himself to more bacon.

Sarah followed her mother past the bathrooms and out the back door, indicating to the agent stationed there they were going for a walk on the beach. He immediately spoke the information into a microphone hidden in his shirt's cuff and opened the door for them.

Lydia headed for the beach and watched as another agent fell in behind them at a discrete distance. She was accustomed to this level of security, but Sarah was unnerved by it. Finally, Lydia slowed the pace and asked, "What's wrong, Sarah? Did you and Daniel not have a good night?"

Sarah grabbed her mother's arm and fought back tears. Her sororal relationship with her mother enabled her to be completely open and pour her heart out, knowing her mother's response would be compassionate without being didactic. "I don't know what's wrong, Mom. I just don't know. Daniel and I had a great night. He's wonderful and I love him so much, but I just can't shake this awful feeling I have. I should be ecstatic, but instead I just want to cry. And I don't know why. I don't know what's wrong with me. I've never felt like this before. I hardly slept. It was the longest night of my life. Oh, Mom, what's wrong with me?"

Lydia found a bench near the entrance to the pier and they sat down, turning slightly to face each other. "Oh, my dear Sarah, I'm so sorry. I should have been far more sensitive to what you've been through instead of playing my little game with you and Daniel. I am sorry."

"Mom, that's not it. I should have enjoyed your antics as much as the crowd. And Daniel was so cute. Like a schoolboy. It was priceless. But instead of elation, I spiraled downward. I don't know how else to explain it. I felt like if I let go of him for an instant, he would disappear. And at the same time, I wanted to push him away and run. I felt so secure in his arms, but then scared to death; almost in a panic. What am I going to do, Mom? I feel like if I have to spend the day with him in a car, I'll go crazy, but if I'm not with him, I'll die. I feel totally out of control. I've never been out of control, Mom. It's just not like me!"

Lydia listened intently, knowing the best thing for Sarah was to talk through her upheaval. Meanwhile Lydia racked her brain for the right words for her daughter. Finally she asked, "Sarah, do you remember the swing set you got for Christmas one year?"

"Yes."

"Your dad stayed up very late putting it together, and Christmas morning when you saw it, you ran for it and started swinging as high as you could with your father watching proudly from the patio, so happy you loved it."

"I remember. I let go with one hand to wave at him and immediately fell and hit headfirst onto my forearm and broke it. Why do you ask?"

"Well, your dad couldn't get to you fast enough. He was so scared, but do you remember his reaction?"

"Yes! He was laughing! I couldn't believe he was laughing. And I was crying so hard!"

"That's right. I was so mad at him for laughing. But later I realized he couldn't help it. It was an uncontrollable emotional response. That's the way our emotions work sometimes. It's like putting ice on someone's back and they feel like it's burning. Our brains can respond to an extreme with an opposite reaction. Let's consider what you've been through recently. You woke up on a perfect Saturday morning expecting a wonderful afternoon with Daniel, but he didn't show up. You found his house in an odd state; watched as a beautiful princess blew herself up after professing her love for Daniel; got chased and nearly killed by a terrorist; waited in agony not knowing if Daniel was alive or dead, and watched as they brought him in, delirious and near death from dehydration after attempting suicide. Then you were whisked away to a safe house with Jonathan to await, alone, an unknown fate. Your idyllic life was destroyed, then suddenly you are in bed with your fiancé. It's emotional overload that has sent you into depression instead of elation, like your dad laughing instead of weeping as he carefully secured your arm and picked you up to take you to the hospital."

"What am I going to do, Mom? I'm so scared. I've never been afraid like this. Never."

Lydia put her arms around Sarah, wanting desperately to protect her from her raw emotions, knowing there was nothing to do but wait and let time do its work. "It will be all right, my dear. I promise it will be all right."

"Are you sure?"

"I'm sure," Lydia said with all the confidence she could bolster. But in her heart, she felt none of that confidence. She knew the dangers that were coming, and knew Brad was particularly on edge. Their daughter and grandson were in grave danger as the evil he had fought so hard to protect them from was insidiously enveloping them and had, in fact, nearly been successful in killing them. Lydia could do nothing now but hold her only daughter and pray.

Daniel had finished his breakfast and headed to the beach to find Sarah, anxious to start their day's journey. He paused in the middle of the street, taking in the scene of Sarah and Lydia on the bench as Lydia put her arms around her daughter. A knot formed in the pit of his stomach as the joy he had been feeling suddenly melted away. He had a gnawing suspicion something was terribly wrong and he could not help but believe it had something to do with him. He fought the urge to run to Sarah and demand an explanation. He saw Sarah glance up from her mother's embrace to see him standing there looking at them, a puzzled expression twisting his face. She released herself and motioned to Daniel to join them. He reacted slowly, afraid of what he was about to hear but unable to do anything except move forward into the inevitable. He saw the remnants of Sarah's tears and was suddenly torn between rage and compassion. She had never looked more beautiful than she did at this moment, her vulnerability tearing at his heart. He wanted to destroy whatever was upsetting her, even if it was him. He willed himself to contain his rage as he forced one foot in front of the other, drawing ever closer to Sarah's outstretched hand.

"Sarah?" he said cautiously, "What have I done?"

"Nothing, Daniel. Nothing," Sarah said quietly. "I think I'm just overwhelmed right now."

"What can I do? Tell me. What?" Daniel fought for words but was helpless.

"Would you mind if I rode with Mom and Dad to 'Possum Trot?"

The question hit Daniel like a sledgehammer as he realized the magnanimity of the request. All the joy of the past twelve hours evaporated, replaced with a feeling of desperation that nearly buckled his knees. He let go of Sarah's hand and gripped the back of the bench, steadying himself as the blinding white light exploded inside his head. His first impulse was to scream, *No. I'll never let go of you!* He looked down into her pleading eyes and melted; the image of Mishael asleep in his arms filled his psyche. He knew now he must do what he was unable to do with Mishael. He had to let Sarah go. If he had learned nothing else from Mishael, he had learned he must listen when his beloved spoke. He must listen and trust; something that was nearly impossible to do at this moment as he realized how totally impossible it had been for him at Stanford. Without the crucible of the past two years forging his emotions, he would never have the strength to let go. He released the bench and walked around to face Sarah. He took her in his arms and whispered into her ear.

"Of course, my love. Go. I will be waiting for you. I will wait forever if need be."

Sarah buried her head into his chest and sobbed, her body convulsing so with each upheaval that Daniel could hardly contain her. He held her tight until the sobs began to subside, then loosened his embrace and kissed her forehead. He released her and turned toward the hotel. He did not want her to see the tears that were nearly blinding him. His body screamed at him to run, but he ignored this impulse and walked ever slower toward his room. He closed the door behind him and fell onto his bed in a fetal position, letting the little boy in him have one last hurrah. He cried until there were no more tears, then he showered and packed. By the time he left the room the Brighams's car was gone. He had never felt so alone in his life.

He found Victor's room and knocked. The door opened immediately and Victor had his briefcase in hand, ready to go. He put his arm around Daniel, patted his back, and said, "Looks like we have our work cut out for us, kiddo. Are you ready?"

"Yes, sir," Daniel said as he picked up Victor's suitcase and headed to the car.

CHAPTER 20

Driving

"Where're we heading?" Daniel asked as he exited the parking lot and turned toward the bridge.

"We'll be headed to 'Possum Trot first, in Emerald Isle, then up the Outer Banks to Carova," Victor answered as he opened his map.

"You'll have to give me some directions, I guess. Sarah was supposed to get me there, but those plans changed just like every other plan we've made on this trip."

Victor sensed Daniel's disquiet about Sarah and did not want to exacerbate the situation with a frivolous remark, so he kept his demeanor serious and to the point. He hoped Daniel was open to conversation so he could try to help, but wasn't going to force the subject.

"Turn right after you cross the bridge, and then left on Seaside Road. That will take you back to 17 North and we can follow that through Wilmington to Jacksonville where we'll pick up 24 to Swansboro. After that you'll see the bridge across the sound onto Bogue Banks. Emerald Isle is the first town on the island."

"All right. Are we still going to meet the Brighams there for dinner?"

"I don't think so. Brad had to go to Camp Lejeune, and I'd like to drop the package and head to Carova. If we time it right we can catch the ferries up the Outer Banks and get to Corolla at low tide tonight. With the low tide and tonight's full moon we can drive along the beach safely to Carova."

"When will I get to see Sarah again? If and when she wants to see me, that is," Daniel muttered, almost under his breath.

"What makes you question whether she wants to see you?"

"Well, she didn't want to be with me today, and I don't know why. What'd I do wrong, Victor?"

"Why do you think you did something wrong? Maybe you're just asking the wrong questions."

"Don't play games with me, Victor. I'm really not in the mood."

"I understand you're upset Daniel, but if you want to have a lifetime with Sarah, you'll have to learn to walk in her shoes sometimes."

"I'm not a teenager. I've been in relationships before, and I know when someone is upset with me. I just can't imagine why."

"Imagination is a powerful force, my boy. Powerful. Edgar Allan Poe understood the power of man's imagination and was a master at using it in his stories."

"And what the hell does Poe have to do with me and Sarah?" Daniel's impatience with Victor was obvious. Victor let it slide and continued his discourse.

"Plenty. You can learn a lot about human nature from him. And a whole lot about what questions you should ask."

"You could just tell me, you know."

"And you could have just told Jonathan to watch the ball, too. You think he would've become the all-star baseball player he is today if you had?"

"Point taken," Daniel conceded. "I guess we've got two hours to Emerald Isle. Talk to me, coach."

Victor chuckled, glad Daniel's mood was lightening up somewhat. "You ever read *The Raven?*"

"Sometime in middle school, I think. Wasn't it about a demon-possessed black bird who comes to take a man's soul?"

"Well that's what most people think, and what the reviewers tell you, but I have a different take on it. What if that bird was a perfectly normal raven doing what birds naturally do, and not supernatural like the literature teachers claim?"

"How so?"

"One day me and your dad found a goose egg down near the pond and decided to take it home with us. Doc Heidi wasn't happy about it, but we couldn't put it back because it already had our scent on it. The goose most likely wouldn't have sat on it anymore. So Dad rigged up a box with a light as an incubator and wrapped it in towels and we waited. One morning it hatched while I was watching, so the little guy bonded to me. I raised him, helped him fly for the first time, and watched him head down to the pond. Beautiful bird."

"So I guess you know something about birds, too?"

"A little. When I grew up in Florida, air conditioning was not universal. We had some window AC units, but none in our bedroom, so sometimes Joseph and I would sleep in the Florida room with all the jalousie windows open. The outside door was aluminum with sheet metal as the bottom panel. One very quiet, moonless night I suddenly heard a rap, rap, rap on that panel, like someone hitting it with a hammer. Scared the shit out of me, and I jumped off the cot and ran for the kitchen. Then I looked back and saw that goose's head peeking over the panel. He rapped the panel again, so I went over and let him in. I still had his cracked corn in his dish, and he ate some, then laid down by my cot and started chewing on my shoelaces like he always had. After that, I'd listen for him at night and sometimes he'd come home, and sometimes he'd stay at the pond. But when he rapped on that door, I'd jump up and let him in."

"So what you're telling me is the raven was just hungry and

knocking on the window to get inside and be fed."

"Maybe that's exactly what was going on. A perfectly natural occurrence."

"Except that he could talk and answer questions about dead people. That sounds like supernatural demon-possession to me."

"Maybe it had to do more with the questions than the answers."

"Aha—so this story does have a point."

"Of course," Victor continued, "Ravens are one of the most intelligent birds and some can mimic words. So it is entirely possible this raven was born and raised in a house, and its owner's favorite word was, *Nevermore*. And maybe, every time he fed the bird he would say, *Nevermore*."

"Could be, I guess," Daniel said, now trying to remember the questions the old man asked the raven in the story.

"We studied that poem in junior high school, and unlike modern lit classes, we had to memorize a poem every semester. When I read *The Raven*, I selected it to memorize because it made so much sense to me after raising my goose. You see, the man dies of fright because of his imagination, not because of reality. It taught me a lot. I ended up in an argument with my teacher over it because I knew the raven's behavior was perfectly normal, but she insisted it was supernatural because that's what Poe wrote about. I told her the true brilliance of Poe was that the man imagined something supernatural out of a perfectly normal phenomenon. And his imagination took his soul, not the bird. She wrote a note home to my parents accusing me of being rude and insubordinate, so I had to defend myself to Dad. No easy task, believe me. I presented my case, and he read the poem. Then he wrote a note back to my teacher. I never knew what the note said, but she didn't bother me anymore. Didn't like me too much after that either. But I didn't care."

"So Doc Heidi didn't say anything to you about it?"

"Oh yeah. He told me to always be respectful to my teachers, especially when they are wrong. He was a great father." Victor chuckled as he remembered the clever rebuke. "So the tough thing in life is to manage our own imagination and act only on reality. Most of us get caught up in our imagined reality and act upon that with horrible consequences. But we can also use that to our advantage. Eric was a classic victim of his over-active imagination, as is common among narcissists. Their imagination makes them delusional. It made it very easy for you and me to take him down."

"You and me?" Daniel interjected. "So you did set up that tete-a-tete in your office when he accused me of stealing the Hudson Building and TGP accounts. I figured as much. Did you play on my imagined reality too?"

Both accounts had been earmarked by Eric as his, although he had never been able to land them. When Daniel brought them in, Eric had protested to Victor, accusing Daniel of violating VCM's strict protocols on interoffice dealings. Daniel had proven to Victor that both accounts had come to him through the owners, who didn't want Eric, so Eric was left out in the cold and the huge commissions went to Daniel.

"Oh no. No need to. You're very easy to predict, so I was confident in your actions."

"Is that a bust on me?"

"Nope. You're easy because you're honest and intelligent, so there's no pretense or ulterior motive. There are very few people with those qualities, by the way."

"I guess that's a compliment."

"You should take it as one. And we wouldn't be talking right now if you weren't like that."

"Oh?"

"Yes. That's the quality the Marine general saw in Brad during his White House meeting. By placing his honesty, integrity, and principles at an unimpeachable level even when it meant the loss of his career, he displayed the character this particular general was looking for."

"I take it that's why you want me to have a conversation with

Brad?"

"Yes, but not until we finish our banking business."

"Interesting," Daniel mused. "But that doesn't solve my dilemma with Sarah, or get me any closer to the right questions. Obviously I'm imagining something that isn't real, and you're going to make me figure it out on my own. I'm really not in the mood for that right now."

"I understand. So let's talk about Poe for a moment," Victor said, not letting Daniel off the hook.

"Whatever." Daniel was sullen, but he had nothing else to do right now except drive and listen to Victor, so he relented.

"You know, about halfway through the poem the old man concedes this is just a normal bird, *caught from some unhappy master*. But the old man doesn't drop the situation there. He starts thinking, and his thinking turns ominous as he tries to give meaning to the word, *Nevermore*, even though it's just a meaningless utterance from a bird. He could have dropped it right there, let the bird stay perched on the bust above his door, let the fire burn down, and waited for morning's light when everything would be fine. But he didn't, obviously. He started asking questions, looking at the ghostly shadows cast by the firelight, and working himself into a frenzy thinking about his *lost Lenore*. So he projects onto this ungainly bird the status of a prophet. Once we, as humans, find a prophet, we immediately inquire about our future. Everyone thinks they want to know their future, and we've been seeking or creating seers and oracles since the beginning of civilization. Almost every civilization, at some point, has sacrificed human lives hoping to get a glimpse into the future. It's an all-powerful aphrodisiac, one that holds the power of life and death. Now the speaker in the poem poses a question, *is there a balm in Gilead*? So he's seeking a cure for his broken heart and questioning whether he'll see his *lost Lenore* ever again. To both questions the raven gives his standard reply of, *Nevermore*, and the downtrodden lover takes this as the truth and acts upon it with dire consequences. What if his question had been, *am I going to hell*? The raven's answer would have been the same, but the lover's soul would have been elated instead of lying on the floor *to be lifted—nevermore.*"

"Nice poem, but it's sheer fantasy. Sarah is upset and I need to know what I've done so I'll never do it again," Daniel said adamantly.

"So you still think *you* did something," Victor said. "Maybe that's your fantasy. Maybe this isn't about *you* at all. Did you ever ask her about what *she's* going through? How *she* feels? Or what *she's* lost? I'll bet you spent the whole night talking *to* her and didn't stop to realize she's been hurting as much or more than you."

"Shit! Shit, shit, shit!" Daniel screamed, banging the steering wheel with his fist. "God, Victor, how can I be so stupid? Of course I didn't ask about her. I was so happy to see her and to be with her. I was like a kid on Christmas morning. It was all about me. Me, me, me! Crap! You'd think I'd know better by now."

Victor let Daniel rant, and after a pause, quietly asked, "Daniel, did Jonathan learn to see the ball by himself? Did you become a great tennis player by yourself? Or do you think I became a billionaire on my own? We all need help along the way. Some of us are fortunate enough to get it, and some of us just strike out and never know why. You haven't struck out, son, believe me. But you need to see that Sarah has lost her life as she knew it. Her job, her home, her friends—all gone. And she almost lost her own life, her son's life, and the person whom she loves most in the world, you." Victor looked over at Daniel and saw the tears streaming down his cheeks into his beard. "In my opinion, she's close to a nervous breakdown, and she's earned it. But I don't think her parents are going to be able to help her. She needs you. And you need to look at *her* reality and be there for her. She will need her time to grieve, just like you needed yours out in the Gulf, and I needed mine on a ranch in Texas. Let her cry, and stop blaming yourself. It won't help her. Your strength and understanding will help her, along with time. We'll rebuild our lives and take care of the business at hand. I know we can, but it will take time and patience. Believe me, we can do it."

"Thank you, Victor," Daniel said quietly as he wiped his cheeks on his shirt sleeve. "And you're right. I never stopped to consider what she's been going through."

"You'll do fine, kiddo. Wake me up in Swansboro. There's a little restaurant there I'd like to visit before we get to Emerald Isle. They have homemade coconut cream pie to die for."

"You certainly know how to enjoy your food, don't you!" Daniel grinned. He didn't want to stop and was still full from breakfast, but Victor was never wrong about food or when to stop, so Daniel followed the directions and enjoyed the quiet time while Victor napped, his thoughts focused on Sarah.

CHAPTER 21

The Blue Sedan

Daniel watched the traffic carefully, not knowing what he was looking for, but his edginess made him suspicious of everything. Cars came and went normally, and he began to feel silly watching. Then he saw the blue sedan. The third time it approached, then backed off, he took note. Either they were a terrible driver, unable to hold a constant speed, or they were checking on Victor and Daniel. Daniel began to watch their movements more closely, trying not to succumb to the paranoia he was feeling.

Victor was awake when they drove into Swansboro and he pointed out the restaurant to Daniel, but Daniel drove past the entrance.

"What are you doing? The entrance is back there," Victor chided.

"They don't have a drive through window, do they?"

"Of course not, and I need to take a piss, so why didn't you stop?" Victor noticed Daniel was watching his rear-view mirror as he turned right onto a small street, then slowed down and pulled into a driveway, still in view of the intersection.

"Watch for a dark blue sedan with tinted windows as it goes through the intersection," Daniel instructed.

Victor was immediately attentive to Daniel's concern and turned to look. He saw the car pause as it went through the intersection and noticed the darkly tinted glass.

"How long have they been behind us?"

"I think since we got onto 17. They're always there, but never very close and never out of sight."

"Drive around the block and back to the restaurant. I'll run in and pee, and we'll see what they do."

"All right," Daniel said as he backed out of the driveway and continued down the road to the next street where he turned back toward the restaurant. The parking lot had a rear entrance, so he took that and found a parking space near the door with enough view of the main road that he could watch the traffic. Victor ducked his head as he got out of the car and ran in.

He returned quickly with a whole pie and started questioning as he slipped into the car. "Where are they?"

"Two blocks down at a gas station. What'll we do?"

"Go out the back way and down several blocks. Let's see if we can get beyond them and into a gas station. While you're getting gas, I'll try to get a photo of them."

"With what?" Daniel asked.

Victor was already reaching over his night bag on the back seat and picking up a box. He set it on his lap, opened it, and revealed a stack of cell phones. He looked over at Daniel and shrugged. "With one of these, I guess." He looked at the notes on each phone before selecting one and turning it on.

"No more having to ask beggars for phones," Victor chuckled. "Brad gave us a few to use in an emergency. I'd say this qualifies. That was very perceptive of you to pick up the tail. I didn't know you were watching."

"Well, I don't know what's really going on here, Vic, but I know it's serious and deadly, so I'm very edgy and very paranoid right now. I've watched a dozen cars as we've been driving, but that one is the only one that has stuck with us. And now that they stopped when we did, I'm sure it's no coincidence."

"Very well done. Try to find a pump around the side," Victor instructed as Daniel pulled into a corner gas station.

Victor pulled his hat down low, got out and quickly headed around the back of the station in the direction of the blue car.

Daniel fumbled with the pump, keeping his head down while wasting time. Finally he saw Victor coming back around the building so he replaced the nozzle, closed the cap, and hopped back into the car.

"We'll know something in a minute," Victor announced as he closed his door. "I was able to get close enough for a shot of their license, but the windows are too dark to get a shot of who's in the car. Let's get back on the main road and see if they follow us."

After Daniel had driven a couple of blocks, he informed Victor, "They're pulling out into traffic now."

"Just drive normally," Victor instructed, "like we were just stopping here for food and gas. I don't want them to suspect that we know they're tailing us."

"I'll do my best," Daniel replied, watching his mirrors closely. "Should we continue on to the Outer Banks?"

"Let's see what Brad has to say first. We still have some time before we have to make that decision."

Minutes later the phone rang.

"Hey. Yeah, uh, what do you have? I'm putting you on speaker so Daniel can listen in."

"Doesn't seem to be anything out of the ordinary here," Brad said. "What makes you so suspicious?"

Victor recounted what Daniel had told him and then how the sedan acted in town.

"What's the speed limit where you are?" Brad asked.

"Fifty-five," Daniel answered.

"You're doing sixty-three right now. How far back are they?"

"About a quarter of a mile. You're tracking us with the phone?"

"Yeah, as long as it's on I can. You'll need to throw it in the water somewhere when you're done. I want you to speed up close to eighty and see what they do. Do it gradually."

Daniel eased up to eighty and passed a few cars. He noticed the blue sedan did the same, but now stayed about half of a mile back.

"Yeah, that's fishy," Brad said. "The license is registered to an Asian family from Winston-Salem. Nothing unusual about them. Two kids, a boy and a girl. I'm sending their passport photos to your phone. If you stop somewhere and can get a look at them, see if they're a match."

Daniel slowed back down to sixty and noticed they did the same, but maintained a longer distance. Obviously they were beginning to get suspicious that Victor and Daniel may be onto them.

The photos came to the phone and Victor touched them to give them the full screen display and showed them to Daniel. The father first, then the mom, the older sister next, then the younger brother. When the boy's photo came up, Daniel recognized him immediately.

"That's the kid who lost his ball under our car on the bridge!" Daniel exclaimed. "I didn't get a good look at the family 'cause they had their backs to us, but I do remember there was a girl with them. It has to be the same family."

"So the kid was under your car?" Brad asked.

"Just to get his ball that rolled under it. He seemed like a nice kid."

"That may have been a way to plant a tracking device on you which would have picked you up as soon as you got on to 17."

"But why? Who are they? And how did they lock onto us, I wonder," Daniel quizzed rhetorically.

"So what else do you have on them, Brad?" Victor chimed in, cutting off Daniel's questioning.

"They seem very clean. He's a professor at Wake Forest and she owns a Chinese restaurant near the campus. Both kids are in private school. No record of any kind. They emigrated here twenty years ago, became naturalized citizens, and the kids were born here. Apparently they were on a vacation in Myrtle Beach until they started following you."

"A Chinese restaurant? That's a little curious," Victor said.

"Why's that?" Brad said.

"I'm planning to go to the Chinese for help when we get to Richmond."

"You still believe Chinese banks are run out of restaurants?" Brad laughed.

"Paul never lied to me that I could tell. I don't know why he would make that up."

"Well, you knew him a lot better than I did. All I really knew about him was Uncle Bert thought the world of him and was pretty upset when he left. You haven't mentioned to anyone you're going to the Chinese for help, have you?"

"Only to Daniel."

"I haven't mentioned it to anyone," Daniel chimed in.

Victor continued, "It's just curious, that's all. I don't believe in coincidences like that, and I don't like it when someone we don't know is following us. It just doesn't add up. Except for dinner at Sunset Beach, nobody has seen my face. And they were obviously on to us before that. Has there been any activity at Jekyll since we left?"

"Nothing. Very quiet there. Even the boat didn't raise any eyebrows," Brad said.

"You think we should skip Emerald Isle and go straight to Carova?" Victor asked.

"No. Stop at the alternate address in Emerald Isle. Go into the garage there and see if you can find a detector. You can carry the baggage down to 'Possum Trot unnoticed along the sound and then stay at the alternate house if you want."

"You thinking we should keep the detector if we find one?"

"Yep. Take it to Carova and leave it on someone else's vehicle there. They'll have to wait for you to come back to Corolla since they don't have four wheel drive. Hopefully, they'll figure you have to come back through there to go anywhere."

"Don't we?" Daniel asked.

"No. I'll get you through False Cape State Park into Virginia at Sandbridge. From there you can pick up I-64 to Richmond. Even if they know where you are, you'll be two hours ahead of them. And, if they pick you up again, we'll have a good idea of their sophistication. If that happens, you can stop in Williamsburg for the night and I'll have someone from the farm check out the vehicle."

"You have a farm in Williamsburg?" Daniel asked.

"No," Victor answered. "That's the insiders' name for Camp Peary, a training facility for covert operations."

"I'll check in with you when you get to Emerald Isle," Brad said. "Get rid of that phone ASAP."

"Will do," Victor said.

"General Brigham, how's Sarah?" Daniel asked hurriedly before Brad could hang up.

"She's doing okay. We've been talking a lot, which helps."

"When can I see her? Is there anything I can do?"

"Thanks for asking, Daniel, but she understands the gravity of the situation, so it's better to wait until we've resolved the issue with Abu before y'all get together."

"I understand. Don't like it, but I understand. Please tell her how much I miss her."

"I will. Thanks for asking about her. By the way, let's drop the *General*. I'd prefer my future son-in-law not be saddled with that. Just call me Brad."

"Sounds good to me," Daniel said. He paused, wanting to tell Brad how much he loved Sarah and how he was looking forward to spending his life with her, but the words wouldn't form, so he just ended with, "Thank you."

"All right. Talk to y'all later." The phone went dead and Daniel saw Victor turn his off.

"So, what do you make of our tail?" Daniel asked.

"Not sure. If they're clean with Brad, then they're squeaky clean. Almost too clean. If they pick us up again in Virginia, we'll know we're clearly dealing with a top-notch intelligence group. But we'll lose them if all they have is one tracking device."

"So, on to Emerald Isle?"

"Yep."

CHAPTER 22

Emerald Isle

The rest of the trip was quiet as Daniel kept an eye on the blue sedan and tried to vary his speed enough to appear natural but also test their resolve. As he crossed the top of the bridge to Bogue Banks and was momentarily blocked from the view of the sedan, he sped up and turned right onto Coast Guard Road then made a left at Reed Road and paralleled Highway 58 until he was close to the alternate address. As it appeared he had lost sight of the tail, he slipped back onto the highway and into the driveway of the address Victor had given him. Immediately the garage door opened and then quickly closed after Daniel was inside.

Victor got out quickly, shook hands with the man who had operated the door and headed up the staircase. "I'm going to watch for our tail. Y'all find that tracker."

"Yes, sir," Daniel heard the man respond as he was getting out of the car. Daniel walked over and introduced himself.

"Hi. I'm Paul," Daniel said as he extended his hand.

"Hi, Daniel. I know who you are," the man said as he took Daniel's hand.

"What the fuck?" Daniel said, exasperated but grinning. "When do I use my alias?"

"Always," the man replied. "You're perfectly correct to introduce yourself that way. Very few people know who you are. I'm just one of the few."

"So do you have a name?"

"Sam."

"Is that your real name?"

"Of course," Sam said, his facial expression stoic.

Daniel studied his face carefully and could not detect whether or not he was being truthful, but assumed he was not, so just changed the subject. "I guess we need to look for a tracker. You know a kid went under the car to get his ball, right?"

"Yep. Where?"

"He crawled under here, and came out there," Daniel said, pointing to different areas of the car.

Sam crawled under where Daniel pointed. Daniel saw a flash from under the car, and then Sam came back out. "Your culprit is under there all right," he said, showing Daniel the photo he had taken with his phone. "I think the kid is guilty, but I don't know what he is guilty of."

"So are you going to take it off?" Daniel asked.

"Not yet. It's magnetic and may have a mag switch, so they'll know when it's removed."

"Oh. So what do we do when we get to Carova?" Daniel asked.

"Well, let's first get some info on it, then we'll figure that out."

Daniel watched as Sam sent out a text with the photo. While they waited, Sam went to a workbench and took out a meter.

"What's that for?" Daniel inquired.

"It's a scanner. I don't assume the car is clean just because I found the obvious, so I'll go over the car with this."

As Sam finished his scan, Victor came down the stairs.

"What'd you find?" Victor said, going over to Sam's phone and looking at the photo. "Is this it?"

"Yes, sir," Sam responded. "That's the tracker. I scanned the car and that's the only one. I'm waiting for info on the tracker before I touch it."

"Okay. While you're doing that, Daniel and I are going to take the bags down to 'Possum Trot. Keep an eye on the blue sedan. It passed us, then came back and parked in a shopping center across the highway. We'll use the path along the water so they won't see us."

Daniel responded by opening the rear hatch and getting the bags. Victor picked up what Daniel couldn't carry and they left through the back door heading toward the sound and the path to 'Possum Trot.

'Possum Trot was several houses away, and Daniel noticed immediately how secluded the small house was even though its lot fronted on Highway 58 and extended to the sound. Very few of the ancient live oaks native to the island had been removed to build the house. It was separated from the highway by the initial dune, and nestled into the second dune line which dropped to the small beach, typical of the property along the sound side of the island.

They climbed a short run of steps up to the deck. Daniel stood still for a moment trying to get a sense of the odd layout.

The home itself consisted of three pods connected by a screened porch that opened onto a small deck with generous steps down the grade to a landing near the water. Two of the pods were triangular and slightly intertwined each other at their base with their roofs soaring to a peak at their apex while two of their adjacent sides created two walls of the porch. The third pod was a rectangle with a single sloping shed roof rising toward the water, its slope mirroring the slope of the land below. Although each pod and the porch squared with each other, the entire composition was slightly rotated on the site so no part of it paralleled the highway or the adjacent homes. This aspect puzzled Daniel and his strong engineering senses wanted to rotate the home back into alignment with the lot.

Victor watched curiously as Daniel set the bags down and studied the house. Daniel then started exploring the home with the fascination of a biologist beginning to examine a new species of flora.

After a few minutes Daniel realized the angle created a perfect viewshed to the sound while simultaneously blocking sight lines to the neighbors. With this seemingly arbitrary touch, the small beach home became a sanctuary, protecting its inhabitants as a quiet haven among the glitz and pomp of the neighboring beach homes, which seemed intent on ensuring the owner's wealth and status would not go unnoticed. 'Possum Trot instead rewarded its occupants quietly with a subdued sense of nesting.

It was quite different than the rectangular boxes of the other beach homes that filled their lots and rose to maximum heights allowed to command views of the sound. 'Possum Trot didn't. Daniel felt its immediate juxtaposition with the sound as if it willed one to be the connection of the land and water. It seemed to participate in this realm instead of rising above it just for the view.

"Who designed this home, Victor?" Daniel asked as he completed his visual mapping of it.

"An architectural student in Raleigh designed it for a friend of the governor. When it was built, it was the only house along this stretch of shoreline."

"So the designer had to anticipate where the neighbors would be to get it situated so perfectly."

"I guess so. I never thought about it." Victor was intrigued by Daniel's fascination with the small house. MALTA had bought it and the adjacent homes to create a safe house and used this one due to its secluded nature. It was not visible from the street and easy to get to by water if you knew which stand of trees enveloped it. If not, you'd miss it among the extreme glass fronts of the adjacent houses.

"So where is the student now?" Daniel quizzed.

"Oh, God, I have no idea. That was a long time ago. I doubt he's still around."

"How about the governor or his friend?" Daniel continued, hoping to get a clue to the student's identity.

"They're both dead. As I said, that was a long time ago."

"But the house is in such good shape."

"We did restore it, and we keep it up. But it had good bones, as the contractor put it. So it didn't need a lot of restoration. Of course we added a very special feature I'll show you. Get the bags and come on."

Daniel picked up the bags and followed Victor into the rectangular pod. It consisted of just three rooms; a bedroom facing the sound, a bathroom, and walk-in closet. Victor went into the bathroom fitted with a glass shower, a small soaking tub, a vanity with two sinks, a toilet, and a bidet. Victor opened the medicine cabinet above one of the lavatories and pressed his thumbs against two fasteners holding it in. The medicine cabinet swung out revealing a keypad. Victor entered a code and Daniel saw a green light come on near the shower. Victor motioned for Daniel to get into the shower. Victor then stepped in and pushed another concealed button and the shower floor began to descend. As lights came on below them, a hidden room was revealed. It reminded Daniel of the fallout shelters he had seen in history books; stark concrete walls with utility shelving packed with various long-term food and water staples along two walls. Another wall had a control desk with several computers, each with a trio of screens. Adjacent to the shower floor were two bunks. As the shower floor was raised back up, a showerhead, lavatory, and toilet emerged. A curtain was recessed into the wall so when pulled across the open sides of the shower, a complete bathroom was created.

"This is incredibly well hidden from above," Daniel commented.

"That's the idea. It can support a team of four for a month and monitor the world."

"Why?" Daniel asked, obviously skeptical of its mission.

"Some people got a bit edgy after Kennedy was assassinated, and the sixties were rather tumultuous, so they built four control centers like this across the country. Now we just keep them updated as a precaution. Comes in handy sometimes."

"Sounds like survivalist mentality to me," Daniel said.

"Maybe, but it's a convenient place to store a lot of money, don't you think?"

"I reckon so," Daniel said as he set his bags down. "But aren't you worried about flooding during a hurricane?"

"It can handle being totally submerged when the shower floor's in place."

"Oh. Nice touch." Daniel did not mask his sarcasm.

"Well, maybe by the time we handle Abu and Babal some of your skepticism will vanish."

"Maybe," Daniel said. "Can we go now?"

"Sure." Victor arranged the bags on the shelves then stepped back into the shower with Daniel for the ascent. The walk back was quiet and Daniel kept looking over his shoulder at 'Possum Trot, etching the design into his memory. He wished he could've known the student who designed it, but obviously that was way before his time.

Sam was waiting for them in the garage with the tracker in his hand attached to a steel putty knife. "Chinese," was all he said as he showed it to Victor.

"And what's with the putty knife?"

"Magnetic switch. It activates when attached and if you take it off the vehicle, it alerts the base station. So the trick is to get it off by keeping it stuck to metal. I slid the putty knife under it and pried it off so the switch stayed engaged."

"Can you be sure of that?" Victor asked dubiously.

"The LED remained green. If it's disengaged it goes yellow and then red, or off if it's compromised or not operating. Don't turn it over though. It's got another safety device for that scenario. Your guys in Seattle were pretty knowledgeable about it."

"Same guys you got to develop my management program?" Daniel asked Victor.

"Same group. They're pretty talented. Not easy to impress, either. But your algorithm certainly impressed them. Now the bigger question: how did they lock onto us?"

"Oh, Brad called while you were out. Wants to talk to you about that." Sam hit the redial on his phone and handed it to Victor.

"What's up, Brad?" Victor said as he placed the phone in speaker mode and set it on the hood of the car.

"We're trying to figure out who these people are connected with and how they figured out where you were. We've been over the security tapes in the hotel, but they don't show anything and obviously they were onto you long before that. You got any ideas?"

"Not really. I've kept out of sight and let Daniel do all the public appearances, so I'm at a loss," Victor responded.

"Daniel, tell me all of your activities since you landed at Jekyll and anyone you saw or saw you," Brad asked.

Daniel went over his activities in detail, including his swim, his encounter with the artist on the rocks, as well as his episode at the bar on the beach. He also told Brad about getting the homeless person's phone. Daniel could hear a lot of background activity while he was talking but could not determine what was going on.

Victor interjected, "I'm pretty sure Joe was working the bar according to Daniel's description."

"Yeah, we just got that from his surveillance tape."

Daniel glanced at Victor with a surprised look. Victor smiled as if to acknowledge the superb expertise of the team.

"Joe sent a text to the DEA and then to New York ten minutes after Daniel's visit, and transmitted a photo of Daniel. Apparently he's working for someone besides the DEA. Something about Daniel piqued his interest. Anything said during the conversation that would do that, Daniel?"

"I've got no idea. I hesitated when he asked my name, but I told him what was on my ID. I will tell you, I'm not a very good liar."

Brad chuckled. "Well, that's an admirable quality, my boy. Joe is an excellent judge of character and probably sensed something amiss. We're checking the New York number and coming up empty. That's very odd. Y'all better be careful with that tail and get rid of them as soon as possible."

"Sam was helpful so we can handle it at our next stop," Victor said. "Talk to you later." The phone went dead.

Daniel noticed Victor had mentioned nothing that would give away their travel plans, so he took the hint and remained silent.

"Ready to go, Daniel?" Victor asked as he got into the car.

"Sure." Daniel got in as Sam opened the garage door and they headed out in silence. Once they were back on the highway, Victor slipped a note to Daniel. It read "Careful what you say. Head to Morehead City then Cedar Island ferry." Daniel nodded.

Victor shuffled through the stash of phones until he found the one he wanted and turned it on. Immediately a text came through. He wrote down the text and started crossing through letters and adding some others. When he finished he handed the paper to Daniel.

Daniel read the note. *Car clean. Take Cedar Island Ferry then go to Carova. Tracking blue sedan. Next communication in Ocracoke.* Daniel nodded and handed the note back.

Victor turned on the radio, found a country station and said, "We can talk now. Until we find out who that is," Victor pointed behind him with his thumb, "let's be careful and keep some obnoxious music going."

"What?" Daniel laughed. "You don't like country?"

"I've listened to Beethoven's Ninth in Vienna," Victor replied. "Country just doesn't do it for me after experiencing music like that. But it should entertain our guests."

"How's that? I thought we were clean."

"A laser on our back window can be very effective, but as long as we're talking lower than the music, we should be okay."

"Oh, all right. I'm talked out anyway. I'll just drive and enjoy the scenery. I love this part of the country. Dad used to say he could spend a week here over a weekend. It sounded silly to me, but like so much of what he said, it makes more sense as I grow older."

"I'm with you there, Daniel. Sure do miss him. I think I'll take a nap." Victor found his hat, reclined his seat, and covered his eyes. Soon Daniel could hear Victor's slow even breathing and marveled at how Victor could sleep at a time like this. Daniel was edgy and in very unfamiliar territory with the threatening environment suffocating him. He longed for the comfort of Sarah's company as the miles ticked by.

The ferry was beginning to load when they arrived, so they didn't have to sit in a long line, waiting. Daniel counted the cars behind him until the blue sedan came into view, and was disappointed when he saw they would make it onto the ferry also. This meant he and Victor would have to wait in the car, pretending to nap so as not to be seen.

Victor woke up as they bumped onto the ferry's metal ramp and were directed toward the right-hand side along the rail. Daniel watched as the blue sedan came onto the ferry and was directed toward the left.

"You watching our tail?"

"Yeah," Daniel replied.

"Where are they?"

"They went toward the other side."

"Crap. I was hoping they'd miss the boat."

"Me too," Daniel said, counting cars going left so he could determine about where they would be. "I think they'll be on the inside lane about four cars in front of our position. But we're out of view. Should we stay in the car?"

"That would be our best move. I was really hoping to get out and enjoy the ride."

"Same here," Daniel said as he reached onto the back seat to get his hat. He reclined his seat and positioned his hat so it covered his face but still gave him a peephole through which he could watch the cabin windows on the upper level of the ferry. After the ferry was out into the sound, Daniel nudged Victor.

"Isn't that the kid who got under our car?" Daniel was motioning upward.

Victor shifted his hat and had to move his seat to get a glimpse of the boy. "Looks like him. Any sign of the adults or his sister?"

"Nope, but I'm watching. I'm tempted to go strike up a conversation with him–see if I can figure anything out about what they want."

"Well, let's avoid that temptation for awhile, okay?"

"Sure. Bummer though. He looks like a nice kid. Wonder who he's mixed up with that he would plant trackers on cars?"

"Good question. I guess we'll learn soon enough." Victor readjusted himself in his seat and watched the calm waters of the Pamlico sound roll past. Finally the docks of Ocracoke came into view signaling the two-and-a-half-hour ride was coming to an end. As the crew of the ferry secured the vessel and started the deboarding process, Victor checked in with Brad. He had nothing new to report on the New York number.

"Hey Brad," Victor asked, "what did Joe do in New York before tending bar on Jekyll? Wasn't he in the restaurant business?"

"I think so," Brad answered.

"Can you find out something about his restaurant?"

"Sure. Why?"

"Just a hunch. Thanks." Victor hung up.

The half-hour ride north on Ocracoke Island was uneventful, and the blue sedan stayed out of sight. At the Hatteras Island ferry it caught up and waited in line several cars behind Daniel. Once across the sound to Hatteras, it lagged behind again, obviously hoping not to be noticed and using the tracking device to keep tabs on Daniel and Victor.

"We're making good time now," Victor announced as he pulled out a tide chart. "Low tide at Corolla is in three hours and we should make it in two, so that will be perfect. We should be at the house before midnight."

"Aren't you hungry?" Daniel quizzed.

"Starving, now that you mention it. We've got an hour's leeway, so let's hit Sonny's Restaurant. We can park across the highway and watch for the tail to pass then sneak in the back and be okay."

After they parked they watched as the blue sedan cruised past. As it went out of sight Victor's phone rang.

"Hello Brad. What's up?"

"You guys stop to eat?"

"Yep. Sonny's. They still have the Blackened Hatteras?"

"As far as I know. We haven't been there in a while. Lydia usually gets the crabmeat imperial, and I'm old school and just get a platter. It's all good and not too fancy."

"You think we'll be okay going in?"

"If I were you, I'd call in the order and let Daniel pick it up."

"Crap. Okay. I'm ready for a break, but I guess it can wait till we get to Carova."

Brad paused as if reading something, then continued, "This New York connection is an odd ball, so it's best to keep out of sight until we know who they are and what they want. Let me call in your order just to be safe. It'll be in my name and paid for. Give 'em twenty minutes."

"What's odd about it?" Victor asked.

"We can trace it to an area, but not a specific location. It's like it's all over a several block area."

"What'd you find out about Joe's restaurant?"

"Hold on. Let me check." Brad was gone for several minutes, then back on the line. "The name of his restaurant was Mekong. His wife is Vietnamese. He met her in Vietnam during the war. Seems it was a unique setup. He ran the bar, specializing in about a hundred beers from small local breweries. Sort of the forerunner to the craft brewery industry. She ran the restaurant."

"Sounds familiar. Didn't they have several children?"

"I'm not sure. We can check."

"Do that, and see if one of them moved to Richmond and opened the restaurant on Broad Street with the same name and setup. I was hoping to go there after I visited the Chinese restaurant down the street."

Daniel shook his head and grinned. Victor knitted his brow as if to ask what Daniel found so amusing. Daniel waved it off for a later discussion.

"Here's a funny coincidence I just saw," Brad said. "His restaurant was in the same area as the phone call. Was that your hunch?"

"It was, and I don't believe that's a coincidence. Joe speaks Mandarin better than me, and I'll bet he sold to a Chinese family."

"You're right. That gives us something to go on to find out about the call. Good hunch, Victor."

"Thanks, Brad. We'll call from Carova." The phone went dead and Victor turned to Daniel. "You've been quiet. What's on your mind, and what'd you find so amusing?"

"That's two very different questions. Which one do you want me to answer?"

"Pick one and go for it," Victor said.

"Okay. Some of the same questions keep nagging me, but they seem frivolous relative to Abu and his cohort. And then there's the money. I want to talk about it but I don't want to appear trite. You understand? I mean, I feel like I should be doing something about Sarah, but I don't know what. Then I start wondering things about you and what's going on, and I feel guilty for even thinking about something other than protecting Sarah and getting out of this mess. What are you smiling at? It's not funny."

Victor kept his grin and replied, "I understand completely, Daniel, and believe me it's okay to think about other things. In fact, it's healthy. For someone like you to be asked to put your brain in neutral for any amount of time creates a very untenable situation. You know, the Marine Corp has manuals about how to deal with down time since a marine spends so much time waiting for action. That's one part of my time in the service I didn't like at all and wasn't very good at, but after a year with Paul, I learned how to let go of the anxious moments and be patient for action. I guess it's a zen thing, but you can use down time effectively. It's really a mindset."

"Is that how you can just drop off to sleep any time, regardless of the situation?"

"Absolutely. Control what we can as best we can, and when we can't—let it go. When the time is right, we act. Until then, we prepare as best we can. Sleep is part of that preparation. Now, it will be very healthy for you to ask your questions. It'll give your mind a break from Abu by focusing on something else. You'll find that when it's time to come back to the question of Abu, you'll be better prepared and your perspective of the whole situation will be far healthier."

"Well, I still feel guilty about it," Daniel confessed.

"You know, I knew a doctor who ran a large mental hospital, and he had an interesting take on guilt. He swore if he could get rid of guilt, he could close his hospital. Just saying."

"Easier said than done, I guess. But I'll try to curtail the guilt so we can talk about other things."

"Like what?" Victor asked. "And what time is it? I like my seafood piping hot, so I don't want it to sit too long."

Daniel grinned again.

"What?" Victor said, noticing the same expression as before.

"Nothing. I'll go on over and wait on it," Daniel offered. "We can talk about it on the way to Carova."

"Good idea," Victor conceded.

Daniel put on his hat, pulled the brim low, and got out of the car. Ten minutes later he returned with a box of food and drinks.

"Brad sure knows how to order," Daniel said, sampling one of the fried shrimp and following it with an onion ring.

"Did he get me the Blackened Hatteras?" Victor asked.

"Yep. Here you go." Daniel set the box on the center console and they proceeded to dish out the food and wash it down with sweet tea. They finished the meal with some of the pie Victor had bought then found a dumpster and cleaned out the debris.

CHAPTER 23

Carova

Satisfied and back on the road, Daniel began watching for the blue sedan. It didn't take long for him to notice them about half of a mile back. He decided to let them be and move onto other issues as Victor had suggested.

"So, Victor, when I woke up in your office, you were praying?"

"Yes, I was."

"You mind if I ask what you were praying about? No, forget that question. What I'm more curious about is what you said about being a religious man. If you're not religious, *why* were you praying?"

"I'll tell you that being religious and believing in God are not really the same thing. But I don't think that's the crux of your question, is it?"

"Probably not, but how do I ask you about that situation? I never knew much about your religious beliefs, never saw a Bible anywhere near you, never knew you to go near a church, but then I wake up to you praying rather fervently over me. Don't get me wrong, I appreciate it. Dad never failed to tell me he prayed for me daily. But I just figured that's what dads do. It never really made much of an impact on me. But for some reason, you praying over me did make an impact."

"Well, Daniel, I'll have to confess. I can't say I ever prayed before in my life, except when I was a kid and had to pray when we went to church. Joseph was the prayer; I was the doer. Always wanting to do something, and never wanting to stop long enough to think about praying. In fact, the only time I felt like I really needed God, and wanted God, I felt totally abandoned."

"Was that when your wife left you?"

"Yes," Victor said, letting out a long breath. "I told Joseph that if God couldn't help me then, I had no use for Him. I'd live my life without Him."

"What did Dad say?" Daniel queried.

"He said he would continue to pray for me. I wanted to hit him, I was so frustrated with him. But he hugged me and kept his mouth shut, so I calmed down."

"So did you ever talk about religion with him after that?"

"Oh yeah, lots. I was always trying to stump him. But he couldn't be fazed."

"Why do you think he was so steadfast? I mean, y'all grew up in the same house but turned out very different."

"Every kid is different, Daniel. I've never raised a child of course, but I've seen plenty and helped with families in trouble. And what I know is that every child is unique. You just can't force a programmed behavior on kids. You can develop them, and you can certainly screw them up, but you can't force them to turn out any particular way. So me and Joseph were very different, but got along and enjoyed the time we could spend together."

"So you hadn't prayed before that? Something must've really changed then."

"A couple of things changed. The first was Joseph's death. That hit me pretty hard, and I felt betrayed again. So all the anger I had worked through over the years with Paul and Joseph seemed to flood back into my life. And once I solved the Abu riddle, I was very anxious to kill him."

"Why didn't you go after him then?"

"By the time I figured it out, he had disappeared. Even Brad couldn't find him, or at least he said he couldn't. But I kept searching, which is why I was very diligent about looking through the Palo Alto paper before it got to you. And that was the pay dirt."

"You said a couple of things?"

"Yes. The other was a letter from Joseph with his will. It was rather lengthy, but the gist of it was about you and also about his relationship with Jesus Christ. He said he always wanted to tell me his story, but if I was reading this letter, then he hadn't told me, feeling I wasn't ready to receive it yet. And now that he was gone he'd leave it to me in a letter and let God do the rest."

"Can I read it sometime?"

"Someday, yes. Joseph asked me to share it with you when you were ready."

"When will that be?"

"Hell if I know, kid. But Joseph said I'd know, so one day when I hand it to you, we'll both know you're ready. Whatever that means. So like Joseph, huh?"

"I guess so. So what was in it about me, and did that or the religious part change you?"

"It was both. He asked that I take care of you. Obviously it was written when you were much younger, but I still respected what he said. I would've done it anyway, but he did have some specific requests."

"Like what?"

"Like that I not give you wealth. He thought it was very important that you make your own way in the world. But so far, you've more than earned your keep, and I'm sure that will continue."

"Thanks, I guess. But truthfully, his inheritance was enough for me to live on if I wanted to. It wasn't wealth, but a comfortable existence, so money hasn't been an issue for me until now."

"What d'you mean, *now*?" Victor looked surprised.

"Those satchels of money are the issue. Obviously they sparked someone's interest, and you seem to be on the run due to money and I'm locked in with you. Not that I want to abandon you or anything, it just seems that wealth has cost me my life, and I'm trapped by it. But without it, Abu would have his way with me in short order. So it's another Catch-22."

"Interesting perspective, Daniel. And truer than you might realize. The wealthiest in the world are the most enslaved, but try to explain that to someone who lives paycheck to paycheck trying to keep up with the mortgage and feed a family. The idea of freedom can be very elusive, indeed."

"Yeah, I guess so. And I'm sorry, I didn't mean to be disrespectful, it's just—"

Victor interjected, cutting Daniel's sentence short. "Hey kid, I appreciate your candor. I hope you don't feel like you have to be reserved with me. We're all we've got, and we're real family. And that's a luxury that has always eluded me, so please, let's keep an open dialogue. And believe me, I trust that you don't mean anything disrespectful."

"Thanks. Now tell me how Dad's letter changed you before we get to Corolla."

"I was still angry with God, but after I read his letter, I started to read the Bible. I didn't expect to get anything out of it, but since he had asked me to, and I felt I might need to so I could take care of you, I started. I got his Bible chocked full of his notes, and started reading. I figured I could just ignore the myths and read it for your sake."

"Myths?"

"Yeah, myths. From what I learned in Sunday School, and what I heard from people who preached, I figured it was riddled with myths. You know, unbelievable stuff, like the entire universe being created five or six thousand years ago. I guess I had learned that in Sunday School, and just assumed the rest of it was more of the same."

"Did you ever ask Dad about that?"

"About creation?"

"Yeah."

"We talked about it once, as I remember. I think it started with a discussion about evolution and morphed into the creation story versus the big bang theory."

"And what was his take on it? Did he believe in creation or evolution or the big bang?"

"Funny thing is he didn't see any conflict in any of it. When I pressed him for an answer, he just told me to read it for myself and decide. He said to pay attention to the time between Joseph's story and Moses. According to your father, God isolated Jacob's offspring in Goshen, and there, his offspring became the Jewish nation as promised to Abraham. And they didn't look like Egyptians which is why Moses knew he wasn't Egyptian, but Jewish. Then, Ecclesiastes talks of seasons and changes, which Joseph said alluded to evolution, which God created. Of course I didn't read it until after his death, but I wish I had. I think our discussions would have been much more meaningful."

"How so?" Daniel was still trying to learn more about his father, so he wanted to keep Victor talking about him.

"Well, our discussions were mostly me asking rhetorical questions in order to poke fun at religion and mock God. But Joseph knew that was just a ruse to cover my pain, so he usually used the opportunity to let me talk. He was always a good listener and never tried to defend God or push some healing words on me. He did ask me a question one time that has always stuck with me. He had a way of doing that, you know. We had a discussion where I said thousands of words and he said about twenty, and the thousand are gone and forgotten, but the twenty seem to be etched on my soul. Funny, huh?"

"Sure. What'd he ask you?"

"He said, 'Vic, if I answered all of your questions, and proved to you the Bible is the true word of God and not a bunch of myths, as you claim, would you accept Jesus as your Lord and Savior?'"

"And your answer?"

"No. I wasn't interested, and I didn't need Jesus in my life. God had already taken everything, so why would I want anything to do with Him?"

"What'd he say to that?"

"He didn't seem surprised. He just said he'd keep praying for me. I told him he could waste his time any way he wanted, but I had become a millionaire on my own and was well on my way to my first billion without any help from God, so I'd just keep it that way, thank you."

"And then?"

"He said, 'Are you sure about that?' I told him, 'Hell yes.' And he just smiled. Damn if he didn't put a cloud of doubt all over my psyche. It really pissed me off. And the bad thing is that even though I'm deemed to be a 'self-made billionaire' in the media, I'm quickly finding out I've done almost nothing by myself. And my only talent, which is my vision to see what a piece of land can be and know how to make it happen, may be, as Joseph put it, my God-given gift. But one thing I know for sure, Daniel, is Joseph never gave up on my salvation, and at your bedside I was praying that God hadn't given up on me either, and that you'd be okay, and that I would get to know you better. I guess I should be more careful what I pray for, huh? As Joseph said, God answers prayers in unexpected ways sometimes. And here we are, on the run from someone we don't know, with a load of hot cash, trying to get to a terrorist and send him to hell, and at the same time getting to know each other. Yeah, I need to be more careful what I pray for," Victor chuckled.

Daniel laughed along with Victor. "Well, Uncle Vic, I don't really understand all that's going on, but I do appreciate you rescuing me and providing the opportunity to have a family I never imagined. By the way, we're coming to the end of the road here. What do I do?"

"Where is our tail?"

"They're still about a half of a mile back. I noticed one of their headlights is slightly brighter than the other, so it's been easy to keep track of them."

"Good. Okay, then, get in four-wheel drive and head straight out onto the sand."

Daniel slowed to a snail's pace and cautiously drove between the two small dunes into the thick sand.

"Don't slow down too much," Victor warned. "Just keep a steady pace until we can see the water." Victor paused, looking intently toward the water. "Looks like the tide chart was right about low tide, so as soon as you get onto the hard sand, turn left and follow the shoreline. Reset your trip odometer and measure nine miles. Keep your bright lights on and watch for tree stumps. They're the remains of old forests taken over by the ocean and they can destroy your car. Otherwise, it's smooth sailing at low tide."

"What do you do at high tide?"

"Then you have to drive up there," Victor said, pointing to his left. "Deep sand up there and slow, rough going compared to this."

Daniel noticed it was like driving on a new highway—smooth as silk. And except for the warning about the tree stumps, it seemed like it would be an easy nine miles. "Looks like a car approaching," Daniel said.

"Just stay to your right. He'll go to your left. There's plenty of room. There may be some fishermen out, but they park perpendicular at the edge of the deep sand, so you're okay."

"All right," Daniel replied. "The full moon sure makes it nice."

"Yep. Beautiful night," Victor said as he looked at the glittering blaze of the moonlight reflecting on the water. "Looks like some nice breakers out there too."

As the odometer flipped to nine miles, Victor instructed Daniel to slow down and look for a flagpole on the dunes. When Daniel found it, Victor showed him where to cross in the opening between the dunes. "Keep your pace up and be ready to give it more gas without breaking traction."

Daniel felt the vehicle bog down as it transitioned into the deep sand and he pushed the accelerator to urge the four-wheel drive through the dunes. The steering wheel started jerking wildly as they traversed the sand moguls, and Daniel felt the computer feeding power to each wheel as necessary to get them over the hump. "Impressive four-wheel drive," Daniel commented as they cleared the dune and turned onto the sand road. "Now what?"

"Drive around till I get my bearings and see something I recognize. All these roads look the same and there're no signs except what some of the homeowners have put up. So I'll have to find a landmark, and then figure out how to get to the house."

"All right."

Daniel drove around the dark roads, avoiding deep ruts filled with water, and following tire tracks around obstacles while Victor instructed him where to turn. Daniel began to notice they were going down the same roads over and over, but Victor just kept prodding him on as he got his bearings. Daniel noticed that many of the dwellings here were little more than pieced together homemade bungalows, all in varying states of repair or construction. It was the very opposite of places like Boca Raton, which oozes ostentatious money-to-burn wealth. But what he also felt was the immense sense of freedom inherent when there is no self-conscious effort shown to impress your neighbor or the world. This community knew how to live in three-quarter time, as Jimmy Buffet would say. And since everything they had here was either hauled up the beach or brought across the sound by boat, there was very little unnecessary fluff. Obviously a relaxed lifestyle was paramount.

Finally Victor had him slow down near a small, orange-painted shack. Suddenly Daniel hit the brakes hard and slid to a stop as a horse ambled into his path looking sideways at him, then disappeared into the pines.

"Stay still for a moment," Victor said. "There's probably another one or two with him."

"Is he loose from somebody's corral?" Daniel asked.

"Nope. He's one of the herd of famous wild horses here. They just roam the area. There's a whole business in Corolla built around bringing tourists up here just to drive around and get a glimpse of them. Sort of like the tourists in Florida who pay for boat rides just to see a wild alligator. For the residents, they're just part of the landscape, leaving piles of poop in their yard to be cleaned up."

"Cool," Daniel said as he watched the roadside for another horse to appear.

While Daniel was watching for horses, Victor took the tracking device, still magnetically attached to the putty knife, and went to the small garage of the orange house. Daniel turned the car slightly to give Victor a little light and watched as he buried the device in the sand near the door. When he got back in the car, he instructed Daniel to turn around and go to the last intersection, then go two blocks over toward the sound and turn right. As Daniel was executing the turn, he asked Victor about burying the tracking device.

"If our tail gets a four-wheel drive and comes looking for us, they'll think our car is in that garage and watch that house. Since there are no windows and you can't see into the garage, they'll sit for a long time before they discover we're not around."

"Good idea," Daniel said. "But won't they just wait for us to come back to Corolla?"

"I hope they do. They'll be disappointed with that also. Tomorrow we'll head north through the state park and go through Virginia Beach, where we'll pick up I-64 and head to Richmond. We'll probably be in Richmond by the time our friends here are able to get a vehicle onto the beach and come looking. Now let's go find the house. I use that orange house as my homing device. Otherwise I'd be very lost around here," Victor chuckled.

As Daniel eased along the road, Victor told him to look for some pine stumps marking a semi-circular driveway.

"They won't look like much, but that's the way I know I'm at the right place," Victor said. "Otherwise the house is kind of hidden by the pines."

Daniel found the short logs standing on end and turned into the drive. The arc of the driveway concealed most of the house as it wrapped around a small stand of pines. The house was a rather typical beach house with a garage on the ground level and steps going up to a second-floor deck and the main living area. A second flight of steps on the main deck led to a small third-floor deck with a satellite dish. Daniel watched as Victor climbed the stairs and fumbled with a control box until some yard lights came on. Victor came back down to the main deck, opened the front door, and motioned for Daniel to go in. Daniel had gathered their clothes bags and the remaining satchel of money, so he turned sideways to squeeze the load through the door and set the bundle down.

"Let's find some food, kiddo. I'm famished," Victor said as he headed for the refrigerator. "You hungry?"

"Sure," Daniel said. "How far is the beach from here?"

"Four blocks," Victor said. "Continue down the road for about a hundred yards and turn right at that cross street. It'll take you straight to the ocean. You going for a walk or something?"

"Thought I might take a swim."

"At night? Alone? With the sharks?" Victor was obviously not happy with the idea.

"I've got to relieve some tension. I want to take a short swim, and I'll jog there and back, so I won't be gone too long."

"Shit. Okay. I'll leave a plate of food out for you. Here have a beer for the road and don't tarry too long, please. Your room is on the left through that door." Victor motioned to the opening beneath the balcony. "I'll take the suite upstairs."

"All right. Thanks."

Daniel was anxious for some alone time and took the beer as he headed out the door. Out on the road, he found jogging was too dangerous since he couldn't see the roughness of the road, so he just enjoyed the beer as he walked toward the ocean. He could hear the waves breaking, and he began to feel his tension dissipate as the sound and smell of the water grew. Looking up and down the desolate beach, he breathed in the heavy salt air and sighed. Looking north he could see the outline of a fence which he assumed was the Virginia border. He hadn't realized how far up the beach they had driven, but at least they wouldn't have far to go in the morning. Daniel took off his shoes and shirt and used them and the empty beer bottle to mark where to go back across the dunes, then headed into the water. As a wave broke over him, he dove to the bottom and swam underwater until he felt like his lungs were going to burst, then he broke the surface and gulped air. *God, that felt good*, he thought. The waves were breaking nicely and he caught one to body surf back to the shore. The tide was apparently running swiftly southward as he had trouble finding where he had left his stash. He laid down on the hard sand with his shirt and shoes under his head and stared at the stars. For the first time since that fateful Saturday morning, he felt a respite of relief. Daniel couldn't help but feel this was the calm before the storm. He knew it would be short-lived as the next day's trip to Richmond promised to be fraught with risk for Victor. But Daniel also knew the sooner Victor concluded his business, the sooner he could be back in Sarah's arms. He fell asleep thinking of Sarah.

CHAPTER 24

Richmond

"Daniel!"

Daniel awakened to Victor's shout and jumped to his feet. "Over here," Daniel replied.

"Shit, kid! You scared me. You know how long you've been out here? Jesus!"

Daniel looked at the moon now hovering close to the horizon and knew it would be morning soon.

"I must've fallen asleep. Sorry, Victor."

"Well, I'm glad you're okay. You ready to head in now?"

"Sure."

The walk back was quiet, both men enjoying the cool predawn air and the peacefulness of Carova. Daniel noticed the eastern sky over the Atlantic was turning a pale pink with the approaching dawn.

Back at the house Victor found enough frozen food to fix a decent breakfast while Daniel showered. As he was buttering biscuits, he heard a helicopter flying low and apparently making passes along the roads. He picked up the phone to call Brad, but it rang before he could push a button. It was Brad.

"Morning," Victor said. "I was just calling you. You haven't left for Africa? There's a helicopter flying around here. Obviously looking for something."

"Getting on the plane now, but I was calling about the helicopter," Brad said. "We had a private jet fly in from China this morning and shortly afterward they rented one of Gibb Aviation's helicopters and headed your way. I'm getting a park ranger to pick you up and take you through False Cape. He'll get you to Camp Pendleton, and I'll have a car waiting for you outside the gate. Cover up when you get in the Ranger's truck so it looks like he's alone."

"Got it. When will he be here?"

"He's on his way. He'll wait to stop until the helicopter's not around so be ready to jump in."

"Thanks, Brad. Any idea who's in the helicopter?"

"Report from Customs just says some businessmen from a land development company looking around. Everything appears perfectly normal with them. I called Andrew and he said he would be flying them randomly up and down the coast. They paid cash up front for the day."

"Thanks."

As Victor was ending the call, Daniel came out of the bathroom. "Smells good for having no food around," he said jokingly as he sat down at the bar and helped himself to bacon.

"Sorry, but we'll have to eat quickly and be ready to leave soon. A park ranger is coming to pick us up and take us to Camp Pendleton."

"What's up?"

"You hear the helicopter?"

"Yeah. Sounded sort of low."

"Brad thinks they're looking for us, so he's getting us through the park and on our way to Richmond in another car."

"All right. Did I hear you say Camp Pendleton? Like, California?"

"Camp Pendleton, Virginia Beach. Not quite as well known as the one in California, but older, and named after a brigadier general who served with Robert E. Lee."

"Oh," Daniel said and grabbed a biscuit before heading to his room to pack.

Victor was watching through the front window when the park ranger's truck stopped on the road, not coming into the driveway. He called to Daniel who immediately grabbed the baggage and ran to the truck. They both got in the backseat of the crew cab and the ranger hit the gas before they could close the door.

"If you hear the helicopter, just lean down so you're not visible through the windows," the ranger said. "They're about five miles south right now, so we should be in Virginia before they can get back up this way."

By the time the ranger had gotten out to open the border gate, driven through and closed the gate behind, the helicopter was flying low along the beach, obviously checking out the truck. Daniel and Victor leaned over toward each other on the seat and placed baggage over themselves for concealment. After a cursory check of the truck, the helicopter turned and headed south, resuming its search along the roads in Carova.

The ride to Camp Pendleton was quiet. The ranger assumed there was an air of secrecy about his early-morning mission, so he kept quiet, waiting for Daniel or Victor to offer any introductions. Daniel followed Victor's lead and also kept quiet while enjoying the park, which gave glimpses of the rising sun over the ocean as well as occasional views of Back Bay to the west. He found it hard to fathom that such a jewel as this existed in an area rife with development. He made a mental note to come back here with Sarah for a camping and hiking weekend.

As they approached the gate at Camp Pendleton, a Marine sergeant motioned for them to turn into a parking lot. He handed the ranger a set of keys and walked away. Victor took the keys, thanked the park ranger, and motioned for Daniel to get out. After the ranger left the parking lot, Victor started walking around while pressing the auto-unlock button and listening for the beep of the horn.

"Nice ride," Daniel commented when he heard the BMW's horn sound off. "A six-series. This should be a fun ride to Richmond."

"Looks like it could be. Brad will surprise you sometimes. This must be his treat to his future son-in-law," Victor snorted as he bent over to get into the low seats.

Daniel moved the seat back as far as it would go, reclined it slightly, and got in. He took a moment to learn the necessary controls and get a feel for the clutch, then put the car in gear and eased out of the parking lot onto Dam Neck Road.

"Where to, boss?" Daniel asked, as he chirped a tire hitting second gear.

"Just follow this road west. It'll change names a couple of times and end up at I-64; I think at the Indian River Road interchange. Take I-64 West and you're on your way to Richmond."

"Okay," Daniel said as he got to the speed limit in second gear and slipped the car into sixth, bypassing the other gears.

Victor reached into his bag and took out a small book with Chinese characters on the cover.

"You going to brush up on your Mandarin?" Daniel asked.

"Yep," Victor said.

"You aren't nervous, are you?" Daniel asked, sensing the similar apprehension as he had felt in the jet.

"Believe it or not, I am," Victor admitted. "I feel like a schoolboy going out on his first date. It's weird. But if this gambit pays off, I'll have a chance at the first real freedom I've had in half a century."

"I hope it does. I'm anxious to get back to Sarah," Daniel confessed.

"I'll do my best for you, kid. I'll certainly do my best." Victor's voice trailed off as he immersed himself in the small book while Daniel tried to follow the road signs west to the interstate.

Daniel found the Indian River Road interchange. He downshifted and eased onto the ramp, accelerating into the curve and feeling the BMW's low profile tires grip the road as if on rails. Victor glanced up from his book, checked Daniel's speed and grinned as Daniel headed west toward Hampton. As he neared the Hampton Roads Bridge Tunnel he noticed three aircraft carriers in port to his left.

"Hey, Victor, look over there," Daniel said pointing toward the carriers.

Victor looked up from his book. "That's Naval Station Norfolk, the world's largest naval base."

"Seriously?" Daniel was impressed.

"Seriously. Pay attention after you go through the tunnel. There's a ton of history in this area. You'll go by Fort Monroe on the right, then later Langley Air Force Base, America's first air base, and also home to NASA Langley Research Center."

"Lots of military around here, I take it?" Daniel responded.

"Yep," Victor replied.

As they came out of the tunnel into Hampton, Victor pointed out Point Comfort and Fort Monroe. "The English landed there in 1607 before going up the James River and founding Jamestown. They named it because as they rounded the point and sailed into calm water for the first time in months, it was such a comfort. They also named Strawberry Banks over there," Victor pointed to his left, "because they found wild strawberries and were able to curb their scurvy," Victor continued as Daniel tried to look around while paying attention to impatient drivers who were accelerating around the cars that had fearfully slowed down when entering the tunnel. "Over there at Fort Monroe is where the first African slaves landed and also where the first slaves were freed during the Civil War."

"How so?" Daniel inquired. "Virginia was Confederate."

"Not Norfolk or Fort Monroe. They remained in the Union. A boat of slaves rowed over from Hampton and asked the commanding officer at Fort Monroe for asylum. The next morning the slave owners came to fetch their property. The colonel told them he considered the slaves contraband property used against the Union, so he confiscated it and freed them. After that, any slave who could get to Fort Monroe was given safe harbor and freed. Interestingly, the Emancipation Proclamation specifically excludes Norfolk since it was still Union."

"Interesting story," Daniel said. "In Florida, we learned American history and Florida history so we learned about Jamestown, but didn't get the interesting details about Fort Monroe, for sure."

Victor was reading the road signs as Daniel was talking and cut him short. "Get off here at Mallory Street and go into Downtown Hampton," Victor instructed. "There's a top-tier men's store near the Air and Space Museum where we can get suits for Richmond."

Daniel followed the signs into Hampton. "I take it that glass building with the double curved roof is the Museum?"

"That's it. Turn onto King Street and drop me off at the door, then park the car."

Daniel parallel parked nearby and walked back to the store, still being conscious to conceal his face as much as possible. He noticed the closed sign on the door as it was opened for him and then locked. For almost two hours Victor discussed clothing for Daniel and himself with the tailor who seemed to know who he was. Once everything was perfect, he paid in cash and pulled out an extra thousand dollars and handed it to the gentleman.

"We were never here. You understand?"

"Yes, sir," the tailor replied, but didn't seem too impressed.

Victor stared intently at him, then emphasized the point. "If anyone finds out we were, you'll never spend that money."

"Yes, sir," the tailor said solemnly, his demeanor totally changed. "I understand completely."

"Good." Victor motioned to Daniel and said, "Let's go."

Daniel was quiet as he picked up the bag of their old clothes and shoes and followed Victor, indicating the way to the car. He found his way back to the interstate and headed toward Richmond.

Victor buried his nose in his Chinese book until they were approaching Williamsburg. He looked up as they were going over a marshland which Daniel had noticed was called Queen's Creek, and pointed off to the right toward a patch of woods bordered by a high fence with signs stating this was property of the US Government. "That's Camp Peary over there. Affectionately called The Farm. Maybe you'll visit it one day."

"Why? Isn't it covert?" Daniel was puzzled.

"Oh, yeah. We'll talk about that later with Brad," Victor said as he resumed his Chinese reading.

"Whoa, whoa, whoa!" Daniel exclaimed. "What are you guys thinking?"

"Nothing. We can talk about it later."

"No way," Daniel said, sensing something was up that involved him, whether or not he approved. "I hate to get testy, but I'm tired of that word *later* every time I ask a question. Why can't you just tell me now? We've got an hour to Richmond and your Chinese sounds good to me, so shoot."

"Brad and I *have* been discussing your future for quite some time, and we do have a few ideas that may interest you. But Brad wants to be in on the discussion, so I promise that as soon as we finish with this money business and get to Maine, he will be there to discuss things with you. I know I've asked for your patience enough already, so please let's get through this ordeal and then meet with Brad."

"As long as it has something to do with dealing with Abu and Babel, I'll be patient."

"Well that's part of it, so bear with us."

Daniel's melancholy began to grip him as he thought about Sarah and the danger he had placed her in. He decided to just be quiet and let Victor and Brad have their say. Then he would figure out how to get his life back and extricate himself from Victor's web.

The miles ticked by quickly as he was lost in thoughts of Galveston until finally the buildings of downtown Richmond came into view and Daniel nudged Victor for directions.

"Just follow the Fifth Street signs into downtown and turn right on Broad Street. We'll park in a deck a couple of blocks from the restaurant where I want to start and then, depending on how that goes, we'll go to Mekong for lunch. I'm curious to see if Joe's family still owns it and maybe get a clue as to why he called New York. Plus, the food and beer selection is the best. If you don't want to eat there, we can try a world-class sub from Black Sheep, or fabulous Italian from Edo's Squid in The Fan district."

"Is there any place you go you don't know the best restaurants?" Daniel grinned as he quizzed Victor. "I get the feeling food is your life's passion."

"I guess I do have two passions, my boy, food being one of them."

"And business is the other, I take it."

"Hell no!" Victor replied emphatically. "Business just facilitates my passions."

"Oh? Food and what, then?"

"Sex," Victor said as nonchalantly as if he had said fishing.

"TMI," Daniel quickly said, hoping to curtail this line of conversation. He had never discussed sex with Joseph, and wasn't comfortable starting a dialogue about it with his newfound uncle.

Victor wasn't put off. "Spend a year with someone like Paul Chang, and you won't be so uptight about the subject, Daniel. But we can drop it for now. Here's Broad Street. The parking deck is about a mile up on the left across from the convention center. I want to walk around and scope things out before we go in."

"Okay," Daniel said, relieved. He felt that what Victor really meant was he wanted to walk around and settle his nerves, so Daniel played along and acquiesced to the request. He found the parking deck, took a ticket, and proceeded in.

"How far up?" Daniel asked.

"All the way. I want to look around."

Daniel followed directions and went to the top level of the deck and found a parking space away from other cars. "Now what?"

"Let's go. You know what to do?"

"Stay at your left hand, behind you, answer no question, and don't look at girls while not appearing bored."

"That's it."

Daniel waited by the car as Victor walked to the deck's edge and studied the street below. Then he followed Victor down the stairs and walked for about a mile along the sidewalks of Richmond until Victor stopped suddenly. He looked around carefully, took a deep breath, and approached a richly decorated crimson door in the middle of a nondescript block of stores. Once inside, Daniel saw it was a very normal looking Chinese restaurant. It could have been anywhere in the country. The wall above the sales counter had faded photos of all of the standard dishes, and the counter had a stack of paper menus with the dishes listed and numbered. Under each number were Chinese characters. Victor took a menu and a pencil out of a rice-filled glass and started scanning the items. Finally he looked up at the young Chinese girl who was patiently waiting for him to order. He took a deep breath and ordered in crisp syllables of Mandarin Chinese. The sublime look of patience on the girl's face turned suddenly to a mix of surprise and then terror. She studied Victor's face for a moment, then looked at Daniel and back at Victor as a vermilion shade of red swept over her face. She then bowed very low as she backed away through the kitchen door.

"Something is terribly wrong here," Victor said quietly to Daniel without taking his eyes off the kitchen door. "I want you to slowly back out and go get the car. If I'm not outside, don't stop. Get the phone with the red tape on it and press redial. Trust whoever answers. Got it?"

"But Victor," Daniel started.

"Get the hell out of here. Now!"

Daniel started backing up as the kitchen door opened and a middle-aged Chinese man came through it. His astonishment was genuine, as if he had seen a ghost. The young girl was close behind him with her head down. Daniel hesitated, not wanting to leave Victor like this. If there was trouble, he wanted to help, but he could not ignore Victor's emphatic words.

"Meestor Veektor!" he heard the man say with a heavy Chinese accent. Then he bowed and said something in Chinese.

Victor responded and Daniel slowed his exit. The tone of Victor's voice did not indicate danger as Daniel had expected. Daniel saw Victor open the palm of his hand by his side toward Daniel, indicating for him to stop. He then continued the conversation with the man, who ended each exchange with a bow. Victor never lowered his head nor looked anywhere except at the couple. Finally he quietly spoke to Daniel, still without moving his head.

"They've asked that we join them for tea in The Golden Room. You see the door in the wall to your right?"

"Yes sir," Daniel responded, his heart racing.

"I'll go in first. If I call you anything but your name, you run. Otherwise, join me."

Victor edged toward the door cautiously and heard it being unlocked from the other side. As he neared it, it opened as well as another panel next to it, creating a wide portal. Waiting on the other side were four women in regal Chinese attire. The two youngest were holding the door as they bowed low, while two middle-aged women indicated with outstretched arms toward a table in the middle of the room. Victor surveyed the room as he walked between them, their bowed heads slightly higher than the younger girls. Although the room was small, it was elegantly appointed in red and gold. Soft lighting from hidden sources illuminated a rich mahogany table with four settings of translucent porcelain china and golden utensils on silk napkins. The walls were adorned with silk tapestries, and a papyrus shoji concealed the opening to the adjacent room, which Victor surmised was the kitchen. As Victor moved, one of the women shuffled her silk clad feet along the lacquered epi wood floor and pulled out his chair. From behind the shoji a man who looked to be about Victor's age appeared, bowed, and took a seat opposite Victor.

As Daniel was intently watching Victor, waiting for a cue as to what to do, two young Chinese men dressed in suits came out of another door on the opposite side of the restaurant. One of them locked the entrance door while the other placed a closed sign in the adjacent window. Then they took up positions behind Daniel. Daniel gauged his distance to the closest chair he could use to smash the front window and escape. He felt that with his size and strength he could carry the two smaller men with him through the window if necessary.

Finally Victor motioned for Daniel to join him, and he entered the room. Daniel walked toward the chair being held for him by the other middle-aged Chinese woman. As he passed through the opening, one of the young women glanced up at him. Immediately the older Chinese man spoke sharply to her and she bowed, then shuffled behind the shoji, not to be seen again. Daniel had been very careful not to return the eye contact. The doors closed behind him, and he heard a lock being set.

As tea was being served, first to Victor, then to the Chinese man, then to Daniel, one of the young Chinese men brought a telephone to the table. Daniel had seen telephones like this in photographs but could not remember actually seeing the real thing. It was a squat, black, boxy object with a headset cradled on top and attached with a coiled wire. A smaller wire was plugged into the back of it and the young man plugged that into a jack on the floor near the table. The angled face of the phone had a metal disc on it with finger holes and a number under each hole, something Daniel had never seen. Immediately the phone rang. The ring was real, not electronic, and the Chinese man picked up the receiver and handed it to Victor. The old earpiece was loud enough, and the room quiet enough, that Daniel could hear the voice on the other end.

"Hello, Victor. This is Mark Chang. I'm Paul Chang's oldest son. I have a letter for you from my father."

Victor's face belied nothing of the surprise he felt, but Daniel saw the color fade from his face and once again sensed the choking aura surrounding his uncle.

The voice on the phone continued, "I'm on my way to Richmond. Our helicopter will land at the airport in twenty minutes. I'd like to join you at the restaurant if that's okay with you. I'll get there as quickly as I can. Meanwhile, please enjoy the tea and a meal with your nephew and my Uncle Chen."

Victor nodded and handed the receiver back to the Chinese man who finished the conversation and hung up. The telephone was immediately unplugged and taken away. Victor waited for the other man to sip his tea, then he placed the cup to his lips as if sipping. Daniel noticed this and did not pick up his cup. The man finished his cup and it was instantly refilled from the exquisite teapot. Victor waited a moment while watching the man's eyes, then sipped the tea. He motioned to Daniel who took a small sip. Daniel considered himself a tea connoisseur, having sampled teas from specialty stores around the country, but this tea was beyond anything he had ever tasted, and the temperature was perfect as well. He surmised the porcelain cups had been preheated. He smiled at Victor, who was enjoying Daniel's introduction to the finest tea the Orient had to offer.

Victor thanked the man and announced they would stay, but would wait for Mark before they ate. Daniel was disappointed, since his truncated breakfast at Corova had long since faded, and he was starving. The man acknowledged Victor's request, but insisted on a small appetizer while they waited. From behind the shoji a Japanese chef appeared with several in his entourage and they set up a small table where he began to prepare sushi and sashimi. "Atlantic Bluefin," he said as he served Victor. "Fresh from Phoebus this morning, of course."

Victor took a set of gold sheathed chopsticks, picked up the raw rice-wrapped fish, dipped it gingerly in the light nikiri sauce, touched it to the real wasabi, which was quite different than the fake green paste normally served with sushi in America, and held it for the Chinese gentleman to take. The man quickly picked up his pair of utensils and expertly took the morsel from Victor and ate it. He then picked up his portion of fish, and Victor nimbly took it and ate. They both gave a slight nod to the chef who then served Daniel. Daniel never knew raw fish could melt in his mouth like this and explode with such succulence. He could have eaten a pound of it, but no more was served. Instead, an entire array of Chinese appetizers was brought out and served by an army of young men and women, each dressed in fine traditional Chinese attire. Curiously, Daniel never again saw the young woman who had glanced up at him.

CHAPTER 25

Paul's Epitaph

As quickly as the appetizers had been brought out, the remains were whisked away, the table cleared and reset in perfect order. The four women took their positions at the double doors and as if given a perfectly timed cue, opened them as Mark Chang walked through. His professed uncle at the table rose and bowed. Daniel followed Victor's lead and stood up when he did and shook Mark's hand. As Mark shook Victor's hand, he bowed respectfully. All of the men took their seats simultaneously and tea was immediately served, followed by two crystal glasses of bourbon on ice for Victor and Mark. Mark raised his glass to Victor as a toast, and after each had taken a sip, Mark indicated that Daniel and Uncle Chen be served. Mark raised his glass again and all four men toasted and sipped. Daniel noticed the bourbon tasted as fine as the Pappy Van Winkle's he'd had on the jet. Finally Mark Chang opened the conversation.

"My dear Uncle Victor," Mark began, his perfect English and accent indicating that he was brought up in the United States. He then slipped into Mandarin and finished his sentence with a slight bow of his head, followed by Uncle Chen bowing slightly lower.

Victor nodded and replied in Chinese then turned to Daniel and translated. "Mark said the Middle Kingdom sends its highest regards and is honored by my presence in their humble restaurant. I thanked him and asked to what I owe such a high honor."

Mark continued in English as the glasses were refilled. "I was dreadfully afraid I had missed the opportunity to meet you and am delighted to find out you were not aboard the ill-fated jet."

Victor nodded but did not respond. Daniel noticed he was being unusually quiet and reserved. Obviously he was trying to determine if this gratuity was genuine or if he was a lamb being prepared for slaughter. Was Mark truly the son of his long-lost mentor whom he assumed was childless, or had he invoked Paul's name to ensure Victor would remain in his clutches long enough to exact revenge for the millions he had scammed from The Bank? And now, since Victor had not died in the jet, maybe the money had survived also, and this man, claiming to be Paul's son, had been sent to coerce the money's location from Victor. Daniel wondered if Victor considered they might use him as leverage to extract information from Victor. Daniel knew that even if he escaped and fled from Victor and his captors, he was helpless against the foes arrayed against him. He knew he would not even make it to the car and the red-taped phone without dire consequences. He watched Victor carefully for any clue as to what he should do, but Victor was stoic, waiting patiently for the situation to present itself positively or negatively. Daniel had to resign himself to an unknown fate at the hands of a diabolical enemy or a fortuitous ally. He took a long sip of the bourbon trying to calm his nerves. It was immediately topped off.

Mark seemed to be aware of Victor's dilemma and proceeded carefully. Victor's quiet demeanor was clueing him in to Victor's distrust.

"Victor," Mark continued, "I know you are unaware of my father's activities after he left Texas. I also know you are unaware of most of his activities before he left Texas. I am prepared to fill in those blanks and fulfill his will concerning you." Mark paused, waiting for

Victor's acknowledgment.

Victor looked around at each person in the room, then back at Mark and shrugged noncommittally.

"I see," Mark said, and motioned for everyone to leave the room. Uncle Chen stayed seated until Mark motioned for him to leave also. He reddened at the insult and loss of face, but obeyed. "Are you more comfortable now?" Mark asked.

"Not really," Victor responded. "Walls have ears, but I'm not too concerned unless you are here to elicit information from me."

"I understand your concern, and I assure you I am here to give you information, not get any from you. But you need to be aware that in order to ensure you know what I say is legitimate, I will be divulging some of your personal life. Is Daniel privy to that?"

"Yes," Victor said immediately. "He can listen to anything. He can stay or leave as he wishes. I assume that will be okay with you?"

"Absolutely," Mark said. "Is there somewhere you feel comfortable talking?"

"Yes," Victor said. "Give me a phone number and I'll call you when I'm there. It's about ten minutes from here and our car is a bit of a walk, so give us about twenty minutes."

"Can we drive you to your car?" Mark offered.

"No, thanks," Victor said.

"Very well. Would you like to eat before you go? We have a banquet prepared for you and Daniel." Calling Daniel by name told Victor that Mark did have information and wasn't afraid to share it.

"Maybe later, thank you," Victor replied.

"We'll fix something for you to take with you, then. Maybe later we can finish." Mark called out loudly in Chinese and one of the middle-aged women appeared immediately from behind the shoji. Mark gave her instructions, and she bowed and left.

"One more thing before you go, if you will indulge me?" Mark asked.

"Certainly," Victor said.

"We have thousands of restaurants around the country, all staffed at the counter by our youngest employees." As he was talking, the young girl who had taken Victor's order entered and stood behind Mark, her head bowed. Mark acknowledged her while continuing to talk. "There is a story each of them are told before they start work. It is about an American man who will come in and order a particular dish, in a particular way, in Mandarin Chinese. So all the menus contain this non-existent fare. Faking the scenario, which has been tried, results in extreme measures against all involved. The legend states that if the employee receives this order and follows very specific instructions to tell the senior person in the restaurant, they will become very wealthy. Now, all the young employees consider this an urban legend contrived to keep them alert at the counter. But I know it is not a legend. It was set up by my father as a way for you to ask for help. He created a fund to be given to the person who takes your order. That fund has grown over the years to a bit over a million dollars." Mark turned toward the young girl. "You have made Michelle a very wealthy young woman." Mark reached into his lapel pocket and pulled out a check. Holding it with both hands he presented it to her. She received it with both hands, looked at it, and fell to her knees, tears streaming down her cheeks.

"Congratulations, Michelle. You have fulfilled a wish of the great Jianhong." Mark helped her up, hugged her, and wiped the tears from her eyes. "May wisdom and truth follow you with this wealth."

Michelle, through her tears, thanked him, then thanked Victor and Daniel. Then the entire staff emerged from behind the shoji, and with great pomp, escorted her to the back of the restaurant and to their banquet. As they left, Daniel noticed two boxes of food had been placed on their table. A note with a phone number had been taped to Victor's.

Mark rose and extended his hand to Victor. Victor rose and shook it. "I look forward to our meeting and offering you the help you came here for." Then he offered his hand to Daniel. "Your uncle is a famous man in our area of China. His presumed passing was a sorrowful day there." He turned back to Victor. "I will keep your resurrection secret until our business is concluded. Then, if you wish to remain dead, so be it."

At that moment the double doors opened, held by the two young men who had closed the restaurant behind Daniel. Daniel shook Mark's hand, picked up the boxes, and followed Victor.

Once on the sidewalk Victor picked up the pace toward the car. "Holy shit!" he said. "Holy shit! What the hell!"

Daniel had never imagined Victor could be rattled by anything, but this experience had rocked his foundation, and he was having a hard time regrouping. Daniel didn't know what to say or how to help, so he just blindly followed Victor's charge toward the parking deck.

Once on the deck Daniel pushed the button on the key fob and heard the BMW chirp as the car doors unlocked. Victor grabbed the handle jerking the door open, plopped down into the seat and threw his head against the headrest. "God, that was surreal." He closed his eyes, then asked Daniel, "Were we followed?"

"I don't think so, but I'm no expert at that. Nobody was moving as fast as us, so if we were followed, they are very good at it. Where are we going?" Daniel started the car and slipped it into neutral, waiting for Victor's instructions.

Victor sat quietly for a while and Daniel picked through the food and munched, waiting. Finally Victor took a deep breath and opened his eyes.

"What's the plan?" Daniel asked. "Do we meet Mark?"

"We have to meet Mark. I need to find out if he's really who he says he is. If so, I can't imagine that Paul's son would want to do me harm. But sometimes benevolence only lasts one generation."

Victor sighed. "There's no running now. Since I don't know anything about Mark's true nature, it's just a matter of where we want to meet the inevitable."

"You think they're after the money?"

"There's a good chance of that. This could be a very elaborate ploy to get to the cash."

"You think they'll use me against you?"

Victor reached into his bag and pulled out the pistol, checked it, then put it in his jacket pocket. "If they aren't successful with me, then you are their ace in the hole. But if I don't check in with Brad at seven o'clock, the money will be moved immediately as a fail-safe, so you will not know where it is. You can tell them the complete truth and it won't matter."

"Will they kill me?"

"Probably not. They'll have nothing to gain by killing you, and I'll be dead anyway so you won't matter."

"So what's the gun for?"

"Me. That's the only way I can protect you. My only option is to choose where."

Daniel's chest felt like it was going to crush under the weight of the situation. He could hardly get the next question out. "And where is that?"

Victor sighed. "The Poe Museum on Main Street."

Daniel started inputting information into the dashboard's GPS.

"Just head east on Broad into Shockoe Bottom. The museum is three blocks south at Nineteenth."

"Okay. Why there?"

"It's safe, it's public, and I spent the happiest day of my life there. Behind Poe's house is a courtyard with a fountain and a portico with three brick arches. I was married there. I'd like to die there if I have to." Victor's attitude was sullen, as if he were tired and defeated.

This was the futility of life that had always gripped Daniel to his core. So much life and living, all to culminate in a bullet to the head in a courtyard in Richmond. So pointless, he thought as the heaviness of depression engulfed him. He had asked his father about this once after a particularly disappointing showing at a tournament. Joseph had no answer, but encouraged him to read Ecclesiastes.

Daniel had never taken the advice. He instead resigned himself to his melancholy. He exited the parking deck and turned right onto Broad Street.

As he headed east, the buildings of Richmond seemed to close in around him, suffocating him, and as he started down the steep hill and under the interstate into Shockoe Bottom, he felt like he was descending into Hell, his soul eternally separated from God. Death felt like just a breath away—so close he could touch it. As he sat motionless at a stoplight, he closed his eyes. He felt his soul depart his body and move through the windshield into the street as the foreboding buildings morphed into empty crypts. The loneliness was more than he could bear as the revelation of separation nearly stopped the beat of his heart. He gasped as his soul returned and he opened his eyes to the green light. Although the episode seemed at least minutes long, Daniel was surprised that almost no earthly time had passed. Had it been a dream or was he momentarily in another realm? But the revelation actually seemed more real than what humans perceive as reality, so he knew it wasn't a dream. What if the physical world was the dream and the spiritual world was the true reality? He just couldn't wrap his mind around it.

Mechanically, he turned right onto Nineteenth Street and parked near Main Street, the revelation of Hell nearly paralyzing him. He looked over at Victor, who had his head down and against the window as if his age had finally caught up with him and he was ready to give up the ghost. Joseph's words came flooding into Daniel's head and he uttered them silently, almost as a prayer. "Get thee behind me, Satan!"

Victor jerked his head up. "Did you say something, Daniel?"

"No. We're here."

"Oh, okay." Victor collected himself and got out of the car, taking the pistol and tucking it into his belt at the small of his back.

Daniel slowly got out and held onto the door tightly to steady himself. Then he closed the door, locked the car, and followed Victor into the courtyard of the Poe Museum.

Daniel and Victor were sitting on one of the metal benches by the fountain when Mark Chang came into the courtyard. He was alone and pulled the other bench close to Victor and Daniel and sat down. Daniel was watching closely and listening for the sounds of Mark's entourage to surround the museum, but he saw no movements and heard nothing except for the rhythmic gurgle of the fountain.

"How was the food?" Mark asked.

"I wasn't really hungry," Victor answered.

"Too bad. I know how much you enjoy a great meal."

"Really?"

Mark's lightheartedness indicated he was either totally unaware of Victor and Daniel's grave concerns about the situation, or he was a fantastic actor playing his part perfectly.

"Well, my father told me he had instilled in you a passion for food and a passion for women. He said it was part of the healing process for you during your time on the ranch. He knew they were poor substitutes for a wife and children, but it was the best he could do. That, and enable you in business so you could indulge those passions."

"Enable me in business?" Victor replied, rather surprised. "He left before I started my first development."

"And who funded your first development?"

"Christopher Chermak and his development company."

"Christopher was the son of Chris, the missionary with whom my father traveled to America. My father rescued him from Mao's cleansing after Chris was murdered by the Red Army. His company was—"

"TOAFP Inc," Victor finished the sentence. "I know. So you're saying Paul was part of TOAFP?"

"Not part. He was TOAFP and Christopher ran it for him. Did you ever consider what the name meant?"

"No," Victor answered. "I assumed they were the initials of the company founders, and Chris was their agent in Texas."

"Turtle On A Fence Post," Mark said, grinning. "Now do you

believe I am Paul's son?"

Victor finally laughed. "Son of a bitch. Paul was slick. So he put me on a fence post in business and created a myth about Chinese banks as a way for me to get down."

"Pretty much."

"But where did he get the money? He was just a ranch hand."

"For forty years he lived on the ranch, spending almost nothing of what he earned. Every month he went into town and sent money to his family in China. One month's wages for him was like a lifetime of earnings for his family in China. He made them all wealthy and instructed them on exactly how to invest the money. Every month he would review the business reports from his village. When Mao took over, he moved all the money back to America. By then he was a legend in his village. You wouldn't believe how many boys were given his name in hopes they would become as great as Jianhong, the Elder. After Nixon visited China in '72, and Mao died in '76, my father began reinvesting in China and followed that wave of economic growth until he died. But his real leap to fantastic wealth came by financing your ventures. And he secretly bailed you out a few times also. He told me you had an incredible vision for business. You have proven him correct many times."

"What about The Bank?" Victor puzzled.

"The Bank is there," Mark replied. "And just as dangerous as you imagine them to be. That is why my father was so careful with how he financed you. It was always through channels that got lost in the Chinese money system. Even The Bank couldn't follow it, but as long as their investments paid off, they didn't delve into what they thought were just small-time investors riding their coattails. He actually had his hands deeper into their pockets than they could possibly imagine. As you made billions, and The Bank made billions, he made tens of billions. And he did it all from his own island in the Keys."

"So he did go to Florida when he left Texas?"

"Yes, and he loved it there, too. He took his wife and a few mistresses, bought an island, and lived into his nineties. He was sharp as a tack till the day he died, surrounded by his children. I'm the oldest son from his wife, so the patriarch of the family and CEO of all the business."

"So how did you find me and why? You have a letter for me from Paul?"

"Finding you was almost pure luck, but not entirely. A bass fisherman depends on luck to get a fish to strike his lure, but he has to get the lure into the water at the right place a whole lot of times hoping for one strike. Otherwise, all the luck in the world won't help. I was in China when we heard about your jet, so I immediately headed back here. My father's instructions about you were two-fold. If you ever came into a Chinese restaurant and ordered, then I was to be summoned to render any assistance you wanted, hence the huge reward to the young lady earlier."

"And the other?" Victor asked.

"Upon your death I was to get with your beneficiary and give them the letter. We assumed Daniel was that person, but weren't positive until we could open the sealed documents with some of your life insurance policies required with some of the loans we issued."

"I always wondered why the life insurance policies were so adamantly insisted upon. It was just a way to get me to declare a beneficiary?"

"That was all. And they all contained Daniel's name." Mark turned toward Daniel. "Your uncle's death makes you a very wealthy young man."

"But he's not dead yet," Daniel replied, trying to process the story and separate fact from fiction.

"No, but he has come to us for help, and the world thinks he's dead."

"What about The Bank? What will they do when they find out he isn't dead?" Daniel asked, watching Victor to ensure it was okay for him to speak. Victor didn't indicate any opposition.

"The Bank really doesn't care about Victor, although they've launched a massive search for the plane under the guise of caring. What they're really looking for is seventy-four million dollars of their cash."

Victor looked over at Mark, feeling now was the time of his reckoning. He placed his hand behind his back and Daniel heard the click of the pistol's hammer being cocked.

"That's very accurate information, Mr. Chang," Victor said quietly. "Are you here to retrieve it?"

Daniel saw Victor had decided to meet the issue head-on and resolve it here in the courtyard dedicated to Edgar Allen Poe. Daniel held his breath waiting for Mark's response.

"I am here to assist you in whatever way I can. I know from your flight plans and activities you were gathering large sums of cash, but I don't know why. Presumably for a venture in Ukraine, but somehow I doubt that. I also believe that for some unknown reason you suddenly curtailed your trip; presumably because you didn't want to be questioned by The Bank's agents, who were on their way to intercept you. When your jet went down, we assumed it was The Bank's doing. But when they immediately launched the search, we delved into why and came up with seventy-four million in cash unaccounted for. That's when we started fishing and got a strike with Joe on Jekyll Island. He called our restaurant in New York and we sent a team to Jekyll, but couldn't find you or Daniel. Our second strike came with the family from Winston-Salem, also restaurant owners who thought they recognized Daniel at a convenience store near Myrtle Beach. They tried to track you, but obviously lost you in Carova. Meanwhile, I flew to Norfolk and rented a helicopter and started looking, while they rented a four-wheel drive and started looking. They found the tracking device buried, so we knew we had lost you. How did you get to Richmond, if you don't mind me asking?"

"Through False Cape," Victor responded, knowing it was futile to be anything except truthful.

"Were you in the Ranger's truck?"

"Yes."

"I had a feeling you were. Anyway, we got the call from Richmond, and I flew directly here."

"So what now?" Victor asked, his hand still on the pistol.

"How can I help you?" Mark replied.

"First, prove what you say is true and not just a ruse to recover the money."

Mark reached into his lapel pocket and pulled out a sealed envelope. Victor recognized Paul's signet ring impression on the seal. The date under it, written across the flap, was from a quarter of a century earlier. Victor examined everything about it before breaking the seal.

"Do you know what it says?" he asked Mark.

"No. I do know I'm bound by whatever it says, and I'm happy to oblige. My father was always impressed by your integrity, so I feel honored to serve you."

Victor nodded an acknowledgment, took his hand off the pistol and opened the letter. As he read it, Daniel watched the tears form and several times Victor had to wipe them away to continue reading. Mark handed him a handkerchief and waited patiently. As Victor read each page, Daniel noticed he would scan down the lines of Chinese characters, pause as if looking for something, then read the English page. Daniel surmised there was a code he was looking for that ensured it was genuine. He finished the letter and reached around to the pistol. Daniel heard the muffled click of the hammer being taken out of the cocked position, and he breathed a heavy sigh of relief.

Victor handed the letter back to Mark and said, "I think we have some business to take care of. Can we get a suite at the John Marshall and get to work?"

"Oh, the John Marshall is now luxury apartments, but I have the entire top floor of the Jefferson reserved," Mark responded. "We can work there. I'll replace the hotel staff with my personal staff, so you should feel comfortable staying there. Discretion is paramount with all of my personal staff. How about that banquet now? Our chefs have spared nothing to present you with the very best."

"I do have my appetite back now," Victor responded. "But first I think I'd like to stop by Hardywood Brewery for a chocolate stout. I hear they're having a keg tapping today."

"I'll have a keg delivered to the restaurant. Will that suffice?"

"I think I'd like that," Victor said. He stood up and Mark followed, extending his hand to shake Victor's. Victor ignored Mark's hand and put his arms around him, pulling him close into a bear hug. "Your father was a great man," he said through his tears. "A great man." He released Mark and headed out of the courtyard.

Daniel and Mark were left staring at each other.

"My father loved Victor as a son," Mark said. "I could never imagine how they could form such a strong bond in one short year, but they did. Victor is a legend in China, you know."

"He is a remarkable man," Daniel said and turned to follow his uncle, the memory of his death revelation still haunting him.

CHAPTER 26

Linden Row

Back at the restaurant, the banquet was in full swing and as good as Mark had promised. The keg from Hardywood arrived shortly after Victor and Daniel, and, as usual, Daniel was impressed with Victor's selection.

Out of politeness, Daniel ate small bits of each entrée, but he had no appetite. He wanted to mention his revelation to Victor as they drove back across town, but Victor's elation at his reprieve, coupled with the promise of Mark's help, had him on a high the polar opposite of Daniel's low.

Daniel longed for Sarah's companionship. For the first time in his life, he did not want to be alone, and Victor's company was not what he needed. He needed to be close to Sarah and to be held by her. He was afraid if he was alone for even a moment, he would slip behind the thin veil separating life and death; the death he had glimpsed on his descent into Shockoe Bottom. It was the most horrific sensation of eternal desperation he could imagine. He felt that if it had been any more than just a glimpse, his body would have shut down, unable to bear the darkness. He fought to maintain a semblance of stability as he watched Victor command attention from the revelers.

Daniel noticed the two women who had served them earlier were now attending to Victor's every need and lavishing attention upon him. Victor was playing his role perfectly; accepting the attention humbly while gently drawing them along, lightly touching their arm to accentuate a point of conversation and laughing lightheartedly when one of them ran her fingers though his thick white hair, obviously lauding his virility.

Finally, Daniel could no longer tolerate the claustrophobic atmosphere. He pulled a chair close to Victor and whispered, "Victor, I'm exhausted. Do you mind if I bug out?"

"Sure, Daniel, but you'll miss dessert, and Mark has promised some sake that will curl your toenails."

"That sounds great, but I'd really like to head to the hotel. Is it close enough to walk? I don't think I can drive tonight."

"All right," Victor said, resigned to losing Daniel for the evening. "Charles," Victor motioned to a young man near the kitchen door, "will drive you and see you to your room. Your things will be there already. We'll be meeting with Mark after breakfast in the penthouse conference room. Okay?"

"Sounds fine," Daniel replied sullenly. "Please thank Mark for his hospitality. See you in the morning." Daniel got up to leave, then leaned back down for one more question. "I don't have small bills for tips. What do I do?"

Victor looked up and replied, "Enjoy yourself. Everything is taken care of, including generous tips." Victor returned to his game with the two women as Charles walked toward him in response to Victor's motion.

"Are you ready for the hotel, Mr. Daniel?" Charles asked.

"Yes, please," Daniel replied.

"This way, Mr. Daniel," Charles said as he escorted him through the restaurant and held a back door open for him. There was a limousine waiting with its back door open as Daniel exited into the private parking lot. Charles closed Daniel's door then got in the front seat beside the driver.

As the limousine began to move, the interior lights came on, softly illuminating the lush interior and revealing a beautiful young Chinese girl in a silk kimono kneeling beside a fully stocked bar. "May I fix something for you, Mr. Daniel?" she asked.

Daniel was caught by surprise at the apparition and stumbled on his words. "Uh, I . . . I think I'd like a ginger ale, please."

"Yes. Of course. May I suggest warm sake, sir?" she replied.

"Sure," Daniel said.

"It will help you sleep, I assure you, Mr. Daniel."

"Fine. Thank you," Daniel said, beginning to get irritated by the constant uttering of his name with *Mr.* tacked on to it, and anxious to be far away from this beautiful young woman who moved as gracefully as a swan on a calm lake and with a demure elegance exuding forbidden sensuality.

She prepared the sake without spilling a drop although the movement of the large automobile over the rough downtown streets seemed to make it impossible. As the car turned a corner, she shuffled toward him on her knees with the grace of a prima ballerina, perfectly balancing the sake. With both hands she offered it to Daniel as her eyes seemed to flutter with an almost imperceptible bow. Daniel thanked her and she bowed again, more with her eyes than with her body, then backed away effortlessly.

"Is there anything else I can do for you, Mr. Daniel?" Her sultry voice as soothing as the warm sake coating his throat.

"No, thank you. The sake is wonderful."

She did not respond verbally, but bowed again, and Daniel noticed the slight flutter of her long, black eyelashes. Then she quietly sat back and watched, waiting for any command from Daniel.

Daniel put his head back into the soft leather seat and closed his eyes, enjoying the quiet and the warm drink.

The door opening broke his reverie and cut short his dreaming of Sarah. He thanked the young girl again as he exited the car into the underground garage. He followed Charles to the elevator and watched as he inserted an electronic key, enabling the elevator to go directly to the penthouse. Getting off the elevator, Charles pointed him to the right and escorted him to his room.

"Is there anything I can get for you, Mr. Daniel? Anything at all?"

Daniel caught the hidden meaning and ignored it, quickly declining the offer.

Charles handed him a gold embossed room key which resembled a credit card. "This card will allow access to this floor and anywhere in the hotel you wish to go. Show it at the bar, the restaurant, or to room service, if you prefer."

"Is there a workout room?" Daniel asked.

"You have access to the private spa and workout area on this floor, and there is a beautiful pool on the lower floor. Would you like me to summon a masseuse for you?"

"No, thanks. Maybe I'll just go for a swim after I get some sleep. Thank you." Daniel entered the room, feeling awkward at not offering a tip, but realizing at this level of service, the paltry tip he could offer would be more of an insult than a gratuity. He was glad he had consulted Victor.

Charles entered the room after him, turned his bedsheets down, and left quietly, closing the door so softly Daniel didn't realize he was gone. He felt a surreal sensation come over him and wanted to sleep, but feared closing his eyes. He walked out onto the small balcony overlooking the Virginia Commonwealth University campus, its tall urban buildings lit and active with students. He was lost. For some inexplicable reason, he craved a cigar. He didn't smoke, but something about the Richmond atmosphere compelled him to want tobacco. He went to the phone by the bed and picked up the headset.

Before Daniel could push a button, a voice said immediately, "Yes, Mr. Daniel?"

For a moment Daniel was too surprised to talk. Then he asked, "Do you have any cigars?"

"Oh, yes, Mr. Daniel. Quite a selection. Would you like the finest

Virginia tobacco or possibly a Cuban from the Dominican Republic?"

"Whatever you suggest is fine," Daniel responded.

"May I suggest a Portuguese port to sip with it? We have Sandeman from Duoro, which is excellent as a dessert wine."

Daniel really did not care and didn't know what all that meant anyway, so he just accepted what was offered. "Yes, that will be fine. I'll be on the balcony. The door is open."

"Of course, Mr. Daniel. Right away."

The phone went dead and Daniel just stared at the receiver, still irritated by the constant use of his name. He felt like he was having smoke blown up his ass, and he wasn't accustomed to being constantly kowtowed to. He imagined he had lost a freedom instead of gaining a luxury, and it reminded him of what Victor had said about the perks of wealth. He replaced the receiver and went back to the warm night air on the balcony, the hum of the city offering some solace. He needed to push all of his thoughts away and consider nothing. He didn't know how to do that, although Sarah seemed to do it naturally. Leaning on the heavy railing, he began watching the twinkling of the buildings' lights while he waited. Daniel leaned back on the cool masonry wall and slid down to sit on the terracotta tiled deck, his knees bent to his chest.

As he watched the city through the ornately cast concrete balusters, his familiar nemesis, melancholy, began to envelop him. He closed his eyes and felt the rough bricks on the back of his head. He heard his door open and listened as a waiter set up a small table beside him, placing his port, cigars, ashtray, and lighter on it.

When he finished, he asked, "Will there be anything else, Mr. Daniel?"

Daniel, without opening his eyes, waved a dismissal to the waiter. His annoyance with this level of attention had reached an intolerable crescendo. He gathered his clothes and decided to find the exercise room to release his frustration.

Before heading out, he studied the hotel brochure and directory from the walnut desk, placed there with a fountain pen and stationary sporting the hotel's logo. After making mental notes on where he wanted to go, he packed a small bag with swim trunks and a change of clothes. He picked up the key and a phone Victor had left for him and left the room.

The solitude he sought in the spa was immediately shattered as every staff member seemed to know who he was and tried to serve his every whim. He needed a run—a long run to clear his head. He retrieved his bag, found a back door out of the spa, and took to the streets.

The sidewalks of Richmond proved challenging for running due to their age, haphazard repairs, and various surfaces. The cacophony of broken brick pavers, concrete slabs pushed up and cracked by tree roots, metal utility service covers set askew, and grating covering the open bellies of the subterranean infrastructure painted a textured landscape dangerously rivaling a rocky country trail. He carefully picked his way along this aged urban path toward the center of the city.

Daniel began noticing the century-old buildings in this area seemed to have ungracefully aged and been brought, kicking and screaming, into the twenty-first century. Classic decorations sported layer upon layer of chipped paint and haphazard repair in a futile effort to maintain a commercial presence. Old storefronts, many from the post-Civil War era, were boarded up waiting for the next urban revival. The plywood covers were adorned with beautiful murals desecrated with spray-painted graffiti, giving even the best commercial intentions a run-down appearance.

Curiously, Daniel felt perfectly at ease here. The imperfections of the urban fabric erased any expectation of pretentiousness. Here, he felt the quiet humility of a defeated culture—its pre-war grandeur erased by Northern carpetbaggers intent on plundering a conquered culture they could not comprehend.

Experiencing Richmond at this pedestrian level gave Daniel the sense of being embraced by a matronly grandmother whose age lines and gray hair could not hide that in her youth, she had been a beautiful, gracious Southern belle.

At Adams Street he decided to veer off Broad Street onto Brook Road, which slices the city street grid diagonally, creating triangular parcels and resulting in uniquely shaped buildings. In one of these, he found Max's Restaurant. Daniel peered through the Art Deco plate-glass facade at an antique bar and decided it was time for a beer.

The friendly bartender welcomed him as Daniel found a seat near where the bar angled to complement the angle of the building.

"What can I get for you?" The bartender asked, placing a small black napkin in front of Daniel.

"What do you have that's dark and maybe from a local craft brewery?" Daniel asked.

"Well, if you're looking for something unique, I have a very sour double IPA. Would you like a taste?"

"No, thanks. I'm not big on IPAs."

"Then maybe you'd like this one. It's dark and aged with cherries—sweeter than an IPA." The bartender poured a sample without asking and slid it to Daniel. Daniel tried it and immediately said yes.

"I get the distinct hint of cherry, but not too strong. Very unusual. What is it?"

"Gnomegang brewed by Ommegang Brewery. Not local, but very good."

"Yes, it is. What appetizers do you have?"

The bartender handed Daniel a menu. "If you're a fan of escargot, ours are the best and a perfect match to the beer."

"Sounds great," Daniel said. "I'll try them."

As Daniel received his beer, a young man returned to his open laptop a seat away from Daniel. He nodded a friendly acknowledgment to Daniel as the bartender took away his empty glass and offered him another. They spoke with a familiarity that told Daniel the patron was a regular. Apparently, he used the bar as a satellite office.

A few minutes later he was joined by a young woman. She sat

next to him, but opposite from Daniel. She was strikingly beautiful, with dark, shoulder-length hair, which, with its natural waves, reminded Daniel of Sarah. As she spoke to her colleague, Daniel noted a hint of a crisp accent, suggesting English was not her native language. Daniel also noted she didn't make any eye contact with him, but opened her laptop and began reading a page of old text, askew on the screen in a PDF file.

Daniel felt the slight brush of a body behind him as another young girl about the same age slipped into the tall chair between him and the other man. As she sat down, she glanced at Daniel, then turned away as the man began introducing the women to the bartender. They all shook hands, Daniel noticing the light touch of the women using only their fingers in the handshake.

As the bartender was gathering their drink orders, Daniel's phone began to vibrate. He had placed Victor's phone on the bar and Victor was texting him on it, wondering where he was. Daniel texted back he was just out for a run. Victor said okay and reminded him of breakfast with Mark. Daniel acknowledged and then turned off the phone.

The girl next to him noticed the shut down and commented, "Freedom now?"

Daniel grinned and responded, pointing to the phone, "You ever wonder what it was like before these things?"

The girl shook her head and turned as the man answered, "I remember a time before cell phones, but I'm forty, and Megan, here, is celebrating her twenty-second birthday tonight, so I doubt she even knows what a dial tone sounds like."

"I do too!" Megan said defensively as she turned back toward Daniel for moral support.

Daniel smiled at her and confessed, "I saw a dial-up phone today for the first time. A real antique with a big metal dial and headset connected to the black box with heavy coiled wire. And the ring was real, not electronic. It was cool."

The look from Megan told Daniel he had rescued her from her

embarrassment and she shifted her position in the seat so she faced the bar instead of being angled toward the man.

The man noted the shift and knew he had lost points to Daniel, but he was very easy about it and reached out his hand to introduce himself. "I'm Russell. Birthday girl here is Megan, and this is Rachael," he said as he released Daniel's hand and scooted his chair back slightly giving Daniel and Rachael unobstructed eye contact.

Daniel noticed the softness of his hands. Obviously, he had spent a lifetime behind a desk pushing keys on a keyboard.

Rachael looked up from her computer screen long enough to acknowledge Daniel with a slight smile and feigned aloofness.

What a nice challenge, Daniel thought as he introduced himself as Paul. He held her eye contact a moment longer trying to decipher the genuineness of her demeanor.

"So, are all of you VCU students?" Daniel asked.

Russell was quick to answer. "Megan has just graduated from the nursing program. Rachael is working on her masters and works part-time with me. Our office is nearby. I'm taking courses, but I'm not a full-time student. It looks like you've been running. You're an athlete?"

Daniel didn't answer immediately as his escargot arrived and he ordered another beer to go with it. In his peripheral vision he noticed Megan's squeamish look at the snails, and then a slight glance from Rachael. Rachael's reaction was positive, as if she appreciated Daniel's adventurous spirit in the cuisine.

Daniel picked up a snail with the small fork, made sure it was soaked with plenty of the seasoned melted butter, then enjoyed it. He chased it with a gulp of the cherry-tinged beer and then answered Russell. "I was an athlete in college. Now I just try to stay in shape. So, Megan, are you going to practice nursing now?" Daniel shifted the conversation away from himself so he wouldn't have to make up lies as a cover. He enjoyed the bar scene and was having fun getting to know these strangers, but having to have a cover story was a real drag and something he definitely wasn't comfortable doing.

"No," Megan confessed. "I really don't want to practice traditional nursing. I'd rather find some sort of research field to pursue."

"Like pharmaceutical monitoring or something?" Daniel asked.

"Maybe. I just don't know."

Russell obviously wanted to know more about Daniel and cut back in at the first opportunity. "Are you from here, Paul?" he asked.

"No. Just here on business for a couple of days." With that, Daniel turned his attention to Rachael, curious if he could entice her away from the computer. "Rachael, what are you studying?"

To Daniel's delight, Rachael seemed willing to forego her work and join the conversation. "Philosophy," she said in a deadpan voice.

"Oh," Daniel said, thinking that may explain some of her demeanor. Daniel figured she had been feigning work in order to assess the interaction of personalities. "So, what do you do with a philosophy degree?" Daniel joked.

"Never take another philosophy course, for starters," Rachael quipped back.

Her smile was infectious, and as Daniel grinned at her wit, he sensed Megan's slight agitation.

Megan was taller than Rachael, and thin, with small features and short brown hair. Alone, she would be considered attractive, but beside Rachael, her looks commanded little attention—and from her body language, Daniel surmised she knew it. He sensed she would assume Daniel would focus on Rachael, and she would be Rachael's wing man, again.

Daniel turned back to Megan, engaging her while surreptitiously watching Rachael. "You're twenty-two today, huh?" he asked. "Any special plans besides Max's?"

"Well, actually my birthday is tomorrow, but Russell wanted to celebrate early, so he offered to buy me a glass of wine."

Rachael had returned to her reading as if nothing had interrupted her. This was the reaction Daniel had been looking for. *She knows her charm lies in her mystique, and she plays it to perfection. Megan is very open and earthy, and has no idea that once the mystique is gone, there is nothing else, philosophically*, he thought as Megan spoke. He covered his inattentiveness by preparing another snail.

He had played this game many times and considered himself very good at it. Suddenly it occurred to him that maybe this was why he had fallen so deeply in love with Mishael. Her mystique was genuine and never faded. It was not a game to her, and Daniel had been thoroughly absorbed by it. To Daniel, Rachael would be a fun challenge, but never a serious relationship. *Rachael's feigned aloofness is her veil of mystique*, he thought, *drawing attention to herself like a siren.*

As Daniel was thinking about the situation, enjoying his escargot, and sipping the sweet beer, Russell was again trying to engage his attention by adding to Megan's answer.

"She likes Pinot Noir. I can't get her to try anything else, sadly." Then he pointed at Rachael. "Rachael is a Pouilly-Fuisse connoisseur. She likes her wine very dry—to match her humor."

Rachael glanced at Russell, but otherwise ignored the gibe.

Daniel finished his beer and, as inviting as the scene appeared to be, decided not to stay. His thoughts were with Sarah, and he wanted to get back to his run while extricating himself from this trio was still easy. Russell seemed intent on drawing Daniel into Megan's birthday celebration—something Daniel did not want to engage in. Another time, a lifetime ago, he would have pursued the party and Rachael, but this evening he wasn't enticed.

"Anywhere nearby I can get some oysters?" Daniel asked, beginning his exit strategy.

"There's a raw bar on Main Street," Russell quickly answered.

"That's too far away," Megan chimed in. "Bistro 27 is only a block away. I've heard they've got great oysters."

Rachael looked up from her work, her interest piqued now that she sensed Daniel was preparing to leave. "Forget those places," she said, "and go to Edo's Squid on Harrison. Judging by the way you were running down Broad Street, it won't take you long to get there." She smiled as she relinquished the knowledge she had noticed Daniel even before Max's.

Damn, she's good, Daniel thought as he noted the attention. Then he caught Megan's slight pout as she realized Daniel would be leaving her party.

"I guess it's Edo's Squid, then. It's hard to turn down that challenge." From Rachael's smirk, he gathered she easily caught the double entendre. Then he smiled at Megan, and lightly touched her shoulder. "Happy Birthday Megan. I enjoyed the company."

Daniel took a fifty out of his wad of cash and placed it on the counter as he nodded to the bartender indicating he needed no change.

"We'll probably be here tomorrow," Russell offered, "so if you're still in town, stop in again."

Daniel thanked the trio and stood up, relieved he could get out before having to refuse a dinner invitation he sensed was imminent. Megan's disappointment was evident, Rachael turned back to her work as if Daniel had never existed, and Russell stood and shook Daniel's hand. "Enjoy your evening in Richmond," he said. "It's a great city. Maybe tomorrow?"

"Maybe," Daniel said, and left.

He headed back toward the hotel and decided to run down Franklin Street for a change of scenery. He turned left onto 1st Street. At the corner of 1st and Franklin, he turned his phone on to get his bearings and find a route. As he was waiting for it to initialize, he noticed Linden Row Inn on the corner and decided to get some information about it. The inn was comprised of a series of pre-Civil War row houses that had been converted into a quaint hotel. Daniel went into the small lobby and inquired about getting a room. The desk clerk was very helpful, so Daniel handed him two hundred-dollar bills and took a key. It was a large brass key to a real brass lock. *How refreshing*, Daniel thought, *to not have to deal with a plastic card key*. He was liking this already. His room number was stamped onto the key, and the clerk gave him directions to his room as he showed him the small elevator almost hidden from view on what was obviously an old rear porch that had been enclosed to become part of the lobby.

"Is there a convenience store nearby?" Daniel asked.

The clerk gave him directions and then Daniel asked about restaurants. Again, the clerk was helpful and told Daniel which ones were his favorites, then showed him a binder on an antique table. The small table was almost dwarfed by the large double-hung window it was sitting under. Daniel noted the glass in the panes was very irregular, distorting the view to the enclosed courtyard. Daniel picked up the binder, which contained information on local restaurants, sank into the well used cushion of the Queen Anne chair, and began looking for oysters. Nothing struck him, and he was still sated from the beer and escargot, so he thought, *Maybe next trip*, and headed to the convenience store.

Coming back through the small lobby with a bag of epsom salts, some toiletries, and a six-pack of hard cider, Daniel asked the clerk for a 5 a.m. wake-up call.

"No problem," he said. "Jenn will be on duty in the morning. I'll leave her a note."

"Thanks," Daniel said and headed to his room.

Daniel opened the large wooden door and entered what he assumed had been the parlor of one of the row houses. Although it was converted to a hotel room, it retained its very high ceilings, coal burning fireplace (now blocked off), large windows, and original wainscoting and moldings. The bathroom was carved out of one side of the room, enclosing one of the large windows.

Daniel poured the epsom salts into the tub, turned on the hot water and opened a hard cider. He let the tub fill to the overflow hole, opened another cider, and slipped into his homemade spa.

Freedom, he thought as his tenseness began to fade. *How sweet this is*. He began reflecting on his time with Victor, nestled in the lap of wealth, and rued the moment he entered that world. He longed for the simplicity of his cottage on the beach and his work at the tennis club. Although his inheritance and his time at VCM had left him a sizable bank account, he invested it and lived within his small pay, saving enough money for he and Sarah to take their weekend jaunts to parks, either camping or staying in inexpensive hotels. Sarah didn't seem to mind the meager budgets and never mentioned wanting anything more luxurious.

Now he felt suffocated by opulence and vowed to extricate himself from Victor's world as soon as possible.

He began wondering what Sarah knew about his relationship to Victor. Although she never gave any indication of being from a wealthy family, or having any wealth of her own—quite the opposite, in fact—she may have had access to information Victor and Brad had kept hidden for years. He desperately hoped she knew nothing about the depth of Victor and Brad's history together, nor about Victor and Joseph's relationship. He knew he would need to find out the extent of her knowledge before they got married. He placed that in a mental box of questions for Victor.

The water was now tepid and becoming uncomfortably cool as he reached for his last bottle of hard cider. He decided to finish this bottle before showering and trying to sleep. His tensions had subsided to the point he was just too lazy to move.

His calm was broken by the thought of money. *Freakin' money*! It angered him to feel so trapped by such an intangible concept. It was finally sinking in that he was like a lottery winner—suddenly flush with money he hadn't earned. It had just fallen into his lap and now he had to deal with it and not lose his life in the process.

It wasn't that he didn't feel prepared to deal with sudden wealth. Joseph had ensured Daniel was well-educated about the trappings of sudden wealth on young athletes. He had told him countless stories of athletes squandering their riches as sycophants gathered around them vying for a piece of the pie. So many of them ended with nothing or tremendous debt after their short professional careers. Joseph had taught Daniel how to shield himself from the inevitable hoard of friends and acquaintances who would feel cheated if he didn't share his wealth.

Daniel could easily handle that. His list of friends and family was very small, and he had no trouble distinguishing the faux friends and keeping them at a distance.

Joseph had also taught him how to deal with the public spotlight—the rote clichés and feigned humility necessary when microphones were thrust toward him. Playing the public while maintaining a private life would not have been a problem for Daniel had he pursued a tennis career. Joseph had seen to that aspect of his education with the same zeal he brought to bear on the mechanics of the game.

What Daniel now felt was different. The claustrophobia of Victor's world coupled with the feeling he would always be running from an unknown evil had destroyed his peace, freedom, and tranquility, something he didn't know existed until it was gone. And not something he would take for granted again.

The water was now cold so Daniel turned on a hot shower and stood under the massaging warmth while the tub drained. He dried off with the luxuriously large towel, dropped it by the tub, and headed to the tall overstuffed four-poster bed. Sleep came immediately as the pillows enveloped his damp curly hair.

Daniel was awakened from a deep dreamless sleep by the phone ringing. He answered it and a pleasant female voice said good morning and told him this was his 5 a.m. wake-up call.

"Wow, a real person," Daniel exclaimed, as he began to get his bearings.

"Yes, I'm a real person," the desk clerk answered.

Daniel stuttered, "I mean, it's just nice to not get an electronic wake-up. Thank you."

"You are very welcome. We'll have coffee ready in the Urban Farmhouse, but not until six-thirty. You can access the restaurant from the lobby."

"Thank you," Daniel said, and hung up. He quickly dressed, wrote a thank you note for the maid and staff, and left a ten-dollar bill with it. He suddenly felt the joy of tipping—saying thank you personally to a caregiver. This was so different than being told a well-paid staff would be "taken care of" as part of a business deal. Daniel smiled and added another ten.

He stopped by the front desk to hand in his key, and Jenn handed him an envelope with his change from the two hundred dollars. He opened it, took out a ten, and gave it to her. "Thanks again for the friendly wake-up call."

"My pleasure," Jenn replied. "Have a great day and visit us again soon."

Daniel picked up a business card and headed out the door for an early morning run to Victor's hotel. The taste of freedom in the crisp morning air was exhilarating, and he decided he would bring Sarah to Linden Row as soon as possible.

CHAPTER 27

Favors

Back at the Jefferson, Daniel got off the elevator and turned toward his room. A door opened ahead of him and the two middle-aged servers from the restaurant emerged. They glanced up at Daniel, and he acknowledged them with a polite hello.

"Hello, Mr. Daniel," they said in unison. Then one of them continued, "Are you up early or out late?" It seemed to be asked as a polite way to fill the silence, not as a curiosity about Daniel's activities.

"Just browsing the hotel, so I guess early," Daniel said. "What about you? Are you out late or up early?"

One responded with, "We're out late," and the other continued, "Your Uncle Victor is quite the man! He kept us up very late." They both smiled, avoiding a giggle that never materialized.

Daniel noted the room number from where they emerged and stopped to let them pass. As the elevator doors opened for them, he said lightheartedly, "Good evening ladies, or good morning. I think I'll get ready for breakfast, now."

"Goodbye, Mr. Daniel," they said in unison as Daniel opened his door. He showered and changed, then went to the restaurant for breakfast. Victor was already at a table drinking coffee and reading.

As Daniel sat down, a waiter immediately poured him a cup of coffee and asked for his order.

"Orange juice for right now," Daniel said, sipping the piping hot black liquid.

"Good morning, my young nephew," Victor said with a liveliness to his voice Daniel had not heard in a while. "Sleep good?" Before Daniel could answer, Victor put down his paper and looked at him. "You look very well rested; like a new person. What did you do all night? Whatever it was, it certainly set well with you."

"Explored the hotel, mostly. My God, this is a beautiful place."

"Yes. It is," Victor agreed.

"Seen Mark this morning?" Daniel asked, diverting the questions about his night.

"He's on his way down for breakfast. I asked if we could meet early so we can finish this business and head north."

"So, what are you going to ask for?" Daniel queried.

"I'll see if we can trade traceable money for spendable money. I'll try to get seventy cents on the dollar, but I'm afraid the best he'll be able to give me is fifty cents on the dollar, since he'll have to hold it for so long. A hundred percent profit isn't much over a ten-year life span. But if we break it up into twenty percent every two years, then he may be more willing to help."

"What if he says no?"

"We'll have to make do with the untraceable cash we have, and I'll have to curtail some of the work I was hoping to do."

"And what work is that?"

"Something that benefits freedom the way Thomas Jefferson visualized for this country."

"Sounds noble. Am I part of that work?"

"I hope so," Victor said, stopping the conversation as the waiter served his breakfast, gave Daniel his orange juice, and topped off their coffee.

"Can I get you something else?" the waiter inquired.

Victor shook his head, and the waiter looked at Daniel.

"I'd like what he has," Daniel said, pointing to Victor's plate, "only cook the eggs more—no runny whites—and a grapefruit half. Thank you."

The waiter nodded agreeably and left. Daniel resumed his questioning. "Is that what Brad wants to talk to me about?"

"Yes. That's mostly it," Victor said.

"I hope he convinces me it's worth the lives of two pilots," Daniel said, still unnerved by his own revelation of death, as well as his discovery of his uncle's debauchery. He had decided to broach that subject when they were back on the road.

Victor put his fork down and looked at Daniel, sensing his disquiet. "Brad has been at war for a long, long time, against enemies you and very few others even know exist. And much of what you take for granted in your day-to-day life is what he fights to protect. Freedom is an on-going battle, and one the media doesn't want to acknowledge. Citizens think wars are fought against Nazis, and communism, and ISIS, and radical extremists bent on destroying America, the Great Satan. But they are not our most dangerous enemies. They're just the ones we are forced to spend young lives and hard-earned money on, and the ones that sell newspapers."

"I hear the words, Victor. And I'm willing to listen, especially if it gets me close enough to Abu and Babel to send them to the grave and keep Sarah and Jonathan safe. I feel like I have no choice in that anyway. But I have to tell you, I'm not as comfortable with all this as you are. I know I don't know nearly as much as what you and Brad do, and I'm young and naive about a lot of things. But I'm not good at following blindly. I'll do what needs to be done, but it would be a lot easier if I knew what that was and why. Hopefully, we can get this money business out of the way quickly and get to Maine so I can hear what you and Brad have up your sleeve. Seeing Sarah wouldn't happen to be somewhere in that mix, would it?"

"I don't know," Victor responded.

Daniel detected a nervousness in his response. "What's wrong?" he asked quickly.

"Brad gave me a cell phone number for her, but when I tried it, the call wouldn't go through."

"You think it's off or is she just out of range?"

"Brad said she's spending time in the mountains, so probably out of range. And with the constant roaming she probably can't keep the battery charged, so we'll just have to keep trying. I'll give you the phone when we're back on the road and you can try."

"I'd appreciate that. Thanks," Daniel said as the food arrived. "When did you say we're meeting with Mark?"

Daniel saw Victor stand up as someone approached from behind. Daniel looked around as Mark was approaching the table.

"Good morning, Mark," Victor said, extending his hand.

Daniel stood awkwardly as his chair caught on the thick rug, tipping it backwards. Mark caught it with his free hand, settled it and shook Daniel's hand. "Good morning," Daniel said through a mouthful of food and some embarrassment.

"Good morning, gentlemen," Mark said as he lightly slapped Daniel on his back and took a seat. "How's breakfast?"

"Very good," Victor said. "What are you in the mood for?"

The server came up with coffee and Mark answered Victor so the server could hear also. "I think I'll have the eggs Benedict with a side of avocado and grapefruit juice. Can you use Virginia ham instead of Canadian bacon?"

"Certainly, sir," the waiter replied and left.

The trio chatted lightly through breakfast, Mark talking about growing up in the Florida Keys, and Victor telling a few stories from his time with Paul on the ranch.

"I didn't know Paul was married," Victor confessed. "I knew he had girlfriends in town. Did he marry one of them?"

"Well, he took his girlfriends to Florida with him, but he brought my mom over from his village. She never saw Texas and never learned

English. She was escorted everywhere by interpreters and ran our house like a Middle Kingdom castle. I'm pretty sure she understood more English and Spanish than she let on, but she never uttered a word other than Chinese and never adopted Western clothing or customs. So our cay was like a little piece of China."

Finally Mark drained his coffee and asked, "Conference room in fifteen minutes suit you, Victor?"

"Suits me," Victor replied and turned to Daniel. "How about you, kid?"

"Sure. I'll get my things from the locker room and see you there. Should I change clothes?" Daniel noticed Victor and Mark were impeccably dressed while he was wearing shorts, sandals, and a collarless T-shirt. He felt very self-conscious.

"It'll just be the three of us. We'll keep it very private unless you want a stenographer to record things," Mark answered.

"You mind taking notes if needed, Daniel?" Victor asked.

"No problem. I'll see y'all up there," Daniel said and left quickly.

Daniel took the locker room elevator to the penthouse, which dumped him close to his room, so he had time to change his shirt, put on some loafers, and grab the fountain pen and stationery from the table. He got to the conference room before Mark and Victor and was at the large, paned window looking out over the city when they walked in together. Daniel noticed it was exactly fifteen minutes from the time Mark had made his request. Daniel let them choose seats and then he took a seat beside Victor. Immediately a server brought in a silver tray with coffee, hot water for tea, ice, a pitcher of water, and soft drinks. He asked if he could serve anything, but Mark and Victor shook their heads, so he left, closing the doors behind him.

Victor helped himself to coffee while Mark thumbed through the tea selection until he found a suitable choice and poured hot water over it. Daniel poured himself a glass of water over ice and waited, anxious for the two men to start their business.

Mark sipped his tea, took a deep breath and opened. "Victor, how can I be of service to you and Daniel?"

Daniel was pleasantly surprised Mark was thoughtful enough to include him, both knowing this was Victor's game and he was just along for the ride.

Victor dispensed with unnecessary pleasantries and got quickly to the point. "Thanks for the offer, Mark. As you can guess it has to do with seventy-four million dollars. A bit over sixty-three million is traceable and putting it into circulation would indicate I am alive and well, something I would like to avoid."

"Figured," Mark grinned. "How'd it end up traceable? My guess is someone in your organization tipped off The Bank and foiled your plans. Do you know who?"

"Good guess. It was Robert," Victor said.

"Your valet?" Mark said, sounding surprised.

"Yes."

"I figured it was one of the pilots. Probably the new one. Douglas was his name?"

"I'm not positive about Douglas, but Steven was in the process of handing me over to Bank agents for questioning, thanks to Robert."

"So, as Sun Tzu has written, spies are a general's most powerful weapon. And your information was just slightly ahead of theirs?"

"Just enough to save our lives, but not enough to complete the transactions that would have left me with all of it untraceable and completely free of The Bank. Since you told me Paul secretly financed much of my business, I was afraid I may have inadvertently gotten some of your monies into the transactions, so I looked through my plans this morning. I didn't find any, and my intentions were solely aimed at The Bank. If you'd like to review the paperwork, I'll restore any that is yours."

"That won't be necessary," Mark replied. "Your plan was obviously airtight and none of our funds were involved. I take it you want me to help make the traceable untraceable?"

"Yes," Victor said, not offering any more of an explanation and hoping Mark would offer a solution first.

Mark didn't take the bait. "From what I hear on the news," he said, "you took care of your pilot problem rather convincingly. With the storms making the water so rough, they've found no trace of your jet. Maybe they're just taking a vacation in the Bahamas?"

"Maybe," Victor replied in a deadpan tone.

"I take it Robert fared better?"

"From what I hear," Victor responded, "he met with some sort of identity theft. All too common these days. Seems his bank account, savings, and retirement funds were wiped out. Then during the investigation, he ran afoul of immigration, so off he goes. I guess he wishes he had taken that Mexican vacation. His secret employers don't appear to really give a shit about their casualties."

"Yeah, that's too bad. Sorry to hear about his bad joss," Mark said. "So, what are your ideas about exchanging the money?"

Daniel scribbled *joss* on his pad. He had never heard the word, and wanted to ask Victor about it later.

Victor wasn't yet ready to concede the initial offer so he asked, "Are you able to deal with that much cash and protect me in the meantime?"

"That's no problem. How long do you consider protection necessary?"

Again, Mark had returned the service to Victor. Victor conceded and answered quickly, knowing any hesitation may be construed as a weaker position than he wanted Mark to believe he was in. "Ten years."

Mark, also sensitive to the significance of hesitation, came back quickly and confidently. "Ten years might be enough if we start in Malaysia and Indonesia." He didn't offer anything further, but waited on Victor.

Victor concluded Mark was not going to offer a solution or acquiesce until Victor had laid out a plan, so he dispensed with the jockeying and proceeded. "What I need is five million a year, totally untraceable. I can provide one million, and I give you six million, traceable, to be held until ten years from today. You provide four point two million untraceable."

Victor paused, knowing this was not an acceptable offer, but a starting point. He waited for Mark's reaction and watched as Mark did a quick mental calculation.

"So you're asking for seventy cents on the dollar, and we make thirty percent over ten years," Mark pondered noncommittally while sipping his tea.

Victor shrugged, waiting for a counteroffer, but Mark offered nothing. Victor knew his position was very weak and Mark probably couldn't agree to any terms without going to his board, so Victor decided to take another approach before giving up. With Mark not making a counteroffer, Victor had to assume fifty cents on the dollar was also not feasible, and that Mark did not want to insult him by offering twenty cents, which was probably the only deal he would consider reasonable. Victor had determined that at fifty cents or less, he could hold the money himself for ten years, use what he had to do some of the work he wanted to accomplish, and enjoy a bit of freedom. "Mark, I appreciate you meeting with us and offering help, and I understand what I have asked is difficult and probably untenable for you, so do you mind helping me put the money into circulation when I feel it is safe?"

Mark didn't answer the question, but instead made an observation and a request of his own. "Victor, I know how closely The Bank monitors your activities, and up until now your record is spotless. I also know they are assuming you and the money went down in the Atlantic, and they really have no concrete reason to question your intentions. Knowing how careful you are, I can assume Robert found no evidence of fraudulent financial activity in your office and that is their only red flag. That's enough to stop you for questioning, but not enough to be sure it isn't business as usual. After all, you've been involved in some unsavory capers over the years, especially in Eastern Europe. Am I correct?"

"You are," Victor said, trying to figure out where Mark was going with this.

"Our sources at The Bank tell us they are following another theory. Apparently your pilots changed flight plans, then had a communications blackout when they were supposed to be talking with The Bank agents. Just as the communications came back, they went off radar and never communicated again. The Bank is thinking they offed you and stole the money. Then flew under the radar to a private airstrip and ditched the plane. The Bank is waiting for the money to start showing up and then they'll have their culprits. They doubt two pilots have the same expertise as you to know what to do with stolen money. And they can't imagine you would ditch your lifestyle for a measly seventy million."

"You've got good sources," Victor commented. "And The Bank thinks more highly of their lifestyle than I do."

Mark chuckled at the dig. "Do you mind if I ask how you were going to complete the transactions, had all gone according to plan?"

Victor nodded agreeably and put his briefcase on the table. He extracted a folder and handed it to Mark. "That's a synopsis of my plan—sort of an outline I was using. For each page of items, I have a complete folder containing the legal documents and banking information I needed at each stop."

Mark took the folder and scanned the information, then began to read it in depth.

Victor and Daniel sat quietly for fifteen minutes while Mark studied the document carefully. Finally he closed the folder and handed it back.

"That's a brilliant plan. But timing was the key. Stopping for an explanation would have ruined it, I gather."

"Yes, it would have. Once I missed an appointment by fifteen minutes, my goose was cooked."

"But if it had worked, you could have gotten away with billions. Why settle for seventy million?"

"It's all Daniel and I could carry," Victor said honestly.

Mark's sudden laughter seemed to change the heavy mood in the room. "I wouldn't have thought of that! Hell, even the two bars of gold and the diamonds would have weighed me down; much less all that cash. You just never consider how much money weighs."

Daniel recalled how Victor had slipped on the rocks in Jekyll trying to carry two bags, and how grateful they were to get rid of a load at each stop. Now Daniel realized that without him, Victor's foray would have been fruitless. Victor had bet a whole bundle of money that Daniel would follow him to Maine and stick by him through the entire ordeal. Of course, Daniel realized Victor held the key to his freedom from Abu's wrath, so it hadn't taken much persuasion for Daniel to agree.

Mark's laughter quieted and he continued. "Victor, I don't know if you've put me in an untenable position or a fortuitous one. But I guess that might depend upon where you sit."

"How so?" Victor asked, a little curious about the fortuitous position.

"Actually, I'm bound by oath to help if I can, so I have to agree to your terms, but I would rather not."

"Then, please don't," Victor interjected.

"Let me finish," Mark asked quickly. Victor nodded as Mark continued. "I think for the first time in your life, you've underestimated your position. Now, maybe you're doing it purposely because you want out with the freedom and money to pursue another dream. I can understand that. The Bank doesn't let go of someone with your knowledge. You are far too much of a liability for them not to have some control device attached to you."

"Control device?" Victor snorted. "That's a kind word for blackmail."

"I would say blackmail is a kind word for what The Bank considers a control device," Mark returned.

"Touché," Victor said, now beginning to worry about this conversation. "But The Bank has never had anything on me I gave a crap about, so their only control has been money. And without their debt, I'm free."

"So they will kill you if they can't control you."

"That's what I figure. So what's your plan?" Victor asked.

Daniel caught the double meaning in Victor's question and also saw Victor's demeanor was different. He wondered if they had walked into a trap Victor had been so carefully avoiding. He also wondered if Mark knew just what a dangerous man Victor was. Daniel watched Victor carefully, waiting for a cue as to his actions.

Mark quickly caught the change also. "Sorry, Victor," he said quickly, hoping to defuse the tension. "I guess you are on edge, so let me ease your tension and lay out my plan. I'd rather not accept your offer because I don't believe seventy million is nearly enough for a man of your talents. I'd rather you start with two hundred and fifty million, untraceable to you, and as long as you return thirty percent each year to us, you can add to your own pot."

Victor was quietly doing the math. "So my seventy-five million is the first year's interest, if I don't perform with your quarter billion."

Mark nodded.

"And I'm in debt to you instead of The Bank," Victor concluded.

"I don't see it that way. The money you will have is untraceable, so you can use it as you like to create more wealth any way you like. I figure your assumed death is a huge advantage with what and who you know, so you will multiply that money with abandon. You can quit any time you like as long as our investment is returned with seventy-five million interest and a favor. That should be a no-brainer for you, don't you think?"

"A favor is never a no-brainer."

"I assure you the favor we ask will be doable by you with no adverse effects and perfectly legal. It's just something nobody else can do."

"If not, I can say no without consequence?"

"Absolutely," Mark said.

"Your offer is extremely generous and tempting. May I ask why that amount?"

"I'll answer your question if you'll answer a related question."

Daniel was enjoying what he perceived as two gladiators circling each other trying to find a chink in the other's armor while wondering if they should be allies or foes. It created a curious situation. Seemingly, Mark wanted to be forthright, but needed to play the game, while Victor was cautiously weighing each word, wanting to continue, but ready to bolt in an instant, should things turn sour. Mark obviously had tremendous respect for Victor so was handling him cautiously. Daniel could only listen, watch, and learn. His biggest question was what Mark really wanted from Victor. He surmised money was not the biggest issue, so something must be in the wings. It occurred to Daniel that Victor had also sensed this and that was keeping him at the table.

"I'll do my best," Victor answered noncommittally.

Mark appeared either not to care the request may not be complied with, or he was confident it was a question Victor would not mind answering anyway, or one he already had the answer to. Mark began. "My father very carefully studied everything you did. He copied much of it, even when he did not completely understand it. He knew you were extremely gifted in business and rarely made mistakes. During the course of his study, he found an anomaly in your finances. One either The Bank missed or didn't care about; he never knew which. But he did know you had a good reason for everything you did, and sometimes that reason didn't show itself for years. Your foresight was incredibly good. So early in your career you started opening small accounts in small local banks across the country. The cash used was never traceable back to you, and the accounts required only a number and a password to access."

Victor was now on the edge of his seat, looking intently at Mark, as if Mark had laid open a secret Victor had assumed was unknown to anyone.

Mark paused, as if gauging Victor's response, then continued. "My father did the same thing. It was small amounts of cash and each bank held no more than the amount of cash they were required by law to keep on hand to protect each account—usually around a hundred thousand dollars. But, given a thousand such accounts, it now adds up to a hundred million dollars accessible almost anywhere in the country as long as it is taken in small doses. So Father saw you were beginning to create a large fund of clean money; unnoticeable if accessed properly." It occurred to Daniel this was probably part of the information contained in the packets he took from the water heater, and it would have become Daniel's had Victor not returned to the plane. Mark continued, "He showed me what to do and ordered me to continue the policy until you acted on it. So my answer to your question is—two hundred and fifty million is what our small accounts are now worth. Each restaurant owner, when given the order, can withdraw one account and deliver it to a central location where it can be collected. Within a week, I can have two hundred and fifty million dollars in cash in my office in the Keys—thanks to you. My related question is: what is your plan? We estimate your accounts are worth over ninety million. That, with the cash you were going after, would give you about one hundred and fifty million to play with, unfettered, with the world as your playground. And if you're a ghost, your possibilities are limitless. So I'm betting now is the time of your action, hence my offer."

"Plus a favor," Victor replied.

"Plus a favor," Mark returned.

"I will need a favor as well," Victor added.

"If it is within my means, certainly."

"I will not be able to seal our deal until after the favor is granted."

"Will this favor take a long time? And will I have your assurance our deal is on once the favor is completed?" Mark asked.

"You have that assurance as long as I'm alive. I'm getting old, so safeguards will be put in place in case of my demise," Victor said.

"So we should drink to your long life!" Mark grinned, raising his teacup.

"Yes. To a long life." Victor raised his cup to meet Mark's and they clinked. "Now, about your favor. If I go through with this I'd like some idea of what your favor will be."

"Of course. I will tell you what all of them will be. I have many children and nieces and nephews. Each year I would like to place one of them with you to mentor, starting with my oldest daughter. She is the smartest and most ambitious and is finishing her MBA at Wharton, specializing in their Global Program which emphasizes political and economic themes across national borders. Teach her all you can in a year. One day I hope she will take my place. And your favor?"

Victor took an envelope from his briefcase and handed it to Mark. Mark removed two photos, each attached to several identity and information sheets. "I would like these two men to find out through their own intelligence networks that Daniel is alive and hiding on a mountain in Maine. They must not suspect they have been fed this information, and I need to know when they receive it."

Daniel caught a glimpse of the photos as Mark was returning them to the envelope. They were of Mishael's father and Babel. *So this was Victor's end game*, Daniel thought. *Use me as bait to lure Joseph's killers to a remote mountain where he can exact his own revenge, assuming Mark can deliver. Wonder where I fit into that scenario?*

"It would seem," Mark said, "our toast may go unfulfilled. These are extremely dangerous men."

"Are you capable of what I ask?" Victor said, knowing that by capable, he really meant willing.

"Yes," Mark said without hesitation. "Yes, we are capable. When?"

"As soon as you can. Then we can have some fun with four hundred million dollars." Victor smiled and raised his cup, "To Joseph and Jianhong."

"To Joseph and Paul," Mark repeated and touched Victor's cup with his. "Let's have some fun."

Daniel watched the two men walk out of the room and felt a foreboding sense of destiny sweep over him. He lingered a moment, slowly gathering the pen and paper, his vision of death poignant in his memory. At the door Victor turned toward him as if to beckon him.

"Coming," Daniel said.

CHAPTER 28

The Road to Quantico

An hour after the meeting concluded, Daniel and Victor were headed north out of Richmond on a route taking them west of Washington, DC. As they settled into the trip, Victor explained this was prime racehorse country and one of the greatest race horses ever was foaled nearby in Caroline County. Daniel nodded, but remained quiet. Sensing Daniel's melancholy demeanor, Victor asked, "What's bugging you, kid?"

"Lots of stuff," Daniel responded. "I just have a creepy feeling about this trip, especially after our meeting with Mark."

"I thought it went great. Far exceeded my expectations."

"So how long do you think it will take him to get Abu to Maine?"

Victor pondered a moment before answering. "A week to a month, I suspect."

"Then there's really no big rush to get to Maine now, is there? I'd like to find Sarah and spend some time with her. You don't know where she is, do you?"

Victor's look turned to concern. "You still haven't been able to reach her?"

"No," Daniel said, fear evident in his response.

"Brad just said she and Jonathan went to the mountains until we get the money and Abu taken care of, but he didn't say exactly where. I know he and Lydia used to enjoy Gatlinburg. They honeymooned there and spend long weekends there when Texas gets unbearably hot. They might be there, and if so, knowing Sarah, she probably has taken Jonathan to Cherokee to learn about their culture and history. But it's not like her to be out of touch like this."

"Can't you just ask Brad?" Daniel said.

"Not at the moment. He flew to Sierra Leone and is probably over the Atlantic somewhere. I sent him a secure text, but I won't get an answer for a while. He and Lydia have a women's education mission there. They're trying to eliminate FGM through education."

"FGM?" Daniel asked.

"Female genital mutilation, sometimes called female circumcision. Really barbaric from our cultural aspect but so ingrained in other cultures that ninety percent of the women in Sierra Leone go through it when they reach puberty. The young girls don't know what's happening until it's done. Some, thanks to international outrage and education, find the strength and support to resist. It's still practiced throughout many Middle Eastern and African countries, but Sierra Leone heads the list, so that's where Brad and Lydia began."

"I'll keep trying," Daniel said. "I guess turnabout is fair play."

"What's that mean?" Victor asked, closing his notebook. He sensed Daniel might be in a talkative mood, and there were still many things to go over with him before they got to Maine.

"Oh, one time Sarah got pretty pissed at me 'cause I went on one of my nighttime swims and left her alone for a couple hours. She was asleep when I left, but woke up to find me gone without leaving a note or taking my cell phone. Now I know how she felt."

"I take it you learned your lesson," Victor chuckled. "She does have a bit of a temper sometimes."

"Yep. And it was justified." Daniel grinned. "So what about Maine? Is there a rush?"

"I really want to get there soon and set up everything for when Abu arrives. Plus, I need you to learn the lay of the land as well, mostly so you'll stay out of danger. We'll need to neutralize any cohorts he brings with him. I'd like to have a little one-on-one with the bastard. Have you ever used a rifle?"

"Dad's twenty-two and shotguns. Nothing fancy. Why?" Daniel asked.

"I want to stop in Quantico and teach you about long-distance shooting. I figure we can set up far enough away from the cabin that you're out of danger, and with a rifle and scope you can monitor what's going on and keep my back safe. We'll have some signals, but if things get too hairy, you can escape without being noticed."

"You really think I'd leave you there?" Daniel bristled.

"You'd better. If you don't swear to me that you will, I won't let you get close to the mountain!"

"I'll think about it," Daniel said.

"Do more than think about it," Victor said adamantly. "I'll need you there, but I'm not going to put you at risk. Is that clear?"

"Clear as shit. I'll still think about it."

"You're a hardheaded little snot, aren't you?" Victor said with a chuckle. "But I'm serious about our plan."

Daniel just shrugged, trying to push the conversation in another direction, his concern for Sarah's whereabouts overshadowing the urgency to get to Maine. "How was your evening with the two women?" he asked.

Victor looked over at him with an inquisitive glance.

Daniel explained. "I met them early this morning as they were coming out of what I presumed was your room. They seemed giddy and praised your virility—or something like that."

"My evening was great, thanks for asking. We played ice and razors," Victor said, trying to keep a straight face.

"What is ice and razors? Or is it some kind of kinky sex game I really don't want to know about?"

"Something like that. It's a game I hope you never want to know," Victor returned.

"Why's that?" Daniel's curiosity was piqued now.

"It's actually part of a conversation Joseph wanted me to have with you if he wasn't around. And now that you're going to marry Sarah, I think it's time."

"Victor! Seriously? I don't think sex, if that's what you're alluding to, is something you have to tell me about."

Victor didn't abate. "It *is* what I'm alluding to, and Joseph would disagree with you, and I tend to agree with Joseph. So you might as well hear me out."

"Okay," Daniel said with a snarky edge to his voice. "Let's talk about sex. What do you need to know?"

"Funny," Victor retorted. "You sound like me when I was on the ranch with Paul. Full of spit and vinegar, and cocky as hell. But fortunately Paul set me straight. I was amazed at what I didn't know, and I had been a married Marine. There's not much we marines don't talk about concerning sex, and after a year of marriage, not much I hadn't tried—or so I thought."

"So what did Paul do? Read to you from the Kama Sutra?" Daniel joked, hoping to end this conversation as quickly as possible.

"That's sex 101. Paul was a PhD in sex, and I had no idea how little I knew." Victor paused, not as if to require a comment from Daniel, but as if he were lost in another time. Daniel let the silence continue and waited on Victor. "You know, Daniel, I was so angry with God, and women, and my life. I really wanted to take it out on someone, and Paul let me rant while we were out on the range working. He let me vent until there was nothing more to vent about, and then quietly started my healing process. I wasn't even aware of it until after he left. But he knew what he was doing the whole time, and he was so smooth when he started. One night after we'd finished chow and the fire was beginning to burn low, I declared to him I was never going to love anyone again, but I was going to go bed with at least a thousand women—all one-night stands. That was my life's goal; screw 'em all is what I told him."

"And how did Paul respond?" Daniel asked, trying to picture a young Victor and his sage, Paul, sitting around the campfire in the middle of Texas.

"He said, 'Well, Victor, I can guarantee you one thing: you're going to leave behind a thousand very disappointed women, and in the end you'll be the most disappointed of all.' And I just told him I didn't give a shit. He shrugged and started telling me about the three kinds of sex."

"Just three?" Daniel piped in. "I figured a PhD in sex would know hundreds."

"Nope. They can all be boiled down to just three, which is why it's so important you know that before you make a lifetime commitment to Sarah."

"So I reckon I'm going to hear this whether I want to or not?" Daniel replied.

"You probably didn't want to be potty trained either. After all, what's wrong with shitting in a diaper? But fortunately someone who knew better took the time to train you, and afterwards you probably were happy to use the crapper."

"Idiotic analogy," Daniel quipped.

"Maybe. But always remember. All of us shit our pants until we learn better. So never take any education for granted."

"Alright, alright. Can we get on with it? What, in your opinion, is the first type of sex?" Daniel squirmed, seeing he was stuck and very uncomfortable with the conversation.

"Rape," Victor said, "and all of its manifestations. Any time there is forced involvement, such as arranged marriages, conquered foes, male domination, mental and physical abuse, or coercion—basically any sex not based on mutual consent and respect for your partner—is rape. It is not only the worst sex in the world, but the most practiced. There are very few societies where women have attained enough power to curtail male domination. Almost every religion preaches it."

"Not Christianity," Daniel argued.

"I'm afraid they do, kid. Jesus didn't, and the Bible doesn't teach it, but preachers who corrupt the Bible do. They can spend an entire sermon on Ephesians 5:22 and conveniently ignore the verses before and after."

"What is 5:22?" Daniel asked.

"'Wives, submit yourselves to your own husbands,' and then some quietly might add 'as unto the Lord,' but they add that part as if to ensure they bow to the man as their lord, not their partner. Very corrupt indeed."

"And the other verses?" Daniel quizzed.

"They are about submitting yourselves one to another, and they expound on how husbands should care for their wives as Christ cared for the Church and was crucified for it so we wouldn't be. That's not the virtual enslavement preached by most religions about relationships between men and women. That's where 'as unto the Lord' needs to be interpreted. Love and care for your wife even unto death, not order her around as you would a slave or a servant and take her to bed at your whim. But it's an easy verse for domineering men to grab hold of and use as a God-given excuse to enslave women. That was the crux of Mishael's war, so even if you had married her, she would have been a soldier first and your wife second. Sooner or later her war was going to turn deadly."

"I never saw that. She hid it so well, but always warned me. All I remember is what a beautiful person she was and how her music had incredible life to it. I naively assumed we would be together forever, but now I realize she knew we wouldn't. She was going to go to war with her father's culture and, although she loved me, she knew she would have to leave me. I was naive, Victor. So naive."

"All of us are naive, Daniel. So few of us have the strength and intelligence to choose what Mishael chose to do with her life. We grow up in cocoons, protected by our opulence. We can't imagine the horrors perpetrated by fanatics like Mishael's father and his lieutenants. So to us, a tennis match means the world when it's really worth no more than chaff in the field. We have the luxury to play, and dine, and drink, and talk, and to choose our own partner as we please. That's what Abu can't stand and why it was so easy for him to have Joseph murdered. His corrupted view of religion rewards hate to the point he cannot know love. To him, God is just an excuse to punish anyone who thinks or acts differently than he does. And shouting 'God is great' not only permits him to commit any atrocity he deems fit, but ultimately rewards him for it."

"So is that why Brad and Lydia are in Sierra Leone?" Daniel asked.

"Yes. Brad went to war one day and never came home, figuratively that is. He has a vision for freedom that is as strong as Mishael's. And he will be fighting for it until the day he dies, just like Mishael."

Victor paused, waiting for Daniel's response. But Daniel had nothing to say or add or comment about. Finally Daniel took a deep breath, as if accepting what Victor had said and wanting to move on.

"So what's sex number two?" Daniel asked quietly.

"Well, the second type of sex is about as far removed from the first kind as you can get. It is purely for the pleasure of all involved. You might think of it as a tennis match."

"I've never equated tennis with sex," Daniel puzzled. "I hope that image doesn't come back to haunt me on the court. Or in bed, come to think of it."

Victor grinned, then asked, "Why do you play tennis?"

"'Cause it's fun, I guess."

"So, sex can be played for the same reason. And consider it this way: a new player can have just as much fun on the court as a seasoned player. And as they learn more about the game and get better, it becomes even more fun. Now if you, at your level of tennis, get on a court with a new player, you'll probably not have a great deal of fun and the new player won't know any better. Y'all probably won't play much of a match; you'll just hit the ball around and maybe you'll give some pointers about how to improve. For you to have fun, you'll need the competition of someone close to your level, and you'll expect them to know what you know. That took years of coaching and practice to achieve. Now does the analogy make sense?"

"I guess so. I take it Paul was your coach?" Daniel asked.

"Sort of. He took me into town after the evening at the camp and introduced me to one of his lady friends. She became my real coach, and her entourage provided my real sex education. Then one weekend Paul took me to Houston to play my first game in the real world."

"What? Like a graduation from sex university?"

"I reckon you could call it that," Victor snorted. "Or maybe my final exam? Possibly orals?"

"Ugh, God! I can't believe you said that, Vic!" Daniel groaned.

"Yeah, losing my inhibitions was my hardest lesson also. But I got over it. And I've had a great time, thanks to Paul. He gave me a great gift that actually proved very useful for my business ventures also."

"How's that?" Daniel asked. "Hopefully you're not going to equate sex with golf."

Victor laughed. "Nope. No golf analogies. Sex is the number one tool The Bank uses to blackmail and control their agents, politicians, and business leaders. Once they have compromised someone sexually, then control is pretty easy. The compromise may be with incriminating photographs, evidence of a perversion, or maybe just a beautiful partner in your life. You think they are your soulmate, but really they're just in your life to spy and influence you. Of course The Bank has something on the partner as well, so they play their part perfectly and The Bank is always the winner. They've played that game since their founding and it's still the most successful control technique in the book. Money is their second option, and it works great too, but sex is the best. I was able to avoid the sexual type of control since I never went out with anyone more than twice, but that was just an unexpected perk in my situation. Paul's real motive was to give me the best substitution possible to the third, and by far the best, type of sex."

"And Paul thought that was beyond you? Why?"

"It took him a while to believe I was serious about never having another long-term relationship. But once he figured out I was committed to only short-term affairs and couldn't have children, he felt I might as well maximize the joy of second best, which is sad but true. Very few people experience the best, and most have to settle for an unfulfilling second since they don't know any better. By the way, you should read Ecclesiastes and The Song of Solomon before you get married."

"Okay," Daniel replied, puzzled. "What does all of that have to do with sex?"

"Well Solomon could have any woman he wanted in the kingdom, and had an entire harem of trained virgins who slept with him at his whim. And after an entire life of indulging in what every man thinks is the ultimate sexual thrill, he concluded it was all vanity. Just vanity without any real joy or fulfillment. And his advice to young men was to enjoy the wife of your youth. Be faithful to one, find joy in one, and grow old together as one. The best sex in the world is lying in bed beside a woman who has been faithful to you, and you both have been true to one another. That sex is destroyed immediately by any infidelity, which is why so few of us ever experience it. Most marriages end in divorce and divorce usually occurs over sexual infidelity, money, or both. So you have the opportunity for the best sex in the world with Sarah. Be true, be ever faithful, and grow old in a joyous union. With that you'll never need to learn all the games I play, nor will you have to settle for second best."

"Well, after being with Sarah, I can't imagine ever wanting to be with anyone else," Daniel said, a bit defensively.

"Every groom says that. Then the seven-year itch happens, along with children, money problems, young women cloying for a married man's affection, older wives looking for the adoration of their youth, arguments that just won't go away, nights in separate rooms . . . it's called life, kid, and you have to persevere through it all, even when you're questioning your entire life. Persevere, and remember the joy of your youth even though it has long since faded. Then one day you'll wake up in bed, an old man, and look over at your wife, now an old woman, and you will know true love, joy, and fulfillment; what Solomon could never experience. He could have anything his heart desired but that. And in the end, that is what he craved the most. So few of us can ever have that. We have to settle for less."

Daniel was quiet now. He knew in his heart Victor was right, and he had every intention of being the best husband Sarah could hope for. If he had learned nothing else in his short life, he had learned that sometimes our best intentions get waylaid by powers beyond our control. He hoped and prayed his life with Sarah would be everything Victor said it could be. To grow old with Sarah; he could not imagine anything finer. He wondered if he was up to the task.

Finally Daniel wanted to conclude the conversation. "So getting married is the easy part, I guess. Fifty or so years of life is the challenge."

"That's the challenge," Victor responded. "Enjoy it, kid. It happens fast. We're nearing Quantico. You'll see the angled spire of the Marine Museum soon. Follow the signs to it."

"Tell me again. Why are we stopping there?" Daniel asked.

"I want to see what you can do with a rifle at five hundred yards. We'll meet a master sergeant who can teach you a few things."

"Sounds fun," Daniel said.

"It's deadly serious. And it's a beginning," Victor concluded.

CHAPTER 29

The Race to Maine

Leaving the Marine base, Victor told Daniel how impressed he was with his shooting ability. "You're a natural, kiddo. You know, putting the crosshairs on a target is easy, but holding it steady and squeezing the trigger without a trace of movement is tricky. And you were rock solid. Did you shoot often with Joseph?"

"A couple times a year he'd take me out plinking, as he called it. I loved it. But the twenty-two is a lot different than the sniper's rifle. You sure know you've pulled the trigger with the A3; and the scope was incredible. I felt like I could count the hairs on a fly at a hundred yards. Thanks for taking me," Daniel said.

"Remember the serious side of this training, Daniel. You may have to put those crosshairs on a human being. And if I give the signal, you'll have to pull the trigger. My life may depend on your steady finger. Are you up for that?"

"If it's Abu or Babel, I'll be happy to oblige. If you're in danger, I'll have no problem pulling the trigger," Daniel said.

"Remember, though," Victor warned, "it's always different in the field. Hesitation is suicide. Overthinking is suicide. The signal and the shot within one second of each other is critical. I brought the A4, which is just like the A3, but with a suppressor so no one will know where the shot comes from."

"I got it. Aren't you hungry yet?" Daniel asked.

"Oh. Shit yeah. What's with me? I never forget about eating. Must be the old adrenalin kicking in that made it slip my mind. Being on the shooting range brought back a lot of memories. Good memories. Blowing things up and shooting things are the fun parts of being a marine," Victor said, laughing. "Let's get on US 1 near Fort Belvoir and go into Georgetown. I know a small restaurant where we can stay out of sight and have a pretty decent meal."

"Now why does that not surprise me?" Daniel quipped.

As usual, the meal was great and as they got back on the road, Victor pulled out a map to study. "Let's try to make it to Woodstock. You think you can drive that far?"

"Sure, no problem. Why Woodstock?" Daniel asked.

"It's a great little village stuck in the sixties. No cameras and no questions. We can get to Maine in about five hours from there, so we can eat an early breakfast and be at the cabin for lunch. Susan usually has some fresh lake trout for us when she knows we're coming."

"Sounds like a decent plan. Have you heard from Mark?" Daniel asked.

"Not yet. He'll leave a message that I'll pick up when I turn on the phone. I'll try him in the morning if I don't get a message tonight. Are you still trying Sarah?"

"Every hour," Daniel replied. "It's really getting worrisome. Isn't there anyone else who might know where she is?"

"I'm sure Brad kept that knowledge minimized for her safety, but I'll call Jeffrey in the morning just on the off chance he knows something."

"Jeffrey? As in my old studio-mate?" Daniel asked. "Why would he know anything?"

"Did you ever figure out what Jeffrey's job was at VCM?" Victor asked.

"I never thought much about it. I assumed he managed properties just like the rest of us. Why?"

"You ever notice how his meetings and your meetings coincided so much?"

"I thought that was Jennifer doing an excellent job of coordinating schedules so the planes were used efficiently. Obviously there was something else going on?" Daniel asked.

"Jeffrey is a translator and an analyst. His father was a Somali warlord who took his mother, a NATO peacekeeper from Finland, hostage in Mogadishu. By the time we got her out, she'd had his child, Jeffrey, who was two years old."

"I don't remember hearing any of that in the news," Daniel said.

"It was a bit before your time," Victor chuckled, "and due to his mother's covert activities it was kept quiet. So, you'll never read about it anywhere. But we did finally rescue her and she settled in America with a Somali who helped facilitate her escape. He adopted Jeffrey. In addition to her native Finnish, she spoke Russian, Farsi, French, and English. She required all communications within her home to be in Russian, so Jeffrey knows the nuances of the language and does a great job translating and interpreting covert communications. The nice part of his job is he can do it anywhere with a laptop. So we gave him other assignments such as keeping tabs on you and seeing you had everything you needed to succeed. He's also a highly trained operative, so if Brad wanted to have Sarah watched, Jeffrey may have been called in. And, by the way, watch your wallet; he's a master pickpocket—a useful talent that comes in handy sometimes."

"Do you do that with all of your new hires?" Daniel asked facetiously.

"Only the best for my one nephew." Victor smiled back. "And we knew you brought some baggage with you from Palo Alto, so Jeffrey was your watch dog."

"Well, I hope he can give us some information about Sarah," Daniel said, not masking his concern. "By the way, when are you going to tell me where my mountain is?"

"As soon as you promise me you will not put yourself at risk," Victor replied.

"As long as I can cover you with the A4 and its glass, I'll stay away. That's what I promise. It's up to you to make sure I can cover you from five hundred yards," Daniel warned.

"When we get to Woodstock, I'll show you the lay of the land. Did you ever wonder who rented it several times a year?" Victor asked.

"I didn't until it turned out that whoever rents it has the same phone number as you put in the want ad. So it must be you or someone you know. Care to fill me in?"

"Sure," Victor said. "It's set up and used as a winter survivalist training camp for top level agents. We run two-week courses there for all of the military branches as well as the CIA and a few close allies. There are hidden observation stations for that purpose, so you will set up in one of those that has a great overview of the cabin area as well as an escape access route. Instructors use those facilities to quietly keep tabs on the students. They can slip in and out without being noticed."

"So, what does Susan do there?"

"She has a research project she's been doing for years," Victor answered. "She knows when the training is going on, so she helps keep tabs on the students while making sure they don't disrupt her project. We've never had a student see her, so she's very good at staying hidden."

"What's the research project about?" Daniel asked.

"Don't know," Victor replied, not being completely truthful. "Nobody knows. All of her notes and data are uploaded to an encrypted server that cannot be accessed without certain specific protocols. Her death is one of those protocols, so we probably will never know what she's been doing."

"That's too bad," Daniel surmised. "She's spent her entire life working on something she'll never see published. It must be very important to her, personally."

"I guess so," Victor agreed.

Victor and Daniel arrived at the Woodstock Inn late that night, and had to wake up the desk clerk for one of the cottages. She pleasantly welcomed them and offered to fix them a late-night snack. Daniel was famished and very happy when Victor agreed.

"Is this what psychedelic looked like?" Daniel asked as he walked through the rustic lobby rife with sixties memorabilia.

"It's about as authentic as you're going to see," Victor replied, then asked the hostess, "How many old guys come in here and announce they were at Woodstock?"

"At least one a week. It keeps this town in business," she laughed.

"I wish I could have been there," Victor lamented. "Man, to have seen Grace Slick sing White Rabbit—that would have been outrageous." Victor's voice trailed off as if he were entering a time warp, then he added, "Best two-and-a-half minutes in rock and roll."

"Have a seat in the bar while I fix your eggs," the clerk told them as she pointed toward a doorway with strings of love beads hanging from jamb to jamb.

Daniel parted them and stepped into the small lounge area with overstuffed floor pillows along the pine-paneled wall and an L-shaped bar with peace signs printed on the tie-dyed seat of every stool. As Daniel looked around he noticed the peace sign dominated the decor, and was used in all manner of eclectic motifs. He wondered if the eggs would come in the same shape.

The eggs and bacon were quickly wolfed down followed by orange juice and green tea for a digestif. Victor looked on the shelf behind the bar and noticed some Wild Turkey Rare Breed Bourbon. "Can I help myself?" he asked the clerk, pointing to the bottle.

"Sure, but only if you share," she said with a seductive smile.

He poured some into his tea, then took two shot glasses and topped them off. Signaling to Daniel, he offered him a shot.

"No, thanks," Daniel declined. "I'm ready for the cottage."

"Number 31. Behind the goldfish pond. The key's on the desk in the lobby," the clerk said as she downed the shot and poured another. "Thanks," she said, tipping the glass toward Victor.

Victor raised his glass and downed the brown liquid, then sipped the hot tea.

"Good night, Uncle Victor," Daniel said, exiting through the beads.

"I'm right behind you, kid," Victor said, then turned to the clerk. "Wonderful late-night snack. Maybe another time?"

"I'm always here," she said, smiling.

To say the cottage was rustic was not a comment on the dated furnishings and faded paint, but more of a statement that nothing in it had been touched or repaired in almost half a century. It was as if it would be a sacrilege to touch the patina accrued since 1969. Daniel looked over at Victor as if to say, "Seriously?" Victor just smiled and said, "We're not at the Jefferson anymore, kiddo, but sometimes it does the heart good to sleep in the past. At least it's quiet. I think we'll have to go back toward town to get cell service. That's a downer. I was hoping to call Jeffrey early in the morning."

"I'll be up around five o'clock," Daniel said, "so we can leave whenever you're ready. I'm anxious to find Sarah. This just isn't like her, Victor."

"Well, everything has been haywire for the last few days, so let's not worry too much yet. Brad should be back tomorrow so that will settle it anyway," Victor said.

"I hope so. I'll try not to wake you when I go for a run in the morning. Good night."

"Good night, kid."

Daniel took a quick shower and found Victor asleep on the sofa when he came out of the bathroom. He took the smaller room with the bunk beds and stretched out, letting the ceiling fan churn the stale air as he tried to sleep and not worry about Sarah. It was a fruitless endeavor, and by four o'clock the walls were closing in on him, so he decided to see a bit of Woodstock in the predawn light. He left Victor a note saying he was going to stroll into town and find a coffee shop.

Daniel perused the streets of the small town until after the sun came up. He happened upon their car parked in front of a breakfast bistro, and found Victor already ordering. Daniel sat down at the small table and turned his cup upright, signaling for coffee.

"Enjoy your run?" Victor asked as he poured Daniel a cup of coffee from the carafe the waiter had placed on the table.

"Yeah. This is a neat little place. You know there's a playhouse on the outskirts where some famous Broadway actors have performed? They're doing *Fiddler on the Roof* right now. Maybe this place does have some redeeming qualities," Daniel laughed.

"Yes, it does," Victor agreed. "That playhouse burned a few years back. VCM donated funds toward the rebuilding and set up a scholarship fund for summer stock. We've helped a few New York actors get their start."

"So you're a little more familiar with this place than you let on. Figures," Daniel said.

"I need these types of hideaways to get some rest sometimes. Vacations at Disney World were never something I aspired to. But a couple of days up here in the Catskills can recharge me better than two weeks at a resort."

"I can imagine it would. Coffee's good. Thanks," Daniel said, tipping his cup toward Victor.

"Try the Jamaican omelet. It'll add a little spice to your morning."

"Sounds good. Then can we get on the road?" Daniel asked.

"Sure. I didn't check out yet. Thought you might want a shower."

"Yeah, that would be nice," Daniel said.

After breakfast, Victor drove Daniel back to the cottage for a shower while he checked out. Daniel was waiting with the car running when Victor finally came out of the main lodge.

"That was quick," Victor said as he opened the door.

"Right," Daniel said with a smirk. "I take it you were making time with the clerk?"

"As a matter of fact, I was. She invited me back after we finish in Maine. I just might take her up on the offer."

"Well, right now I'm anxious to get down the mountain and find some cell service," Daniel replied.

"Oh, yeah, I tried Jeffrey when I was in town, but he didn't answer. Hopefully, he'll call back soon."

"I hope so," Daniel said as he traversed the rutted gravel road out of the inn. Once on the main road, Victor's phone rang.

"Hello," Victor answered as he put the phone in speaker mode.

"Hey, Victor. Mark here. How's your trip going?"

"Fine. We had a quiet night in Woodstock and are getting an early start to Maine. What's up with you?" Victor asked, hoping to dispense with the small talk and find out if he could help with Abu.

"All's okay here. Lily and Lani were disappointed you left so quickly."

"Lovely ladies," Victor said. "Hope to enjoy their company again one day. Any success with Abu?"

"That's a curious situation," Mark replied. "This guy you call Abu, he's Syed Ahmed Hussain?"

"That's right," Victor said, trying not to let his impatience surface.

"And his cohort is Habib Hafiz?"

"Yes. What do you have?"

"You know they have a very sophisticated intelligence network in the US?"

"Yes."

"Well, they're looking for Daniel and they don't believe he's dead. They've been concentrating their efforts around Brownsville and Matamoros, thinking he went to Mexico to escape Habib. Babel as you call him."

"And?" Victor was restless for Mark to get to the point.

"They went to Williamsburg and then headed toward Maine. We've had a tail on them, but lost them during the night. If their destination is the same as yours, they'll get there before you. My guess is they're going to check it out, so I didn't need to feed them any information. Of course, if they don't find Daniel there, then they might leave before you arrive. But I'd be very careful when you get there."

"Shit!" Victor exclaimed. "That certainly changes things."

Daniel grabbed the pad and pencil that Victor always kept handy and scrawled a quick note. *Didn't Eric get into law school at W&M?*

Victor nodded affirmatively then said, "It's in Williamsburg."

"What?" Mark said.

"Nothing. Daniel and I were wondering who they talked to in Williamsburg. Do you have anyone available to check out someone there?"

"Sure," Mark said. "Who?"

"Hold on a moment, Mark," Victor said, then turned to Daniel. "Why do you suspect Eric?"

"Well, a couple of days after our confrontation with Eric in your office, when you gave me the packet with information about Maine, Jeffrey suggested I start locking my office door when I leave. I thought it was odd since I assumed the building and our suite were secure, so I never worried about my office. Maybe he suspected Eric was going through my files. I'm pretty sure he would've had to in order to get some of the information he tried to use against me. And if Jeffrey was assigned to covertly watch me, it would make sense he would warn me to lock my door."

"What'd you do with the envelope I gave you?" Victor asked.

"It sat on my desk for a week or so until I had time to study it," Daniel answered.

"That would be plenty of time for Eric to study it, if he actually was rifling through your papers. So he might've given Abu information about the mountain." Victor turned back to Mark and gave him Eric's full name, spelling out his last name. "He's a law student there. He has a wife and two kids. I don't have an address. Find out if Abu and Babel talked to him and if he told them anything about Daniel."

"Mark, this is Daniel. Do you know if they talked to any of my studio-mates or people from the racquet club?"

"Hi, Daniel," Mark replied. "I'm not sure. They spent time in Houston, so I'll check with your colleagues. You mind if I call them?"

Daniel looked at Victor for guidance. Victor answered for him. "Please do check them out. It's possible they're being watched, so do it carefully. We'll send you names."

"Will do. I guess a few people are going to get Chinese takeout today."

"Huh?" Daniel grunted.

"We go almost anywhere unnoticed when we're in a delivery van with takeout. And can knock on any door. We sometimes walk right up to a surveillance vehicle and offer them the food under the pretense of a canceled order and check them out while we're there. We've even gotten credit card info and photos when they pay. Pretending not to understand English gets us some amazing info, too."

"Nice trick," Daniel said as Victor nodded in agreement.

"Okay. Anything else?" Mark asked.

"No," Victor answered. "We'll get to Maine in less than four hours. We'll need all the info you can get before that."

"Will do," Mark said as he hung up.

As soon as the phone was off, Victor opened his passport and thumbed through the pages until he found what he was looking for, then began dialing a number. Daniel watched curiously. As the phone was ringing, Victor explained. "The stamps in the passport look like normal customs stamps, but in reality, this is a covert phone book. Names, numbers, and passwords are hidden in plain sight if you know how to read them. I have Jeffrey's covert number right here," Victor pointed to a stamp from Somalia. "Read the visa number backwards and you get Jeffrey's emergency number." After four rings, Victor hung up. A minute later he redialed. Jeffrey picked up on the second ring. Daniel could hear Jeffrey's familiar voice, but didn't understand the words. Victor answered, "Nyet." It sounded to Daniel like Russian. Then he heard Jeffrey say, "Angliyskiy?" and Victor say, "Nyet, nyet."

Jeffrey responded in English as Victor pushed the speaker button. "Great to hear your voice, sir."

Victor responded quickly, "How's Kansas?"

"Golden," Jeffrey returned.

"Good. We're looking for the general's daughter. Have you seen her? She hasn't been answering calls."

"Yeah," Jeffrey answered. "She lost her phone, but ordered a new one she should get today."

"Where is she?" Victor asked, relieved by the explanation.

"I promised her I wouldn't tell. She wants to surprise the kid."

"He's with me. We're on speaker," Victor said.

"I figured as much," Jeffrey said. "So don't tell her I told you and act surprised when you get there."

"Where?" Daniel said with a sudden flush of anxiety.

"Where you're going. She's already there. I dropped her off last night."

"Oh, shit! No!" Daniel and Victor both screamed at the same time.

"Tell me she's not there!" Daniel yelled.

"Wha-what's the problem?" Jeffrey's surprise made him stutter. "I-I thought you'd be h-happy!"

Victor cut in and took the phone off speaker. "Abu and Babel are there. Where are you?"

"Just south of the city. Probably five hours away with the heavy traffic building."

"Get back as fast as you can. I'll call the sheriff. Oh, my God! Just hurry. Please hurry. We had no idea she would want to join us. This is a freakin' nightmare. Shit!" Victor was shaking as Daniel grabbed the phone.

Daniel's voice was quivering, "We're a little closer than you. God, please hurry."

Victor took the phone and turned it off, then smashed it against the shift lever until it was in little pieces. He gathered up the pieces and tossed them out the window. Immediately he grabbed another phone and dialed.

Daniel's speed was approaching triple digits by the time Victor realized he was speeding. He grabbed Daniel's leg and shouted, "Don't get caught, or we'll never get there. I can't call anyone in New York to let us go. Just keep it at ten miles over the limit and be careful."

"How the hell can I do that? Sarah's . . ." Daniel lost his voice for a moment. Then quietly said, "They'll kill her."

"I know, Daniel, but our only chance is to get there without a stop. Any kind of a stop. Understand? They won't kill her before we get there. It's you they want."

"Shit!" was all Daniel could say, exasperated as he backed off the accelerator. He heard the click of the phone being answered.

"Cornish Sheriff's Department. May I help you?"

"Is Sheriff Tratton there? This is an emergency," Victor said, trying to keep his voice under control.

"He's down at the library. Can Deputy Colcered help you?"

"Tell him to get the sheriff now. A life is in danger. Hurry. You've got this number?"

"Yes," The woman said. Victor hung up and handed the phone to Daniel. "You answer that one." He reached into the bag and found the last two phones. He picked one and turned it on. He picked up Mark's card from the center console and dialed the number. Mark answered immediately. Victor didn't wait for any pleasantry. "You got anything yet?"

"I've got someone on the way to his house and another guy on the way to the law school, but haven't heard anything yet."

"Call me on this number when you do." Victor hung up before Mark could respond. He opened his passport and found another number.

Daniel heard a *hello* from the other end and Victor immediately said "Kansas." Then Daniel heard the faint "Golden."

Victor continued, "How are things in Arizona?"

"Fine sir. Great to hear your voice. Hope all's—"

Victor cut him short. "The general's daughter is at the northern retreat. We believe Abu and Babel are there also." Daniel heard the curse from the phone as Victor continued. "How fast can you assemble a team and get there?"

"If we can commandeer the G650 and find two pilots to replace the others, then it will take an hour to get everyone to the airport. We have a cart in the security locker loaded and ready for an event like this, so we'll prep on the way." Daniel detected a pause on the phone and presumed the person on the other end was doing some fast calculations. Victor held the phone slightly away from his ear so Daniel could listen in. "Fast flight will be about two and a half hours. We'll transfer to a helicopter for a thirty-minute trip, so fastest possible is a bit over four hours, sir."

"Do it immediately. Heavy arms, sniper in helicopter. Use authorization code victor740bravo52, level one for everything including the helicopter. See if you can get a message to Brad."

"Yes, sir," was the immediate answer.

"Any questions?" Victor asked anxiously.

"Your ETA?"

"Four hours."

"This number?"

"Negative, negative," Victor replied.

"Got it, sir."

Daniel heard the click of the phone going dead, and turned to Victor. "Why not use that number? We only have one phone left and it hasn't been used. Who was that, anyway?"

"A double negative is a yes," Victor replied.

"Like nyet, nyet to Jeffrey?"

"Exactly."

"So you're talking code?" Daniel guessed.

"Absolutely. Cell phone calls are constantly monitored even when you think they're secure or private. If Abu is as good as Mark hinted, then he has a mole in our intelligence community. A couple of names or places mentioned that they are scanning for and they'll hear our conversation within minutes, pinpoint our location, and track us."

"So that's why you destroyed the other phone?"

"Yes."

"And what is it with Kansas?"

"Code for use no names."

"And golden?"

"Appropriate response for understood and recognize who you are. Any other state, like Arizona, is just to talk enough to ensure my voice is recognized. Brad and I would like to train you in covert operations when we finish with the Maine business."

"Is that what he wants to talk to me about?" Daniel asked.

"Yes," Victor said quietly as he tried to calm down and formulate a plan.

"What are we going to do when we get to Maine?" Daniel asked. "And who was that on the phone?"

"That was Billy. He was responsible for getting an agent to your house when Babel was waiting for you. His fast actions saved Sarah then, but I don't think he can make it in time to help in Maine. And neither will Jeffrey. With Brad out of the country, I'm afraid we're on our own. God, this is a nightmare, Daniel. Let me think for a minute."

"All right," Daniel said quietly. He noticed his hands were trembling as he tried to drive carefully at the maximum speed he could risk. He knew if the police tried to stop him, he would probably attempt to outrun them, even though he knew it would be futile. But if he couldn't get to Sarah before Babel, everything else would be futile anyway. His life would be over. Finally, Victor sighed and looked at him.

"Daniel, hopefully the sheriff will get there before Abu and Babel and get Sarah to safety. When we get there, if we're not sure about the sheriff, then you should take the A4 to the first outpost while I go to the cabin and check things out. If you see Abu or Babel, or anyone you suspect to be with them, shoot them unless I'm holding my hand up. That's a fail-safe sign. I'll keep one hand up. If it goes down, you pull the trigger."

"I can do that, but I'd rather go to where Sarah is," Daniel said, almost pleadingly.

"I'm trained. You're not. The best thing for Sarah is for me to get to her and you to cover me. I can take care of myself in close quarters. Understand?"

"I understand," Daniel said as Victor's phone buzzed.

Victor answered without a hello. "What have you got?"

Daniel recognized Mark's voice as Victor touched the speaker button.

"Abu and Babel have visited all of the former studio-mates except J. Apparently he's been out of town since the kid went missing. They also visited everyone at the racquet club and got no information. But when they went to Williamsburg they talked to the law student while he was studying in the library. Unfortunately, when our guy went in to see him, he was slumped over his books, dead. People around just thought he was asleep. He's in the middle of finals, so it wasn't odd for him to be there studying and napping."

"Is your guy still there?" Victor asked.

"He's outside the building waiting for instructions."

"See if he can go back to the cubicle and look for any drink. Anything liquid he would have ingested. If so, tell him to take it to Camp Peary. I'll have someone meet him at the gate. Tell him to be very careful with it," Victor warned.

"Will do. I'll call back." The phone went dead immediately.

Victor opened his passport and thumbed through it until he found a number to dial. The phone was immediately answered by an official military aide who spouted several acronyms and announced the line was not secure. Victor requested a secure line and a return call, then hung up. A minute later the phone rang and Victor answered with a number code. After a short wait, Daniel could hear a voice come on the line. Victor hadn't put it in speaker mode, but Daniel could still hear the faint voice. "Colonel Ames."

"V540, are we secure?" Victor asked.

"Yes, sir," came the crisp reply.

"Within the hour a man may come to the gate carrying some sort of drink. Take it carefully and send him away quickly. Secure the liquid and the container. It will need to go to Fort Belvoir for K24 analysis. Dispatch immediately. Understand?"

"Yes, sir."

"I want you at the gate to meet him. No one else. Is that a problem?"

"No, sir."

Victor turned the phone off.

"You think Eric was murdered?" Daniel asked.

"If he gave Abu the information about Maine, then Babel will eliminate him just to cover their tracks. Looks like his nosiness got him killed. Too bad," Victor said facetiously.

"He did have a wife and children, Victor," Daniel said sullenly.

"You're right," Victor responded. "I've become way too callous in my old age. Eric probably thought he was just helping with a missing-person case. The death penalty is a harsh punishment for snooping."

"Yeah," Daniel said as he was thinking about the danger to Sarah.

The phone buzzed and Victor picked it up and hit the speaker button. "What have you got?"

It was Mark, and Daniel noticed there was no introduction or mentioning of names. Obviously Mark knew how to follow covert protocol in dicey situations. "Big Gulp. Half full. On the way." The phone went dead.

"I guess Mark knows how deadly these guys are now?" Daniel asked rhetorically.

"Yep. He'll be extremely careful from now on," Victor concurred.

Daniel's phone buzzed and he looked at the number noticing the Maine area code as he handed it to Victor to answer.

"Hello," Victor said.

"Sheriff Tratton here. Can I help you?"

"This is Susan's friend from the mountain. Do you recognize my voice?" Victor asked.

"Oh yeah, V—"

"The mountain is infested," Victor cut in, covering the sheriff saying his name. "Listen carefully. We believe we have an innocent there with a team on the way to do harm. Can you rescue?"

The line was quiet for a moment, then the sheriff asked, "Should I call in the state police or the national guard?"

"It may be too late, but you should."

There was another delay, then the sheriff spoke. "Sorry, sir, but I thought you were dead, so I'm just a little surprised."

"I am. Keep it that way, please. And hurry," Victor said solemnly.

"Okay."

Victor turned the phone off and laid his head on the headrest.

Daniel decided to use the cruise control since he was too nervous to keep his speed constant. All he could do now was drive and pray. Feelings of helplessness swamped him.

Except for occasional directions from Victor, both men were quiet until they were close to the turnoff to go up the mountain. Victor had used the time to draw a detailed map for Daniel and write notes in his journal. Daniel assumed they were notes to Brad. Victor pointed to the nearly hidden road, and Daniel turned quickly onto it. Victor began reviewing their plans and options with Daniel as he was concentrating on keeping the car on the rugged, one lane mountain road.

As Daniel made a sharp left turn, following the ruts, the sheriff's car came into view fifty yards ahead. The lights were flashing and the driver's door was open.

"Stop here!" Victor shouted.

"Let's get closer," Daniel countered.

"No! Stop!" Victor demanded as he opened his door. "Get the A4 and let's go. Stay alert. The path you need is just beyond the sheriff's car. I'll take a shortcut up the mountain to the cabin. Put a round in the dirt near me when you're in position."

Daniel grabbed the gun case and followed Victor. He figured he could assemble the rifle on the way to the lookout. As they passed the sheriff's car, they could see him lying on his back in the road, motionless. His throat had been slit.

"We're too late, Daniel. Get up there fast. Don't wait for me to get into position, just shoot the sons-of-bitches. There's the path. Go!"

Before Victor had finished the sentence Daniel was on his way, running as fast as he could while trying to read the map, follow the small trail, and find the marker for the lookout. "God, please don't let me miss it," he kept praying.

The moment Daniel saw the dark figure emerge from behind a tree, he felt his guts explode from a sudden jab, then sensed a bright flash of light as he was propelled forward by a blow to the back of his head. He was sent sprawling to the forest floor, unconscious.

CHAPTER 30

The Consecration

Daniel's head felt like it was in a vise as he regained consciousness. Slowly, he opened his eyes and started to jerk, but immediately felt the sharp pain in his nostril. He looked up into Babel's grimace.

"No, no, my young infidel. Be very still or you will lose half of your little bitty white nose," Babel laughed as he held the large hunting knife's tip in Daniel's nostril, applying enough pressure to hurt, but not cut.

Daniel tried to move his arms and legs, but they were bound tightly and Babel was sitting on his chest with his legs pinioning Daniel's arms.

"You rotten son-of-a-bitch," Daniel screamed. His head exploded with pain as Babel hit him just above his ear.

"You will learn respect before we kill you, or you will die with even more pain." Babel spit the words into Daniel's face, his eyes inches away from Daniel's.

Through the pain, all Daniel could see was the evil in the dark irises. He had never imagined such evil could display itself. Daniel winced as he spat back, "Swine!" and the pain again exploded as Babel's fist landed hard above Daniel's other ear.

Babel sat upright and returned the knife to Daniel's nostril, daring him to move. "Oh, what a joy it would be to kill you now. How unfortunate Syed wants that pleasure. He was so delighted watching me have my way with your bitch."

Daniel screamed and again tried to writhe free, but Babel had him pinned perfectly. He felt the blood drip into his throat as the knife sliced his nostril.

"Be still, you imbecile," Babel shouted. "Syed will cut you. He wants you all to himself. But I will do your sweet lady friend as you watch. Ah, what a glorious day this will be. God is great!" Babel smiled as he looked toward the sky.

"Satan is your only god, you rotten piece of pig shit."

Again Daniel felt the intense pain of another blow. He was now having trouble focusing after the repeated head blows, but he was in no mood to keep quiet. His physical pain was nothing compared to his angst over Sarah. It occurred to him if he could buy enough time for Victor to get to the cabin, then Sarah might have a chance. And if he could get Babel to hit him hard enough to be fatal, then they might let her go. "You really think you're a Muslim, you asshole?"

Again, the blow, but Babel knew just how hard to hit for maximum pain and little damage. "What do you know about my religion, infidel?" Babel spat back.

"Your religion?" Daniel managed to laugh. He knew he now had Babel engaged, so he milked it, trying to get the anger level rising. "You're no more Islamic than Jim Jones was Christian. You just drink the Kool-Aid and practice evil in the name of a false god. That makes you a son of Satan." Again, the splitting pain encompassed Daniel's head as Babel landed another blow.

"I'll teach you to blaspheme God!" Babel screamed.

Daniel was grappling for anything that would get to Babel, so he kept talking through the pain. "So your boyfriend likes to watch you prey on innocent women? Same with little boys? Do you enjoy hearing them scream, coward?"

Daniel braced for the blow, but it was a moment later than he expected. Babel's timing had been interrupted by that sentence, and Daniel's finely honed sense of his opponent's emotions told him he had hit a nerve; a truth nerve, perhaps. *Was it the rape? Or the comment about young boys?* Daniel realized it must be the boyfriend. *Abu was his boyfriend!* He seized on that tidbit of information and drove it into Babel's black heart. "So you use that little pecker of yours on Syed!" Through the double slaps Daniel shouted, "You can't satisfy a woman with that tiny prick, so you pick on boys and suck your boss's dick!" Daniel's face was numb from the repeated blows, but he didn't relent. He knew he was buying time for Sarah, and Babel was playing into his scheme. "You're not even a real man, you cock-sucking son-of-a-bitch."

At that moment Daniel felt Babel's body convulse in a sudden orgasmic shudder as an arrowhead appeared protruding from his ribs. Babel looked down and touched the pulsing barb with his free hand as another arrow emerged from his gut. Daniel heard a gurgle as Babel tried to speak, but the words were just a bloody froth filling his mouth. Daniel's quick pelvic thrust threw Babel onto his side and he grabbed the knife from Babel's limp hand. Daniel sliced the cords binding his hands and rolled on top of Babel, breaking the arrow shafts as he shoved Babel onto his back. With both hands, he plunged the knife into his throat. Babel's body jerked spasmodically as the knife severed his spine. His eyes rolled into his head and he was gone. Daniel sat on the lifeless body, afraid to let it go; afraid it wasn't dead.

"Let's go, Daniel. We've got to hurry," Daniel heard a woman's voice say as he stared at Babel's contorted face. Then he smelled an overpowering stench of urine, feces, and dead, rotting flesh. He leaned over and puked, then looked up at Susan.

"Hurry, Daniel," she urged as she started running up the trail.

Daniel grabbed the knife and cut his feet free, then ran after Susan as he realized the stench was coming from her, not Babel.

As Daniel caught up to her, they heard a single gunshot. She stopped and held her hand up motioning for Daniel to be still and quiet. She shouldered her bow, then cupped her hands behind her ears as she rotated her head side to side. Then, as if locking onto a signal, she ran into the forest. Daniel followed, amazed at how nimbly she slipped through the underbrush. Suddenly she slowed, stepping stealthily along. Daniel tried to follow her as quietly as he could, but he was no match for her skillfulness. He caught up to her at the base of a small hill beneath the cabin area. She was crouching beside Victor who was sitting with his back to a tree.

"You're bleeding," Victor said as Daniel noticed his shirt was red with blood from his nose.

"So are you," Daniel said as he looked at Victor's hand over his gut with blood oozing out between his fingers.

"Yeah, the son-of-a-bitch shot me. I was hoping you'd get them with the A4. What are you doing here?"

While he was laboring to talk, Susan was getting bandages from her side bag, laying Victor on his back, and pulling up his shirt to expose the wound. She expertly applied the bandage and pressure, taking both of his hands and placing them in the best position to stem the flow. She talked as she worked.

"Did you see who's at the cabin?" Susan asked.

Victor winced with pain as Susan adjusted his hands. "Damn, Susan! That hurts!" He inhaled sharply, then spoke haltingly. "Two outside with rifles. I think Abu and Babel must be inside with Sarah." Victor paused again as pain gripped him. "I slid down the hill to get away after they shot me."

"Babel's dead," Daniel said. "He ambushed me on the trail and Susan saved me. Did you see Sarah? Is she all right?"

"Sorry, Daniel. I didn't get a look into the cabin and I didn't see the second guard until it was too late. God, is that my guts that smell so bad?"

"No, Victor," Susan said. "It's me. Part of my research. You stay very still and keep the pressure on. We'll be back for you." She reached behind her waist and took a small, handheld crossbow and several bolts, and handed them to Daniel. "You know how to use this?" she asked.

"Yes," Daniel said, pulling the stirrup to cock the steel limb and placing a bolt in the barrel.

"Good," Susan said. "I'm going to survey the cabin. You go that way about fifty yards. You'll see a yellow bush. There's a stairway hidden behind it that leads to the cabin area. I'll meet you at the top in about ten minutes. Stay hidden until I get to you. Got it?"

"Yes," Daniel said. He put his hand on Victor's forehead. "Stay still, Uncle Vic. We'll get them, then we'll get you to the hospital. I promise."

"Be careful, son. Be careful, please," Victor said quietly as he closed his eyes.

Daniel whispered to Susan, "Will he make it?"

"If we can get him out of here quickly, he will. But nobody will make it if we don't get to the cabin. Let's go."

She took off to the right along the base of the hill and Daniel headed to the left looking for the bush.

At the top of the steps Daniel lay prone, surveying the cabin area. He watched as the two guards paced back and forth on the porch. The door opened once and Mishael's father stepped out to say something to the guards, then quickly went back in. He seemed very small standing next to the guards, but they were obviously subservient to him.

Daniel felt a slight pressure on his leg as the stench again filled his nostrils. He looked down to see Susan sidling up beside him. He had not heard her approach.

She whispered into his ear, "Rear clear. Just the two guards. If you can get to the corner of the house, I'll signal you when the guard is there and turning. Use the crossbow on him and I'll get the other guy at the same time, then we'll rush the door. Sarah's tied up on the bed in the back bedroom, and the other guy is sitting on the couch watching the door. If we surprise him, we have a good chance. Listen for a chickadee whistle. That's when he'll be turning around. Ready?"

"Got it," Daniel said.

"Try to be quieter. I could hear you from the other side of the hill." She pointed at the guards and said, "They don't know what to listen for, so you're probably okay, but just go easy. We've got time."

"I'll try," Daniel said and slid backwards to get below the sight line of the guards. As he moved along the side of the hill, he became aware of every snapping twig and the rustling of leaves. He slowed down and began watching every step, looking for the quietness. It seemed like an eternity until he got to the cabin. He eased along the wall to the corner and waited, knife in one hand, crossbow in the other, ready to strike. He could hear the steady rhythm of footsteps on the slightly elevated wooden porch. He listened carefully as the footsteps paused, then heard the chickadee. He rotated around the corner and extended his arm to get the bolt close to the guard's back, pulled the trigger, then grabbed the guard's legs and jerked him off the porch, thrusting the knife under his ribcage toward his heart. He shoved the guard's face into the dirt to muffle his scream and held him there until he felt no more movement. From his crouched position over the body he could see along the porch where the other guard had fallen to his knees, two arrows piercing his chest. Daniel leapt onto the porch and kicked the rifle away as he hit him in the head with the haft of the knife, then with a backstroke, sliced his throat open. The guard gurgled as he tried to scream, then fell forward, dead. Susan was now behind Daniel on the porch and motioned toward the door. Daniel reloaded the crossbow and handed it to Susan. She motioned for Daniel to stand beside the door as she kicked it in, but Daniel shook his head. He knew that with his size and strength he could easily take the door off its hinges, then Susan could use the crossbow on Syed, hopefully before he could react. Susan nodded agreement and signaled the count of three.

Daniel used the entire force of his body against the door and it shattered easily, sending him reeling into the room. He rolled once and was on his knees at the couch as the bolt whizzed by him into Syed's shoulder. The suddenness of the attack caught Syed off guard and as he tried to yell, Daniel hit him in the face with his fist holding the knife. The knife handle acted like brass knuckles and Daniel felt Syed's jaw crush under the force of the blow. Daniel leapt to his feet, grabbing Syed's collar as he stood and jerked him off the couch. He kneed him in the groin, then threw him to the floor as easily as he would a rag doll. He was surprised by the delicate lightness of Syed, almost as if he were a child. Daniel heard the crunch of bone as Syed's arm folded behind him when he hit the floor. He yelled from terror and pain.

"Habib! Habib!" he cried, his outburst garbled from his broken jaw.

Daniel stood over the crumpled body, reached down, and slapped him across the face with enough force to pop his eyeball out of its socket.

"Your precious boy toy is dead, you godless bastard!"

Syed just continued whimpering, "Habib. Oh, Habib."

Daniel felt Susan brush past him in the melee and head toward the bedroom. He quickly regrouped and followed, leaving Syed to his agony.

Susan got to Sarah first and immediately felt for a pulse. She was naked on the bed, lying on her stomach with her hands and feet bound. Daniel couldn't tell if she was dead or unconscious.

"Oh, God, is she alive?" Daniel shouted at Susan.

"She is," Susan said. "Just unconscious. Let's get her covered up."

Daniel sliced the bindings, trying to be careful not to move her too much.

"Let's get her on her back as we wrap the blanket around her," Susan said.

Daniel blindly obeyed, gently rotating her. He felt the stickiness of her blood on the sheet as he wrapped her.

"Her pulse is very weak. She may have been drugged. She'll need to get to a hospital as fast as possible. Where is your car?"

"Behind the sheriff's. He's blocking the road."

"We'll have to carry her," Susan said. "We can use the cot as a stretcher. It's in the closet. Get it while I look around to see if I can figure out what they gave her."

Daniel got the cot and snapped it open as Susan searched the cabin for evidence of drugs. She came back into the room with a medical bag and dumped the contents on to the bed, then began shuffling through the various bottles, reading labels.

"I'm pretty sure this is what they gave her. It requires an antidote every hour or she'll die. It's a terrorist's ploy so if they're killed, their captive dies shortly after."

"How do you know all that?" Daniel asked.

"Side-effect of my research. I spend weeks sitting very still in trees and have a lot of time to read books on medicine, anatomy, physiology, and anything that has to do with human and near-human bodies."

"Near-human?" Daniel puzzled.

"Great apes and the like. Look through these bottles for small red capsules. I'll read labels. Maybe I'll recognize the antidote." Susan was in constant motion as she talked, carefully searching through everything that had fallen out of the bag.

As Daniel picked up the first bottle, he heard heavy footsteps on the porch. He grabbed the knife and ran to the main room ready to attack whoever it was. Three soldiers in full gear were coming through the door, covering the entire room with their assault rifles.

"Hit the floor, now," one of them shouted to Daniel as he saw the brilliant red flash of the laser pointing at him.

Daniel stopped and raised his hands, ready to take the bullet.

"Get down, now!"

Daniel dropped to his knees.

"Who are you?"

"Daniel Furman!" Daniel shouted back.

The soldier lowered his rifle. He came over to Daniel and held him by the chin as he surveyed his face. "Jesus. Sorry, Daniel. I didn't recognize you. You've taken quite a beating. I assume this sack of shit crying on the floor is Syed Hussain?"

"Yes, sir," Daniel said.

"And those two on the porch? Are they his?"

"Yes, sir," Daniel responded.

"Mike!" the soldier called to one of the other men. He pointed to Syed. "What's he chewing on?"

Mike bent over and opened Syed's limp jaw and took out a pill as Syed screamed in pain. "Looks like a cyanide pill, sir. His jaw's busted so bad he can't bite it."

"Well, isn't that a shame," the soldier said facetiously. "Shove his eye back in its socket and get him to a helicopter. Brad'll want to have a chat with him."

Mike grabbed Syed by his belt and carried him out like he was toting a puppy. He was still whimpering as Daniel watched him go, his arm dangling uselessly.

"Anybody else we need to know about?"

"Babel's down the trail, dead. The sheriff's on the road with his throat cut. Victor's at the bottom of the hill. He's hurt bad."

"Jack," the soldier yelled immediately, "take Rob and go find Victor. Move it!" Then he turned back to Daniel. "Who's in the bedroom?"

"Sarah. She's bad. Susan's with her."

At that moment Susan appeared in the doorway. "Billy, good of you to drop in. I haven't seen you since you almost froze to death here."

"Damn, Dr. Stratford, is that you who smells so bad?"

"Shut up and get Sarah to a hospital. Here's a note for the doctor. Make sure he reads it, or there's a good chance she won't make it."

"Yes, ma'am," Billy said, then clicked on his shoulder microphone. "Clear. Come in quick. Lower stretchers. Two down who need medico. ASAP."

Daniel heard the helicopter come in low and fast over the cabin, stop, and hover. He went to the porch as two soldiers were fast-roping down while two more were getting baskets to the ground.

Daniel watched as Billy immediately organized getting Sarah to the lowered basket, then went to the edge of the hill to check on Victor. Two soldiers were getting him up the hill. Daniel hoped he was just unconscious since the soldiers were being so careful with him. Daniel recognized one of the men as the corpsman who had given him the drug in the helicopter over the Gulf.

"He's lost too much blood," the corpsman reported to Billy. "He won't make it to the hospital and he won't make it at all if we don't give him some blood. I don't have any and I don't know his type anyway."

"We're related," Daniel shouted over the noise of the helicopter. "Can you use mine? I'm O negative."

"It might kill him, but he'll die soon anyway. We have the best chance with your blood type," Doc shouted back.

"Can you take mine and give it to him?" Daniel asked desperately.

Doc looked at Billy for direction. Billy nodded.

"Get him to a bed inside," Doc told the soldiers carrying the stretcher. "Come on, Daniel. We'll have to hurry."

Daniel ran in as Sarah was being carried out. He stopped and kissed her swollen face. "I love you, Sarah. Stay with us, please."

The soldiers carrying Victor prodded Daniel through the door and he headed to the bedroom. Doc worked at lightning speed to set up the transfusion.

"You know this is dangerous, Daniel?" Doc warned.

"Do it!" Daniel said.

As Daniel felt the large needle pierce his arm, he looked up to see Brad coming into the bedroom. Brad took his hand and squeezed it.

"You saved her life, son. Thank you," Brad said.

"Is she going to be all right?"

"Susan found the antidote for the drug, and we sent the bottles with her to the hospital. They'll know what to do, so she should be fine. I'm headed to the hospital. You take care, you hear?"

"Yes, sir," Daniel said. He was feeling very weak now and thought he was going to pass out. The last thing he heard was Brad ordering Doc to take good care of his future son-in-law.

"Think as I think," said a religious man,
"Or you are abominably wicked;
And we will kill your sons,
Rape your wife and daughters,
And gouge out your eyes
As you beg for death!"
And after I had thought of it,
I said, "I will, then, think as you think."

—What Stephen Crane might have written had
he lived beyond the idealism of youth
and experienced the reality of terrorism.

The End

Acknowledgments

Thank you to my typist, editor, friend, tennis partner, punctuation guru, first reader and sympathetic critic: Helen Anspach.

Thank you to my manuscript consultant, Amanda Rooker of Split Seed Media, for her guidance.

Thank you to my pre-readers: Mike Curtis and Gerard Healy, author of *Originally from Dorchester: A Memoir*.

A special thank you to my sisters, Laura Scott Rash and Susan Allred, for their help and advice.

Writing is a passion, and without a great publisher, the writing withers on the vine. So I thank the Koehler team, editor Becky Hilliker, and John Koehler for giving me the opportunity to share this story with readers.

Daniel and Victor return in
The Bank, the third book of the
Turtle on a Fence Post series.

When Daniel comes to accept his new station in life, he becomes embroiled in a world of technology that can change the course of history, provide for the welfare of the Earth, and define the center of world power.